I0768885

THE FORGOTTEN EARTH

BOOK ONE OF
THE FORGOTTEN EARTH SERIES

BRILYNN O'NEAL

To those fighting for a better world, whether in small or large ways, visible or invisible ways, I see you. Keep fighting.

Author Note

This novel contains descriptions of violence, rape, and trauma (no explicit rape scenes), as well as open-door romance.

Tarraco
Home
Coria
The Forgotten Earth

PART I

Chapter One

Willow

It's easy to take the things you value for granted and forget how easily they can be taken away. Humans are notoriously forgetful, and we've forgotten what we've lost.

But not me. I knew what we'd lost, and that made me dangerous. It made me a target. How easily I'd forgotten that too.

The book lay face down, the pages crumpled beneath its worn binding—abandoned the instant the soldiers walked through the doorway. Evidence of my treason. Evidence of how easily things can be taken away.

The soldiers' rough leather boots padded along the worn tile floor, and my terror increased with each step. Their patrol schedule was off, and it was never off. They weren't supposed to be here for another hour. I relied on the general's obsessive attention to detail and schedule adherence to keep myself safe in the forbidden part of the city.

Something was wrong.

I inched further into the shadows of the library shelves, my hands trembling fiercely. I clutched the wood behind me to steady them. My breath rasped out of me in sharp bursts. The sound of it was ready to give me away, and I could do nothing. I had no weapon, no way to defend myself.

I heard the footsteps, two pairs, stop only a few rows over from me, and my breath halted with them.

"I don't understand why the general keeps this trash. It became irrelevant a hundred years ago." The drawl of the soldier's voice suggested disgust as I heard him flipping through the pages of a book.

"He should have turned this place to ash."

"I suppose it doesn't matter now. We'll be gone in a few days."

Gone? No one left the walls of Coria if they wanted to live.

I perked up, trying to catch their words as the direction of their footsteps turned the other way. They were leaving as quickly as they had come.

"The Claeg will claim this place . . ." A twisted laugh followed the words, and then there was nothing but the sound of a squeaky hinge as the door closed, leaving nothing but my still-ragged breaths.

It took me many minutes to calm down enough to stand. The fading light filtering through the dust-covered windows indicated I was running out of time. Curfew was approaching.

I hastily wound my way through the shelves, retracing the steps I took when the soldiers first entered. I found the book where I'd dropped it. *The Rapid Decline of Earth's Ecosystems: How We Failed to Save Our Home.* The R's and the E's were faded almost to the point of disappearing.

I stared at it, my hands still trembling.

How much was a book really worth? How far would you go for that knowledge? Would you die for it?

The questions swam in my head, mixing with panic.

I reached down and grabbed the book, then raced to the worn leather chair by the window that overlooked the forbidden part of the city. I looked down at the stack of books I'd collected—the books that held the knowledge that kept our food supply intact and kept our dying city limping along.

Except, no one knew that. It was safer that way.

I stuffed the books into my torn and patched backpack: books on botany, plant identification, medicinal plants, bioengineering, food crops, and a book that recently caught my attention: *Celtic Lore.*

I threw the bag over my shoulder, then froze, scanning the Coria City Library, hoping it wasn't the last time I'd see it. Hoping the soldiers were wrong. Because if they weren't, then what hope would we have?

I had to beat the sun. It was a ten-minute walk back to the fence and the safety of the outer edge of the inhabited part of the city.

I took my usual route, sticking to the shadows and ducking behind gutted buildings. I stayed away from the main streets that soldiers often patrolled.

The buildings here had been ransacked and destroyed. The Elite had extracted every possible resource from them. What was left was a skeleton city—nothing but the bare bones of buildings that once housed the lives of people long lost to history.

The sidewalks were cracked, but my feet flew across them, racing the light. I'd memorized every dip and every hole that had once housed a tree or plant that had died over a hundred years ago. All that remained were empty pits at regular intervals in the broken concrete.

I ran until my lungs burned and I saw the fence that separated the forbidden part of the city from where we lived and worked. I swerved left, ducked behind an old, empty warehouse, and peeled back the broken wooden boards that concealed a hole in the side.

I squeezed through and sprinted across the bare concrete floor. Now, the light barely filtered through the cracks in the roof.

I moved a few empty wooden crates to the other side, revealing a hole in the building that extended through the fence. I crawled in, pulling the crates back in place, and then I walked out of the tiny metal shelter on the other side. Making my way through the sad excuse for homes, I found myself face to face with a man whose clothes were so torn I wondered why he even bothered to put them on.

A crooked smile formed on his face, revealing missing and rotted teeth.

"I'm surprised you waited this long. It's dangerous," I said, reaching into my bag and pulling out a book I'd taken just for him.

His face twisted into something resembling glee. "I'm already half-dead, child," he replied dismissively as he eagerly reached for the book.

I placed it in his outstretched hands before glancing at the sky. "I have to go. The soldiers will be here any minute."

He was already absorbed in the book as my hands began to tremble again at the thought of soldiers.

"Bill," I said, "you need to get inside." I barely concealed the desperation in my voice.

He waved his hand at me. "I'm going. I'm going."

"Keep it hidden," I added, but I couldn't help the smile that spread across my face at his reaction to the pictures.

I pushed away from the broken picnic table we always met at. "Yeah. Yeah."

"See you tomorrow!" I waved before hurrying toward Sixth Street and my studio apartment.

If I'd been smart, I wouldn't have given the book to Bill. Not this close to sunset.

If I'd been more careful, I would have noticed the soldier watching from the shadows.

Chapter Two

Liam

I hated patrol, even more so after returning from an extended assignment outside the wall. It was a mindless job, one I felt was below my rank and not worth my time, but I couldn't voice that opinion if I valued my life.

I stood on what used to be a flat sidewalk, leaning against a crumbling building as the light faded around me, keeping an eye on the fence.

A fucking fence.

The exhaustion of my last assignment seeped into my bones as I watched people hurry away every time they noticed me—bowing their heads, never even making eye contact. Not that I blamed them. Contact with a soldier almost always ended in death. Something I knew all too well.

Almost everyone was inside. They didn't want to be caught outside after curfew with the sun nearly gone. Eager to be inside myself, I turned to leave a few minutes early when a small man dressed in rags stumbled toward a single picnic table situated next to the fence.

I stopped in the shadow of the building and stared at the man. He was one of the Forgotten. A man I'd seen often, though he never noticed me. He mostly kept to himself, constantly talking like he wasn't alone. I wondered who he thought he was talking to. Likely a dead loved one. There was no shortage of people lost here.

The man sat atop the table, still chatting to himself, watching the fence.

I straightened, peering over his head into the distance, wondering if he was expecting someone to walk right through it. Maybe this evening would be interesting, for once.

The person didn't come through the fence, though. She came from the mass of shelters the Forgotten used as homes. The homes were tucked together in a small area next to the fence. Most were unoccupied, as the Forgotten had dwindled to a population of no more than twenty people, which was why my patrol seemed even more useless.

Until today.

I assessed her like any target—mid-twenties, average height, wisp thin, poor eyesight. Smashing her eyeglasses would be an advantage, but she didn't look like she'd be able to put up much of a fight anyway. She wasn't one of the Forgotten, but she wasn't part of the Elite, either. Mid-tier worker then. Clearly not manual labor—her hands weren't cracked or calloused. Must be something intellectual. Why'd she come from the Forgotten settlements, then?

I immediately forgot that line of questioning as she smiled and pulled out a book, handing it to the man.

I stared at it, unblinking. Of course books existed in this city, but most had been destroyed or belonged only to the Elite. It had been years since I'd seen anyone carrying books around.

I knew I should question them. I knew I should take the book. I knew I should at least alert them to my presence, but I stood there completely frozen in the shadows by some unknown force. All I could do was watch.

The man opened it as her hands trembled ever so slightly. I couldn't see his expression, but I could see hers. She beamed at him as he flipped through the pages, and I found I couldn't stop staring at her—at the unfiltered joy caused by whatever was in that book. I had the urge to see for myself, but I was still rooted to the ground, unable to take a single step.

A moment later, her lips still upturned in a stunning smile and her hands steady again, they said their goodbyes and she took off down the street as the man called after her, saying something I didn't catch. She waved back once and then she was gone. The man went back to perusing the book on his lap.

I stared after the woman as if I half-expected her to return.

After several minutes of nothing but the sound of the wind, I shook my head slightly and pushed off the building, heading back to my office and the patrol report I'd have to write before I could finally sleep.

On the long walk, I thought of the joy on the woman's face. But it wasn't just joy, it was something else. Something I hadn't seen in a long time—hope.

As I typed my patrol report, the general came barging into the office I shared with three other captains, only one of whom was present. The general was a burly man with a long, dark-red beard and a large scar on his left cheek that was as raised and angry as he often was.

I immediately shot to my feet, my legs pushing the chair away from me with a loud scraping sound.

"At ease, Captain," the general said, coming to stand next to me.

I relaxed my shoulders but didn't sit back down.

"There's an unruly band of men intent on stealing food from the warehouse. There have been several attempts to stop them, but to no avail. We don't know where their weapons are coming from. They need to be taken care of. I expect the situation to be handled immediately," the general said, with more annoyance than anger.

My shoulders dropped even more at the thought of delaying my much-anticipated night of sleep.

"Just me or with my men?" The question seemed innocent enough, though I rarely questioned the man. His temper often ended in a curious soldier becoming a snack for the Claeg.

"I expect it to be handled quickly and quietly, so that decision is up to you, Captain." The general left no more room for question or debate and was gone an instant later. The sound of his footfalls echoed down the hallway. Even his steps sounded angry.

I sank back into the chair and pushed my unruly, long, blond hair out of my face.

My men would only cause a scene, even if it'd be easier to use them. Easier for my conscience, at least. Whatever was left of it.

I could do the job quickly and discreetly on my own—that wasn't the issue. I knew the men stealing food were only trying to feed their families. It felt wrong to end them because the Elite had failed to provide them with their basic needs.

But that was my job. A job I was good at. Too good. It didn't matter how I felt about it—I was surviving, just like everyone else.

Or so I told myself.

"You're going alone, aren't you?" Marvin, the only other captain in the room, asked me, though I wasn't sure it was a question.

I looked over at him. He was a large man, with rich umber skin, and built like a brick wall. Though we were the same height, he probably had fifty pounds on me. His promotion to captain came around the same time as mine. We were the longest surviving captains.

If I had any friends, he'd likely be my only one.

"My men would only fuck it up," I grumbled.

Marvin huffed a short laugh. "Were we that stupid?"

"Probably had the same egos, but I'd like to think we got promoted because we weren't nearly as dumb," I replied, standing and grabbing my bag of various weapons. I pulled out the short sword, strapping it to my back, and slung the bow over my head. I attached daggers to the holsters on my legs and tucked a few into my jacket.

Marvin laughed at my response, eyeing the weapons I was securing to my body. "No guns?"

"Too noisy. Draws too much attention," I explained, securing the last of my arrows.

"Take 'em out quickly." His voice sounded as exhausted as I felt.

He didn't mean take them out quickly because that was the assignment, he meant take them out quickly so they wouldn't suffer.

I gave him a firm nod and then I was gone, headed for the warehouse where I'd add twenty more innocent names to the ever-growing list of people I'd slaughtered in the name of the Elite.

I was their slave. We all were.

No matter how much I tried, there was no escaping the monster I'd become.

Chapter Three

Liam

I had to wait until midnight. I knew the men wouldn't steal in the early hours. They were too intelligent for that if they'd managed to evade the Elite's soldiers who were finally sending me in. The Elite must have been desperate, so I had to be smart and quick about it.

I sat, crouched on the metal rooftop across from the warehouse, facing the back entrance of the building. I stayed in the shadows so no one from below could spot me. The back of the building was the most accessible and least heavily guarded. Whoever was stealing would use this entrance, but they wouldn't escape tonight.

No one faced me and escaped. Not unless I wanted them to.

Long past midnight, I waited in the same position, not even registering the slight cramping in my legs. I wouldn't have noticed anything if the light from under the warehouse door hadn't picked up the plume of dust from the men's movement. When I finally spotted them, I noticed they were dressed from head to toe in black, moving fluidly as one unit among the shadows, creating the illusion that it was nothing but a nearly imperceptible shift of the dark.

I watched them, counting all twenty men before the back doors. The frontman scanned the area and then gave the rest of them some sort of signal.

I waited, knowing that shadows were hard to strike but that the light from the warehouse's interior would give me a better chance at taking them out quickly.

The group leader cracked open the warehouse door, illuminating only a small piece of dirt. The rest of the men remained in shadow, but it was just enough light for me to distinguish them.

I silently strung my bow and released my arrow, striking the leader in the head. The person instantly crumbled to the ground, and before any of the others could react, I'd taken out five more.

The rest fell out of formation, darting in different directions, looking for a place to hide.

Their terror made them easier targets.

Those that ran were shot down without much effort, but a few were smart and slunk further into the shadows. I lost their movement.

When silence fell and no one flinched, I counted sixteen dead bodies, all of which had fallen in under a minute.

The last four were missing, and I swore under my breath as I slung my bow over my shoulders and pulled out two daggers instead. I'd wanted to take them all out with the bow. It was easier that way. I didn't have to get close to them. I didn't have to see what I'd become reflected in their terrified faces.

I stayed low, sticking to the darkest parts of the rooftop as I crept closer to the edge—just far enough to peek over the side.

One person was directly under me, pushing themselves up against the side of the building. I could see their chest moving rapidly up and down in an erratic pattern.

They were likely in shock.

I released a dagger, striking the person in the top of their skull. They fell almost soundlessly against the wall and tumbled to the ground.

Their death spurred another one of the three remaining people to move just enough that I spotted them. My second dagger flew before they could even glimpse me. It caught them in the eye, and they instantly fell.

The remaining two were not underneath or across from me. There wasn't a single sound, as if they'd completely stopped breathing. I knew I'd have to draw them out.

I jumped from the roof to the ground in one fluid movement, landing in a low crouch and swinging my body toward my blind spots.

It worked. The men instantly moved from their hiding spots and drew their guns.

Shit. How'd they get guns? Only the Elite had access to guns.

I shot to my feet, drawing two more daggers.

The man holding the gun had his face covered with a black cloth, but I could see his eyes. He hesitated for a moment, but there was no tremble in his grip. It was as if he already knew his fate.

"You're the famous captain." His voice was steadier than I imagined it would be.

When I didn't say anything he continued. "You're fighting for the wrong people."

I cocked my head to the side. I knew I was, but what choice did I have? What choice did anyone have?

"There are people who will follow you."

I didn't get a chance to form a response as the man gave an imperceptible nod and his friend put a bullet through his head and then turned the gun on himself.

The tang of blood filled my nose as an eerie silence filled the space the gunshots left behind.

Death was always so silent.

I stood there, stunned, with the man's words echoing in my mind, and took in the twenty dead bodies around me—their dark forms lying in unnatural positions on the dirt. Clouds of dust drifted past, slowly falling back to the ground. I watched it settle briefly, then walked back to my office as if nothing had happened.

Except, I'd just killed twenty innocent people in the span of two minutes.

"It's done," I announced wearily, peeking into the general's office.

His head shot up from the computer before him and he grinned, cruelly. "All twenty?"

I nodded once.

"And not a speck of blood on you," the general observed, standing and walking toward the door.

I straightened myself as he approached.

He clapped me on the shoulder. "I have good news for you, Captain," he started, leading me into his office.

I sat in the large chair in front of his desk as he walked over to a table covered in multi-colored bottles of alcohol. He poured us both a drink from a dark bottle.

He handed me the clear glass filled with a strong brown liquid, and I accepted it, taking a small sip as he sat down across from me.

He took a large swig from his glass, almost downing the whole thing. "We're getting out of this hell hole," he continued.

I raised a brow as I took another small sip.

"The Claeg are gathering in the thousands outside our walls. The time has come for us to leave this place and join the northern city, Tarraco. Join the emperor. They have far more resources than we do. No more living in poverty for us." The general beamed.

My eyes widened involuntarily before I caught myself and returned my expression to one of neutral disinterest.

"You are to report to the wall with your men the day after tomorrow, before dawn. Other units will be arming the citizens, but you'll stick close to the Elite. Protect the Elite at all costs. Most of the Claeg will be gone by the time the Elite leave their secure homes, so it should be simple," he added.

"What about the other citizens?" I asked. I couldn't quite process what I was hearing.

Thousands of Claeg could only mean one thing. Death. No, not just death—genocide.

The general waved his hand casually, downing the rest of his glass. "Don't worry about them. They're the bait. We'll arm them—give them a fighting chance."

Bait?

"We can't keep the entire city alive on the five-day trip north. We're taking only what's necessary to survive," he added in way of explanation, as if he hadn't just suggested that we were going to leave the majority of the city to die at the hands of the Claeg.

"And Marvin's unit?" I asked the general, my panic growing.

This was not in my plan.

"They'll be accompanying us. Most soldiers and units will remain behind to escort the Elite to the city. You'll get explicit directions the morning of," he said, standing and gesturing for me to finish my drink. I swallowed in one gulp before handing the glass back to him.

He walked back to the table and poured himself another one. "You'll have a better life, Captain. You should be grateful," he said without facing me.

"Yes, sir. Thank you, sir," I replied out of pure habit, though my pulse kicked up. Killing twenty men for stealing precious resources was one thing. Hell, killing a hundred was one thing, but knowingly sending thousands to their deaths? That was something else entirely—especially in a world where humans were almost extinct.

He turned and grinned again, downing another glass. "You're dismissed, Captain."

Chapter Four

Willow

The early morning sunlight, muted by the constant dust in the air, woke me from my dreams. I slowly sat up and reached for my mangled wire glasses. As I put them on, I stood, aiming for the window, the bottom of my torn and patched socks picking up the brown dust as I moved across the floor.

The city was just waking up around me as I looked toward the horizon. The view was blocked by the city wall keeping out the Claeg that prowled the dead and wild Earth beyond.

The broken buildings in front of me housed most of the people in the city. Some apartments only had three walls. People made do with what they had, their lives a constant struggle to survive. I did the same. We went through the motions daily, pretending we weren't on the precipice of total collapse.

I sighed at the further decomposition of the city's buildings and streets before grabbing my brush off the cluttered table in my tiny kitchen. It was missing most of its teeth. I ran it through my waist-length curly hair, simultaneously scooping up my personal notes and shoving them into disorganized piles.

I then stuffed an old, stale piece of bread in my mouth while running a damp cloth over my dust-caked skin before pulling on a clean cotton shirt and pants. The shirt was just as hastily patched as my socks to keep it from falling apart. New clothes were a luxury only the Elite enjoyed.

After grabbing the piles of paper on the table, I laced up my black leather boots and rushed out, already late for work.

Before the door shut behind me, I remembered the glass vial on the counter. It held a collection of seeds I found scattered among the city's debris, blown in by the wind. I went nowhere without it.

I had a dream of one day getting the seeds to sprout. It was a foolish hope—one of many.

My hand closed on the vial by the door, and I carefully wrapped it in a dirty cloth to protect it, then gently placed it in my pocket, patting it lightly before heading out the door.

"Willow!" my best, and only, friend, Olivia, shouted, waving her hands frantically at me from across the street as I emerged onto the sidewalk.

I smiled, pushing my broken glasses further up my nose, and clutching the handful of papers close to my chest, I hurried over to her.

She wrinkled her nose as I approached, studying me intently.

"You're giving off really intense, mad scientist vibes. You know, there are these things called hairbrushes?" she said as she reached out her hands to help me.

I snorted, handing her a stack of papers as she dramatically pretended they weighed a ton.

A grin split across Olivia's bright-red lips. She looked down at the papers in her hands. My hand-drawn picture of the life cycle of a seed was sitting on top. "You take your job way too seriously, Will. Who does extra work at home? And actually *enjoys* it?"

I snatched the picture from her hand, but the next one only gave her even more fuel. She stared down at it with an amused expression. "Reading fairytales, are we?"

I'd drawn a picture from one of the Celtic mythology books I found. It depicted a Fae wielding elemental magic—Earth Magic. There was just something about it. It wasn't my usual reading material, but it did show plant growth.

I grabbed the rest of the papers from her hands with a huff. I didn't dare give her any more ammunition. Instead, I headed for the bioengineering lab we both worked in, not bothering to wait for her to catch up.

She chuckled behind me.

"The usual stop?" She asked as we turned the corner.

I nodded.

She sighed, returning my smile with a tentative one of her own. Olivia was easily a head taller than me with rich, black hair that fell just past her shoulders. She was beautiful, with long, graceful legs and sharp, but not severe, features. Her lips were bright red, which was the first thing anyone noticed about her, except maybe her height. Her lips stood out even more because they always seemed curved into a sarcastic grin as if she found the world far funnier than it was.

I looked at her sideways. "I don't need it."

"Have you looked at yourself lately?" she asked, incredulous, although her eyes still sparkled with mirth.

I huffed again, picking up my pace.

"Willow!" Bill shouted from his picnic table, already expecting us.

"Morning, Bill. How's Leslie feeling?" I asked, setting my papers on the table and shrugging off my backpack. I pulled out a small, dense loaf of bread and handed it to him.

Bill took it from my hands and shook his head. "Died last night," he said, tearing into the loaf of bread before adding, "in her sleep."

No remorse or sadness shone in his eyes. He had seen this kind of death so often it was as if he was simply reporting the weather.

"Shit," was all I could think to say in response, though my heart sank at the same time red-hot anger rose dangerously close to the surface.

Olivia eyed me warily, knowing exactly what I was thinking, and likely already anticipating me trying something stupid to fix it.

"And no one has come from the lab to provide more food or medicine?" I asked him.

Bill shook his head again, swallowing. "Why would they?"

"Because you are all just as much a part of this city as everyone else," I snapped, the anger almost pouring out of my throat now.

Bill shrugged as he popped more of my food into his mouth.

"I'll talk to my boss," I added.

Olivia rolled her eyes. "You'll just get in more trouble."

I glared at her. "Have a better idea?"

She held up her hands in mock surrender.

"Have you two heard the rumors?" Bill cut in, still chewing the bread.

We both turned our attention to him, expecting the worst. We were always expecting the worst here.

He took another bite and grinned at me—an almost sinister grin. "I've heard hundreds, if not thousands of Claeg are camped outside our walls right now."

I heard Olivia's sharp intake of breath next to me.

"You're sure?" I was skeptical of the information, but that didn't mean I wasn't also terrified it was true.

Bill nodded, his mouth too full to respond.

"They've never done that," I commented. "They're nomadic."

"Read that in a book, eh?" Bill asked, his words muffled from the food in his mouth.

"Quiet," Olivia whispered harshly, and Bill glared at her before returning his attention to me.

"Thanks for the heads up about the Claeg," I said, grabbing Olivia's arm and dragging her toward the lab. "We'll see you tomorrow."

"I'll be here if I'm not dead." I heard him chuckle as we rounded the corner leading to the bio lab.

I shivered at his words. They felt less like a joke and more like a premonition.

"Willow, I don't mean to be negative, but you know what they do to people who push too hard."

I stopped in my tracks and wheeled around to face her. "That was the *last* child of the Forgotten. There. Are. No. More."

Olivia let out a long breath, and when she didn't respond, I turned and continued.

"What about the Claeg?" Olivia asked with a shaky voice. "I can't lose you too."

I knew she was terrified. I knew that's how she lost her wife, Kat, three years ago. I knew I was all she had left, and she was all I had left.

"I know," I said as I shut my eyes and took a deep breath.

I grabbed her hand and squeezed gently. She pulled it back and dramatically wiped it on her sleeve, as if my palm were a sweaty mess. I choked on a laugh, and she gave me a small smile in return. Leave it to Olivia to lighten the mood.

I was still simmering as we passed through the front doors of the bio building and got in line, waiting to be scanned into the lab.

"Are you going straight to Marcus?" Olivia whispered in my ear from behind me.

I nodded.

"Go easy on him. He doesn't rank that high. He's a nice guy."

I huffed. It didn't matter who you were, if you were part of the Elite, you could never be classified as *nice*.

"Wrist," said the guard standing by the lab's doors.

I held my wrist over the scanner, and the automated doors behind the guard opened, letting me through. I paused on the other side and waited for Olivia to stumble in after me.

We both worked in food production, engineering basic grains used to make simple bread, crackers, breakfast mush, or other not-very-creative concoctions. Technically, the grains were plants, but there was no healthy soil or water to grow them in; they were so heavily genetically modified that they never produced any green. We pumped enough synthetic growth hormone into them to at least get them to grow into brown plants, eventually creating a pathetic amount of grain to turn into food—just enough to feed our declining population.

The building we worked in was just as pathetic as the food we grew. Old fluorescent bulbs hung from exposed wires, almost none of which worked anymore, creating a patchwork of light and dark throughout the hallways. Large swaths of the walls had peeling paint, exposing worn-down sheetrock underneath. Ceiling tiles were missing, exposing broken pipes and wall studs.

Most of the employees—the few that were left—walked around like hollowed-out husks of human beings. There was no joy or passion to be found, everyone was just going through the motions. Most were forced into these positions out of necessity. I was one of the lucky ones who was forced into a job I truly enjoyed.

Olivia and I walked to our lab stations in silence, and I slammed the papers on the table and shrugged off my pack.

"We'll figure it out," Olivia said across the room.

I didn't respond as I strode out of our office. I heard Olivia's deep sigh as I reached the door to Marcus's office and pounded on it. Hard.

"Come in," a flat voice said from the other side.

I pushed the door open and slammed it behind me.

Marcus jumped in his chair and peered at me over one of the three computers on his desk, which were beeping frantically.

"What is it this time?" Marcus's words held an undercurrent of amusement.

"Am I that predictable?"

He smirked but didn't answer me. Instead, he motioned for me to sit.

I felt his assessment of me as I moved to the chair in front of his desk. Checking if I was sick or hurt. He was overly concerned about me. I found it somewhat endearing, if not a bit odd for an Elite.

Marcus was dressed immaculately, as the Elite often were. They must have been repellent to the dust because it never seemed to accumulate on them like the rest of us. Marcus was tall and elegantly built, and though he was attractive, he wasn't rugged or rough around the edges. He wasn't a fighter. He was polished, which stood out in our world.

"We need more medicine, food, and working tech so we can increase crop output," I stated as his eyes finally found mine again.

At that moment, his computer started beeping and flashing the color red. His eyes dipped briefly to the screen before returning to me.

"Is that all?" he asked, almost mockingly.

"No, it's not, now that you mention it . . ."

Marcus cut me off with a laugh, holding up his hand. "I may be an Elite, Willow, but I only have authority in food production."

"So, get us more tech so we can do our jobs properly."

"There isn't any more tech. You know that. We've used and reused everything we can in this city. Even the military is running out of weapons."

That was more information than Marcus had ever given me, and it made me sit up a bit straighter.

"So, then what? Our last PCR machine goes out, and that's it? No more food? We starve?"

"We're doing everything we can."

"Are you?" I practically shouted, "Because what it looks like to me is that the Elite are only protecting themselves. Leslie died last night, Marcus. There are no more children. Do you understand what that means?"

Marcus's face paled. He knew she was the last child because I'd begged him for medicine for her.

"The medication . . ." he began to say, his words shaky.

"It wasn't enough."

Marcus shook his head. "I'm so sorry, Willow. I'm so sorry, I couldn't have done more."

I wanted to remain angry at him. I wanted to blame someone, and he was an Elite, so it was easy to put the blame on him. The reality was, though, that he'd risked his own life trying to help me and my reckless quest to help those who needed it most.

None of it was his fault.

I sighed, dropping my head into my hands.

I heard his chair push back, and before I knew it, he was kneeling in front of me, pulling my hands away from my face.

My glasses slipped down my nose, and he gently pushed them back up.

I didn't want to meet his eyes. I wasn't sure I could handle what would be staring back at me. Staring through me.

"Please don't do anything reckless," Marcus whispered. "Especially not now."

My eyes widened slightly. "What's going on?"

He pulled back, dropping my hands and running his own through his short, black hair.

"You can't tell me, can you?" I whispered.

He shook his head, and I tried to ignore the utter defeat on his face.

"Don't go far for the next few days. Stick close to the lab. Promise me."

He sounded so desperate, and I wanted to press him on it. Wanted to squeeze the information from him, but I was too afraid to put him in danger. Too afraid someone was listening on the other end of the cameras behind his desk.

Before I could agree to his wishes, his computer started blaring. His eyes widened, and he rushed in front of the monitor. His eyes shot to the camera in the corner of the room and then back to me.

A pleading washed over his face as I stood, understanding what he couldn't say.

We had said too much.

I made my way slowly to the door and opened it, my heart rate increasing.

"Be careful," he called after me.

It was hard to be careful when I didn't know what I was up against.

"Any news?" Olivia asked, twirling around in her desk chair like a child as I walked back into our shared office.

She studied me with narrowed eyes as I practically fell onto my desk, burying my head in my arms.

"We're fucked," I mumbled.

"What about the new dirt samples? Any luck getting something to grow?"

"Maybe," I replied, not lifting my head.

I heard Olivia rise from her chair and plop on my desk. "I seem to remember you mentioning something about using your own shit to increase the soil's nutrition?" Her voice held a hint of teasing in it.

I raised my head only enough to see the grin on her lips. "So?"

Her smile grew wider. "Perhaps you could continue that *personal* study using our seeds. No need for working technology if your poo will make the seeds sprout."

I gave her a wry grin and then plopped my head back down. "I've been doing that already. For weeks now. How do you think we were able to increase our output this month?" My words were muffled through my arms.

"You're shitting me?" Olivia sounded genuinely shocked.

I lifted my head again. "Pun intended?" I smirked at her.

"I knew it!" Olivia ran her hands through her hair. "Why didn't you tell me?"

"I wanted to see what they'd do first. The fewer people involved, the better."

Her expression turned to confusion. "If you can grow food *without* tech, just using the seeds, then aren't our problems solved?"

I finally sat back up. "I can only get the genetically modified seeds to sprout." I paused, pulling out the vial of seeds from my pocket, studying them. "The wild ones won't."

She looked at the vial and then back to my eyes.

"The Elite has to know about the increased output. Why haven't they inquired about it? It seems to me that this could solve a lot of problems."

I sighed. "They don't want to solve problems."

"It hurts them too, doesn't it?" Olivia asked, but she knew the answer. "At the very least, why not kill us all and keep the resources and knowledge for themselves?"

I knew she was joking, but something akin to a warning bell went off inside me.

Chapter Five

Liam

"We have a situation," the general barked as he stormed into our office the following day. "Someone's been sneaking into the forbidden part of the city."

"Stealing weapons?" I guessed. The Elite's primary weapons warehouse was there.

The general shook his head. "Books."

My mouth almost fell open. "Books?"

"Yes. Books. I need you to investigate immediately. We apprehended a man with an illegal book but found no others. He claims he was given the book. I need you to find the person responsible. You know what to do," the general said with a wave of his hand.

"Excuse me, sir, is execution really called for here?" I dared to ask him.

His expression immediately hardened. "It's treason." His tone left no room for debate, so I dropped the subject. "The man we apprehended is in holding cell B. I expect the situation to be handled within twenty-four hours."

"Yes, sir," was all I could say as he turned and stalked out of the office.

I stared after him.

"They're sending *you* to investigate someone stealing *books*?" Marvin sounded just as confused as I was. "When was the last time someone was found with an illegal book?"

"I haven't heard of it since we were kids. I thought all the illegal books had been destroyed."

"Seems the Elite are hiding something else," Marvin commented casually, clicking his tongue. "Want me to go with you?"

"If you want."

He beamed at my response. His smile was as big and charming as he was, and I knew women fell hard for it.

I stood, and Marvin followed me to the basement of the building where the Elite held people for questioning.

The words from the food warehouse thief echoed in my mind as my boots pounded on the concrete floor of the prison.

You're fighting for the wrong people.

I froze as we entered the cell, staring at the Forgotten man who'd received a book from the mysterious woman. I hadn't told anyone about him, or the woman, so how did he end up here? And where was she?

My body tensed at the thought of harm coming to her. An unusual response I didn't want to think too much about.

"Like I told the other people, I was given the book by someone I don't know. They left it for me on the table I usually hang out on by the fence. It's an innocent enough book. Nothing harmful in it."

The man spoke, and I couldn't help but stare at his missing teeth and tattered clothes that hid absolutely nothing.

Marvin stood and leaned against the wall opposite me, flipping through the book. His brow creased and his mouth firm as he stared at it.

I moved my gaze back to the man in front of me. "Does this person sneak into the forbidden part of the city often?"

"Like I said, I don't know, but she does leave extra food sometimes." His eyes lit up like he thought he'd just saved her by revealing that little fact.

All it did was bring her one step closer to her death. A strange sort of anger washed over me, and in that moment, I was almost certain I couldn't carry out her murder. Because that's what it was. Murder.

"So, you do know her?" Marvin interrupted.

The man clamped his hand over his mouth, finally realizing how much he'd just revealed.

"Listen, we just need to know a name or an approximate location, and I promise no harm will come to her," I said, leaning closer to him. My entire body constricted at the lie that slipped so easily from my mouth.

"I don't know where she lives, but her friend lives on Third Street, close to the fence." He sounded afraid.

I stood up, the metal chair scraping on the concrete floor. "Thank you," I said before turning and motioning for Marvin to follow me out.

"Have you seen this?" Marvin asked in wonder as I closed the door behind us.

I shook my head. "I'll question the friend and let my men take care of him."

Marvin looked at me, his eyes assessing. "Liam, have you *looked* at this?" he asked again, more seriously this time.

I glanced down at the open page in his hands. It was our world, but it wasn't. It was full of color and life. Life I'd never seen before.

"What else are they hiding from us?" Marvin asked in a whisper.

Chapter Six

Willow

We made it through the night and most of the day without any more word on the Claeg gathered outside our walls.

Olivia and I pushed our way out of the bio building doors and onto the scorching sidewalk. "I'm gonna check on Bill. It's unlike him to miss a meal."

The city had become eerily silent since the rumors of the Claeg gathering had started yesterday, and I wondered what everyone was doing. We hadn't heard anything more, and there had been no official notice from the Elite. It all felt wrong.

"You could afford to eat your own food every once in a while," Olivia said as she scanned my frame, smirking.

I looked down at myself, the clothes hanging loosely off me, and pursed my lips. "I'll eat more when there's more to eat and the Forgotten are taken care of."

"You'll be dead by then," Olivia commented drily.

I shrugged.

"Good to know you've got your best interests at heart," she said, giving me a sideways glance.

I gave her a pointed look as we neared the suspiciously empty picnic table.

I looked around at the city streets and then at the small group of shelters that housed the Forgotten at the city's outer edge. Everything was silent and still. The only sound was the wind passing through the metal roofs and siding, vibrating them slightly. There were no voices, no shouts, no laughter—nothing.

"Where are they?" I asked her as my eyes darted past the fence. I tried not to sound panicked, but something was wrong.

"Hell if I know. But something tells me now isn't the time to be doing anything stupid." I could hear the slight edge of fear in Olivia's voice as something caught my eye in the distance.

"Is that . . . smoke?" I asked, pointing past the fence.

Olivia followed my gaze and cocked her head slightly. "I can't tell if it's smoke or a dust cloud. The wind has picked up since this morning." She paused and looked back at me for a moment. "I know what you're thinking, and it's a terrible idea. We should be going home. Right now."

"First, you have no idea what I'm thinking, and second, I agree, you should go home."

"Without you? No fucking way."

I finally looked at her, and for the first time, I noticed some fear in her eyes. "I need to find Bill."

"Need or want?"

I couldn't deny that it was a solid point.

What I wanted to do was risky, but I couldn't shake the feeling that the suspicious cloud and Bill missing were somehow connected. And

I couldn't live with myself if I knew something was wrong and didn't at least try to help him.

"Go home, Olivia. If I'm not back in thirty minutes, come find me," I said, making for the metal shelter and the hole in the fence.

"Willow," Olivia hissed at me.

I stopped and turned around to face her. "I'll come back. I promise."

She let out an exasperated sigh but nodded, knowing that arguing with me in the middle of the street would likely raise the suspicions of the soldiers, which was the last thing we wanted. If I was going into the forbidden part of the city, then we didn't want them anywhere near us.

I gave her one last look before I ducked into the metal shelter and through the hole in the fence, following the same discreet route through the buildings to avoid anyone spotting me from the other side.

As I approached the library, I knew it wasn't dust. It was smoke. I also knew the only two things that were flammable here anymore were toxic chemical barrels left over from when this part of the city was functional. And books.

It didn't smell like a chemical fire.

My heart picked up speed as my feet did. My mind threatened to crack from the dread I felt.

If the books were gone, then I had nothing. If the books were gone, then no hope remained for us. No one knew how much those books kept our food supply intact. Not even Olivia knew how much my research had helped our food security. I kept it to myself for her safety—for everyone's safety.

As I rounded the last corner, it wasn't the library up in flames that caught my attention, it was what was in front of the building.

Hanging from a lopsided old streetlamp was Bill. He was wearing the same tattered clothes, but his body was lifeless. The color had drained from his face, and his entire body hung limply, swaying lightly in the breeze as the flames engulfed the building behind him. Fire was already spilling out of the library windows, and I knew nothing would survive.

I fell to my knees, and that's when I noticed it. Below Bill, propped up against the lamppost, was the book I gave him the other day.

I turned my head away and clutched my stomach, bile rising in my throat.

I had done this to him. I had doomed him the moment I gave him that book. Hell, the moment I started having any contact with him at all.

My shock and guilt quickly turned to panic. If the Elite knew about Bill, then Olivia may already be in trouble.

I didn't think; I turned and sprinted back, ignoring the fact that my whole world was burning behind me. Someone I considered a friend had just been murdered as a message to me, precious information in that library was now gone forever, and I may have just sentenced my best friend to death.

I sprinted back into the city's outer edge, not caring who saw me. If I was caught, so be it, I just had to get to Olivia. I had to warn her before it was too late.

I ran as fast as I could, my lungs and legs burning with the effort, my glasses slowly slipping down my nose. I dodged trash and rubble, almost tripping on a sizable crack in the sidewalk as I turned the last corner onto Olivia's street.

I pushed open the double doors of Olivia's building, trying to avoid the missing fifth step in the stairwell leading to the second floor. By the time I reached the third floor, I was dripping sweat and breathing heavily, but I didn't stop. I raced down the hallway to her corner apartment. The hallway and the building were silent, as was the rest of the city, and most doors were closed. That is, if they had doors that were still intact. Usually, Olivia's building was full of life and laughter. People had to rely on each other in this city to survive, and this building was particularly close-knit. I didn't stop to wonder at the oddity of it.

Olivia's door was closed. I couldn't tell if that was a good sign as I knocked loudly, shouting her name.

I heard muffled footsteps and the scraping of some furniture across her tattered wooden floor. Then, the door swung open, revealing Olivia's worried face.

"What the hell happened?" she whispered harshly a moment later, dragging me into her apartment by my shirt and slamming the door shut again as she pushed a heavy dresser in front of it.

I didn't know what to say or where to start, so all that came out were more questions. "Why is your building so quiet? Why are all the doors shut? And why is there a dresser in front of your door?"

She inhaled deeply, the lines on her face easing slightly. "We were visited by a soldier not fifteen minutes ago."

My eyes widened.

"He was asking questions."

"About?"

"Books."

"Shit," I replied, walking over to her sparse kitchen.

"What happened?" Her question was a cautious one.

"They murdered him. Bill. He was hanging outside the burning library, the book I gave him at his feet." My voice was shaky and breathless from my run, and the emotion threatened to pull me under.

I went to the cabinet where she stored rare items, avoiding Olivia's face, not wanting to see the horror and the grief. I grabbed a bottle of amber liquor. I didn't know where she'd gotten it, but I'd known it was there.

"Willow," Olivia's concerned voice drifted over to me.

I ignored her and took a swig straight from the bottle, the tears suddenly springing free in a torrent down my dry cheeks.

"It isn't your fault." Her voice was careful.

I took another large drink, swiping away the dampness beneath my eyes, and peered at her across the room. "If you believe that, you're a fool."

Olivia glared at me. "If you want to get drunk, fine, get drunk. I won't stop you. But it won't bring him back."

"You don't think I know that!? You were not the one to see his lifeless body hanging from a lamppost while your entire world burned behind him! You don't get to judge me," I snarled at her.

Her voice lowered. "I'm not judging you. You know what I was like when Kat was taken. You know what I did for months."

I wanted to stay angry at her. I wanted to be able to blame someone else for what happened. But I couldn't. It was my fault.

I slammed the bottle on the table, and then stormed to the door. I needed to get out. I needed to go home. I needed to protect my remaining books. I needed to do something.

Olivia cut me off before I reached the door, blocking it. "I'll let you go. I'll even give you the bottle, if you promise to go straight home. If you promise not to stop, no matter what you see or hear."

I took a deep breath, backing up a step. She dropped her arm and waited for me to answer.

"I promise."

Olivia walked over to the counter and grabbed the bottle, shoving it in my arms. "Be careful."

I nodded, knowing I should say something. Anything. But I couldn't.

She opened the door for me, and I walked out, taking another long drink from the bottle then tucking it under my arm.

It was nowhere near sunset, so I allowed my pace to be slow as I took in the city. It was silent. As if everyone knew something big was about to happen. Hadn't Marcus all but confirmed that? Hadn't Bill?

I rounded the corner of Olivia's street, stumbling off the edge of the sidewalk and barely catching myself in the process.

That's when I saw them. A soldier and a woman. Alone in the shadows across the street from me. I heard her begging, even though I couldn't make out her words. The soldier's back was to me, but he had her hands pinned to the side of the building above her head.

It wasn't the pleading that made me hesitate, it was her eyes. Wide with fear. Knowing that she had no way out. No one to help her.

My hands began to tremble, and the bottle slipped from them, the glass breaking and the remaining liquid running down the concrete and disappearing in between the many cracks.

The soldier hadn't heard, too wrapped up in abusing the woman in front of him. I knew I should keep my head down and walk away. I knew I had promised Olivia. I knew there was nothing I could do. I knew it would only mean there'd be two victims instead of one if I stepped in.

The alcohol swirling in my gut and beginning to make my head spin made me bolder, and I ignored the shaking hands and my own better judgement as I reached down and grabbed a large chunk of the broken glass bottle.

Was I really doing this?

Apparently, as I found my legs crossing the street, my arm held out in front of me, the jagged edges of the bottle leading the way, giving me more confidence than I had.

Before I knew it, I had the broken bottle pressed up against the neck of the soldier. "Get your hands off her," I growled, the bottle shaking like a leaf in my trembling hands.

The soldier released the woman's hands, holding up his own. He let out a mocking laugh as he noticed my fear. He knew I'd already lost. I knew it too.

"Back up," I commanded, but failed at keeping my voice from shaking.

He laughed again but obeyed. I struggled to keep the bottle at his neck.

I mouthed "run" to the woman, and she didn't hesitate as she slipped away and sprinted down the street.

The soldier waited until she was out of sight before he moved. His movement was too quick for my increasingly drunken state, and he easily swatted away the bottle, grabbed my wrist, and slammed me against the side of the building, knocking the air from my lungs.

I tried not to crumple to the ground, but my legs gave out, and I fell onto the broken glass, feeling the shards rip the skin of my hands. The blood ran hot, and poured onto the concrete sidewalk, disappearing between the cracks as the alcohol did. I watched it for a moment before the soldier grabbed my shirt and hauled me to my feet.

I finally looked at him, knowing there was no way out. I'd saved the woman just to sacrifice myself. More importantly, I'd broken my promise to Olivia.

The soldier sneered at me, a twisted smile forming on his face. It was then that it hit me. What a dead Earth did to us. It stole every piece of humanity, turning us into monsters. That's what we were becoming. We were becoming the Claeg.

The thought, along with the alcohol, had me giving in. Giving up. I sagged against the soldier's grip, lowering my head in submission.

I didn't notice him at first. The fear and alcohol running through my veins made me blind to my surroundings, but then his deep, commanding voice cut through the air. "Step back, Private."

The soldier holding me seemed to recognize the voice and instantly dropped my wrists and took a step back.

That's when I finally looked at the other soldier that had silently appeared before us. His presence was as commanding as his voice. He had messy blond hair that fell across his forehead and was much taller than the younger soldier. He looked as though he could crush him in an instant. But it wasn't so much his size, as it was his eyes that caught my attention. Eyes so blue they appeared to glow.

I shook my head as if to clear the image, chalking it up to the alcohol that now began to churn in my gut, making me feel queasy.

"You're not my captain. You have no authority over me," the private sneered, trying to hide his own fear of the captain in front of him.

The captain took a step closer. I watched as the soldier shrank back.

"She's mine." The captain's deep voice held no room for argument. He pointed a dagger in my direction. One I hadn't noticed until now.

The soldier looked between the captain and me, fear and loathing coated his features for a moment before he abruptly strode off, mumbling something under his breath.

That's when I felt the cold bite of steel against my neck.

Chapter Seven

Liam

I noticed her right away, my silent rage coming out of nowhere and sending my feet across the street to stop the soldier pinning her to the side of a crumbling building. I had no real authority over this soldier. He was one of Marvin's, but that didn't stop me. Nor did the fact that my orders were to get rid of her.

That's how I found myself holding a dagger to the woman's throat as she cowered against the building, trembling. I was careful not to hurt or touch her.

Being suddenly so close to her had my eyes traveling down her body. I instantly knew she was drunk. Her eyes were wild, her movements slow and sloppy. But, this time, I noticed her dark brown hair tumbling down to her waist, coated in a thin layer of dirt like the rest of her. She was almost emaciated—her cheeks were hollow, and her loose clothes gave no hint of curves. But she was attractive, that was obvious. Beautiful even.

As my gaze slid to her hands, I saw the blood and the broken glass.

Noticing where my attention was, she balled her fists, trying to hide them.

As the private disappeared around the corner out of sight, I finally dropped my dagger and took a step away from her. She straightened and turned a defiant chin toward me.

"What did you do?" I asked her, not moving, not really knowing why that was my first question.

"Me!?" she shouted. "What did I do?" She laughed. "You're deranged if you think that situation was my fault."

I cocked my head to the side, studying her. Her amber eyes held mine.

I shook my head. "What happened?"

She narrowed her eyes, assessing me. Probably wondering if I was a threat. Wondering how much she should reveal. "He was about to rape a woman. I stepped in."

No one interfered with a soldier's business. It was a death sentence. Her bravery was impressive, but ill-advised.

I looked from her eyes to the ground, noticing the broken bottle.

"Your weapon?" I asked, pointing to the glass.

She nodded once, and then unexpectedly heaved the contents of her stomach all over my leather boots.

Her cheeks instantly stained red as her sheepish eyes widened and met mine.

For some reason, I wanted to laugh, but a split second later she pushed off the building and started racing down the sidewalk. Stumbling was more apt of a description.

At first, I was so stunned I just stood there, but when she disappeared around the corner, I followed her. I told myself it was because I wanted to make sure she made it home safely, but the reality was, I knew. I knew why she was drunk. I knew why she had been reckless.

I'd murdered her friend, and she knew he was dead.

The next morning, as everyone finished packing to evacuate, I was left alone with Marvin. "I'm not going with you," I blurted out.

I'd been planning to escape for a long time. Every mission outside the wall helped to solidify my plan. I'd been mapping my route, studying each town and village for a safe harbor. Well, as safe as one could expect out there.

I'd also been secretly stockpiling supplies for months, taking food and weapons one at a time so that no one would notice the loss.

Marvin stopped and looked at me, no hint of surprise. "You have a plan?"

I nodded.

"Of course you do," he sighed, running his hand over his smooth bald head and glancing at the closed door.

I lowered my voice even more. "You're welcome to come," I offered with an attempt at a smile.

Marvin shook his head, devastated. "I can't. The less I know, the better."

Shit. I was putting him in danger.

I went to speak, but he held up his hand. "You're not staying. I know the risk I'm taking by staying. You know the risk you're taking by going."

I tried to say something else, but he stopped me again. "For what it's worth, I hope you find what you're looking for. And when you do, come find me. I'll be waiting."

I wanted to ask him what that meant. I wanted to ask him a million questions. Hell, I didn't know if he'd ever been married, had kids, had a family, or any of those typical things friends talked about.

It was safer not to know, though. Safer to simply have no one close enough that the Elite could use against you.

Even if he felt like a friend, he was still a stranger to me.

"You'll always be welcome, wherever I end up," I told him.

He gave me a half-smile and a wink as he picked up his bag of weapons and strode out of the room without another word.

I fell back into my chair, the dagger strapped to my leg cutting into the side of my thigh.

If my plan was going to work, I had to make sure my death looked believable.

Chapter Eight

Willow

The city was still deathly silent the next morning, and I wondered how long it would last. How many people had been questioned by soldiers the past few days and were either killed or too scared to show themselves?

Olivia and I walked to the bio lab in silence, scanning our surroundings as if a soldier would pop up at any moment. She still hadn't mentioned what happened yesterday, and I was glad. I didn't want to lie to her about the soldier and the captain.

No one was in line at the scanners, a new phenomenon that didn't leave me feeling any less afraid.

"Wrist," the guard mumbled as he stared blankly at us.

Walking down the hallway to our lab, I spotted Marcus in a discussion with a soldier, and I froze.

Oliva tugged on my right hand, urging me forward, but I couldn't move. My hands trembled, and I stuffed my left in my pocket.

Marcus finally noticed us and mumbled something dismissive to the soldier, who bowed his head and glanced at us briefly. His face twisted into curiosity with a hint of amusement before he took off in the opposite direction. It was the same soldier who'd tried to hurt me.

I finally let out a breath as he disappeared, approaching Marcus slowly.

"Output numbers are due by the end of the day." Marcus's words stuck out in stark contrast to the concern in his tone.

"They're already done. On my desk."

"Good."

Marcus's eyes slid down to my hand, and I pulled it behind me, not wanting him to see the cuts from the broken glass.

The movement had Olivia finally noticing my hands, and I heard her slight intake of breath.

Marcus knew too. I could see it in his face as he met my eyes.

I didn't give them time to ask about it, instead blurting, "Something's going on."

Marcus halted, the concern still there in his face, but now he looked almost pained. "I don't know what you're talking about."

"You're a shit liar."

Olivia gasped, slapping her hand across her mouth.

Marcus didn't even register her reaction as he stared down at me, searching my face. "What have you heard?"

"Rumors."

"Office. Now," he said, waving his hand in the direction of his office as he took off down the hall, expecting me to follow.

But we didn't reach his office before the alarm sounded and we all froze.

I heard Marcus's sharp intake of breath as he whirled on me, placing a hand on my lower back. "Stay here. I'll be right back."

He didn't give me a chance to respond as he slipped into his office.

"Willow." Olivia's voice held a warning in it.

I turned to see soldiers filing into offices and pushing people out into the hallway, everyone as confused and scared as I felt.

The soldier Marcus had just been talking to was among them, and, as he locked eyes with me, I knew his intentions without him having to speak. I grabbed Olivia and dragged her down the hallway that was quickly filling with people.

"What're you doing?" Olivia hissed.

"Getting us to safety."

I heard Marcus calling my name over all the commotion. I waved him off, concentrating on keeping my hold on Olivia.

I heard his voice become more insistent as we were pushed further down the hallway by the growing mass of people. I registered Marcus's look of panic as the crowd was pushed out the main doors of the building and onto the street.

We were met with hundreds, if not thousands, of other people making their way down the road, all headed for the city's main street. The one that led to the only gate into and out of Coria.

Olivia halted, her voice trembling. "Where are they all going?"

"Let's try my apartment," I suggested, though I already knew we wouldn't make it. Based on the number of people in the streets, the soldiers were obviously rounding us all up.

I had to try, though. I had to keep Olivia safe.

Olivia didn't argue as I led her across the street, weaving in between the crowd of people headed in the same direction.

When we reached Sixth Street, I made a hard left, pulling Olivia behind me. I halted in the shade of a building when I spotted a line of soldiers blocking our way. They all dressed identically, with brown leather jackets, white shirts, brown pants, and brown leather boots.

Unlike the captain who saved me, each of them had their rank flaunted on their jackets.

They were outfitted with daggers, swords, and guns.

My hands began to tremble again as we slowly backed away from them. I squeezed Olivia's hand harder in an attempt to hide the shaking. Olivia squeezed back.

"All able-bodied people are required to fight," one of the soldiers said as he walked over to us and shoved us back toward the main street.

We both stumbled but managed to keep our feet under us.

"Doesn't that mean you should be out there?" I snapped back, earning me a knock on the head with the butt of a gun. My vision blurred momentarily before a throbbing sensation began at my temple.

The same soldier shoved me to the ground, and Olivia lost her grip on my hand. She backed up a step, wide-eyed, her breaths coming in shallow bursts as she stared in horror at the soldiers in front of us.

The soldier bent down and put a knee on my chest. I felt like I couldn't pull enough air into my lungs.

"What should we do with the mouth on this one?" He seemed far too delighted at the prospect of hurting me, and the images of my parents came into view as my vision threatened to black out.

Not again.

The soldier leaned down and whispered in my ear, "Might have one last ride before you turn into Claeg food."

My whole body was shaking. My fear held me hostage. I lay there with no fight in me. I was completely frozen.

Olivia snapped me out of my trance. She snarled at my captor, reaching for me like she would pull me out from under him.

"Go," I snapped at her.

She didn't make a move to obey.

The other soldiers moved at once, descending on both of us. It was enough of a distraction for me to ram my knee up into my captor's balls. He let out a groan of pain and released the pressure on my chest, just enough for me to slip out from beneath him.

What I didn't expect was his swift retaliation as the sharp end of a blade tore downward, ripping my shirt from collar to waist. It left a shallow gash in my chest, and I felt the warm blood trickle down my torso.

I didn't have time to register what was happening as Olivia grabbed my hand and turned us both. She pulled me back toward the main street and we both took off running.

One of the soldiers shouted from behind us as we reached the crossroads.

We didn't look back. We kept sprinting toward the safety of the crowds on Main Street. I focused on that single goal, not letting my mind wander to my torn shirt or the blood that was now soaking the band of my pants.

We were out of breath and sweating, but we made it—instantly blending into the thousands of other people jammed together and barely moving forward. I finally looked behind us to see a few soldiers scanning the crowd for us, but I quickly turned away, slumping down amongst the people that filled the streets.

I shook my head, feeling the throbbing sensation where I'd been hit. I seemed incapable of processing what was happening around us. My vision was peppered with black dots, and I felt like I couldn't stay on my feet. I swayed in motion with the rest of the crowd, trying to regain my senses.

I focused on my immediate needs as I tugged my shirt back together, tying it into a sloppy knot. It was the best I could do.

Then, I surveyed our situation. My brain instantly focused on the evidence in front of me.

"We stick together no matter what, OK?" I said to Olivia, unable to keep my voice from shaking.

She nodded, focused on the closed gate ahead of us and the sounds that began to percolate toward us from the other side. Sounds of fighting. Sounds of pain.

As we approached the gate, I briefly registered that a bow and a few arrows were shoved into my arms.

"The Elite have guns, and we have these?" someone ahead of us asked in disbelief.

"This is a lot of people, Willow," Olivia said, finally pulling her gaze from the gate and looking at everyone around us. "Might be the whole city—"

I didn't know what to say.

"Are they going to give us any directions?" someone asked next to us.

"Unlikely," someone else replied.

"So, this is a suicide mission?" the first asked.

No one responded.

We finally halted before the closed gates, and it felt like my legs were made of lead. Olivia stopped scanning the crowd and returned her gaze forward. Some people chatted nervously, but most seemed like they were in a state of shock, like I was.

It felt like an eternity, but as the gates began to ratchet open, a silence descended on the crowd. We could hear fighting beyond the wall. It was likely that the city's meager military had already begun our defense.

"We don't fight, we hide. The Claeg are attracted to the scent of blood, so we must get as far away from other people as possible," I whispered to Olivia, who looked white as a ghost watching the gates.

I looked down at the blood on my shirt and pants and knew we wouldn't get far. All I could hope was that we could find somewhere to hide before the scent of my blood hit any of the Claeg.

"Hold onto me and make a sharp right as we exit. We'll go along the wall until we can find somewhere safe. They fight in packs, drawing you to the center, so we'll stay with our backs to the wall to avoid becoming trapped," I added, remembering all the information I read about them in books I stole from the library.

It was the only plan I had, and it was a shitty one at that. I had no idea what we were going to find outside the walls. I didn't have a clue if there was even anywhere to hide. My knowledge of the outside world was limited to books written one hundred and fifty years ago, and the maps in those books were likely incomparable to the world now.

I only hoped we could find *something* to conceal us until the Claeg moved on, because I knew they eventually would.

Olivia didn't respond verbally to my plan but inclined her head slightly to let me know she heard me.

As the large crowd moved forward again, we heard the first screams, and everyone around us froze. I started pulling Olivia to the outskirts of the crowd, afraid it might become a stampede if people started trying to get back into the city. Even if the soldiers were there to make sure we went through. She followed without protest. Her skin was pale and clammy as she stared forward, clutching the bow and arrows with her free hand.

"Don't look!" I yelled at her over the screaming and panicked voices. I focused solely on getting her out of the chaos and away from the stench of iron-rich blood that began to assault my senses.

We reached the gate's opening the exact moment we came to the outside of the crowd, and I pulled Olivia through the gate and along the wall. We quickly but quietly made our way along it, covering as much distance as we could.

My brain couldn't register much of what was happening in the commotion. The dust made it hard to see more than ten to fifteen feet in front of me. I caught glimpses of the Claeg as they appeared and disappeared into the dust, apparently knowing exactly how to maneuver in this environment.

The Claeg looked precisely as described in the book, and I found Olivia staring in horror at them as they came and went from our line of sight. They appeared almost human, but their skin was gray and sagged off their bones, which could easily be seen under their skin. They were hunched at the shoulders and only had a few strands of black hair that came out of their scalp. Their most defining features were their teeth and eyes. Unlike humans, all their teeth were sharp and pointed, resembling shark teeth, and were designed to tear apart animal flesh. Their eyes were all white and lacked any visible irises, but that didn't appear to affect their vision. They moved through the desolate landscape, killing easily. Killing on instinct.

I yanked her forward, willing my body to keep moving.

There was nothing but a smooth wall to our right. There were no structures, no rocks, and no changes in the landscape ahead of us.

No place to hide.

My hands shook, and I squeezed Olivia's hand even tighter. I could feel my heartbeat racing in my chest. I knew we only had moments before the Claeg noticed the smell of my blood. They were everywhere, as were the screams of the people attempting to fight them off.

As we continued along the wall, we came upon a brief window in the dust where we could see further into the distance. I heard Olivia gasp beside me as she stared at what appeared to be thousands of Claeg stretching on as far as the eye could see.

"I thought they only fought in small numbers?" Olivia gaped.

I didn't respond, unable to explain, as I yanked on her arm again and picked up my pace. We were quickly approaching the outer edge of the battle. After a few more minutes of sprinting, we'd put some distance between us and the fighting. I didn't stop but slowed my pace slightly as I felt Olivia struggling to keep up.

That's when I saw them—another small pack of Claeg attracted to the scent of so much blood behind us. They were scavengers, killing and coming back long after to eat the dead. When the Earth began to die, that's when they showed up, seemingly out of nowhere—speeding up the demise of the Earth. Speeding up *our* demise.

I halted, Olivia almost crashing into my back. I scanned the area for something—anything—to help us. Our weapons would be useless against so many, even if we knew how to use them. I quickly tossed mine aside, and Olivia did the same. The weight would only slow us.

Sheer luck had my eyes landing on a slight break in the wall ahead of us. We were too far away to see if we could fit through it, but we had no other option.

Despite our evident exhaustion, I grabbed Olivia, urging her to sprint as fast as possible. We had approximately ten seconds before the Claeg were on us, and I wasn't sure we would make it in time.

"Faster!" I shouted at Olivia, who felt almost like a dead weight behind me. The rasping of her breath was all I heard as I made one last push toward the opening.

I didn't hesitate as I shoved Olivia through the crack first and then turned to squeeze myself through. At that exact moment, the leading Claeg dove for me, clawing through the fabric and skin on my leg and grabbing hold of my ankle.

I screamed as its sharp nails dug into the thin layer of skin at my bone and held tight. The warm blood trickled down into my boot; It licked its white lips as it inched closer to me.

I kicked at its hand, trying desperately to separate it from my ankle but it was much stronger.

"No!" I yelled as I crashed onto my side, the Claeg dragging me out of the opening in the wall. I clawed at the ground in desperation.

The next thing I knew, strong hands grabbed me under the shoulders and pulled, simultaneously cutting off the hand of the Claeg with a sword.

The creature made an ugly shrieking noise and pulled back.

The other pack members were instantly on us, trying to claw their way through the opening as I was dragged inside.

Through sheer luck, they were slightly too large to fit through the wall.

I was dragged further into the darkness when the hands finally released me, and I fell back onto the cold dirt.

A low, deep voice asked, "Are you alright?"

And, suddenly, I was staring into familiar, bright-blue eyes, illuminated only by the light filtering in through the crack in the wall.

Chapter Nine

Liam

I wasn't expecting her. Hell, I wasn't expecting anyone, but especially not her.

She scrambled away from me the moment she saw me, clutching her ankle, her other hand covering her torn shirt. She was trembling fiercely.

I stared at her, not knowing what to do or how badly she was injured.

I didn't have much time to think about it, though, as a ripping noise had my gaze snapping to the wall's opening and the Claeg pack trying to claw their way in. They had managed to widen the opening by another inch.

"We have to move," I growled, reaching for her hand.

She hesitated, her eyes darting between the monsters and me as if she didn't know which was more dangerous.

When her eyes widened at something behind me, I was already moving.

The smallest Claeg had finally pushed its way through the opening, racing toward us. It was the Claeg that had originally grabbed her, its missing hand oozing blood all over the dirt. It was moving quicker than I expected.

I wheeled on the creature, slicing my sword through the air, aiming at its neck. My hit was a half-second too slow and instead of slicing off its head, I tore clean through its leg. It stumbled and fell, letting out a loud roar in the process.

I quickly turned to the two women who had pressed themselves up against the far wall, both staring in shock at the Claeg now clawing its way toward them on the ground. Toward the scent of their blood.

I took two giant steps in their direction, pulling out two daggers.

I handed the first to the taller one. She didn't hesitate to take it but looked as though she didn't have a clue what to do with it.

I pressed the second dagger into the smaller woman's hand, and her eyes met mine briefly.

Fear. That was definitely fear I saw there. But, for a brief moment, she stopped trembling, resolve taking over.

"Follow me," I commanded, dropping her hand and turning to chop the head off the injured Claeg. Its shrieks instantly stopped.

The two women side-stepped the Claeg, eyeing its grotesque form and mutilated body.

I forgot what it was like to see them for the first time. I forgot the terror. I forgot the sounds. I forgot how twisted and monstrous they were.

I pulled out a flashlight and led them further into the wall, away from the pack still trying to claw their way in. I secured the area once we rounded the bend, ensuring the Claeg couldn't get to us.

I had a decision to make, and I needed to make it quickly. I had minutes before the Elite caught on to my absence. I hadn't planned on taking others. I had perfectly prepared everything I needed—I didn't have enough for anyone else.

To leave them would be a death sentence. But to take them would probably lead to all our deaths, mine included. One was injured, and they'd likely never been outside the wall. They'd slow me down. They'd be a liability.

That was my military thinking.

"Where are we going?" Her unsteady voice, full of pain, pierced the eerie silence as we walked. We were approaching the northern end of the city now. Farthest from the battle.

"Not much further," I said, not looking at them.

I knew she was in pain, but she didn't utter a word as we finally approached where I had stockpiled my supplies.

I set down the flashlight on a few wooden crates stacked against the city wall's interior, so that it illuminated the area. When the light fell on the two women, I noticed how pale they were and worried the woman with the glasses might pass out from blood loss.

"Sit," I commanded, pointing to another set of empty wooden crates.

The taller one gently lowered her friend onto them. She slumped against the wall, wincing as she finally relaxed her injured leg.

"I have a few medical supplies," I explained, rummaging through one of my packs.

I found what I needed and walked over to her. She tensed, hands shaking.

"I'll do it," her friend cut in, taking the supplies from me.

I looked between the two women—understanding dawning. I suspected they recognized me, but I didn't let on that I remembered them. I didn't want to make the situation any more complicated than it already was.

The taller woman bent down and began unbuckling the boot of the injured one. I heard her hiss through her teeth as the boot fell off and a stream of blood trickled down her foot, landing on the ground.

"Does it need stitches?" I asked, stepping back.

The injured woman assessed her leg, before meeting my eyes. "I don't think so."

She held my gaze for longer than I was used to, and I couldn't help but notice that even though she looked fearless now, her hands were still trembling.

I walked back to the crates, pulling out packs of supplies.

Her voice drifted over to me, stronger this time. "Going somewhere, soldier?"

I cringed at the term, halting my packing to face her.

"I would have thought that was obvious," I retorted.

"Care to explain what's going on?" she asked, clearly annoyed at my response.

"I know about as much as you do," I replied, rearranging supplies.

"I highly doubt that. Though your jacket doesn't reveal your rank, you're clearly an experienced soldier."

My eyes were on hers the instant the words were out of her mouth. "And how do you figure?"

She nodded toward the supplies. "You've been planning this. Your supplies indicate you know what you need to survive past the wall, which means you've done it before. Likely many times."

I stared at her, trying to see beyond her matter-of-fact words.

"I can't take you with me." I didn't know why I said it, even if it were true.

Her friend's head shot up at my words. She looked between the two of us. "Why not?" she sounded surprised at my admission.

I took two strides toward them, and the injured woman recoiled against the wall. Her reaction shocked me so much that I halted mid-step.

"I don't have enough supplies to take you with me, and your injury will only slow us. The Claeg'll hunt us down before we make it five miles."

"And what do you expect us to do then?" Her voice sounded downright baffled by my response.

"What would you have done if I weren't here?" I shot back at her.

"You are here."

I went to open my mouth, but her friend beat me to it. "We're getting nowhere."

The injured woman looked at her friend, her shoulders visibly relaxing. But only slightly. "Fine. Leave us here if you want." She didn't say it meagerly—it was a challenge.

Fuck.

I ran my hands through my hair, grappling with what to do.

I pulled out a knife and lighter. "If you're coming with me, you'll have to cut the trackers out of your wrists."

It was a scare tactic. I knew it. But if they were going to come with me, it needed to be done. If they didn't want to, that was on them.

The taller one shook her head, exaggerating the movement, but the other stood on shaky legs, hobbling toward me with an outstretched hand.

My eyebrows rose as I handed her the knife and lighter. I couldn't help as my eyes traveled down her torn, blood-stained shirt and I assessed her injury.

She noticed my gaze and turned away, hobbling back to the crates.

That's when I noticed it—the thing that was more likely to get us killed than the Claeg.

Chapter Ten

Willow

The soldier grabbed my arm before I could return to my seat.

As I went to protest, he growled, "Take off your shirt. Now."

I tried to free my arm, but he held on with an iron grip. "I will do no such thing!" I yelled at him, fixing him with a stare equally as harsh.

"Who are you?" Was it fear I detected beneath his firm voice? And didn't he already know who I was? Or, at least, have an idea?

"I'm nobody," I replied, still trying to pull my arm away.

He looked down at me, and I glared back. "You have an Elite tracker on your shirt. Where did you get it?"

"A what?" I asked him, completely dumbfounded.

"A tracker the Elite use for their own. One that doesn't get embedded in your wrist but is worn on clothes. Why do you have it on your shirt?"

I shook my head, and my pure confusion must have convinced the soldier I wasn't lying because he dropped my arm an instant later.

"They'll be here within an hour, maybe less. Someone important wanted to keep tabs on you. I'm surprised they even let you out of the city with that thing on." He paused and sighed, pushing blond strands out of his eyes. "Shit," he said, shaking his head, still grappling with something. "You have a decision to make, and you need to make it quickly. We're running out of time. I cannot be here when the Elite show up. You either come with me immediately or wait for the Elite to come get you."

Bile rose in my throat at the thought of going with the soldier but also at the thought of being in the Elite's hands. If they knew about the books, I'd be dead the instant they found me, but that wasn't even what scared me the most. It was the fact that I'd be putting Olivia in danger, too.

It was an impossible decision. There was no correct one when death was likely the result of both choices.

Luckily, I didn't have to make the decision. Olivia made it for me. "Cut the trackers out."

The soldier didn't look entirely convinced he had heard her right. I sighed, tugged at the knot holding my shirt together, and shimmied it off my shoulders, painfully aware that the soldier could see every rib through my gaunt skin.

I studied the Elite tracker. It was a small, round disk no larger than my thumbnail. It looked like a computer chip and clung to my shirt where the small of my back was.

I sighed as I balled the shirt and threw it at the soldier.

He smirked as it hit him in the face, but only responded by throwing me a new one.

When I finished with Olivia's wrist, I glanced at the soldier's. It was bandaged with a dirty cloth, blood already seeping through the outside of it. I refrained from telling him it might become infected as he carefully cut open my wrist to remove my tracker for me since Olivia had vehemently declined to do so.

I clenched my teeth, trying not to make a sound. He was quick and efficient.

When he finished, he gently let go of my hand, and I finally turned to face him.

He was studying me intently.

"Thanks," I murmured, holding my wrapped wrist against my chest.

He nodded. "I'm Liam."

"Willow. And this is Olivia."

We both turned to look at Olivia. She gave him an awkward wave, keeping well away—her eyes trained on his every move.

Liam headed toward the crates. "We need to be far away from here by nightfall." He paused and looked at the two of us as if trying to determine if we could make it. "I have basic supplies that will last us a few days. We'll have to stop at an abandoned community, about a two-day walk from here, to re-stock. You'll have to move as quickly as you can."

"Where are we going?" I asked. He had to have some final destination in mind.

Liam seemed as if he was contemplating whether to answer or not.

"To find a new home," he finally said.

I wasn't sure how to respond. My head was flooded with questions, but I refrained from asking them. Now didn't feel like the right time.

Liam knelt and dug out two more packs from the crates, handing them to us. He then proceeded to strap two bags, two canteens of water, a bow and arrows, and a bag of weapons onto himself. That wasn't including the sword already strapped to his back and the hidden knives and daggers that were likely all over his body. I couldn't imagine the weight he was carrying.

Olivia was downright gaping at him. Mouth open. I almost laughed at her expression.

She threw me a sideways glance, and I smirked at her.

"Don't say it," she warned, but I could hear the sarcasm returning.

"Wouldn't dare," I said, still smiling.

Liam was watching us both but didn't say a word. His face remained impassive, his body stiff and alert.

"Ready?" he finally asked.

"Seriously?" Olivia said.

Liam didn't take the bait. He just turned and started walking.

With my ankle bound and the bleeding stopped, I was able to walk with only a slight limp. I ignored the pain, gritting my teeth and doing my best to keep up.

A few more minutes of walking inside the wall brought us to another opening. This one was even smaller than the one we had entered through.

"You'll have to shove your packs through first," Liam instructed us. "I'll go ahead."

The speed at which he got all his stuff and himself through the opening was impressive.

"Gotta work on my fitness," Olivia whispered.

I snorted, holding back a laugh. "Even then," I responded, shoving my bag through the opening, "you'll never come close to that."

Olivia let out a small chuckle as I got on my stomach to shimmy through the opening.

I instinctively covered my eyes and felt Liam grab my elbow to help me. "Thanks," I muttered.

I didn't know if he heard me, though, because he was already busy helping Olivia.

I stood in the dappled sunlight and squinted at the barren landscape ahead of me. Sounds of fighting were nothing more than a murmur this far away, but my whole body tensed anyway, all my senses on high alert. I swiveled my head in all directions watching for any movement. Watching for the now familiar movement of a pack of Claeg.

"This way," Liam murmured as he finished helping Olivia up. Then he started walking north, away from the massive wall behind us.

I couldn't help but wonder if we'd made the right choice in following this soldier.

Olivia wrapped her hand around mine and squeezed. Neither of us could say the words, so we let them pass unspoken. We started walking, following the soldier in front of us—stumbling toward some unknown future.

What I knew of life outside the wall was limited. What I learned came only from whispers, diluted stories, and myths.

There was nothing but dead dirt below my feet that crunched unnaturally with every step we took. The land was flat and endless in front of us, the horizon blurred by the constant dust suspended on the wind.

Large rocks and small crevices, that may have once been streams or creeks in another time, dotted the landscape. Everything was so wind-blown that any indication of what truly existed was lost long ago. My imagination couldn't even piece together what the land may have looked like before it died, even though I'd seen pictures.

"You get used to it," Liam's voice drifted toward us from where he had stopped for a moment.

"You should have left us back there."

He raised his eyebrows slightly, but I didn't explain further.

I stopped a few times to pick up seeds in the dirt, adding them to the collection in my pocket. I felt Liam's eyes on me as I bent down to gather them, but he never said anything.

For miles, nothing changed in the landscape. It was as dead and hopeless as it was when we first set out. The only evidence we had gone anywhere was the aching in my muscles and joints, the fire I felt where the Claeg had torn my ankle open, and my stomach rumbling. The wind had destroyed all evidence of our movement, and the sun setting was our only indication that any time had passed.

We walked silently for so long I almost forgot how dangerous it was out here when Liam suddenly shouted, "Run!"

I glanced behind me just long enough to see a dust storm quickly descending on us—the cloud blotting out everything around it. It was a monster itself, devouring everything in its path. It's wind strong enough to throw you across the landscape, and sharp dirt and rocks forceful enough to put holes in you.

"Over there! Between those rocks!" he bellowed, pointing ahead of us.

We raced toward the rocks, crouching down between them. Liam pulled his bag off his shoulders, grabbing a blanket, and threw it over the three of us.

When the windstorm hit, he practically threw his body on top of us, taking the brunt of it. I heard the stones bouncing off the rocks above us and falling down on Liam like rain.

He didn't make a sound, concentrating on keeping us completely covered. His breath was steady against my back, a rhythm that seemed to keep me from shaking, despite how close he was.

We all listened as the wind died, not daring to say anything.

When Liam finally crawled off us, pulling the blanket aside, I could see the storm's damage. The blanket wasn't completely shredded but was torn in several places, as if someone had taken a knife to it. I couldn't imagine what his back felt like. The landscape around us was covered in a new, thick layer of dust. That included us.

Liam watched as we rose to our feet, dusting ourselves off. His military eyes silently assessed our every movement.

"We'll stay here for the night," Liam finally said, and I held back my relief. I didn't think my body could take any more walking.

As we silently set out our sleeping blankets, I assessed Liam too. I watched him pull his shirt over his head, wincing slightly as he did. Though I couldn't see his back, I could only imagine what it looked like, as the shirt he threw on top of his bag was covered in blood.

I wanted to say something—to thank him for what he did. I wanted to help him, but I didn't know how. Instead, I focused on setting up our camp as he threw a clean shirt on and proceeded with his own sleeping arrangements, not muttering a word about his shredded back.

"Here," Liam said, holding out a bag of food for the both of us.

Olivia hesitantly grabbed the bag he offered her, and I nodded my thanks as I took mine.

An audible gasp escaped my lips as I opened the bag to find dried meat. Out of the corner of my eye, I saw Olivia staring at the bag in her hands, dumbfounded.

"What is it?" I could almost hear the concern in Liam's voice.

"Nothing, we just haven't had meat in years." I sounded like a schoolgirl, unable to hide my excitement.

"Years?" Liam responded, his eyes widening slightly.

"We're only fed the basic grains we can grow in the lab. Crusty bread, mush, flatbread—that's it." I shrugged.

"No wonder you two are so emaciated." Liam paused but added quickly, "No offense."

"None taken," I mumbled as I took my first bite and practically moaned at the taste of it. What he said was true, there was no denying how malnourished we were.

I could hear Olivia eating as though it were her last meal.

Liam looked over at her, a hint of a smile forming on his lips. "Take it slow. It might make you sick the first time," he advised, and Olivia slowed her pace.

We consumed the rest of the meal in silence, and I wondered if the soldier would ever say anything other than barking instructions.

"I'll keep watch. You both need to rest," Liam finally said as we finished our meal.

Olivia gave me a quick, concerned glance.

"We aren't comfortable with that," I calmly tried to explain to him.

"Do you have a better idea?" He sounded almost amused.

"No, but we sure as hell aren't trusting you while we sleep." I couldn't help the slight clip in my tone.

"I wouldn't touch either of you," he practically growled, once he realized what we were implying. His eyes drifted to my chest as if he could see the truth of what happened with the soldiers. As if he were remembering what almost happened the day Bill died.

I started to tremble slightly at his stare, remembering the way the soldiers looked at my mother before they slit her throat in front of me.

"Come. I'll help you get that wretched dust off," Olivia said before turning to glare at Liam.

He must have gotten the hint because he turned, carrying his stuff a hundred feet away, and settled himself against a rock.

He didn't look back at us.

Chapter Eleven

Liam

The next morning, Willow sat bolt upright, completely panicked.

"What is it?" I called from the rock above her, my heart rate increasing at the look on her face.

Before she could reply, something caught my attention and I strained my eyes, looking for movement or changes in the landscape around us. From my vantage point, I could see in every direction.

"Get up!" I yelled as I caught sight of a new plume of dust kicking up not a half-mile away from us. "Quickly!"

Olivia and Willow scrambled to put their blankets back in their packs as I leapt down from the rock and grabbed them, practically dragging them further into the rock outcropping. I wedged us down into a small crack barely big enough for the three of us. We were so close to each other I could hear their breathing. Olivia's breath was fast and shallow, while Willow seemed like she wasn't breathing at all.

We didn't have to wait long before we heard the grunting from a small group of Claeg that had somehow picked up on our movement. Willow tensed beside me, still not breathing.

I shifted, my leg pushing up against hers. I kept my gaze straight ahead and heard her breath slowly return. Her warmth seeped into my side, easing something inside me, too.

We waited for what seemed like hours. The waiting was the hardest part. I knew they were scared, and I couldn't do a damn thing about it except keep them hidden. I knew the presence of a soldier—my presence—only made it worse.

Long after the sounds of the Claeg vanished, I finally grabbed the rock in front of me and pulled myself through the small opening in one fluid movement.

They both emerged back into the sunlight, slightly dazed. I almost missed Willow's shaking hands as she shoved them behind her.

"Re-pack your bags. We need to be moving in the next ten minutes," I said to them both, falling back into the familiar role of captain.

Willow didn't move while Olivia bent down and rearranged the hastily packed supplies in her bag.

"We're *not* your soldiers." her voice was low but firm.

I didn't know how to react to that. She was right. But that's who I was—a captain of soldiers. Or who I had been for the past five years, anyway.

Olivia's eyebrows rose, and a half-smile tugged at her lips as she patiently watched us.

Willow continued, "Why don't you teach us something instead of just ordering us around?"

I wasn't expecting her to ask anything of me. "What do you want to know?"

"Let's start with the Claeg. How can we defend ourselves against them?" Her arms fell to her sides, but she kept her hands in fists to hide the shaking. Little did she know, I noticed everything when it came to her—every look, every movement. After what I'd done these past five years, I was surprised I even had the capability of caring enough to notice anything at all.

I sighed deeply. She was right, although I didn't want to admit it. I wasn't sure I'd be around much longer to help them. "First, you won't be able to fight them. They're too skilled and too strong, and you're too . . . small and inexperienced," I said somewhat awkwardly. "If you're smart, you might be able to injure one of them at least enough to run away and hide. They travel and fight in packs, making killing them harder. Usually, their packs are small, ten to fifteen at most."

"But then, why were there so many at the wall?" Olivia interjected.

"We don't know. Our scouts saw them gathering in larger and larger numbers. It's very unusual behavior. They're normally on the move, not stopping anywhere for very long."

I paused, considering what to say next. I didn't know how much I should tell them about what happened. I was afraid the truth would only paint me as more of a villain. If I was going to keep them alive, I needed them to listen to me. To trust me—if only a little bit.

"I have a bow and arrows, two swords, a few daggers, and a gun with limited ammunition. I can teach you how to use everything but the gun. The ammunition is too precious to lose. But we can't stay still for long. Even though we removed our tracking devices, the Elite might still send out a search party. They have skilled trackers—better than I am—so we need to keep moving."

"Why go through all the trouble?" Willow asked, picking up on every detail of what I said.

"I don't know," I lied, "you're the one with the Elite tracker."

I could tell she didn't totally buy it.

I couldn't blame her. I was a liar and a monster. I could have left them to the Elite. I probably should have. Someone wanted to keep tabs on Willow—the Elite tracker on her shirt made that obvious. The tracker wouldn't have been necessary if they truly wanted her dead. The Claeg would have taken her out without them lifting a finger, so the tracker was there for another reason. A reason I couldn't quite figure out. Was it to keep her safe or hunt her down to use her for their benefit? The latter made me terrified for reasons I didn't fully understand. I knew she was wanted for the books she stole, but what else made them want to keep track of her?

Then there was me. The reason the Elite wanted to track me down. A whole other issue.

"OK, teach us," she said after a moment, determination punctuating her words.

"We should really start with conditioning. But we have to cover a lot of ground quickly, and you are too malnourished to do both. So, until you gain some weight, we'll skip the conditioning drills," I said to them both.

"How thoughtful," Olivia replied sarcastically, and I noticed Willow smile at the comment.

I sketched a bow as I replied, "I aim to please. We'll start with archery. You have a better shot at killing a Claeg with an arrow than in hand-to-hand combat."

"Let's be honest, shall we? We don't have a shot at all," Olivia commented, as she stood there with her arms crossed.

Willow almost laughed, and I watched her mouth as she tried to hold it back.

"Not with that attitude," I responded with a half-smile of my own, before continuing with my instruction. Willow studied my words with an intensity that unnerved me a little.

It turned out Willow wasn't horrible at the bow. She wasn't entirely devoid of athletic skill, that was obvious, but years of sitting in a lab and malnutrition didn't help.

She was about to string her bow when I walked over. She didn't notice me right away as she paused and bent down, gathering something small in her hand. She mouthed something silently, and an instant later, a breeze ruffled her hair, pulling it over her shoulder.

She stood, leaning the bow against her good leg as she reached into her pocket, pulling out the same glass vial I saw her with earlier. She deposited the tiny, oval-shaped object in the vial and returned it to her pocket.

When she finally noticed me, she froze.

"Don't let me distract you," I said, waving my hand at her.

"Your presence is distracting," she responded. I cocked my head at that, a smile itching to form, but she quickly added, "Anyone staring at me would be distracting."

I didn't say anything as I walked a hundred feet away and sat down on a rock, pretending to stare at something in the distance, instead.

I caught Willow turning back toward the target and smiled to myself. I watched her out of the side of my eye. When she released the arrow, it went too high and missed the target by a foot or so.

"You need to hold the bow higher," I yelled from my seat, unable to help myself.

She smiled, and it threw me a little as she grabbed another arrow.

This time, she followed my advice and held the bow higher but still missed the target by a few inches.

I silently walked up behind her as she strung another arrow.

When she finally noticed me, she almost jumped out of her skin and mumbled, "Shit."

"Sorry. Didn't mean to scare you. May I?" I asked, inclining my head toward the bow and arrow.

She nodded slowly, but I could see her hesitation.

I walked around behind her and was close enough to feel her body's warmth. I closed my eyes for a moment, trying to compose myself. "Raise the bow," I said quietly into her ear.

She lifted the bow to a ready position.

"Your back elbow needs to be up more. In line with the arrow," I said, my head in line with hers, staring down the length of the bow toward the target.

She lifted her back elbow an inch or so.

"Now try," I said.

She released the arrow and sure enough, it hit the target.

"Good," I said as I reluctantly backed away from her.

I didn't go far this time, and she didn't seem to mind. She strung another arrow and released it, hitting the target again.

"Once you hit the same target a hundred times, we can move on to something more challenging," I called to her.

"A hundred?" she gaped at me. "That seems excessive."

"You need to build muscle strength more than you need to practice your aim."

She frowned.

I smirked. "Better get to work. You have ninety-eight more to go."

"Asshole," she muttered before turning back toward the target. I chuckled under my breath.

She hit the target about twenty more times before her arms gave out. I watched her improve with every shot, amazed at how quickly she picked up the skill.

"Let's move. There'll be more time to practice later," I called out as I walked back to our temporary camp, where Olivia was already packing up.

Willow followed me back and bent down to help Olivia without a word.

I left them together as I scrambled up the rocks to scan the area for Claeg or humans. Suddenly, a bout of dizziness hit me. I stumbled but didn't fall, stopping to let it pass. I held up my wrist.

No wonder I was dizzy. I was still losing blood.

Chapter Twelve

Willow

"So, how come I didn't get any close one-on-one instruction?" Olivia said, waggling her eyebrows as she shouldered her bag.

I narrowed my eyes, knowing exactly what she was implying, but I didn't get a chance to respond as the sight of Liam stopped me.

Something was wrong. Something was *very* wrong.

He seemed the same, with the same stoic look on his face, but his eyes were glassy. I scanned his body and finally noticed his wrist. It had been almost two days, and it was still bleeding. The deep-red blood stood in stark contrast to the white of the bandage.

"Your wrist," I said, pointing.

"I've had this happen before. It'll be fine," he replied, dismissing me and turning to finish packing up.

"It could already be infected. Will you at least let me look at it?" I said to his back, trying to hold in my growing panic.

He paused and faced me again, holding out his arm in silent invitation. I walked over to him, taking his hand in mine. I instantly felt the heat and knew the wound was infected.

"Fuck, Liam, what were you thinking? Why didn't you say anything?"

He just gave me a blank look.

Olivia watched us.

"We have nothing to help with an infection, but I can at least clean and change your filthy bandage. Olivia, can you grab a clean cloth and some water from my pack?" I said, still clutching his too-warm hand.

I turned it over and slowly unwrapped the filthy, blood-stained bandage. When I did, the blood gushed further, running down his arm, big red droplets landing on the ground. I cursed him again as Liam began to sway on his feet.

"Sit down," I commanded, and he obeyed without a word.

Olivia came back with my shirt and some clean water. I washed the wound as best as I could, and tightly tied the clean cloth around it. Liam still didn't make a sound, watching my face as though he was trying to read my thoughts.

"Rest here for a few minutes until the bleeding slows," I said, standing and walking away before either of them could stop me.

The last thing I heard as I crested the rocks was Olivia. "You're almost human with those flushed cheeks. It's a good look on you."

A small smile tugged at my lips despite my growing concern, as I picked up my pace, increasing the distance between us.

I walked further into the rock outcropping, my mind racing. I brooded over every possible situation. Given the limited first-aid supplies, the lack of proper shelter, little rest, zero medication, and little food, the chances of fighting an infection like that were near impossible. I had seen the exact situation over and over again with the Forgotten.

What would we do without him? Despite the risk of trusting a soldier, he was the only one that knew how to survive out here. I wasn't too proud to admit that.

I sighed and sat down on a rock. I tilted my head toward the sun's warmth, letting it seep into my sore muscles and wary soul. I didn't intend to stay long, just long enough to calm my restless brain.

When I finally turned away from the burning sun and back toward our temporary camp, the color green flashed in my peripheral vision. I halted momentarily, blinking before slowly swiveling my head toward the color.

Tucked between some of the rocks, about a hundred feet from where I was sitting, nestled four or five plants. I stared at them for a moment, dumbfounded, before slowly approaching them. I assumed they were an illusion, and I blinked repeatedly, fully expecting them to disappear as I inched closer to them.

They didn't.

I bent down to get a closer look. I didn't know what to think. My brain went into overdrive again, trying to explain the unexplainable, as I touched the leaves, my nose filling with an earthy scent. White flowers bloomed in groups from long stalks, and the feathery leaves spread out in a bushy pattern below them.

I had spent so much of my life studying plants—knowing they once existed, knowing they once had names and scents and beautiful blooms. But I had only ever seen them in pictures. And no matter how many photos I had studied, nothing compared to meeting them in real life.

A single tear escaped down my cheek, landing on the dry earth below, instantly absorbed, leaving no trace of the moisture behind.

I knew this plant. I had studied her properties extensively and seen many pictures. This was yarrow. A warrior's plant. A plant of protection and healing.

I hesitated long enough to ask permission to take some of her leaves and flowers. I wasn't expecting an answer, of course, but to my astonishment, I could have sworn I *felt* one.

I didn't overthink, quickly plucking a few of her leaves and flowers. Then I gathered some dried flower heads and spread her seeds on the barren Earth in front of me.

"Thank you," I whispered before getting up and racing back.

If I had waited a moment longer, I would have heard a response in a long-forgotten language.

If I had just turned back, I would have seen more plants sprout from the seeds I had just spread.

When I returned, Olivia was sitting a reasonable distance from Liam, eyeing him, not with concern, but amusement.

I didn't want to know what they'd talked about.

Liam seemed detached from everything. He was sitting with his back against a rock, arms falling limply at his sides. His eyes were still glossy, and the color in his cheeks indicated a rising fever.

When Olivia saw me, she bolted up, racing over.

"I found something," I said to her as I held the plants and flowers out for both of them to see.

Olivia gasped as she inched closer, her eyes on the plant in my hand. "Where? How?"

"I stumbled across them, close to where we hid from the Claeg and the dust storm earlier. Four plants. I just can't figure out how we missed them the first time," I responded.

Her face looked utterly bewildered, and I almost laughed.

Liam was oddly silent.

"Have you seen any plants out here before?" I asked him.

He shook his head deliriously.

"Olivia, can you heat some water so I can make tea?"

She nodded, her eyes hovering on the plant in my hand for a few more seconds like she thought it might disappear at any moment.

I walked over to my pack and rummaged around, trying to find a cup. Liam finally broke his silence. "I have a cup in my bag."

I moved over to his pack.

"It's in the front pocket," he said to my back.

I opened the front pocket and moved things around, looking for the cup. I hesitated when my hand grazed a picture. It was a photo of a woman slightly younger than Liam. She had beautiful blonde hair and a brilliant smile.

"Did you find it?" Liam asked when I froze.

"Yes," I said hurriedly over my shoulder, quickly putting the picture back where I found it. I pulled the cup from the bag and held it up for him to see, wondering who the woman was and *where* she was. Had she meant something to him? Or maybe, she *still* means something to him?

I didn't say anything as I filled the cup with water and placed it on the hot coal that formed from the fire starter. While the water was heating up, I sat beside Liam. I took a few leaves and chewed them up. Their taste was somewhat bitter, but earthy. I had never tasted anything like it.

I slowly unwrapped Liam's wrist and placed the chewed-up leaves over his wound, completely covering it. Then, I tightly wrapped his wrist again with a clean bandage. When I looked up at him, he looked right into my eyes. I still couldn't read him, but his gaze was softer than it had been. I gave him a slight smile and a reassuring nod as I stood, amazed I wasn't shaking. Progress.

I repeated the process for the wound on my leg and chest.

"We'll need to stay here another night. You have to sleep this time. If you don't fight this infection, we don't stand a chance," I said, walking over to the cup of hot water and dropping in the remaining leaves and flowers.

If Liam had an opinion, he didn't voice it. I could only pray we wouldn't run into any trouble while he was out.

Watching him, Olivia sighed deeply before whispering, "He doesn't look so good."

"I thought you said he looked better like that?" I gave her a knowing smile.

She smirked right back at me.

I lowered my voice. "I found a picture of a woman in his pack."

"His latest victim?" Olivia responded.

"Maybe you two have more in common than you think," I added.

Olivia's grin disappeared.

When she said nothing else, I grabbed the hot tea, testing it out, and brought it to Liam.

"Drink this," I said, handing the cup to him.

Liam silently took it from my hands and ventured a sip. His eyes widened at the taste of it and a smile tugged at the corner of his mouth.

"Have you ever tasted anything so wonderful?" I asked, smiling back at him.

Liam looked up at me, pausing as if trying to figure out if he had. He shook his head.

"It tastes so . . . alive," I added.

He nodded, not taking his eyes off of me. "Thank you."

I smiled. "When you're done, get some sleep."

He didn't object.

"I've been thinking." Olivia said when I sat beside her, leaning against her tall frame. "Shouldn't you go back and get more of the yarrow? We may need it."

"I agree. But I just can't bring myself to take more than we need. As you can see, plants aren't exactly abundant. I spread some seeds, though. Maybe one day they'll grow."

Liam moved slightly beside us, and I wondered if he was listening.

"Hey, Willow, you think there are more plants out there?" Olivia asked with a small yawn.

"I don't know, but I hope so."

Chapter Thirteen

Liam

I woke up just as the sun was rising. Olivia was on watch, sitting with her back toward me, watching the sky change color. Willow was fast asleep on the other side of our camp, tucked up next to a large rock as if she were trying to steal warmth from it.

I felt surprisingly better than I had the previous night. When I pulled my arm free of the blanket and looked down at the bandage covering my wrist, I was surprised to find no blood. I didn't feel anything. No pain, no heat, no fever. Nothing.

I stood up, walked over to Willow, and softly touched her shoulder. She opened her eyes and blinked a few times as I backed up a foot.

"How're you feeling?" she asked me, her voice rough from sleep.

"Take a look for yourself,' I replied with a small smile, offering her my hand.

She sat up slowly, rubbing the sleep from her eyes, and reached for her glasses.

She studied my hand briefly before slowly unwrapping the bandage. She was gentle, and I smiled as she finished her task.

A quiet gasp escaped her lips when she saw my completely healed wrist. My smile broadened. She hastily bent down and unwrapped her ankle, revealing nothing more than a few red marks where the Claeg had torn the skin.

"My fever is gone too," I explained, adding with a small laugh, "What kind of magic is in those plants of yours?"

She huffed.

I wanted to hug her, but all I did was say, "Thank you," when she didn't respond.

She shrugged, waving off my thanks. I found myself just looking at her.

She eyed me like she knew what I wasn't saying. "What is it?" she asked me carefully.

I shook my head slightly. "I gave you no reason to help me."

"Why wouldn't I? You were hurt." She seemed confused by my question.

"You don't know me."

"Do I have to know you to help you?"

She was afraid of me. She knew what soldiers were like. They could easily have let me die, taken my supplies, and gone on without me.

"I could be your enemy," I said to her.

"Are you?"

I shook my head and lowered my gaze to the ground. "I don't know."

She believed I was helping them. But even with my best intentions, I'd likely get them killed. I felt like we were all on borrowed time. Some better option must exist for her.

She placed her soft hand over my rough, scarred one. I tensed slightly but didn't pull away. "We wouldn't be here without you. We would have either been Claeg food or torn apart in that dust storm on day one. We owe you our lives."

I pinned her with my eyes—the truth tumbling from my lips. "I'm not so sure you wouldn't have been better off with the Elite."

Her face twisted in surprise as she yanked her hand free of mine. I flexed my fingers slightly at their sudden absence.

"They would've killed me. Even if they hadn't, what life would have been waiting for me?"

I couldn't answer her. The Elite had access to more resources but that didn't make their lives any easier. They were cruel, even to their own. Competition, violence, and rape were common among them. I'd seen it many times. But out here? Death was the inevitable conclusion—and I'd brought them along with me.

I shifted the conversation, trying desperately to erase the look on her face. "How did you know about that plant?"

Of course, I had my suspicions about her. I knew she read books she wasn't allowed to. But I wanted her to be the one to tell me.

She took the cautious route. "I'm a bioengineer. It was my job to know edible plants."

I narrowed my gaze.

"That's not the whole truth, Willow," Olivia said, walking toward us. She must have been tending to personal matters because she disappeared shortly after I woke.

Willow gave her a sharp look, and Olivia only winked back at her.

"Fine. Might as well get to know each other. My job was to bioengineer food crops, not medicinal plants. I didn't even know medicinal plants existed and no one in our lab was working on them. As far as I know, I'm the only one who knows these plants ever existed," Willow continued.

"She sneaks into the forbidden part of the city and spends all her free time reading books. But you already knew—or at least suspected—right?" Olivia interjected.

I raised my eyebrows at Willow.

"Well, that's the simplified version of the story," Willow said, pushing her glasses up and shooting Olivia another stern look.

Willow continued, "I used to go to the city's outer edge to leave extra food for the Forgotten. After months of doing that, I worked up the courage to sneak beyond the fence. I knew it was dangerous. They—you—could've come looking for me, but I couldn't help it. I found the city library, which seemed completely untouched. I was curious. I spent hours there almost every day, soaking up everything I could about the past. I soon learned I had a particular interest in plants. It's been three years since I first started visiting the library."

"And you never got caught or stopped?" I inquired, entirely baffled by what she just revealed. How had she evaded the Elite for so long when she had a tracker on her wrist? How had she evaded my patrol? How was she even still alive?

She shook her head. "Not until you came around asking Olivia questions."

I arched my brow, and the corner of my mouth kicked up. I turned to Olivia. "I didn't think you recognized me."

Olivia shrugged, letting Willow continue. "Why didn't you turn me in?"

"Honestly, I was annoyed that they tasked me with that as the Claeg were gathering in the thousands outside our walls. It seemed an insignificant problem, comparatively." It was half the truth, anyway.

"But soldiers don't just let you go. Not even for small things," she replied softly.

There it was. Just as I suspected—something terrible had happened. Something that was likely irreparable and would forever forge a wall between us.

"Maybe we should take this conversation on the road since we've been delayed an entire day?" Olivia suggested. Willow sagged in relief, and we were both grateful for the change in subject.

When we finally left our camp, no one looked back. We were all too focused on what was ahead of us. If we had, things may have unfolded very differently because tucked against the rocks where Willow had slept were ten more plants—unfurling their leaves and reaching for the sun.

Chapter Fourteen

Willow

We walked for a while. No one said anything. We were back to our old routine, focusing solely on moving forward, one step at a time.

The landscape didn't change much during the first half of the day, but the longer we walked, the more my mind played tricks on me. I'd scan the horizon, watching for dust storms or oncoming Claeg, but all I saw was a lush landscape. An oasis of plants spread out before us. A vision of what the Earth used to be. It felt like all I had to do was walk a little further and that world would materialize. It was a cruel trick of the mind, and I felt myself getting more agitated with each step. The seeds were the only thing tethering me to our current reality. There were so many more seeds out here than there were in the city, and after two days my vial was almost full.

I hadn't noticed Liam as he stopped ahead of me, and I crashed into his back with a loud grunt, almost dropping my seeds.

"Sorry," I mumbled, quickly backing away.

Liam turned and watched me as I stuffed my hands into my pockets, along with the vial.

When his gaze returned to my face, he lifted a strap on his back, producing his water canteen. He held it out to me without a word.

"I have my own," I commented, not moving.

"Take it."

I hesitantly grabbed the water from him with shaky hands, confused by his command.

He watched me intently as I took a swig. When I lowered the canteen, Olivia swiped it from my hands.

"Thanks!" she chirped before guzzling the water.

When she returned it to Liam, he looked somewhat amused, shaking it to see how much she'd taken.

"Never offer Olivia anything. She'll take it all."

"Excuse me, but he didn't offer it to me—just you—which is extremely rude," she said, feigning hurt.

I snorted, pointing to her canteen. "You have your own."

"Not the point," she shot back.

I caught Liam holding back a laugh as I said, "Let's go before I can't move my legs anymore."

No one protested, and Liam threw the canteen strap back over his head. I tried not to notice the corded muscle in his arm as he did.

When he caught me staring, I wheeled around, clearing my throat, which felt dry and full of dust even though I'd just had water.

I didn't look his way the rest of the walk. Though I felt his attentive gaze on me.

Hours later, when we finally stopped to rest, we settled on some barren rocks and Liam handed us more dried meat and crusty bread.

"So, what's your story?" Olivia finally asked him.

Liam turned to her, slightly baffled. "There isn't much to say, really," he replied, suddenly finding the food in his hands fascinating.

"Oh, I doubt that, *soldier*," she said. I cringed at her tone, not sure how he would take it.

He didn't flinch. He looked at her blankly and replied, "I was born in the city. My parents died when I was young, just like everyone else's. I had no interest in academia, so I spent my days fighting with my older brothers. My brothers eventually went off to fight and never returned. I took up a new interest after that, this time in women. One of them put me in my rightful place. I eventually married her. We weren't married for long before she was recruited and never returned. After that, I volunteered to fight instead of waiting to be recruited to die. I've never had a particular skill for self-preservation, and yet, here I am."

The matter-of-fact way Liam spoke made me wonder what he felt for the people he lost as he continued. "After a few years, I was promoted to captain. The knowledge I've gained these past five years made me realize this battle won't be won by fighting, and I was going nowhere. I wanted out. That's when you two found me. Is that a satisfactory story for you?" he asked, glaring at Olivia, daring her to ask more.

"That'll do," she replied, pausing for a beat before adding, "for now."

The landscape slowly began to change as we continued. It was still barren, but the slight uphill grade and my burning lungs indicated we were slowly gaining elevation. The rock outcroppings became more frequent and closer together. I silently wondered how the plants may have changed with the increased elevation.

I was deep in thought again, studying the slight change in the color of the dirt beneath my feet and collecting more seeds, when Liam stopped abruptly ahead of me. He held a finger to his mouth to ensure we remained silent and bent down, studying the ground.

"Hide between those rocks," he said firmly, pointing to our left about a hundred feet from where we were standing. "I'll be right back." Then he was gone, pulling his sword from his back before either of us could protest.

Olivia grabbed my arm and pulled me with her. We wedged ourselves between two rocks just as we had the last time the Claeg passed us. We didn't speak, afraid of what might be out there that we couldn't see or hear.

After a few minutes, a shrill cry broke the silence, and my stomach knotted up. I remembered what Liam had said about the Claeg and how they were almost impossible to kill on your own. Without thinking, I quickly squeezed myself out of our hiding place, simultaneously pulling the bow from over my head and making sure my arrows were within easy reach.

"What are you doing?" Olivia hissed at me. "Are you crazy?"

Maybe I was crazy, but I couldn't sit there and do nothing. So, I ignored her and crept over the rocks, heading toward the shrieking Claeg.

I moved quickly but quietly, ready to shoot or run. My heart was beating so fast that it felt like it might break straight through my chest.

I scrambled up one more rock and I could see the Claeg below me. There were maybe ten of them. Two were on the ground, bleeding and not moving. The color of their blood stood out in contrast to their pale gray skin and white eyes.

There were too many of them for one person. Panic started to grip me.

Liam moved with lightning speed—almost inhuman—as he dodged a blow from the Claeg in front of him, circling behind it and stabbing it in the back. The Claeg screeched again, and I could feel the sound vibrate in my bones. Liam wheeled around to dodge a blow from another one that had snuck up behind him, but he became wedged between them instead.

Before I could react, he had all three bleeding on the ground. He didn't seem to notice three more of them pushing him further toward a crevice in one of the large rocks. I did the math in my head and realized the fourth Claeg was nowhere to be seen.

They were setting a trap.

I quietly crept around to where Liam was being corralled, making sure none of them saw or heard me. I had to find the fourth one.

As I got closer, I noticed Liam was now trapped on three sides. Two of the three Claeg were still standing. Bile rose in my throat.

Then, I heard it—it's rough breathing. The fourth Claeg was waiting to attack from above, and Liam had no idea.

As Liam dropped another Claeg in front of him, I strung my bow, moving closer to get a better aim. I was shaking so hard I didn't know how I would be able to shoot accurately. The Claeg was crouched down, leaning over the rocks, its eyes focused on the scene below. It didn't see me as I silently willed myself to be still. I aimed and fired my arrow.

The arrow pierced straight through the Claeg's skull, and it fell forward through the crack in the rocks.

As it fell, Liam looked up. The distraction was just enough for the remaining one to have a chance at a death blow. I let out a roar of my own and before I realized what I was doing, another arrow pierced the last Claeg through the center of its chest. It fell with a thud on top of its sword. It was deathly silent. Even the wind seemed to halt its relenting motion.

Everything had happened so fast, and I was shaking so hard I thought I might collapse. I put my hand on the rock next to me to steady myself. I turned around slowly, and Liam was already standing there staring at me, covered in blood and dirt, with a look I couldn't read.

Aside from a shallow gash that went from his bicep down to his wrist, he seemed unharmed.

I couldn't hold it together anymore. I pulled my shaking hand from the rock, buried my face in my hands, and sobbed. Before I knew it, Liam had closed the distance between us, standing so close I could feel the warmth of his body and hear his heavy breathing. But he didn't touch me.

His eyes held so much concern that I finally took a half-step toward him, leaning my head into his chest and wrapping my shaking arms around his waist.

He tensed as if he wasn't expecting it. Then, a split second later his steady arms encircled my shoulders as he gently placed a hand on the back of my head, fingers lacing through my hair.

He didn't say anything as I leaned my full weight into him, surrendering entirely.

When my shaking slowed and the tears stopped falling, I looked up. Olivia was there. Liam turned his head and waved her over. He gently peeled me away and transferred me into her arms. She nodded a silent thank you, and he inclined his head before walking away.

He looked back briefly before he disappeared behind some rocks.

After a minute or two, Olivia peeled back from me. "You OK?"

I nodded, not trusting my words yet.

"What were you thinking?" she asked gently, clearly afraid I wouldn't answer her if she scolded me.

"I don't know. I wasn't thinking."

"Damn straight, you weren't," she responded.

I smiled a little despite my tears. "I'm sorry," I replied. "Won't happen again." Though I was unsure I could promise her that.

"Better not," she said sternly, before adding, "Let's find Liam and get the hell out of here."

The scent of blood filled our noses, wafting up from the dead Claeg below. I didn't argue with her as we held onto each other and walked in the direction Liam had gone.

We rounded the corner, and I heard Olivia gasp just before I saw it—a crystal-clear pool of water.

Liam was crouched down next to it, washing the dirt and blood from his body. I froze, staring open-mouthed at the pool of water.

"Where'd it come from?" I asked, my voice still shaky.

Liam had removed his shirt to wash it and now I couldn't find any words. I looked at the pool of water and back at Liam, whose torso was crossed with dozens of scars, similar to his hands. Some were white, others were slightly pink as if they were newer and still trying to heal. What his body must have endured these past years was something I couldn't even begin to wrap my head around.

"I don't know," Liam replied. "It wasn't here before the Claeg showed up."

Olivia seemed skeptical. "How do you know?"

"Because I tracked them past this exact spot, and it was bone dry fifteen minutes ago."

Olivia walked toward the pool to inspect it, shaking her head in disbelief.

Liam mouthed, "Are you OK?"

I nodded quickly, though I could tell he wasn't convinced.

"Thank you," he said.

"For what?" I asked, confused.

"For saving me. Again."

"Oh," I responded, not realizing that was what I had just done. "You're welcome," I added, a bit awkwardly.

"How'd you learn to shoot so well?" he asked with a wink, amused despite everything.

I just huffed at him in response. He smiled and I couldn't help but return it.

We stood there in silence, just staring at one another. It was as if we were having a whole conversation without using any words. Except, I wasn't at all confident I actually knew what he was thinking.

And then I felt a tug. Like someone pulling on an invisible thread connecting us. I stayed rooted where I was, shocked at the strange feeling and unsure how to react.

Olivia was the one who finally broke the silent tension. "I can't make sense of this. It seems to be an underground spring that's bubbling up from below. There's no stream of water coming in or out. I thought there was only deep groundwater left?"

"I thought so too," I said before finally peeling my eyes away from Liam. "Let's clean up and fill our canteens," I offered because there was no logical answer to her question. There was no logical answer to any of it.

Liam finally looked away from me, scooping up his wet shirt. He walked around the pool, handing me a wet cloth to clean myself with, and then he left us, returning to where we had hidden our stuff.

"Where the fuck is *my* wet cloth?" Olivia scoffed, looking between my hands and where Liam had disappeared.

"Guess he likes me better." I patted her on the shoulder.

Olivia huffed but didn't respond, giving me her best side-eye.

I went to make another retort when I felt something. Another pull. This time, it wasn't coming from Liam's direction.

I tentatively followed the feeling back toward the dead Claeg. When I rounded a large rock, I froze. Before me was a sea of green.

"Holy shit," Olivia commented behind me, disbelief filling her words. "Do you know these plants?"

When I turned to face her, Liam was there. He was dressed, with his sleeve rolled up past his wound. He stared at the plants before us, just as shocked as we were.

I glanced at his bleeding arm and then back to the plants. "It's comfrey. Heals shallow cuts and broken bones."

Olivia's sudden intake of breath was all I heard as we continued to watch the plants in front of us. They blew lightly in the breeze, the dust kicking up around them. The veins stuck out in stark contrast against their large, bright green leaves. I couldn't help but think of the veins in Liam's arms creating a similar pattern.

"Maybe we should collect some and keep moving?" Olivia finally suggested.

Liam moved without another word, heading toward the plants.

I stayed rooted in place—too amazed and shocked to move. But I felt something else. Something familiar. Something that made me tremble.

Fear.

Chapter Fifteen

Liam

Willow silently chewed the leaves, covered my wound with them, and then wrapped my arm in a clean cloth as she had done before. Her movements were just as gentle and careful, and I wondered how someone like her could survive in this world.

I stole glances a few times and wanted to ask her a million questions but thought better of it each time.

As if she could read my thoughts, she finally asked, "What is it?"

I hesitated, but then my curiosity got the better of me. "You're afraid of me." Of course, it wasn't really a question.

"I'm not afraid of you," she replied, standing up and walking toward where Olivia was packing our stuff.

"What is it you're afraid of, then?" I asked her back.

She halted but didn't turn. "This whole godsdamn world."

After hours of traveling, Willow fell unceremoniously onto her rolled-out blanket, and all I could think about was how close I'd been to losing them today. How close I'd been to dying and leaving them on their own.

I hated that I couldn't protect them. Not really.

Before Willow could close her eyes, I said, "We need to scout the area before we rest. Make sure it's safe. I want to show you what to look for. Both of you." I nodded to where Olivia had rolled out her sleeping blanket not far from Willow.

Willow slowly pushed back to her feet, stifling a yawn, but didn't complain. Olivia grumbled something inaudible as she came to stand beside us, glaring at me as if I'd asked her to strip naked in front of us.

I ignored it and waved for them to follow me.

I showed them how to find the highest point to scout in all directions. What to look for in the air, such as increased dust plumes, fires that would indicate a camp, or groups of tracks that might indicate a large group of Claeg or soldiers. I taught them to look at tracks and determine how old they might be, where they were coming from, and where they might be going.

Willow yawned often, but her attention to detail never wavered. I could see her brilliant brain working as I explained everything, memorizing every word. I knew if I could teach them enough skills then maybe, just maybe, they'd be able to go on without me. If it came to that.

"You were quiet," I commented to Willow on our walk back to camp.

She gave me a curious look. "Exhaustion will do that to a person." She paused momentarily, debating whether to say more. "As will killing your first ever living being."

I didn't respond, and she turned away from me. It hadn't even occurred to me that her exhaustion might be so much more than physical. We had been in survival mode—no time to process anything. Shutting it all out seemed so much easier. Safer.

"We'll reach the abandoned community tomorrow. Depending on timing, it might be dark when we get there," I said, stopping in front of her bed roll.

She collapsed onto it, not bothering to respond or cover herself.

I waited a few feet from her until she was asleep. Then I made to leave for my watch when Olivia's whisper drifted over to me. "Go easy on her, she's got more scars than she shows. We all do."

I hadn't stopped to think about what her scars might be. Or Olivia's. Somehow, I was so caught up in my own miserable life that it hadn't even occurred to me that maybe she was battling just as many demons as I was.

I grabbed a blanket and walked back to cover Willow, aware of Olivia's watchful gaze. Then I climbed out of sight, taking the first watch.

"Are we going to keep ignoring it?" Olivia finally asked the next day, after we'd been walking for a few hours.

We were still gaining in elevation, but nothing else had changed. The sun was starting to set on the horizon, a ball of bright red burning through the dust-filled skies—our only indication of time passing.

"The plants, you mean?" Willow asked her.

"The plants . . . and him," she said, aiming her thumb at me.

"Me?" I couldn't help my surprise.

Willow reigned in a laugh.

"Yes, you. You know I've never seen anyone move like you, right?" Olivia commented.

I sighed. Perhaps it was time for a little more truth. "I'm aware that I'm . . . different."

"*Different*?" Olivia asked, incredulously.

I took a long breath, staring straight ahead, not meeting their eyes. "I didn't know I was different until I volunteered to fight. I thought I was stronger, faster, and better because I always fought with my brothers when I was younger. But it didn't take long for me to climb in rank because of my unique abilities. Before I left, the Elite started taking an obsessive interest in me. I didn't know what they wanted—or still want—with me. I didn't stick around long enough to find out. But I do know they won't be happy that I'm dead, or rather, they won't be happy to find out I faked my death."

"You think they know you're still alive?" Willow asked me.

I shrugged, "I don't know for sure, but they seem to know many things before they even happen."

"Who are they?" Olivia inquired.

"I don't know, but it isn't just the Elite of Coria. They are connected somehow to another city. The fight you were forced into was a way for them to get rid of the majority of the people in Coria. I was informed of the plan as the Claeg gathered a few days ago." I probably looked as defeated as I suddenly felt.

"What did they want you to do?" Willow asked, and I couldn't gauge her reaction to the information I just revealed. I knew she suspected it, but I never confirmed. She was oddly calm.

"To help safely evacuate the Elite."

"But what was the incentive? They couldn't have expected you to let everyone die without a revolt."

"No, they offered us money, security, and power—considerable power—in the new world they claimed to be building." I paused before I added, "I'm sorry. I should've told you earlier. I thought if you knew, you might not trust me."

Willow studied me thoughtfully, and I tensed, expecting her anger. She surprised me again by ignoring the revelation.

"What about your unit? Did they go along with the plan?" she asked instead.

"Yes." The thought of Marvin left me feeling guilty.

"Why?"

I shrugged. "People will do anything when they're desperate."

"And you aren't desperate?"

I considered for a long time before I answered. "Yes and no. I didn't have safety or security, and most days I had very little to eat, but—" I paused for a second and took a deep breath. "But I'm not afraid of death. And I had nothing to lose."

She nodded as if the answer didn't surprise her, and I found that we had both stopped walking. Looking down into her eyes, I felt like I couldn't breathe. We were too close. I felt the need to run, yet I was rooted to the spot.

Willow's hands began to shake slightly, and she pushed her glasses up.

I instinctively reached for her hands as they dropped to her side when Olivia's voice pierced the silence. "I think we made it."

I quickly stepped away from Willow, and she walked over to where Olivia was standing before a large wire fence. The two stared at it as if they were confused about why it was there.

"It's electrical. Or, it once was," I explained and then pointed to our right. "There's a hole in the fence over there."

We squeezed through the hole and the two of them froze, taking in the town before us.

There were forty or so houses scattered throughout the rocky area. Each house was small but probably once housed a family of six or more. The houses were spread out, with considerable distance between them. There appeared to be walking paths between each house, made of smooth stone, as if neighbors often visited one another. Some houses had old metal swing sets overrun with rust. The swings swayed slightly in the breeze as if a child had just gotten off to go inside for dinner. The houses were built of stone, the windows broken. Their tattered curtains blew in the breeze that wove through the glass shards still clinging to the windowpanes.

"Most of these houses were raided for supplies, but the house on the cliff remains untouched," I explained. When Willow looked at me, I realized I'd been staring at her and dropped my gaze immediately.

"Why?" Olivia asked, looking past the house closest to the fence and toward the jagged cliffs behind.

"It's a tough climb to get up there and the paths are narrow and steep—hard to carry supplies down."

"You mean to tell me that *soldiers* couldn't get up there, and you think *we* can?" Olivia asked.

"The climb isn't the only reason no one's made it up there," I replied.

Olivia crossed her arms.

"There is some"—*How do I put it?*—"superstition surrounding the house. You'll see when we get closer," I said, motioning for them to follow. "By the time we get up there, scouting the area will be dark and difficult. I'll sweep the house before we sleep, but we should stay together for the first night."

"Why was this place abandoned?" Willow asked me.

"We don't know. I suspect they used the house on the cliff as a lookout and spotted an attack coming long before it got to their doorstep. They likely abandoned the village before there was any chance of a fight."

"Where would they have gone?" Willow pushed.

I, once again, debated how much to tell them. I could feel Olivia's eyes on me and knew she suspected the same thing Willow did—that I wasn't telling them the whole truth.

"There are other villages close to here. One is due west. I believe there's a large city to the north—Tarraco, as the Elite call it—but I've never ventured far enough to confirm it," I answered.

"You were sent here? Why?" Willow asked, trying to coax more information from me.

"To raid the houses for supplies. To check for survivors," I shrugged. "I wasn't given much information."

"But you had your suspicions, didn't you? Otherwise, why would you abandon your position and travel all this way, completely alone?" Willow's fists clenched, but this time I knew it wasn't out of fear.

Her frustration ignited my own. They had no idea what we were up against. They had no idea who they were standing in front of. They blindly trusted me. Suddenly, I wanted to shout the whole truth in their faces. I wanted them to see what kind of monster they were dealing with.

"What are you implying?" I asked, irritation evident in my voice.

"I'm not implying anything!" she was suddenly shouting. "I just want the truth."

I stepped closer, close enough to feel her breath coming in shallow bursts, "I've never lied to you."

"Omission is a form of lying."

"You wouldn't understand." My voice was a low rumble now.

"Try me." She held her ground, her amber eyes locked on mine.

I huffed, then turned and walked away. She was entirely too observant and, dammit, if it didn't make me feel exposed.

I heard her sigh deeply and knew she had picked up her pace to follow me, but she didn't push me further.

The house was barely visible at the top of the cliff. If we didn't look closely, we might not have spotted it. We couldn't make out any details in the dark, but the house was massive, taking up most of the space at the top. It melted into the cliff behind it, making it impossible to guess its true size from the outside, even if you were standing right in front of it.

The path was difficult for Willow and Olivia. It took quite a lot of effort for them not to trip on the rocks that littered the path, threatening to throw them over the side into the dark abyss below. A walk that should have only been ten minutes took us almost an hour.

I walked with the flashlight pointed behind me so that it illuminated their steps. I didn't need any light to illuminate my own, as I was already familiar with the path. I never spoke of it, but my eyesight was better than most for reasons I didn't understand or care to explain.

The house was easily three stories high with massive windows dotting the front, carved into the stone facade. Glass doors opened to massive stone balconies that hung over the cliff, offering an unobstructed view of the town below and the surrounding area. Something about the dark stone caught my attention—as I stared at it, it felt as if it were alive.

"I see what you mean," Olivia said, looking up at the house in front of us as the moon rose on the opposite horizon, casting eerie shadows on the stone. "If I weren't exhausted, I'd probably run in the opposite direction," she added, taking the first step up the stairs with me on her heels.

"As I said, my men were highly superstitious."

"So, it's the local witches' house, then?" Willow said, laughing and following behind us.

We all stopped in front of the massive stone door and wooden handle. Willow stood still, studying it. The stone was carved into intricate swirls and loops, and there was a sizable eye in the center of it. She ran her hands over it. I could tell something about it was familiar to her. I had never seen anything like it before.

"It's Celtic," Willow offered.

"I feel like the house is watching us. You think it's booby-trapped?" Olivia asked, and I almost laughed. Not because I disagreed, but mostly because I was a little afraid of the same thing.

"That's ridiculous," I replied, though I didn't sound all that convincing. I caught Willow's knowing smile as I pushed the heavy stone door open. The hinges creaked, and Olivia jumped at the sound; the three of us peered into the darkness beyond, listening for any movement.

We were met with total silence. After a moment, I stepped over the threshold and swept my flashlight around the entryway. Olivia and Willow followed me in, staring at the house's enormity. The ceiling was three stories up and had carved openings letting the moonlight in. The light illuminated small areas of the entryway, and I noticed thick stone tiles, almost black, interrupted by the occasional light-colored stone tile. They must have made a pattern, but it was too hard to tell in the darkness. A wide staircase to the left of the door circled to the top of the house, disappearing into the stone above. Where it led, I had no idea. The staircase railing was made of intricately carved wood, made to look like vining plants.

As I moved to the right, they both followed me, no one saying a word. We walked through a set of doors, and Olivia gasped. I looked over her shoulder to find that we had entered the kitchen. If you could even call it that. It was more like a mess hall or cafeteria, designed to hold and provide for a lot of people. There were many stoves and ovens that lined the far wall and a large doorway to the left of them.

I walked through the doorway and disappeared. "Holy shit," I yelled shortly after, and Olivia and Willow both raced in behind me.

As I swept my flashlight around the room, my mouth dropped open in disbelief. I had never seen so much food in my entire life. There were floor-to-ceiling shelves that were completely stocked with food. Food I had never seen before. Food I didn't even know existed.

"Looks like you and your men missed a large opportunity," Olivia commented, whistling at the abundance before us. "I'm pretty sure this could have fed our entire city."

My mouth hung open as I moved my flashlight over the shelves, illuminating box after box, and bag after bag of perfectly preserved food.

"We should find someplace to sleep," Willow finally said, motioning for the doorway. "We can raid this pantry in the morning."

Olivia and I both nodded, though Olivia seemed reluctant to leave the food as if she thought it might disappear overnight.

We chose a huge sitting room with two large glass doors leading out to two enormous balconies. There were floor-to-ceiling windows, three couches, many plush chairs, and a sprawling fur carpet in the center of the room, with a single large table in the center.

"I've never seen a room so large," Olivia commented, walking around the couches and running her hands along the soft fabric.

"How come it doesn't have any dust?" Willow asked. I hadn't noticed it before now, but she was right. The house seemed *lived-in,* like someone was caring for it. It should have been dusty and musty smelling. It shouldn't have had so much food or rooms that felt so alive.

Olivia and I both shrugged. "I'll look around and make sure no one's here," I said, heading for the door. I turned at the last moment and yelled, "Heads up!" before I tossed a flashlight at Willow.

She fumbled with it but caught it. "Asshole," she murmured, and I chuckled as I slipped out the door.

Chapter Sixteen

Willow

The morning sunlight danced through my eyelids, pulling me slowly out of my dreamless sleep.

I cautiously blinked my eyes open, stretching my hands above my head, listening for any sign of voices or movement. When I heard nothing, I turned toward the large windows and saw Liam on the balcony, staring at the town below.

I got up and walked to the open doorway. The cool morning breeze instantly hit my warm skin, making me shiver.

"It's beautiful," I commented, staring past him at the horizon and the rising sun.

He turned slightly. I couldn't read the look on his face. "Olivia moved to a more comfortable room," he replied, dismissing my comment and looking back toward the horizon.

"I'll leave you, then," I said, spinning away from the door.

Liam's voice stopped me. "There's enough here; we can stay a while. It's secure enough too, if I can get the fence working again."

I turned slowly to find him standing in the doorway to the balcony, leaning casually against it, his arms crossed over his broad chest, the early morning sun creating a halo effect around him. "If that's what you think we should do," I replied.

"No opinion?" he asked, slightly amused.

I narrowed my gaze, taking a single step toward him. The pull I felt earlier was suddenly stronger. "This is all new to me." My voice was lower than I intended it to be.

Something in the way he looked at me made me shudder, and instinctively, I took another step toward him. I stopped mid-stride when my hands began to shake.

Liam's gaze dropped to them briefly before meeting my eyes again. He pushed off the doorway, uncrossing his arms. "You know far more than you give yourself credit for."

I snorted. "I know of a world that no longer exists, except in books. Doesn't help with this one."

"I wouldn't be so sure."

I didn't know what to say to him, so I just stood there, unable to look away.

He moved toward me, pulling something from his pocket and holding it out. "This is for you."

He was out the door before I could ask what it was, leaving me feeling oddly chilled.

I studied the tin and then opened the top, a small gasp escaping my lips. It was a healing balm made from animal fat. Given the lack of animals left, healing balm was so rare I never expected to come across any, let alone be able to use some.

I dipped my finger into the tin, spreading the balm across my permanently dry and cracked lips which had worsened since leaving Coria. I practically moaned at how good it felt.

I found Olivia in the kitchen, going through everything in the pantry, trying to figure out the food and where it came from.

"You look a bit frustrated," I commented.

She held out a white box of unknown contents. "I haven't heard of half of this stuff. How is it here? And how has it survived this long?" she trailed off, reading the words on the outside of the box. "What's rice?"

"It's a grain. Like the wheat we grow in the lab."

"Oh," she said, putting the box back on the shelf and picking up another one.

"Liam thinks we should stay here a while," I finally said, scanning the shelves myself.

Olivia paused her browsing. "Why?"

I shrugged. "Your guess is as good as mine. He doesn't explain much."

"No kidding." She looked at me funny. "What's on your lips?"

I smiled, pulling out the tin. "Liam gave it to me. Want some?"

Olivia smirked, lifting her brows. "Did he now?"

I scoffed. "Oh, fuck off. You want some or not?"

She chuckled, snatching it out of my hand. She proceeded to smear an obscene amount on her lips.

"Don't waste it," I chided. "That's all we have."

She waved a dismissive hand at me.

"I think you two might want to see this." Liam's voice came from the doorway to the pantry. It was so sudden, I practically jumped out of my skin.

Liam gave me an apologetic look, and Olivia glanced between us, reluctantly giving me back the tin, her grin still plastered on her face.

I cleared my throat. "Lead the way," I said to Liam.

We walked past the grand entrance again, which was even more spectacular in the daylight. Details were carved into everything, but I didn't have time to stop and study them as I hurried to keep up with Liam and Olivia.

We walked to the opposite side of the house, and Liam stopped next to a large wooden door that was intricately carved with a large tree. Instead of leaves, though, there were animals at the end of the branches.

"The Tree of Life," I whispered, admiring the detail, not realizing that Olivia and Liam were staring at me. "What?" I asked when I finally noticed.

Olivia smirked at me, shaking her head. Liam looked at me thoughtfully for a second before turning and pulling on the large wooden handle.

I froze when I saw what was beyond the door. It was a circular library with a central, red velvet couch on top of a bright white rug. A fur blanket spanned the back of the couch. But the couch wasn't what caught my attention. It was the bookshelves.

They were wooden shelves intricately carved into vining plants. You might have thought they were alive if you looked at them quickly.

They felt alive.

Something stirred in me as I took them in. A familiarity. A knowing.

I took a hesitant step into the room and noticed the sunlight streaming in from the windows above the shelves, illuminating them.

The books seemed completely untouched by time and dust, and, once again, I felt like the place was somehow being taken care of, though there was no evidence of other people.

I inhaled deeply, and the scent of leather books and the Earth filled my nose. I'm not sure I'd ever smelled anything so wonderful in my life.

I didn't realize I had tears in my eyes until Olivia whispered, "You OK, Will?"

I turned away from the books and smiled at her. "More than OK."

I spent that whole first day in the library, exploring every nook and cranny, pulling books off the shelves at will, and flipping through them. No one bothered me.

Liam went off to scout the area and then fix the fence and electricity while Olivia mumbled something about taking stock of all the supplies in the house.

As the sun fell toward the horizon and the library took on a golden glow, I suddenly felt him, though he wasn't there. I stared at the doorway, knowing he would walk through an instant later, and the idea that I could *feel* his presence startled me so much that I didn't realize I was just staring at him, unblinking.

Liam halted, and the look on his face shook me out of my temporary state of shock. I finally spoke. "You need something from me?"

"No. Olivia made dinner." His voice was hesitant—careful.

"You know she can't cook, right?" I said, placing the book I was reading on the couch next to me and smiling at him.

His eyebrows rose slightly. "Should I be worried?"

"Very," I said, standing.

He let me pass and followed me to the kitchen. We didn't speak, but I could feel him watching me, even though I couldn't see his face.

"There you are!" Olivia shouted with delight as we both walked through the kitchen door. I halted at the feast before us.

"What—where—" was all I could manage to mumble as I walked over to a table made for the Elite. There were fake flowers in vases, linen tablecloths decorated with green ferns, candle holders in the shape of deer antlers with beeswax candles on top, various types of colorful crystals, and clay plates painted with all manner of woodland creatures.

And that was just the decorations. The food was even more spectacular. Food I'd seen in books but had no idea of their names.

What stood out the most about the food was the colors. There was red, green, white, orange, brown, and even purple.

Olivia stared at the feast she created, still grinning from ear to ear.

I was completely speechless.

"What's for dinner?" Liam asked, sitting beside me but keeping his distance.

"I have no idea. Some of the food had cooking directions, thank goodness, or else I wouldn't have known what to do with it," Olivia said, still beaming. "But we have wine," she added, waggling her eyebrows.

I rolled my eyes but didn't hesitate to pick up the glass and take a sip. Liam watched me curiously before also picking up a glass and taking a big gulp. I smiled, wondering if the alcohol might break down a little of the wall he kept around himself.

"Taste test? A little of everything?" I asked expectantly.

Olivia nodded and winked at me before we grabbed whatever was closest to us.

A few bites, and a few sips of wine in, and I think we all realized what we had lost. It wasn't just the taste of the food we had never had but also the variety. Never had I had so many different things in one meal. Knowing now what was possible, it would be hard to go back. Impossible, even.

"Want to hear what Willow used to do as a kid?" Olivia asked through a mouthful of food after we all silently ate our first few bites, eyes wide at the taste of it all.

"You wouldn't dare," I threatened.

"Too late now, he's already interested," she replied, pointing her fork in Liam's direction.

I groaned and finally looked at Liam, who was desperately trying to hide his smile. Color dotted his cheeks, likely from the wine.

"You're next," I said to him, almost laughing now. "She takes no prisoners."

"I do have a talent for squeezing the best stories out of people," Olivia replied with a wink, doing her best to sound arrogant.

"True talent right there," I said, rolling my eyes.

"Shut it, Will, and start talking."

I sighed, still smiling, and leaned back in my chair. "Well, as you know, I have a bit of a habit of going places I'm not supposed to." I paused, and Liam looked at me expectantly. "It started when I was a kid."

Liam raised a brow, taking another sip of wine.

"I was smart. No shock, there. My teachers trusted me, and my science teacher gave me a key card one day to gather extra supplies from the warehouse. She never asked for it back. You can probably imagine what I did with it."

The corner of Liam's mouth kicked up. "I take it you didn't give the card back?"

"Hell no. Do you know the things the Elite hoard? The key card was magic to a kid like me. At first it was just about my curiosity, but once I knew what they had, it became about so much more. At first, it was just books. But then it turned into more than that. I began stealing extra food for the kids in my class."

I took a breath and found Liam looking at me like he'd seen a ghost. "What?"

He shook his head slightly, putting down the fork in his hands, but the expression remained. "I knew you," he said quietly, "or rather, I knew *of* you."

I waited for him to elaborate.

"You stole medicine too." It wasn't a question, and now he looked almost sad or guilty.

"Yes," I confirmed in a whisper, desperately wanting him to continue, though I already knew what he would say. My hands started trembling then, and I was grateful they were under the table where no one could see them.

"My mother got sick when I was a kid. Bacterial pneumonia. We didn't have access to any medication. A friend mentioned that there was a girl who could get us some. He came back the next day with a full vial of antibiotics. It saved my mom's life and gave me more time with her."

Olivia's mouth was practically in her lap, and I'm sure I didn't look much different.

"Well, that was a surprising turn of events," Olivia finally said, as Liam stared at me. I felt him. The sadness, the surprise, the gratitude. Genuine gratitude, and there was something else there that I was too afraid to name.

I shook my head as if to shake away the feeling of him and went to say something, but Liam cut me off.

"Thank you . . . for the millionth time, it seems," he said, and all I could do was nod and give him a small smile before Olivia spoke again.

"You know, Will, I think that may be the first time anyone's ever thanked you for all that."

"Really?" Liam sounded surprised.

"Many people died or disappeared before they could ever thank me. Most didn't even know it was me. I wanted it that way. For my safety and theirs."

Liam looked as if he was struggling with something, but before he could say anything else, Olivia cut in. "So, what were you like as a kid, Liam?"

His face changed from contemplative and almost sad to something feral. A wicked grin formed on his face before he said simply, "I haven't changed much."

"So, you were a brooding, unpleasant beast of a child?" Olivia asked, that lovely sarcastic grin plastered on her cherry lips.

Liam's grin remained. "Pretty much."

"Well, don't just sit there. Give us examples," Olivia said impatiently.

"There is one story . . ." The look on his face made my stomach flip, and I clenched my hands tighter under the table.

"I wasn't an easy child," he began, and Olivia snickered at that as she began stuffing more food in her mouth. "I was the youngest of four boys, which I realize was super rare to have a family that size, even then. My parents were too busy trying to feed so many mouths that my brothers were the ones who raised me. They knew I was different, but they didn't treat me any differently. They honed my fighting skills, and ended up with more broken bones than we could count."

Olivia's eyebrows rose as she put down her fork, nestling her chin in her hands.

"One day, they thought it would be a good idea to have me break into the food warehouse and steal food so that our parents could take a day off."

Olivia bristled, "Do you know how many soldiers guard that warehouse?"

Liam nodded and smiled. "Oh, I'm aware."

Olivia laughed a little and then returned to her pasta and dried apples as Liam continued, "Their brilliant idea was to have me serve as a distraction while they snuck in. I was to keep the soldiers busy but conscious."

"Ha! Right," Olivia commented sarcastically.

Liam smirked at her. "I tried to act like an innocent ten-year-old who was just curious. My questions were enough distraction to get my brothers in, but not a minute later, shouts started up inside the warehouse, and I panicked."

Liam stopped and gauged both of our reactions. Olivia was practically on the edge of her seat with anticipation.

"Before I knew it, all the guards outside the warehouse were down and unconscious. They never saw it coming. I panicked after that, barreling through the side of the warehouse. I didn't even notice that the impact had dislocated my shoulder. My brothers must have heard me crash through the wall because they instantly changed direction and sprinted for me, their hands full of food, half of which was spilling all over the ground."

He stopped his story briefly and smiled at the memory.

"I thought they would look pissed, but instead, they looked triumphant as they sprinted past me, through the broken wall, and yelled back at me to run. So, I did. I hauled ass back to our apartment. Luckily, I had knocked out so many of the soldiers that they didn't have men left to pursue us."

Olivia was staring at Liam, completely awestruck.

"We made it home in one piece, and the food lasted us almost two weeks. It was the best two weeks of my life." Liam stopped shortly. "After that, my brothers came up with lots of dangerous plans. Surprisingly, we never got caught. I think I knocked out too many witnesses," he stopped, then grabbed his fork and put more food in his mouth, washing it down with more wine.

No one said anything for a few moments. Olivia just stared at Liam as if she was trying to unlock some secret within him, and then she grinned at me. "Perhaps you two have more in common than you think."

Liam's eyes turn toward me, but I continued to look at Olivia. "Our methods are quite different." It came out harsher than I intended.

"Two sides of the same coin, if you ask me," she said, then returned to her food, picking up the dried apple slice and studying it intently.

I sighed. "And what about you, Olivia? Don't you think you owe us a story?"

Olivia put the apple down again and grinned at me. A mischievous sort of grin. "We left the best for last," she said, and then launched into a lengthy description of her childhood, and we all laughed until our stomachs ached from the effort of it.

I had heard her stories before but never tired of hearing them. How she delivered them made me wonder what she might offer, if the world were different. The stories she could tell. The joy she could bring to people.

When I looked at Liam, he was smiling genuinely, and I'm not sure I had ever seen anything so lovely.

"It's getting late," Liam finally commented after consuming every morsel of food on our plates, including the chocolate bar we all shared in stunned silence. "We should get some rest."

Olivia nodded slowly, and I rose to clear away the dishes, stacking them and walking them toward the sink.

"I think we should stay for a few days." Liam's voice drifted over to me from the table. "Scout the area, figure out what our next move is."

I didn't say anything as I set the dirty dishes in the sink and returned to the table to collect more.

"How can we help?" Olivia asked him sleepily as she handed me some empty plates.

"Take stock of the supplies here. Prepare for a quick escape if need be. Practice some self-defense so you're not vulnerable while I'm gone. Eat so you can put on some weight," Liam shrugged.

Olivia snorted. "Well, eating doesn't sound so bad."

I smiled as I wiped down the dishes, my back to the two of them.

"You've been quiet," Liam observed, coming up beside me and grabbing the clean dishes to put away.

I didn't look at him as I continued washing. "It's a good plan."

Liam paused, and I could feel him studying me.

"If you have something to say, just say it," I said to him, cringing as it came out sharper than I wanted.

He didn't react, simply responded, "Olivia found a room we think you'll like."

I stopped cleaning, but he had already turned away, putting away the rest of the clean dishes in the cabinets. Content, it seemed, to put some space between us.

Olivia sauntered up to me and whispered, "I have a surprise for you."

I turned and smiled at her. "Another one? Wasn't this meal enough for one day?"

"I saved the best for last," she said, and then grabbed my hand and pulled me out of the kitchen and down the hall, further and further into the interior of the house and the cliff itself.

There were no windows in the interior of the house, and the darkness consumed us. The only light that illuminated our path came from the flashlight. The hallway was lined with many doors, presumably leading to various rooms, but they were shut. I wondered what all the rooms were used for and who might have walked these halls before us.

I caught glimpses of the artwork along the walls as Olivia's flashlight illuminated them briefly before plunging them back into darkness. The artwork all had a theme: nature. A world long gone.

She stopped at a wooden door that was carved with a beautiful tree. Its trunk was wide, its branches gnarled and twisted, with broad leaves at the end. The tree was an ancient oak.

She opened the door slowly, then motioned me in. I stepped through and waited for her flashlight to illuminate the rest of the room.

The room was spacious. The bed was bigger than anything I had ever seen, and in the center of the room was a dried-up rock pool with carved rock steps leading down into it. It had a large faucet at one end and a drain on the floor. Once upon a time, it must have been used as a large tub.

Twisting vines and beautiful trees covered the carved stone walls. My gaze drifted behind the bed, and suddenly my breath caught.

Olivia noticed where I was looking. "That's why I picked this room for you. It's a weeping willow."

I nodded. I couldn't find the words.

"This place keeps surprising me," Olivia added, looking around at the carvings and handing me the extra flashlight.

"Liam's room is right next to yours," she said with a wink, "and mine's just next to his on the other side."

I ignored her wink and walked over to the willow tree, shining my light over it. The detail was exquisite. Roots were carved into the floor and wrapped around the bed. Its ornate trunk rose on the left side of the bed, and its draping branches and leaves fell elegantly along the wall behind it.

Without warning, the lights flashed on.

"Liam must've gotten the power working!" Olivia sounded delighted. "He's been at it all day. He thinks the house runs on geothermal power. There's steam coming out of the cliffs. He thinks there's a hot spring under here," Olivia told me, a hint of awe in her voice. "Well, the power makes things easier, doesn't it? I'll leave you to get settled." She hurried out the door.

I continued to take in the details of the room. I ran my hands along the rock carvings, wondering who created the intricate designs. They must have known a lot about plants.

I wandered over to the tub. It was also carved, but this time with what appeared to be aquatic plants, though I had limited knowledge of them.

The whole room appeared to pulse with life, yet I was the only living thing there.

On a whim, I decided to try the faucet. To my astonishment, water flowed from it. It was dirty, but it didn't take long to clear. It was warm to the touch and had a slight sulfur smell. It must have been coming from the hot spring inside the cliff. I laughed at the wonder of it.

I let the pool fill with delightfully hot water. I didn't know if I had ever taken a bath. Maybe as a child, but the memory failed me.

I was staring at the falling water when there was a light knock on the door.

"Come in," I shouted, not taking my eyes from the pool of water.

"It works!" I could hear the amazement in his voice.

I looked up at Liam. "It's amazing."

"Olivia thought you'd love this room. She said the tree behind the bed is a willow tree?"

"It is," I replied, smiling.

He looked at it in the light and grinned back at me.

His smile faded as a silence descended on us. The water became the only sound filling the room.

A few moments later, Liam turned for the door and said, "After breakfast, I'll teach you and Olivia some defensive skills if you're up for it. Then you can have the rest of the day to yourself. I have to scout the area and finish the fence."

"Sounds good."

He hesitated a moment and stared past me at the filling tub. "Enjoy your bath."

He was gone before I could say anything else.

Chapter Seventeen

Liam

The next morning, I brought Willow and Olivia down to the flat area at the base of the cliff underneath the house to lead them through some self-defense drills. We started with conditioning which had them both sweating and breathing heavily, almost to the point of total collapse.

"If this is what it's always gonna be like, you can count me out," Olivia whined as they walked back toward me. I held out a few daggers and could tell that each step they took was a considerable effort.

I smirked at Olivia. I couldn't help it. "It'll get easier. I promise. But you'll probably have trouble walking tomorrow."

"Tomorrow!" Olivia practically shouted. "I'm having trouble *now!*"

Willow let a laugh slip from her lips, and I turned at the sound.

"I set up a few targets against the base of the cliff. I want you to work on hitting within the circle," I explained, handing them each a dagger and expecting both of them to refuse the task.

Olivia groaned, and I watched as she tried to raise the dagger into a throwing position. Her arms were shaking with the effort. It only made her groan louder.

"We can call it for today if you want," I suggested, and Olivia instantly dropped her arm, relief flooding her face.

"Thank goodness because I don't think I could even pull it back far enough to throw it more than a few feet." Olivia sounded so grateful for the invitation to stop that Willow almost laughed at her again.

Olivia gave her a *what are you smirking about?* look, and Willow just smiled broader.

Something had changed in Willow since last night. She seemed more at ease. More joyful.

I hated to think that everything I'd been hiding would steal that from her.

"Oh, you think you're better than me?" Olivia taunted Willow.

"I don't think, Liv. I *know*," she replied, keeping her face and voice deathly calm and steady, though the corner of her lips twitched slightly.

Olivia crossed her arms and shot back, "So, you think just because you killed a few Claeg with arrows, you can throw daggers? Let's see it then. An extra helping of food at dinner tonight says you can't hit the circle on your first try."

Now, it was my turn for my mouth to turn up slightly as I watched them go back and forth.

Olivia must have noticed it because she wheeled on me and asked, "You want in on the bet?"

I held my hands up, "I don't think I want to get in the middle of this."

Willow let out a sharp laugh. "Wise choice."

Her gaze landed on me for a fraction of a second before she faced the target, positioning her feet and raising the dagger into a throwing position, desperately trying to keep her fatigued muscles steady.

"Arm goes straight back and straight forward. Don't throw across your body, and don't flick your wrist," I said softly behind her.

"No helping!" Olivia reprimanded, and I raised my arms in surrender, smiling unintentionally.

Willow took a deep breath, pulled the dagger straight back, and then flung her arm forward, releasing it. To my utter shock, and hers as well, it hit the inner edge of the circle and bounced off the stone with a loud clang.

"Beginners luck," Olivia mumbled, her disappointment evident. Not because of her pride but because of the food she had bet on.

"Liv, you can still have the extra food. I think the handle hit the target, not the blade, so it doesn't count," Willow replied, slowly walking forward to retrieve her dagger.

"It—" I began to say, but Willow whirled around and cut me off with a look that said, *if you say it, you're a dead man.*

I wisely shut my mouth and followed.

"A bet is a bet, Will. I'll give you this one," Olivia shouted from where she stood behind the throwing line, not wanting to move.

"How about two out of three?" Willow yelled back, bending down to retrieve the dagger from the dry dirt. Her dagger had made a slight divot in the stone, marking where she'd hit.

"You hit it with the blade," I whispered behind her as she silently studied the rock and the target circle I had drawn. "You have impeccable aim and good form for someone who's never wielded any weapons."

She turned to face me, and I realized I was closer than I intended, though I didn't want Olivia to overhear me.

"Afraid I'll soon be able to beat you at your own game?" she taunted.

I took a step closer and glared down at her, but it wasn't anger that filled me. It was a challenge. "Never," I whispered, handing her a second dagger, my hand lingering on hers longer than it should have.

"I'll remind you of that when I beat you one day," she responded, winking at me as she walked back to where Olivia stood by the line.

I took a deep breath, the feeling of her skin lingering for a moment.

"Care to try? I'm sure your arms are functional by now," Willow asked Olivia with an encouraging smile.

Olivia shook her head dramatically. "I don't care to get my ass whooped by the two of you until I've had a proper meal," she said with a huff, turning and making her way toward the path up to the house, limping slightly.

Willow laughed. "Your loss," she shouted after her.

Olivia flipped her off as she rounded the corner up the cliff, and Willow chuckled next to me.

"Best of three?" I asked, beaming at her, holding two daggers of my own.

She gave me an eye roll and nodded, positioning her feet again. "What do I get if I win?" she asked, even though she knew she had no chance. Even if she hit the circle all three times, she knew I would hit the very center of it every throw.

"Whatever you want, Willow. I'll give you whatever you want."

She raised her eyebrows. "Risky bet, soldier, but you're on," she replied, turning back toward the target.

Of course, I won, though she was able to hit the interior of the circle each time, continuing to amaze me with how fast she learned.

I felt her watching me every time I threw, studying my movements and concentration. Her eyes didn't leave me even when the dagger hit the target, rebounding off it, the sound reverberating throughout the valley like a gong. It was as if she knew I'd hit the very center of the target and didn't even have to watch. That little fact didn't give me as much satisfaction as her eyes on me did.

"Next time," I said, turning toward her, grinning like a child.

She rolled her eyes again and stalked off to grab her daggers. I followed her, and then we both silently walked up the path to the house, the sun now clearly above the horizon, the heat making beads of sweat roll down my back and glisten on her chest.

I noticed no trembling in her hands and found some part of me relieved at that small detail.

When we reached the kitchen, where Olivia was hungrily stuffing food into her mouth, I announced, "I'll leave you two."

They both nodded, too tired to respond and then I was gone, back through the front door, headed to the top of the cliff to scan the horizon in all directions. Wondering the whole time at the increased speed of my heartbeat.

Chapter Eighteen

Willow

I pulled out an old wooden table stuffed between some of the shelves. It was an effort to move it, not just because of its size but because my muscles were still shaking from the effort of the conditioning drills. I wondered if I'd ever be truly capable of the physical demands of life outside the city. Life that was chaotic, unpredictable, and demanded more physically from me than I ever imagined.

The only positive I saw in our situation was the freedom. The feeling of being able to explore what I wanted, read what I wanted, sleep when I wanted, and eat when I wanted. It was all new to me.

My life had been dictated to me from the moment I was born, down to each minute of the day and each morsel of food I was allowed to eat. Even my career was assigned to me at a very young age. I had no choice. But now, I felt lighter somehow. Freer to be myself.

When I finally got the table to the center of the room, I went off to explore the shelves of books. I had no real plan. I was just interested to learn what was there. To see if there were books I had never seen or books that sparked something in me.

I scanned each shelf carefully. Pulling out books as their titles spoke to me. The books were organized by topic and then alphabetized.

Similar to the library in Coria. It didn't take me long to find the plant books.

I pulled various ones and put them on the table. Everything from edible plant books to garden design, growing your own food, and medicinal herb gardens.

As I flipped through each one, I set the books on the table. Each one opened to a page that was either new to me, inspiring, or beautiful.

Before I knew it, every inch of the table was covered with books, displaying a colorful collage of plants. A whole ecosystem on a table. A dream. A foolish dream.

I felt him walk up behind me, completely silent, and wondered how he could move without making a sound. More importantly, I wondered how I knew he was there long before my senses picked anything up. The feeling intrigued me more than it scared me.

I didn't turn toward him right away, as I half-pretended to rearrange the books on the table. Something to keep my hands from starting to shake in his presence.

"This was really what it was like?" he finally asked me, amazement filling his voice, and I found him studying each picture intently, his eyes wide.

I shrugged. "Some places, but there were so many different ecosystems. All differed depending on location, soil type, water, sunlight, and overall climate."

Liam looked away from the pages and at me, his brows furrowed.

I let out a short laugh. "Sorry. I sometimes forget all this stuff is completely foreign to everyone."

Liam turned back to the books and was silent for a long time. He ran his hands softly along some of the pages. I didn't think I had ever seen him so careful, so gentle before, and I couldn't take my eyes off his hands.

When he glanced back at me, I pretended to study one of the books closest to me.

"Could it ever be this way again?" His words were tentative, as if he were afraid of the answer.

"I don't know how," I responded truthfully, unable to hide the small crack of sadness in my voice, as I pushed my glasses up and then put my hands behind my back.

"The plants we found. Is there any way to multiply them?" he asked, genuinely curious, as he continued to observe me.

"Only by spreading their seeds and watering them. Given there's no rain, we'd need to care for them to give them any sort of chance."

Liam's eyes wandered back to a picture of a field of wildflowers. "I don't understand. Why would they keep this from people?"

I knew he meant the books.

I didn't respond immediately, unable to form words from my swirling thoughts. "Books are dangerous. They give you ideas. They give you possibilities. They open doors. They allow you to see what the world could be. And most dangerous of all, they give you hope. Unrelenting hope. That is why they don't want us to have them."

"That's what they've given you?" It wasn't a question.

"Perhaps too much. Perhaps foolish hope." I knew I sounded exhausted. Like the hope had taken all of me.

"Or maybe that hope will one day defy the impossible."

I let out a sardonic laugh and reached into my pocket, pulling out a small glass vial. "I cannot get these to grow no matter what I do, and yet, I still collect them. I still have this foolish hope that one day, I'll find the answer in all these books that will get them to sprout and that everything will be different. But the reality is that they are most likely dead. Dormant for so long that they lost their ability to live again."

Liam stared at the seeds in my hand. One small line creased the center of his brow, and I desperately wanted to know what he was thinking.

After a moment, he pushed past me toward the bookshelves. I watched his broad back as he disappeared behind them.

When my gaze returned to the picture he had run his fingers over, I did something truly idiotic out of pure instinct. I ripped it out and carefully folded it, placing it in my pocket.

I didn't know why, but I would give him this world, somehow, even if it took all of me.

A minute later, I found him in the botany section. He was flipping through a book on plant anatomy and identification when I stopped before him.

"It's hard to commit those identifiers to memory without ever having seen them in real life," I commented, pointing to the book in his hands.

"I'm just amazed at all the different types of plants," he said, then gave me a small smile before closing the book gently and putting it back on the shelf.

A moment later, he reached toward the top shelf and a leather-bound book I hadn't noticed until now.

As he pulled it down, I couldn't see a title or any writing on the outside. It was made of cracked brown leather, fading slightly around the edges. The only indication of its age. There was a leather strap that wound around the outside of it and tied it closed at the front.

Liam looked from the book and then back at me, eyebrows raised.

I held out my hands, and he gently placed the book in them. His fingers brushed mine lightly before he pulled them away, and I felt that pull again. I didn't look up at him as my hands began to tremble in earnest this time. I kept them busy by opening the book.

As the book fell on the first page, I couldn't help the slight gasp that escaped my lips, and something deep inside of me clicked into place, though I ignored that feeling as much as I ignored the pull I felt.

I stepped back from Liam, open-mouthed, and flipped through more pages.

"Willow?" Liam said with a hint of unease.

"It's a handwritten journal," I explained, turning over another page, "A personal account of working with plants." My face pinched as I stared at a hand-drawn diagram of something I didn't understand yet felt was important. "I've never come across anything like this. The books at the library were printed books. Never handwritten."

After a few moments of silence, Liam finally said, "I'll leave you to your reading. I just wanted to let you know that the fence is up and running. We're safe here for now." Before I could respond, to thank him, or ask why he was so abruptly leaving, he pushed past me, his arm brushing lightly against my shoulder, and I felt the thread snap. My heart almost stopped in my chest.

I clutched the open journal and took a deep breath. Though I didn't want to admit it to myself, something had just changed, and I wasn't sure if it was the journal or the man who had surprised me for the first time with his gentleness and curiosity. With his *humanness*.

I turned and stared past the shelves to the door he had just exited through as if he would walk back through them. As if he *wanted* to walk back through them. Instead, I wondered if it was me who wanted him to walk back through those doors.

I shuddered at the thought and then strolled back to the table in the center of the library, still clutching the journal to my chest.

Chapter Nineteen

Liam

I woke up with a start, sitting up abruptly, rubbing my eyes, and blinking into the darkness. I leaned over and switched on the light. I had no idea what time it was, but I knew, after the same nightmare I had all too often, that I wasn't going back to sleep, so I swung my legs over the side of the bed and threw on a pair of pants.

I had no idea where I was going, but somehow, I ended up in the library, staring out at the dark horizon. Maybe it was no surprise that I was there. The place felt safe. It felt a little like Willow and all her big dreams.

My thoughts drifted to the nightmare that plagued me almost every night. It was always the same. The faces of all the innocent people I'd killed. Even the faces I'd never seen haunted me. A constant reminder of the person I'd become. The person I could never escape.

The library door opening snapped me out of my thoughts as Willow came in and practically ran straight into me. She only wore a short, white cotton shirt and white cotton underwear. Clothes she must have found in the house. Clothes that were too big for her, but somehow hid nothing. Her legs were bare, and I suddenly couldn't stop staring at the shape of her.

She stumbled back and mumbled, "Sorry." Color rose to her cheeks.

We stood there in silence for a moment, and the silence made me all too aware of her lack of clothing.

"Couldn't sleep?" I asked in a gruff voice.

She shook her head, still rooted to the same place, only a few feet away from me. "Weird dream woke me."

I nodded once and then reluctantly tore my eyes away from her and toward the windows and the rising sun. I didn't want to turn away, but I didn't want to frighten her. The irony, though, was she was beginning to terrify me.

"How are you feeling?" I asked.

"Sore," she admitted.

"I'll try to keep it light today," I replied, the edges of my mouth turning up slightly, guiltily thinking about how I might challenge her again.

"Gee, thanks," she said sarcastically, crossing her arms, covering her chest that was almost completely visible through her shirt. I tried not to notice the movement, her half-naked body, or her taunting tone.

This wouldn't end well. Not for either of us, so I pushed past her without responding, saying as I went, "See you on the field in a half hour."

I didn't want to see her reaction, so I practically sprinted out of the room and wound my way down to the training area.

There was so much pent-up emotion I didn't want to unpack, so I did what I always did. Trained—pushed my body to its breaking point.

I had every intention of doing that when the color green stopped me, and I stared blankly at the tall plants at the bottom of the cliff, easily as tall as I was.

I tentatively stepped toward them and somehow knew they were connected to Willow. I had suspected it before, but now, I could *feel* it.

I didn't touch the plants but studied them from a few paces away. I'd never seen anything like them, though they looked familiar from some of the books Willow had scattered about the library.

She likely knew what they were and their uses.

When I had taken in my fill of them, I turned and finished what I'd come down here to do. I trained until I was dripping with sweat, and my muscles felt like they might give out.

Panting, I walked back to the plants and watched them as a slight breeze picked up. Their scent wafted to me, and I inhaled deeply. I didn't turn away, not even when I heard Willow and Olivia chatting and walking down the cliff above me.

I could hear Olivia's grumpiness, likely from the soreness, and found myself smiling at the conversation I couldn't quite make out.

When they got closer, I heard Olivia moan, "He better go easy on us, or I'll poison his dinner." I couldn't quite tell if she was serious.

Their conversation suddenly halted, and I knew why, but I didn't turn quite yet. Too many thoughts still clouded my head, and I feared what might come out of my mouth if I faced them.

"Is it the plants or the half-naked man in front of us that you're gawking at?" Olivia whispered to Willow, clearly thinking they were still too far away for me to hear, but, as with my eyesight, my hearing also seemed to be better than others. I heard every word.

Willow elbowed her away and Olivia grunted at the contact. "The plants," Willow replied roughly.

I turned as they approached. "You know these?" I asked Willow, though I already knew the answer.

She nodded slightly, staring past me at the tall plants that leaned slightly toward the sun that had risen just above the eastern horizon. "Hemp. High in a compound called CBD. Excellent for inflammation"—she paused a moment, clearing her throat—"and muscle soreness."

Olivia's mouth dropped open, and Willow almost laughed at the sight, but she shrugged instead. "There's a single leaf growing out of one of the bookshelves in the library. I found it just before I came down here," she added, which didn't help the look on Olivia's face.

Willow laughed like she was a bit self-conscious. "I'll collect the plants after we finish. Make an oil from them for our sore muscles."

Olivia stepped forward until she could touch the plants. She ran her fingers along their five-pointed leaves. "They have a strong scent," she observed.

Willow nodded, though she had probably never smelled them before. "They have a high volatile oil content. All plants with high volatile oils smell strong," she informed us as she walked over to touch and smell them, pointedly trying not to look at me.

I did, however, watch her.

After a moment, she said, "Shall we?" pointing toward the empty dirt in front of us.

I inclined my head, and then we moved to stretching and conditioning drills.

Now that I was tied to the two of them, I wondered when my past would catch up to my present. As much as I didn't want it to, it was inevitable. I just hoped I could survive it when it did because I wasn't sure I could let Willow go, even if it was what was best for her.

When we finished training, Willow went over to the plants and mouthed something silently, and then closed her eyes and waited for a moment before reaching out her hand toward it. The wind picked up slightly as if whispering something at the same moment she touched the plant.

She shook her head as if to clear it, and then she finally tore a stalk of leaves off the plant, the smell of it wafting into the air. She poured water over the base of the plants, silently saying something, and the wind picked up again as if they were conversing.

If Willow heard or felt anything, she did not mention it. In fact, when she turned to walk back to the house with Olivia, she looked like nothing had happened at all. Like the plants growing here, and her silent conversation with them, was completely normal.

Chapter Twenty

Willow

We spent the next week in the same routine. We trained in the morning and then split ways—Olivia headed to the kitchen after snagging cookbooks from the library and experimenting with the new food, and Liam headed off to scout the area. In the late afternoon, he'd sneak into the library, grab a random book from the shelves, and sit down next to me on the couch, our shoulders always touching, with neither of us wanting to be the one to move away first.

In those moments, I noticed I was no longer shaking. His touch grounded me in a way I didn't quite understand. I think he noticed it too, though he never mentioned it.

His smile. It's what I noticed the most about him. The casual way something in the book would make his lips quirk up without him realizing it. I kept those moments to myself. Savoring the feel of them, smiling inwardly.

I knew he was still hiding something from us, but I didn't push it, mostly because I was still too afraid of what it meant for all of us. I was getting too comfortable here. It felt almost like a true home, and I didn't want anything to change, so I kept my questions to myself.

As for the journal—something about it lured me into it each day, and I spent the early part of the night, before I fell asleep, thinking about it. It wasn't just a book about plants, though that was the meat of it. It was also about elemental magic.

It had diagrams that I couldn't understand but seemed to illustrate how one might manipulate and use the elements for various purposes. There were often lines drawn on the diagrams, crisscrossing randomly across the page. Not forming any particular pattern but connecting various points. The diagrams changed throughout the journal, getting more detailed as they went. From points to pictures of objects, people, animals, plants, and elements. One diagram even had the lines crisscrossing a drawing of the entire Earth.

I didn't understand what any of it meant. The descriptions of the diagrams were vague at best, as if the author didn't understand them either. The lines weren't labeled, and there was no mention of what they might represent. Looking at the diagrams, one would think a toddler drew the lines, but I could feel they had a purpose. I just couldn't figure out what that purpose was.

Somehow, it was all connected. I just didn't know how to find out what it all meant. My logical brain begged me to forget the journal, but something about it kept me returning until the diagrams burned into my memory, and I couldn't get them out.

"You're no longer afraid of me," Liam commented out of the blue one evening.

My eyes shot up from the book I was reading on tinctures, and I peered at him over the top of my glasses. "I was never afraid of you."

He gave me a quizzical look, and I laughed, snatching the book from his lap and pretending to look at it. "It was never you, just what that brown jacket represented. A trauma response I can't shake."

Confused, he watched me fiddle with the pages of his book. I finally peered down at it. A quiet chuckle rumbled through my chest, and his cheeks turned pink. The great captain, embarrassed by a book.

"You're reading fairy tales?" I asked, his choice of reading material rendering me almost speechless.

He shrugged. "No one in my family ever told me stories as a kid."

His confession only made my giggling fit worse, and he looked mortified.

"I'm sorry," I choked out. "I just didn't peg you as a stories kind of guy."

He lifted an eyebrow. "And how would you have pegged me?"

"Military arts?" I answered, knowing full well how ridiculous that sounded.

He feigned being hurt by that, putting his hand on his chest. "These *stories* tell me far more about what it means to exist in this world than any nonfiction book. There's a human element to them that doesn't exist in those plant books of yours," he said, nudging my book with his hand, brushing against my knee.

I wrinkled my nose, and he reached out to flick it. I swatted his hand away.

He chuckled. "Not everyone can be as smart as you," he added. "Someone has to be the dumb oaf in this relationship."

My eyes widened. Relationship?

"Dinner's ready!" Olivia beamed from the doorway.

When I caught her eye, I wondered how long she'd been standing there. Her look told me it was long enough to get a pretty good idea of what was going on.

But what was going on?

Liam stood in one fluid motion, reaching back for me.

I hesitantly took his hand, and he helped me stand, bending down to whisper in my ear. "Those *fairytales* are how I've learned all this charm."

I stifled full-on laughter. He smirked, stepping aside to let me pass.

I stared past Olivia, already knowing the look she was giving me.

Olivia held out a hand, stopping Liam before he could squeeze through to the hallway. He eyed her with amusement.

"Dumb oaf," she chuckled.

Liam rolled his eyes. "That's my new nickname, isn't it?"

Olivia only laughed, finally releasing him.

Two weeks after the plants appeared on the training field, Olivia and I found Liam on the field at dawn, and it was clear he was in a mood.

Olivia nudged me and whispered, "Should we just go back to the house?" as she stared wide-eyed at the anger in his eyes, a blue fire alight within them. A fire I'd never seen before.

The sight of us did nothing to quell his anger, and I swore he heard what Olivia whispered as he growled, "Warm-up drills. Now," pointing to the flat expanse of dead Earth in front of him.

Olivia glared at him and even stuck out her tongue before turning and walking to where he was pointing.

We warmed up and went through our conditioning drills without a sound. Liam twirled a dagger between his fingers, sitting on a rock close to the cliff, his features twisted in anger and confusion.

I wanted to know what had gotten him in such a mood, but I didn't dare ask him. Not with that fire in his eyes.

When we finished with our usual drills, he stood up, grabbed three swords, and stalked over to us. He shoved them into our hands, and Olivia stumbled back a bit from the force of it, grunting slightly.

I couldn't help the snarl that came out of me. "You don't have to be so rough."

His eyes widened, the blue fire growing brighter. "You want me to be more gentle, huh? The Claeg won't be *gentle*. The soldiers won't be *gentle*. The Elite won't be *gentle*. Hell, the whole world won't be *gentle* with you. It's about time you learned that," he growled at me, baring his teeth.

I took a determined step toward him. "You don't think I know that? I live in the same world you do."

Liam took a few more steps toward me until he was within arm's reach. "You know *nothing*," he growled.

I bit back the sudden emotion at the insult and threw my own. "Maybe we *would* have been better off with the Elite."

Something changed in Liam's posture as if I had struck him in the chest. A moment later, he got right up into my face and, in a deep, low voice, edged with anger, replied, "Fine, then teach yourself," and shoved the sword into my hands, brushed by my shoulder, and stalked off back toward the house.

He didn't look back.

As he disappeared up the cliff, Olivia finally broke the silence. "You think maybe that was a little harsh?"

"No!" I snapped at her, shoving the sword into the dirt. "And why are you taking his side!?"

Olivia studied me for a moment. "First, I'm not taking anyone's side. Second, you think maybe what you're both feeling right now is, in fact, sexual tension?" she asked seriously, but she had a big grin on her face that gave her away.

My anger only grew at her question. "It is NOT sexual tension. It's I'M GONNA MURDER HIM tension," I shouted and then stalked off back toward the house, simmering.

"Isn't that the same thing?" she asked, following me as I began to climb the steps.

I whirled around and glared at her. "It is NOT the same thing!" I screamed, but it only made Olivia giggle, and she clamped a hand over her mouth to try to stop herself.

I hissed at her, wheeled around, and continued climbing, ignoring her comments.

When we reached the house, she walked past me, no doubt heading for the kitchen.

I turned left and headed toward the library, trying to ignore what Olivia had just said.

I didn't notice him at first, lost in my thoughts, but when I looked up, he was sitting on the red velvet couch, hunched over with his elbows on his knees, lost in thought. When he saw me, he straightened up as if readying himself for whatever I would throw at him.

I flinched at his reaction, and as I walked over and sat down next to him on the couch, I couldn't help the trembling that started in my hands. I looked down and rubbed them together. I needed to lean into him, wanting to stop my shaking, but I was too afraid.

"What's wrong, Liam? And don't deflect like you always do."

He glanced at me out of the corner of his eye, not moving closer, but not moving further away either. "There is so much you don't know about what it's like out here. There's just so much death. So much that I cannot control."

There it was. The reason for his anger. He wanted to change things and felt powerless to do so. He wasn't alone.

I stared at him for a long time before working up the courage to offer him my own truth. To tell him what burned inside me, slowly eating away at my soul.

Some part of me *needed* to tell him. I needed at least one person to know. One person who might understand.

"I was ten. I had already shown interest in reading, and my parents indulged me by bringing home books of all kinds. Ones I couldn't get at school. Ones that came from our friends' secret stashes passed down for generations. One day, they brought home a book they'd been looking for for a long time. It was my birthday, and they were so excited to give it to me. Still, they waited until after I had consumed every morsel of extra food they'd stashed for the occasion." I paused and sucked in a breath, not sure I would be able to finish, my hands already trembling even harder. "But they didn't get the chance to give me the book before two soldiers burst into our apartment, knocking down the door. They ripped the book from my mother's hands and told us it was treason to possess that book. A crime punishable by death. I didn't even know what the book was about."

I could see the pain in Liam's eyes. He already knew what I was going to say.

"I thought . . . I thought that the death would be the worst part, but it wasn't. One of the soldiers held my father with a knife pressed against his throat and a gun pointed at me, while the other soldier . . ." I couldn't help the trembling that now consumed my entire body. No force of will would stop it at this point. It was a part of me. A constant struggle.

"You don't have to say it," Liam whispered.

"Yes, I do." I paused and took one more deep breath before finishing. "The other soldier raped my mother in front of us, made us watch, and then slit her throat. Her screaming is what I remember the most. The sound of it and the helplessness I saw on my father's face. My father tried to save her, but when he did, they slit his throat too, and then they left me there, not bothering to remove my parents' bodies. I desperately wanted them to have killed me too, so I wouldn't have to bear their deaths by myself. I spent months scrubbing the apartment until my hands were raw. The only reason I survived any of it was that I met Kat, Olivia's wife, a few days after I buried them. She became the only person in my life for a really long time. Until Olivia came along." I paused again, feeling completely numb and detached from my body as if I were floating above myself, watching the whole thing unfold from some other place. "I've never told anyone about what they did to my mother. Not even Kat."

He moved closer to me.

"It's my fault they died," I whispered, unable to look at Liam.

I had never admitted that piece of myself, either, and I fought the self-hatred and guilt as it reared its ugly head once again. "It's my fault Bill died too."

"Bill's death was my fault," Liam cut in.

My heart stopped in my chest, and my eyes shot to his.

He looked like he might be sick. "The general somehow found out about the book you gave him. Bill was detained before I could do anything. I couldn't defy the general's orders. Not if I wanted to live."

Now, I felt like I was the one that was going to be sick.

"I wasn't the one to murder him, but I also didn't stop it." Liam's voice cracked at the admission, and the shock I felt prevented me from saying anything.

I didn't even move.

"I saw you give him that book, Willow, and I just . . ." He didn't finish his thought. Or he couldn't.

My eyes snapped to my shaking hands, and my chest was so tight I felt like I couldn't breathe.

"Willow?" Liam asked tentatively, reaching for my hand.

I jerked away from him, and he pulled back. A sadness bloomed in his eyes that I'd never seen before.

"I envy your strength," he said after a long silence.

"What strength? I'm a trembling mess who knows *nothing* of this world."

He shook his head. "I shouldn't have said that. I didn't mean any of that. I've seen far less trauma break people. Drive them mad, but all you've done is gain more empathy for those around you. All you do is help people. People that many believe aren't even worth helping, myself included. If that isn't strength, I don't know what is."

"But what good is empathy?" I practically pleaded with him. "All it's given me is more heartbreak. More death. And I can help all the people in the world, but it won't change the fact that my parents are dead because of me. Sometimes, I feel it would be better to be a monster in a world full of monsters. Maybe then, it'd be easier."

"It's not. Trust me."

I looked at him then. Long and hard, as if I could erase the million scars etched on his heart and mine. "You aren't a monster," I whispered. "If you were, we'd be dead or in the hands of the Elite."

"There are far worse deeds than killing people. Even innocent ones."

"Such as?"

Liam stared into the distance, not answering for a while, clearly grappling with something I couldn't see. "Such as standing by while innocent people, like Bill, are killed and doing *nothing*. *Letting* it happen. It shreds your soul into far smaller pieces than being the one holding the knife."

"And if you had tried to stop it?"

"They would have killed me, along with the innocent people," he replied matter-of-factly.

"You were doing the only thing you knew to survive."

He let out a sadistic sort of laugh before answering, "Death would have been a more honorable alternative to standing by and doing nothing."

"You're doing something now."

He raised his eyebrows, but the sadness in his eyes was still there. "Or am I just running away?"

"Is that what you're doing?" I had the sudden urge to hug him, to erase the sadness in those beautiful ocean-blue eyes, but I was a coward. I was too afraid to move or get too close to anyone else for fear of losing them, so I didn't budge.

"I don't know," he whispered.

After a few moments of contemplative silence, Liam said, "Don't lose your empathy, please. It's the only light in this horrible world."

"I think that's the nicest thing you've ever said to me," I replied, surprised.

He glanced at me sideways, a small smirk twisting the sadness in his features. "Don't get used to it."

His low, gravelly voice stirred something in me, though I fought the feeling, pushing it further into myself. "Oddly enough, I'm getting rather used to you ordering us around. It'd be a shame to stop now," I replied, my voice edged with sarcasm.

His lips twisted into a feral smile. "Well then, we have more work to do."

I groaned, but a smile also tugged at the corner of my mouth. "No more conditioning drills, *please.*"

"And here I was thinking you *liked* them."

"They'd be much more enjoyable without your nagging," I said, finally standing up.

The sudden change in his voice stopped me in my tracks, though. "I don't deserve you."

Those words broke me, and I froze, unable to move. "No one deserves to be alone," I whispered.

"I do," he said as he suddenly rose from the couch and pushed past me, the passing air brushing my cheek lightly, the scent of earth and honey filling my nose, and then he was gone through the door before I could say anything.

I fell back onto the couch behind me, put my head in my hands, and cried until no more tears were left.

Chapter Twenty-One

Willow

"Willow?" Liam's soft voice broke through the darkness of my room in the early morning. Knowing him, it was just before sunrise.

I rolled over to face him, though I couldn't see him through the blackness.

"Mmm?" I mumbled, my voice rough with sleep.

"I think you should see this." There was something like amazement in his voice.

I groaned as I reached for the lamp. The light flooded the room, illuminating Liam standing by the doorway, smirking at me.

"You look lovely in the morning."

"Asshole." Sitting up and grabbing my pants from the side table, I clumsily pulled them on while Liam waited for me with quiet amusement.

"This better be worth it," I whined to him as I put on my glasses and passed him through the doorway.

"It is." I could feel him still smiling.

As we reached the front door, Liam stepped around me, pulled the handle, and swung it open.

The scent hit me instantly. A smell I had never experienced, and yet it was familiar somehow.

The scent of wet dirt.

"What?" I stammered as I almost stumbled down the steps.

Liam grabbed my elbow. "Rain."

I squinted in the darkness, the morning light appearing on the horizon, and registered the slight darkening of the dirt at the bottom of the steps. I hurried down them, feeling a softening of the earth beneath my feet.

I bent down slowly and felt the dirt under my hands. It felt smoother somehow, like the sharpness had disappeared. As you walked on it, there was no more crunch, like even the rocks had melted into the earth.

I scooped up a handful of dirt. It was wet but not soaked, like it was still thirsty. I brought it to my nose and inhaled deeply. I felt him watching me, and, as I let it fall back to the ground, I angled toward him.

"How?" I whispered, though I knew there was no explanation.

Liam bent down next to me, reaching his hand down to feel the moisture. I watched his hands splayed against the earth, slowly moving back and forth.

"I don't know," he whispered back.

We stayed that way for a while, content to take it all in as the horizon grew brighter.

"What's that intoxicating smell?" Olivia's voice drifted to us from the top of the stairs.

I rose from the damp earth and turned to face her, a smile forming. "It rained last night."

"You're kidding," she said incredulously, walking down the steps and planting her feet on the ground. Instead of a sharp crunch, she was met with near silence.

"I'd ask how, but I'm guessing there's no real explanation," she added, bending down to feel the wet dirt beneath her fingers.

I shook my head slightly. "The Earth is somehow awakening. I think the better question is, why now?"

Change was coming. It was already upon us, but I had no idea where that change would lead. From the looks on Olivia and Liam's faces, I wondered if they were thinking the same thing.

"Training?" Liam finally offered.

It was a better alternative than staring blindly into the unknown, so I nodded, heading back to the house to change into more appropriate clothing. Olivia and Liam were on my heels, and we spent the rest of the day in our normal routine.

In fact, we spent the next few days going through the same motions, and besides a few more rogue leaves on the bookshelves, no more plants popped up, and no more rain fell. I was starting to wonder if maybe it was a fluke or something we imagined.

A fool's hope.

I sat in the library in my usual spot on the red velvet couch. The late afternoon sun was streaming through the windows, and books were strewn everywhere now. On the table, on the floor, on the couch. All of them were open to seemingly random pages, no longer a beautiful collage but a beautiful mess.

Desperate for answers, I had taken to studying water in the days following the rain. How it was created and how it moved through ecosystems.

Without trees and plants, there wasn't enough transpiration and evaporation to form rain, even if the ocean still existed. According to my research, the rain that fell was an impossibility.

Yet, there I was, sifting through the journal again in a desperate hope that it would reveal something I had missed.

I felt him again, as I did almost all the time now, and I looked up to find him standing in the doorway, leaning against it with such ease and comfort, a lazy grin on his face.

"I brought you dinner since I doubted you'd emerge from here before nightfall," he said, pushing off the door, holding a plate of something that smelled divine.

I inhaled deeply as he reached out to hand me the plate.

"Thanks," I said around a bite.

"Find what you were looking for?" he asked me, glancing around at the giant mess of books I had created.

I shook my head, my mouth full of food I had never tasted. Olivia was still finding new food here and trying new recipes from her books. The result was that we had both put on considerable weight. My skin no longer sagged off my bones, and my ribs were barely noticeable through the skin on my torso. I had also gained muscle, something I had never known was possible.

Liam sat beside me on the couch, pushing aside some of my books to make room for himself. He studied me silently as I ate, and I wondered if he was thinking the same thing about me.

"I've been thinking about why no new plants have popped up anywhere and why there hasn't been any more rain," Liam finally said, glancing down at an open diagram of the water cycle I had been studying.

"And?" I asked through a mouthful of food.

"It can't be a coincidence. The three plants that grew were three plants we needed at that specific time."

"I've thought of that too, but *how?* It's not like we just waved our hands over the dirt and made the plants pop up. Everything I've read is explicit about how plants grow. Seeds need light, water, and healthy soil with tons of nutrients to grow. They did not have those things and grew into mature plants in the blink of an eye. An impossibility."

"Maybe you were on to something about waving your hands and making plants grow," he teased as the corner of his mouth curled into a wicked smile.

I put my plate down and smacked his arm playfully. "Don't get cheeky. I'm serious. Maybe you're right, though. Maybe it is magic. Maybe there is no answer."

"My fairytales are looking less silly now, huh?" he joked, stopping to look around the room at all the books scattered everywhere. "How do you even have time to read all these? Or keep track? Remind me not to take lessons from you on organization."

"Asshole," I murmured through my last bite of food.

He let out a short laugh, reaching for my empty plate.

"Maybe this is just a fool's errand. Trying to figure this all out and also trying to figure out why it hasn't happened since. Perhaps I should just give up."

"You? Give up on studying your books. It would be the end of the world if that day came," he replied dramatically.

I rolled my eyes. "Leave me alone. Go pick on someone your own size."

"You're shit out of luck on that, I'm afraid," he said, winking at me.

I flipped him off and then pretended to go back to reading.

He chuckled lightly and then strolled out of the room. I pretended not to watch him go.

Chapter Twenty-Two

Willow

A light knock on my bedroom door later that night brought me out of my trance as I watched the water fill the tub in the floor. I hadn't stopped taking my daily baths, a luxury I didn't think would last forever.

"Come in!" I yelled over the flowing water. I already knew who it was, so I didn't take my eyes off the water as Liam came through the door and halted just beyond the threshold, holding clean sheets in his hands.

"You can leave them on the bed," I said, finally peeling my eyes away from the water and watching him walk across the room.

As he set the sheets down, he paused as if he wanted to say something but thought better of it and headed for the door again.

"Stay." The word slipped out before I could stop myself.

Liam froze and didn't turn or say anything for a few moments. My hands began to tremble again, and without thinking, I stuffed them in my pockets.

"I can't," he whispered, still not facing me.

"Why not?" I dared to ask him, though I feared his answer. It wasn't the rejection I feared. It was what it meant if he *did* stay.

"I'm afraid," he said quietly, still facing the door.

His answer caught me off guard. I wasn't expecting such raw honesty. I stood there, frozen, and it took me a moment to whisper back the truth. "Me too."

He turned around then, and his eyes searched my face, a question lingering. His eyes revealed more than his words ever could. I began to tremble more, but then he stepped closer and said softly, his voice low and deep, "I think your bath is ready."

I looked toward the bathtub, the water still spilling from the spout, and then back at Liam, "There's room enough for two."

His eyebrows rose slightly, and the corner of his mouth twitched up. I watched his lips, my breath hitching.

"Will you help me with something?" I asked him a bit hesitantly. He tilted his head slightly in a silent reply, and I took a deep breath, trying to compose my nerves. I pulled my hands out of my pockets and held them toward him. They shook violently. "Will you help me?"

His eyes darted from my face to my hands. When his eyes met mine again, there was a blue fire lit behind them. Fire I usually only saw when he was angry. "Get in the tub," he commanded softly. The low grumble of his voice sent my heart pounding again.

"I don't think I can take my clothes off," I said, not wanting to admit that my hands wouldn't be able to complete that task.

"Keep them on," he said, not breaking his stare.

I slowly walked to the stairs leading to the tub. I stepped carefully into the warm water, my clothes instantly feeling heavy from the weight of the water they absorbed. I made my way over to the faucet and turned the handle. The water slowed to a trickle and then stopped completely.

When I turned, Liam stood in the water a few feet from me. He had removed his shirt, and I could see the strong muscles in his torso crossed with dozens of white scars. Some were raised, others flush against his skin. I suddenly had the urge to trace those scars with my fingers.

"Turn around," he ordered, his voice like gravel.

I did as he told me, my hands still shaking violently.

The current of his movement hit me before he came to a stop, inches from my back.

Liam leaned down and whispered in my ear. "Focus only on the single point of contact. Don't think about anything else. Just the feeling of it. And breathe slowly."

How I would breathe at all was beyond me, but I did as he said, letting my arms hang loosely at my sides.

He started with my right arm. The tips of his fingers touched me lightly at the point where my arm and the water came into contact.

I couldn't breathe. I felt too much. I trembled more violently than I ever had because it felt like I couldn't hold it all.

He didn't move his hand as he waited for me to start breathing. When I finally allowed myself to take a few deep breaths, he slowly and lightly began to trail his fingers up my arm.

I narrowed my focus to just his fingers and my breathing, and ever so slowly, I felt the trembling begin to ease. Everything begin to ease, as if all it took was his touch to erase every terrible thing in this world. It should have frightened me. The power he seemed to hold over me, but it didn't. Instead, all I felt was hope and something far more dangerous—desire.

As his fingers reached my shoulder and the sleeve of my shirt, he ran them slowly around the seam and then dipped them back toward my elbow. He left a trail of warmth everywhere we were connected, and goosebumps rose along my arms. He slid his fingers back down to where he started. He did the same thing on the left side, and by the time he returned to the start, my trembling was all but gone, replaced by a strange tingling feeling

He pulled his hand away, and a feeling of floating above myself suddenly overtook me, as if his touch was the only thing keeping me tethered to myself and this Earth.

I shuddered involuntarily, and his hand was instantly on my arm again, as if he also sensed it.

"May I take off your shirt?" he whispered, leaning down, his breath tickling the edge of my ear.

I swallowed, but nodded, and then his hands were around my waist, tugging my half-soaked T-shirt over my head. Liam tossed the shirt onto the floor next to the tub and said quietly, his voice still coarse, "Keep focusing."

How could I focus? Standing in only a bra, a shirtless soldier behind me? A soldier who had somehow become a friend. A confidant. Despite everything.

His hand started on my right arm again. His touch was instantly soothing. He took his time running his fingers up my arm, but he didn't stop at my shoulder this time. He continued to the base of my neck, and I instinctively angled my head to the side, letting my hair fall away from the right side of my neck, exposing it completely. His hand hesitated momentarily and then continued slowly up my neck to just below my ear.

I held back the sound gathering in the back of my throat as his fingers came back down and wound their way across my upper back. I didn't have to try to focus anymore. My attention was locked on every subtle movement of his fingers on my bare skin.

I was in deep trouble now as his fingers ran themselves up the left side of my neck and then traced the contours of my ear. I sucked in air, trying desperately to keep my breathing even.

Liam's fingers made their way back to the point where my neck met my shoulder and lingered there.

I started trembling involuntarily at his touch, and he pulled back instantly as if I had shocked him.

The need for him to touch me was so overwhelming that I backed up into him. Crushing my back against his firm torso. "I'm not trembling out of fear, you idiot. I'm trembling out of desire for you to touch me," I choked out, and then I reached back and grabbed his hand, placing it on my chest, just below my collarbone.

A silent invitation.

Liam splayed his fingers flat against my chest and didn't move.

Just when I thought he might pull away, he lowered his mouth to my ear, his hand still on my chest. "Where would you like me to touch you?" His voice was so deep it was as if the words vibrated into my very core, and my legs threatened to give out at the sound of them.

"Everywhere," I whispered back, my voice still unsteady.

A low growl of approval came from deep within his throat as he grabbed my waist with his free hand and crushed me further into the front of him. The hand on my chest moved slowly down my center and then over. His fingers ran along the edge of my bra, dipping under the fabric, brushing my nipple.

His touch elicited a soft moan from my lips, and I bent my head back against his shoulder, exposing my neck and chest further.

The next thing I knew, his mouth was tracing the edge of my ear, his hand completely under the fabric of my bra, as he massaged and tugged at my nipple.

I arched further into his touch, my ass rubbing against him. He let out a hiss at the contact, and I smiled as his mouth started down my neck.

He sucked slightly at the junction between my neck and shoulder. I let out another quiet groan, my breath coming in shorter bursts.

I was burning, wanting more from him.

I twisted out of his grip and turned my body to face him. A bit of surprise flashed briefly across his face before turning toward something resembling joy. His eyes lit like blue embers.

"What is it?" he whispered, studying my face intently as if he could read my mind.

I shook my head. "It's nothing," I whispered, hungrily pulling his lips down to mine.

He stopped me, holding his lips above my mouth, and smiled. A feral grin that had me almost pleading with him before he covered my mouth with his.

It wasn't a gentle kiss. It was a kiss that spoke all the unspoken words between us. All the things we hated and loved about each other. All the desire we had bottled up for fear of what it might mean. All the years of feeling so utterly hopeless, lost, and alone. We poured everything into that kiss. A tangle of lips and teeth and tongues and breathless moans.

When it felt like too much to hold, and I could hardly breathe, Liam pulled away, bent over, and before I could protest, he swept me up in his arms and leapt out of the tub in one fluid motion. Water sprayed everywhere as he set me down gently on the bed and tugged at my pants.

"So greedy," I laughed as my pants fell with a wet thud onto the stone tile next to the bed.

"Wasn't it you who wanted me to touch you *everywhere*?" Liam practically purred as he climbed on top of me. Water fell from his body and his soaked pants onto my skin as he reached for my bra.

"Yes," I replied breathlessly, not wanting to argue, only wanting him to touch me again.

Before I could blink, my bra was on the floor, along with his soaking pants, and Liam was staring at me as he knelt between my legs.

"You're beautiful, and I've thought so since I first saw you. It's taken all of me not to touch you," he whispered gruffly, his gaze devouring my entire body.

I shuddered slightly, then reached up and grabbed his head, pulling his lips to mine again.

And then, the lights went out.

We both paused, pulling our mouths apart. I could feel him assessing the situation.

"Please don't stop," I begged him.

I felt him turn his attention back to me, and he reached out, brushing his finger lightly across my bottom lip. "Oh, I have no intention of stopping now. I'll just have to learn your body from touch and taste alone."

"Fuck," I moaned, and he laughed into my mouth.

His hands and mouth traced every inch of me, learning and memorizing every part of me as he promised.

Every place his mouth touched left a trail of fire, and I was happy to burn.

"*Please*," I begged him, my voice barely more than a whisper, as his mouth traced my upper thigh.

I felt him raise his head, and the absence of his touch made me squirm with impatience.

He chuckled. "Say it again. I want to hear you say it again. Just like that."

It wasn't hard to beg for his touch. "*Please*."

And then his mouth was on me, swirling around my center, and I arched my back, needing more.

He groaned when his fingers slid inside of me, and he felt how much I wanted him. How ready I was for him. His fingers pulsed in and out of me, his tongue dragging up my center. I moaned loudly, completely lost in the feel of it.

"You. I want you," I ground out, still needing more. Needing him inside of me.

He was on top of me in an instant, and his lips found mine again in the darkness. He tasted of honey and my own desire.

"Fuck, Willow," he moaned as he found my entrance and pushed into me.

I arched into the feeling of him, every muscle tightening around him as he continued to fill me. And nothing had ever felt so good. So right.

I clutched his shoulders as he moved within me, both of us lost in the haze of desire. Our breaths intertwined as we continued to discover every inch of each other.

"Liam." I wasn't sure if it was a warning or a plea. His name was like fire on my lips.

He groaned loudly, and it almost sent me over the edge.

"Say it again. Say it as you come."

Those words were all it took as I practically shouted his name, and our bodies fell over the edge together. Liam pulled me closer, holding me through every pulse of pleasure.

When he finally pulled away, I started trembling again, this time from the cold. He gently wrapped me in a blanket and held me close. I put my head on his bare shoulder and took in his scent. He smelled of earth and honey.

We lay there for a while in complete silence, enjoying the warmth and feel of each other. After a while, I started to trace slow circles on his chest, tracing along the raised scars as if I could erase them with my touch.

"Careful," he growled in a hushed tone.

"Well, it's only fair, isn't it?" I asked, a hint of mischief in my voice.

"Mmmm," was his only response as my fingers trailed down his torso, memorizing every part of him.

I went slow, not wanting any of this to end. The feel of him, the taste of him, the smell of him. It was my undoing.

My mouth traced the same line my fingers did, going slowly, eliciting deep groans from him. I smiled into his skin as my tongue drifted lower.

Before I got to where I desperately wanted to be, he stopped me and pulled me on top of him. He stared at me in the dark for a brief moment before he drew my mouth to his. "I want all of you," he whispered, and then I was lost again, lost in him; we were lost in each other. We moved together as if it was something we had always done, as if we were only remembering, not doing for the first time.

The release had us both shaking. I collapsed my full weight onto him.

When our breathing finally slowed, the exhaustion hit me like a wall, and I found I could barely keep my eyes open. Liam must have sensed it because he rolled me off him, pulled the blanket over my shoulders, and kissed me lightly on my forehead.

I closed my eyes, close to sleep; Liam's voice drifted over to me. "There's something that's been bothering me," his voice was contemplative.

"Mmm?" I mumbled, forcing myself to stay awake.

"If your parents were killed because of a book, why did you risk going to the library?"

I inhaled deeply. "Because I thought if I were caught, it would be what I deserved."

Liam tensed, his breath halting for a moment. "Do you believe that now?"

I didn't respond immediately. I wasn't entirely sure what I felt anymore. "I don't know. Everything has changed." It was the truth and the only answer I could give him.

Chapter Twenty-Three

Liam

We woke to Olivia screaming. I was instantly up, groping for the flashlight. I found it quickly and was almost at the door when Olivia barreled through it. She was breathing heavily but seemed uninjured.

"What's wrong?" I asked her, trying to keep my voice steady.

Suddenly, she was looking from me to Willow and back again. A wide grin formed on her face. She ran the flashlight slowly from my head to my toes. I knew what was coming, and I grinned in advance of it.

"Mmmm, I see why you like him," Olivia said to Willow over my shoulder.

"Olivia!"

"What? You two aren't exactly hiding anything. Literally."

I chuckled at that, completely unfazed that I was standing naked in front of her. I saw Willow's smile despite her supposed shock.

It was then that Willow and I noticed the green. She quickly got up, grabbed the flashlight from me, and scanned the room with it.

"I think the whole house is covered," Olivia explained. "I screamed not out of fear but shock."

We were all speechless.

The vines that had once been carvings were now living. They were covered in broad, deep green leaves and snaked around the room like they had always been there. What should take years to grow seemed to have happened in the blink of an eye. They turned the entire place into a living greenhouse.

"How?" Willow whispered, barely audible.

I stood there, staring at the vines, wondering what had changed, and my mind drifted to Willow. To what happened last night.

"So, you don't know if it's everywhere?" Willow asked Olivia.

Olivia shook her head.

"I'll go fix the lights," I finally said, pulling on my pants. I walked over to Willow and held out my hand for the flashlight.

When she handed it over, I could see the million thoughts racing through her mind. All I could offer her was a light kiss, but the shift in her body was palpable. The creases around her eyes softened and she smiled up at me. It was all the reassurance I needed before I was out the door.

From what I could tell, headed for the utility room, the whole house was covered in living plants. Their aliveness created a smell I had never experienced before. It smelled like I imagined all those pictures of gardens would. It smelled like color. It smelled like life. It was a smell that was almost as intoxicating as Willow. In fact, their scent was eerily similar to Willow's, and for some reason that didn't surprise me. Once the lights were back on, I returned to Willow's room and found her staring in disbelief at the willow tree behind the bed. Its leaves hung down over the bed, creating a living curtain.

"What the hell?" Willow sounded like she was somewhere between denial and disbelief.

Olivia just stood there staring at the tree.

"You should see the rest of the house."

Willow and Olivia wheeled around to face me, and the tears gleaming in Willow's amber eyes almost took my breath away.

"It's incredible. Especially the library, Willow," I added.

She didn't say anything as she practically sprinted to the library, ignoring the plants everywhere, covering every surface.

I finally caught up to her as she reached the library doors and froze in front of them, staring at the handle like she was afraid of what she might find behind them.

"You OK?" I asked her.

"I'm scared."

I didn't ask her why. Deep down, I already knew why.

I nodded toward the door, encouraging her to open it. She placed her hand back on the handle and pulled.

I heard her sharp intake of her breath, and then the tears fell. They were tears of joy, of disbelief, of awe. This was everything she'd dreamed of, and now it was real. I couldn't imagine what that felt like, but I was damn glad I had the opportunity to witness it through her.

"But how? It's not real. It can't be." Her voice shook so much that she could barely get the words out.

"Does it feel real?"

"Yes. It feels so alive. I can feel it in my bones."

I searched her face, wondering how someone in this world could look upon anything with such wonder. How could someone have this much hope, and how the hell could I ever be worthy of her?

I reached down and brushed the tears from her cheeks. I tilted her chin up and kissed her gently. Her lips instantly parted, and I felt her body press against mine, and I had to force myself to pull away.

"Can we just stay here forever?" Her voice sounded so hopeful that my heart instantly dropped.

"I wish we could, Willow. There's nowhere else I'd rather be, but we can't survive here on our own. We'll run out of food eventually. We need other people."

Her face fell, and her gaze dropped to the hand she had placed over my heart.

"We'll come back here one day, I promise," I added, though I didn't know if I could keep that promise.

In reality, I wasn't sure we'd make it a step into any town or city without the Elite killing us on sight, and the guilt that it was all my fault reared its ugly head. "For now, while we plan, let's just enjoy this place. Enjoy each other, OK?"

She met my gaze again and smiled, then kissed me long and hard, and all those thoughts drifted away. It was only her and me, and damn if I didn't want that kiss to last forever.

"I'll take that as a yes." I laughed against her lips.

When we finally separated, the realization of where I had to go hit me. "I have to go far today. There is a town west of here that I've been to before. I was hoping to see if anyone was still there, or if there was any chance there were supplies they could trade. I won't be back until dinner. Possibly later."

I purposefully kept my fears of what I'd find there from her. I didn't want to burden her with it, nor did I want her to know what part I'd played in the possibility that the town no longer existed.

I could tell she knew what I wasn't saying.

"Meet me here later?" she asked, as if she feared I wouldn't return.

"Only if I get your full attention when I get back," I said, unable to pull my gaze from her lips.

"I'm yours," she whispered in my ear.

She had no idea what those words meant to me, and I couldn't stop myself as my mouth crashed into hers again. My hands trailed down her back and over her hips. I wanted to touch every inch of her again. A small moan escaped from deep in her throat.

"Careful," I warned, "or I might not be able to leave."

"I would be OK with that," she replied, grinning.

"I would be too, but I need to scope out the town," I said, resigning myself to the truth, even though my body protested. Even though I wasn't even sure I'd return to her.

She stepped back and waved me off. "I know. I'll see you later. If you see Olivia, can you tell her I'm here?"

"Sure thing," I responded, and then I was out the door before her pull kept me there.

It took me much longer than I expected, and I was utterly drained when I walked through the doorway. The kitchen was still lit, and I knew Olivia and Willow had dinner set out for me. I could see the soft light from the library spilling into the hallway on the other end of the house and knew Willow would be waiting for me.

I took a few minutes to eat the dinner. Olivia outdid herself with a new curry recipe from a cookbook that lay open next to the stove. Its pictures were blotted with some of the ingredients, and I smiled at the mess still on the counter and in the sink.

What an odd thing to be happy about. A mess. It was such a simple thing, an ordinary thing, but it made this place feel a little bit more like a home, a feeling I hadn't had in a long time.

The feeling didn't last long, as the day's memories came flooding back to me. Deep down, I knew that even if this place felt like a home, it could never be a home. No matter how hard I would try, this world would take it from me, just as it had taken everything else.

The thought sobered me as I strolled down the hallway toward Willow and what I knew I'd have to say to her.

When I walked in, she was staring at me as if she already knew I'd be there, and my breath caught slightly at the relief I saw in her eyes.

"That was a long day," she said to me hesitantly, as if afraid of what might come out of my mouth.

"It's not what I expected. I had to go a lot further than I wanted to."

"Did you find what you were looking for?"

"Yes."

When I didn't elaborate, she asked, "Did you eat?"

"Yes, thank you for the dinner."

I didn't move from the doorway, suddenly frozen with fear and something else. And it didn't help that a moment later, Willow walked over to me, wrapped her arms around my waist, and leaned her head on my chest.

I tensed at the contact, even though I wanted it. Needed it.

"Where are you?" she asked, looking up at me.

I searched her face for a moment, warring with myself over how much I should reveal. Some selfish part of me wanted her to always look this way—always feel this way. Her eyes were alight, more than I'd ever seen. She was happy, and I was about to ruin all that.

She ran her thumb over my brow, down my cheek, along my jaw, throat, and chest, and finally came to rest her hand over my heart.

I tensed even more at her touch, everything screaming at me to walk away from her. That she'd be better off, safer, with anyone else. That I would ruin her. That I'd kept too much from her, and once she discovered all the truths, that she would never look at me the same way again.

I'd lose her.

She looked up from where her hand lay over my beating heart to my eyes, pausing for a brief moment, before she reached up and pulled my lips to hers.

Every warning bell in my head went off. Everything in me told me to stop, but I couldn't. Her pull was too strong. I kissed her so deeply I felt like I might drown in it.

I pulled back only for a moment, long enough to breathe. "Fuck, Willow, it's all too much," and the next thing I knew, I had her pushed against the bookshelves, our clothes on the floor, and there was nothing left but our unrelenting hunger for each other.

Willow finally collapsed into my arms, and I carried her to the couch, setting her down gently. She pulled the blanket up to her chin.

I looked around the room at the plants, the books still scattered everywhere, and our forgotten pile of clothing. Another small thing that made this whole place feel so ordinary. So much like Willow. So much like home.

I dropped my head into my hands. "I'm sorry," I finally said, my voice so full of grief.

"What's wrong, Liam?"

I released my hands and looked over at her. Her brow was creased with worry.

"I can't protect you. I can't give you this." I motioned to the room.

"You don't have to. I just want you."

"It's not enough. *I'm* not enough," I said, my voice trembling now.

"Why isn't it? Why aren't you?"

"Because you don't know what we're up against," I almost shouted at her, then lowered my head into my hands again.

"Tell me, then."

I shook my head. I couldn't tell her.

"No! You don't get to shut me out. That isn't fair."

I could see all her anger, frustration, desire, and passion on her face, and I cracked.

"Do you even know how precious you are? Not just to me, to everyone and everything?" I motioned around the room again, "This is your creation, Willow, whether you want to believe it or not. People will hunt you for this. People will kill for this. People will use you and manipulate you and twist you into someone you don't even recognize anymore. Do you know how I know? Because they did that to me. For five years, they twisted my soul into something I no longer recognized. And you know what? I found you, and . . . and . . ." I trailed off.

She put her hand on top of mine, and I stared at it for a long while. Mostly in awe of how steady it was.

"You brought me back, Willow, and I could never repay you for that. If you only knew what I've done and what I've seen." I shook my head. "I'm scared. I don't want to go back to how it was, and I can't protect you."

Willow suddenly got up and knelt between my legs. She brushed my lips slowly with her thumb. I grabbed her hand and kissed the inside of her wrist where the tracker used to be, and she closed her eyes for a moment, a quiet, breathy sound escaping her lips.

I felt my whole body relax at the feel of her. Like she stole all the tension from me simply by touching me.

She deserved the truth. "There's a village due west of here, similar to this one. They . . . they . . ." I was suddenly choking on my words and paused briefly, taking another deep breath. "They murdered the whole village. Women, children, everyone, and put their bodies on stakes. They were serving them to the Claeg." I was shaking as the images flooded my brain again, and a single tear escaped my eyes.

Willow stood up, sat on my lap, and wrapped her arms and legs around me. I leaned my forehead into the crook of her neck and tears I hadn't let spill for five years suddenly poured out of me and down her chest.

"It's not your fault," she said. "There's nothing you could have done."

I felt her tense.

"I knew it was happening. I knew, and I did nothing to stop it." I lowered my head again as the shame, the guilt, and the self-hatred flowed into my blood.

I felt Willow tremble a moment before tears fell from her eyes, and I knew it wasn't just me she was crying for. She was crying for this horrible and broken world.

Chapter Twenty-Four

Willow

"I think you two might want to come outside," Olivia said, her tone serious.

I was still half-asleep on the couch, and the sun had just begun to rise, casting a soft glow across the library floor.

"We need to stop meeting like this," she said to Liam with a wink and a grin as he pulled his pants on.

I couldn't see Liam's face, but I could guess at the look he was giving her given Olivia's chuckle.

"Busy night, Willow? Get a lot done?" she asked wheeling on me, sarcasm dripping from every word.

I ignored her, pulling my shirt over my head. "What'd you find?"

"You might want to see it with your own eyes."

Olivia led us to the front of the house and opened the door, and suddenly, there was nothing but green. Liam sucked in a breath, and Olivia watched our reactions.

The land was completely covered in plants. Not just around the house but encompassing the entire community. All variety of plants, from ground cover to mature trees. The image resembled all the pictures I had ever seen of the ecosystems of the past.

I was in complete shock.

"That's not all," Olivia said, a huge grin forming.

"What else?"

She motioned for us to follow her, and we walked around to the other side of the house. I heard it before I saw it.

"A waterfall," my voice was barely a whisper.

Sure enough, around the corner, a large waterfall tumbled down the cliffs into a small pool at the bottom and continued in a stream that meandered through the center of the community. Looking at it now, it seemed obvious that a stream belonged there, but I hadn't noticed it before.

"So, I have a question, what the hell happened last night?" Olivia asked us, arms crossed, the grin still plastered on her face.

I looked at Liam. He hadn't said anything, and his face was blank. He was staring at the waterfall and landscape beyond.

"You think it had something to do with what happened last night?" I asked her.

"I don't have a clue, but *something* happened last night."

I went over the night's events, trying to piece together the information I had learned from my research and what Liam had revealed. I didn't see the connection, but something about Olivia's question tugged at some invisible thread within me.

"Well, you two seem to have a real gift," she laughed.

"And how do you know it's not you?" I barked at her defensively.

She gave me a stern look. "It's not me, Willow, and you know it."

I looked at Liam to see if he would respond, but he was lost in thought.

"Well, we might want to figure out why this is happening because I'm not sure we can hide from the world if, everywhere we go, entire ecosystems start to pop up," Olivia observed.

"She's right," Liam finally said. "We're an easy target now. We can't stay hidden here any longer."

It took a moment for his words to sink in. To even think that this would be a bad thing was completely unfathomable. The plants were a miracle, but they were likely to get us killed in this world, even if we had nothing to do with their existence.

My heart sank. The world I dreamed of was somehow returning, and now we had to leave. Abandon it.

"How long?" I asked, unable to hide the crack in my voice.

"We should have a few more days before anyone catches on," Liam responded, and part of me knew he was allowing us more time here because of me. Because of how attached I'd become to this place.

The captain in him was likely fighting him on that decision. Fighting to leave immediately.

"I'll start the preparations," he said, returning to the house.

I grabbed his arm, and he looked down at me. "I'm so sorry."

Those three words broke me. "It was never going to be forever. I knew that." Although I tried to sound strong, my voice wavered.

He pulled me into a hug. I rested my head on his chest, listening to the roar of the waterfall and his heartbeat all at once.

"Olivia, can you help me with the packing? I know you took stock of everything," Liam finally asked, slowly peeling away from me. The captain was back.

"Sure." Olivia's smile was gone now.

"Willow, are there any of these plants we could use? Take with us? Medicine? Food?" he asked.

I nodded. "I'll look around."

"Take your bow, and if you see any Claeg, run."

I nodded again, words failing me.

We all walked back to the house in silence. Liam squeezed my hand and kissed me on the forehead before heading toward the kitchen with Olivia. I headed to our room and grabbed my bow and arrows.

The first thing I noticed was the smell. If green had a smell, this would be it. I'm not sure I had ever smelled air this fresh in my life. I took a moment to look at everything from above. I noticed a grove of oak trees, some willow trees along the stream, fields of wild grasses and flowers beyond the oaks, and many shade-loving plants among the trees and along the houses.

I turned and followed the path up and over the house. It was already a long trail, but my pace slowed at so many useful plants.

My pack was almost full when I reached the bottom of the trail. The land spread across a field of grasses and wildflowers ahead of me. I spotted some poppies and collected some of her seeds for pain. As I moved across the field toward the stream and the houses beyond, I spread seeds and water in my wake. I hummed as I collected the plants that I had waited my whole life to meet, a melody of joy, and I swore I could hear them answer with their song.

I made my way to the stream and dipped my now empty water bottle into the clear water. I stood watching the water flow, washing away the dead and dying land, carving it into something new. I never thought I'd live to see this.

From the stream, I made my way toward the oak grove. Once there, I searched for familiar plants beneath their branches. I spotted miner's lettuce, wood sorrel, chickweed, and nettles. All of them were edible and nutritive. I picked some to snack on and packed some away for dinner later.

When I finished, I sat beneath the mother oak and pulled out the rest of my snacks. I looked over the field as the wind blew the grasses and wildflowers into a beautiful dance. The colors shifted and changed as they moved. I closed my eyes and listened to the wind find its way through leaves and branches.

When I finally stood, I wandered over to the clear line between the now-living Earth and the dead Earth beyond it.

Curiosity got the better of me as I bent down to feel the difference between the dead and living soil beneath my hands. I stepped out onto the dead dirt; the feel of it was harder, sharper.

I should have been more careful. More aware. But I was so lost in my observations that I failed to notice them.

I screamed as a gray, dead-looking hand grabbed me, its claws digging into my wrist, my blood forming bright-red droplets on my skin.

I tried to yank my hand free, and that's when I noticed the rest of the Claeg. They were all crouched down below the line of plants. Hiding. Waiting.

When the smell of my blood reached the others, they all leaped into action. There must have been two packs of them. Probably thirty total.

I yanked my hand harder, but even if I could get away, thirty was too many. Even for Liam.

I shouted, though I knew no one could hear me.

The Claeg holding me hissed back, a grotesque smile forming on its colorless lips as it pulled me toward its sharp teeth. This one was slightly larger than Liam, and much stronger than me.

My pulse increased as adrenaline pulsed through me. I had become too comfortable here. I'd almost forgotten the terrors beyond the house and the tiny world we created within its walls. This creature brought down that illusion in an instant as it drove its sharp nails into the fragile skin at my wrist.

I dug my heels in as the others raced closer. A second later, I lost my balance and fell backward. The force of my fall ripped the claws from my wrist, and I screamed, clutching it close to my body. I inched further from the Claeg, trying to lose myself in the field of wildflowers.

It took me a moment to realize they weren't following me, even though I could hear their shrieks and hissing.

Then it hit me. What I'd read about them.

They couldn't pass the line between the dead and living Earth. They were never found near any plants, and it was theorized that they killed humans to prevent them from growing plants.

Well, here was the proof. They were creatures of death and destruction, and the living world, it appeared, was not habitable for them.

I stood and took one more look at the Claeg, who looked as though they didn't know what to do. Terror and hope swam through my head as I took in their panicked back-and-forth motions and listened to their frustrated hisses.

The truth was, I didn't know what to do either.

When I walked up to the front door, I heard their laughter coming from the kitchen. The sun began to set in the distance. I could still see the Claeg, but they seemed to be moving north now. I wondered where they came from and how they knew exactly where I was. It was as if they were *hunting* me. Or hunting us? Were they connected to the Elite? Or were they drawn to the plants somehow?

I shook off the questions and walked into the kitchen. Liam and Olivia were preparing dinner, and Liam was laughing at something Olivia had just said.

"Willow!" Olivia shouted, and Liam stopped and turned, still smiling.

I smiled back, setting my full pack on the table.

It was then that they both noticed my bleeding wrist and their faces turned white.

I waved off their concern, pulling my pack off and searching for the needed herbs and bandages.

They watched in stunned silence as I patched myself up.

I laughed at their bewilderment. "The good news is that the Claeg can't cross the line between the living and dead Earth."

Their mouths fell open simultaneously.

I laughed again because I didn't know how else to respond.

As we ate, I explained everything. They were silent throughout the story, not interrupting me at all.

"I told you it was confusing," I said through a mouthful of food. "I'm just grateful for the knowledge that we're safe from the Claeg here, even if I don't know the why or the how of it."

"But are we safe from other humans?" Liam asked, his voice losing its joy somewhat. "And what about the fact that you thought they were *hunting* you? If they're hunting you, they know who and where you are. What if they were *sent*? What if the Elite are somehow controlling them?"

"Is that even possible?" Olivia asked. Her smile had faded as well.

Liam was silent for a moment before responding, "I don't know, but it wouldn't surprise me if the general was working with the Claeg. You saw the numbers in Coria. That wasn't a natural occurrence for the Claeg."

"That's crazy," Olivia said, completely stunned.

"I know it seems that way, but there's something bigger and more complicated going on here," Liam responded.

"Yeah, no shit," Olivia said. "My head hurts from all this information."

"What do we do?" I asked.

Liam sighed. "We continue with our plan. There isn't anything else we can do. The Elite know we're here; if they didn't know before, they do now. All they have to do is follow the color green."

I knew he was right but didn't want him to be. We ate the rest of our meal in silence, each of us lost in our own thoughts.

Olivia broke the silence and solemn mood first. "So, I read in one of those cookbooks that chocolate is an aphrodisiac. I had to look up what that meant."

I laughed before I could help myself, which rewarded me with Olivia's sly grin. She knew that I already knew where she was going with it.

"As I was saying," she continued as Liam gave us a confused look. "I was just wondering if any of your plants have the same effect? Not that the two of you need any more reason to jump each other."

I had to hold back my laughter, and my body shook with the effort of it. "So, if it's not for our benefit, who's it for?"

Olivia shot me a sharp look.

"Is anyone going to explain what's going on here?"

This time, I actually laughed because Liam looked so confused and out of place.

"It's not for anyone, just a curiosity," Olivia was able to get out through her own laughter.

When I calmed myself enough to speak, I patted Liam's hand on the table next to me. "Aphrodisiac foods and plants help increase libido by increasing blood flow and stimulating hormones."

Liam shot Olivia a look I couldn't see.

"What? Don't tell me you aren't at least a little intrigued," she purred at him.

Liam slowly met my gaze. "Oh, I'm intrigued, all right."

I rolled my eyes at the two of them, but I'm pretty sure I was blushing. "Unfortunately, most aphrodisiac herbs don't grow in this type of ecosystem, and I haven't had the pleasure of coming across the few that do."

"Good thing I made a chocolate cake then!" Olivia said far too enthusiastically.

"A cake?" I asked incredulously.

Olivia's smile grew wider, and it seemed to be contagious.

"You may share it with me if you promise to keep your hands to yourselves, at least until I'm out of eyesight and earshot. Because, well . . . gross."

"Deal," Liam and I both said in unison, and then we all devoured the cake like it was our first (because it was) and, likely, the last time we'd ever taste anything like it.

Chapter Twenty-Five

Willow

The next morning, I was rifling through the pantry when I heard the front door open and close. Olivia was packing our belongings, and Liam had gone out to scout the route we would take the next morning.

"Liam, is that you?" I called, reaching for a bag of flour on a high shelf, standing on my tiptoes, arms extended.

It didn't occur to me that it was too early for Liam to be back, and when I finally reached the bag, I heard two sets of feet slowly entering the kitchen, not one.

I froze, and my trembling hands dropped the bag of flour. It exploded in a shower of white as two soldiers appeared in the doorway, blocking my exit.

"What do we have here?" the taller of the two sneered, looking around the fully stocked pantry.

"Looks like we hit the jackpot. Plenty of supplies, the captain's around here somewhere, plants everywhere, and a pretty little thing all by herself," the other soldier said, twisted glee on his pale face as he took a step closer to me.

"Captain?" I asked, trying to play dumb even though dread consumed me, and I felt a familiar tremble start in my hands. Despite everything Liam taught me and how far I'd come, I still feared the soldiers and everything they represented.

"Oh?" the tall one smiled. "What was the name she called when we first walked in?" he asked the smaller soldier.

"Sounded like she was calling the captain's name." He took another step closer to me, and my mind raced for a way out, but there was nothing I could use as a weapon. There was no exit but the one they were blocking.

"You must have been hearing things," I replied, backing up against the back shelf and keeping my shaking hands behind me as they took another step closer. As much as I wished Liam were here, part of me was relieved. The gun visible in the holster on the taller soldier told me they were leaving with Liam one way or another. Dead or alive. And I knew Liam wouldn't let them take him alive.

They sneered. "We know you're lying, but that's OK. If you want to do things the hard way, it's more fun for us anyway."

I knew they expected me to fall to my knees, begging them not to hurt me, but I would give them no such satisfaction. Before I lost my nerve, I threw two fistfuls of flour in their eyes and bolted for the door, slipping through the small gap between them.

I had almost made it through when the taller one grabbed the back of my shirt and yanked me back. The force of the pull, combined with the flour on the floor, made my feet slip out from underneath me, and I fell hard on my back, knocking the wind out of myself. My glasses went flying.

As I gasped for breath and tried to stand, the smaller soldier crunched my glasses under his boot. The *snap* echoed through the pantry. He then moved his boot onto my chest, pinning me to the ground.

He slowly wiped the flour from his face. "Feisty little bitch we have here."

I squirmed, trying to remove his boot, but he only pushed harder, making it impossible to breathe. I felt a rib give way, and a *crack* sounded in the silence between words. The soldier smiled, and I fought the urge to scream.

"It's easy, princess. Tell us where Liam is, and we'll let you go," the smaller soldier said as he bent down and put his face inches from mine, while keeping pressure on my broken rib with his boot.

"Go to hell." I spat in his face.

He stood, wiping his face with his shirt sleeve. He removed his foot from my ribs. The relief was short-lived, as a second later, he kicked me in the same place my ribs had snapped. The pain was blinding, and though I wanted to scream, nothing came out. I couldn't pull enough air into my lungs to mutter a sound, and blackness swirled around the edges of my vision.

"Say that again," the soldier snarled at me.

"Cool it, Tom, we need information from her," the taller one said, holding out his arm to stop Tom from doing any more damage.

I groaned in relief, finally pulling some air into my lungs, though my breath came in shallow bursts. It felt as though I were breathing tiny shards of glass.

The taller soldier bent over and put his face close to mine. "We need just one little answer."

Beyond the two of them, I could make out Olivia just outside the doorway to the pantry. I didn't dare look directly at her for fear that they would see her, so I growled, "Get out."

I prayed she knew I was talking to her.

The two soldiers laughed. "I don't think you're in much of a position to be telling us what to do, princess."

Out of the corner of my eye, I watched Olivia back up from the pantry and head for the front door.

Relief flooded me as I lifted my trembling hand and gave them both the middle finger.

The taller soldier's face twisted into pure rage, and he stood abruptly, grabbed the end of my hair, and dragged me out of the pantry.

I clawed at his hand, my ribs protesting with every movement. My eyes watered at the pain, and my breath began to come in even shallower bursts as I fought to stay conscious.

He dragged me to the front entrance. I tried to keep my head from smashing onto the floor as he dropped my hair, and I was mostly successful, but my head still rebounded off the hard stone. Agonizing pain pierced through my skull.

Before I could regain any sense of myself, Tom tore my shirt off. Not a second later, he kicked me in the stomach so hard that I crumbled in on myself, curling into a tight ball despite my screaming ribs.

I had no sense of time. Of how long it was between kicks. They blended in a constant stream of pain, and before I knew it, the taller soldier grabbed me by the hair and yanked. I was forced to come out of my tight ball and look at him.

"You want more? Or are you gonna give us what we asked for?" he asked, smiling wickedly. I wanted to plunge a knife through his throat, but all I could manage was spitting in his face. This time, though, it was blood that came out; the tang of iron lingered on my tongue.

He slapped me and released my hair at the same time, my head snapping backward and bouncing off the floor. This time, I knew I was going to lose consciousness, and I begged for the darkness.

"Don't lay another finger on her." I barely registered the low growl coming from the front door, now ajar. Liam was standing there with a rage I had never seen before. The blue fire lit behind his eyes, ready to explode and consume everything in its path.

"Well, well, well," Tom said, stepping toward Liam, who had his sword in his hand and pointed it at the two soldiers.

"The mighty captain has finally returned." His disdain for Liam was apparent.

"We've been looking for you," the tall soldier added, bending over me but not touching me.

Liam stepped forward, his eyes darting between the three of us. Assessing, calculating, flaming eyes.

"Tsk, tsk," said Tom, taking out a knife and holding it to my throat. "We'll have to kill her if you come any closer. Shame, though, such a pretty little thing."

"Perhaps we'll have a little fun with her before we do," the tall soldier snickered, winking at Tom.

Liam let out another low growl.

The two soldiers both laughed mockingly. "Getting soft on us, Cap? You used to love watching us do this, didn't you? Don't have a stomach for it anymore? Or maybe it's because you actually like this one," the tall soldier said, glancing down at me briefly.

"The captain, who never touched a single lady in any of the villages we pillaged, finally has a bit of a crush." Tom laughed again and then grabbed my hair, pulling my face toward him, "Wonder what makes you so special that the almighty *captain* would take an interest in you. Does it have to do with these plants, perhaps? Or maybe you're fun to bed? Huh?"

Liam hissed, raising his sword.

"I wouldn't do that if I were you," Tom said, pressing the knife further into my neck, causing a small trickle of blood to fall to my chest.

"What do you want?" Liam spat, his hands trembling with restraint.

"You know they want you. Don't play dumb. For the life of us, we cannot figure out why the hell you're so special that you deserve both human and Claeg chasing after you, but"—Tom shrugged and trailed off for a moment—"they are paying us double to bring you in, so here we are."

"Seems like it might be more than double, given the plants. There's a larger reward for bringing in any information about what's happening with the sudden plant growth," the tall soldier added, licking the perimeter of my ear and groaning.

My whole body trembled at the contact, a reflex I couldn't control.

"I'll go with you if you leave her," Liam replied.

Were his eyes glowing?

"You don't have any power to negotiate, I'm afraid."

Liam cocked his head to the side and gave them a predatory grin. "No, I believe it's you who doesn't have any power to negotiate," he said as a dagger appeared in his hand. An instant later, the dagger was embedded in Tom's eye, and before Tom even dropped the knife from my neck, the tall soldier's head was on the floor next to his falling body.

Then, everything was still and silent all around me.

I looked up at Liam, my vision still blurry. His eyes were *glowing* as he stared down at the two dead bodies, blood splattered across his shirt and face.

"Liam," I whispered.

He finally tore his eyes away, and a moment later, he was on the floor next to me. "I'm so sorry."

"Willow!" Olivia shouted as she raced over and fell onto the floor next to me. "What can I do!?"

"My ribs are broken. Right side," I barely choked out.

Liam walked to my other side and gently lifted me off the ground. I groaned at the pain that seemed to pierce every inch of my body.

He was gentle as he walked me to my room and set me down carefully on the bed, trying his best not to touch the right side of my body. When he had me settled as comfortably as possible, I instructed them on the plants to collect that would help.

Olivia hurried off to find what I needed while Liam sat on the edge of the bed, his head in his hands, miserable.

"What is it?" I managed to croak out.

He raised his head. Tears were streaming down his face.

The tears took me so much by surprise I almost reached for him, but the pain held me pinned to the bed.

"I failed you." His voice was barely a whisper as he stared blankly at the tub in the floor.

"This wasn't your fault," I managed to say through clenched teeth.

"How can you believe that?" he practically shouted at me. "I led them here. I *knew* my men could get past the fence. I *knew* it would only be a matter of time before they came looking for me here. We should have been long gone."

I stared at him for a few moments. "You couldn't have predicted when, and this wasn't your fault," I repeated, pleading with him now. "And when are you going to realize that you're *worth* something? That you're *better* than them? You *chose* to leave to do something better. It's what you're doing *right now* that matters. The rest doesn't matter."

"How can you say it doesn't matter? You heard them. I did *nothing* to stop them from doing the same thing they did to you to countless other women! I stood by and *watched*. And it's worse than that, Willow. I did things I cannot ever atone for. I've killed countless innocent people, and I didn't kill your friend, Bill, but I did nothing to stop it either. I was cowardly enough to make my men do it, which I did when I couldn't stomach doing it myself. I deserve nothing less than death, and yet, the one person who doesn't deserve a moment of pain has endured more than any of us." He turned away from me then and shook his head. "I'm only making this worse."

"Look at me," I demanded.

He didn't turn toward me right away, and I thought maybe he wouldn't. I could see the tears again, an ocean of them pouring out of his depthless eyes.

"You're a fool, Liam. You're a fool who is blind, and I won't let you die, no matter how many times you tell me you deserve it." I paused, sucking in a painful breath. "You act like death is the only thing you're capable of. As if what you've done to keep us alive, or what you've taught us, or what you've helped us build here isn't worthy.

You act like you're the villain, but I don't see a villain, I see beautiful possibility."

Liam laughed, but it was a humorless laugh. "You're the fool, Willow," he sneered, and then he stormed out of the room, slamming the door behind him.

That's when I let the tears fall. Tears that I had bottled up since the soldiers first walked through the door; the sobs that racked my body produced a greater pain than I had ever known.

Hours later, after Olivia had done her best to ease my pain with poppy seeds and meadowsweet, wrapped my broken ribs with comfrey, washed the blood from my body, and fed me small bites of food, Liam suddenly appeared in the doorway.

Olivia mumbled some incoherent excuse to leave and hurried out, stopping briefly to glare at Liam.

"I'm sorry," he said, not moving from the doorway. "I'm sorry for storming out. I left you broken on the bed, and I shouldn't have. But"—he paused and sucked in a breath, looking away from me and toward the beautiful living willow tree that hung above the bed—"I'm mostly sorry for not telling you about what I did. For all the villages we raided. All the people we killed. All the women who were raped while I stood by and did *nothing*. I was so broken after I lost my wife and my family. After I just *let* them be taken and killed. I didn't think I deserved to live. I didn't think I had anything to live *for*. I wanted to burn this entire miserable world to the ground. That's the worst part,

I think. That I felt like *everyone* deserved a terrible fate. That there was nothing left in this world that was worth saving."

I went to interrupt him, but he held up a hand to stop me. "I wanted to tell you all the terrible things I did before I met you. I wanted to tell you the whole story so you could have the choice to walk away if you wanted to. I wanted you to know who I was underneath all of it. And I had every intention of telling you everything, but then you told me about your parents, and I just *couldn't*. I was a coward. I was too afraid to tell you because"—he paused and choked on his words for a moment—"because you were the first wonderful thing to come into my life in so long, and I didn't think I would survive you walking away. Each time I told myself I would leave because you'd be safer or you'd be better off without me, something held me here. I can't explain it, but I felt something profound would break inside me, and there would be no recovering from it." He looked at me then, and I could feel a pain so deep I thought I'd drown in it.

"I wish you could see what I see." It was all I could offer him.

He finally walked over to the bed and sat beside me, grabbing my hand and stroking it softly. Something in his touch soothed me in a way I couldn't explain. A deep-rooted soothing, so subtle but so profound, that eased the pain slightly.

"And I wish you could see what I see," he whispered into my hair as he curled up on the bed beside me. "You can't logic your way out of all this," he added, motioning to the leaves above us. "It's pretty clear to me that all of this has something to do with you."

I didn't know how to respond to that. Whether I believed it had anything to do with me didn't seem important. At this moment, it didn't matter *how* it was happening. I was just so grateful that it was happening because it meant that there was some small hope for a future. Some way out of this mess.

Chapter Twenty-Six

Liam

"You think maybe it's about time you tell us what we're really up against?" Olivia's tone was harsh, which threw me a little.

I deserved it, though. If I'd told them the whole truth, Willow might not have been lying immobile on the bed right now.

"The general mentioned escaping Coria with the Elite was all part of a bigger plan put in motion a long time ago by a man who calls himself the emperor."

Willow sucked in a surprised breath, coughing and clutching her ribs. "Emperor? You're serious?" She squeaked out through clenched teeth.

Olivia watched Willow, her brow furrowed.

I nodded. "He's in a larger city the general calls Tarraco."

"What's his plan?" Olivia asked, her attention still on Willow's every pained movement.

"To build an empire," Willow wheezed, trying to sit up.

I raised a brow, and Olivia reached out to help her get into a more comfortable position.

"He's conquering nearby villages and cities and either bringing them under his control or eliminating them if they don't serve his agenda," Willow explained.

I nodded. That was what I'd suspected based on my orders and the information the general let slip occasionally.

"How did you know that?" Olivia asked.

"Books," Willow explained, smiling. "There have been many empires built over the last ten thousand years. Some lasted a long time, others collapsed quickly."

"What's his goal?" Olivia addressed the question to Willow, but I answered.

"Ultimate control."

Both of them snapped their attention to me.

"He wants to control everything. He wants to be a god in the eyes of the people."

Willow narrowed her gaze, but Olivia spoke first. "What does he currently control?"

I didn't want to tell them. I didn't want the already dire situation to become an impossible one, but the soldiers coming here and destroying what we'd built gave me no choice.

"Everything."

Olivia gasped, and Willow's gaze burned into me.

"There's no rebel organization? No one fighting against the emperor?" Willow asked.

I shook my head. "That's what I've been looking for. Even the evidence of some sort of separate society out of his control. There's none. Not even a whisper of one. Not within a fifty-mile radius. He's been at this for a very long time."

Olivia's head fell into her hands. Willow's eyes burned with rage, temporarily overshadowing the pain.

"What do we do?" Olivia's voice was shaky with emotion. I couldn't tell if it was fear or grief. Probably both.

"We keep looking," I said, because what other choice did we have? "We have to be gone today. When Tom and Leo don't return, the rest of them will be after us."

"How long?" Olivia sounded worried.

"As soon as possible, but I'm not sure Willow can travel."

"I can manage," she said.

I looked at her skeptically, and Olivia's concern was evident in the slight downturn of her lips and narrowed eyes.

"I can manage," she said, louder this time. "My legs work just fine." She swung her legs over the side of the bed and stood.

Olivia shook her head.

"You do look like you've improved," I commented, and she wrinkled her nose as if taking offense to my simple observation.

"I can move. Slowly. Not sure I can carry anything, though."

Olivia's seemed skeptical as she stared at Willow, but she sighed and asked me, "What can I do?"

"Finish packing. I'll make sure we have enough weapons. Willow, are there any books we should take?"

"I'll look," she replied, her breath coming in shallow bursts again.

I nodded back, still studying her, knowing she was likely trying to hide most of her pain so she could get us all to safety.

"I can manage," she said more firmly when I didn't break my stare.

"Your glasses were broken beyond repair," I said.

"I only need them for reading. I wore them all the time out of habit. I'll survive without them." She gave me a small smile in hopes of reassuring me.

"Let's move." Olivia sounded impatient, but I agreed. We had run out of time.

We left in the late afternoon. I didn't look back at the house, afraid I'd never leave if I did. I saw Willow scanning the landscape as we walked, taking in everything around her. It had rained while we were preparing to leave. Likely while she was unconscious. The rain made the plants come alive even more. The water droplets on the leaves reflected the golden light from the setting sun, creating a beautiful glow.

I saw Willow trying to memorize every plant as we neared the edge of the living landscape. I also saw the tears she was trying to hold back.

She didn't say anything as she dropped to her knees onto the dead dirt in front of us, and I jerked, reaching out to steady her.

She let me hold onto her arm as she reached into her pocket and held out her vial of seeds.

"I just thought . . ." she didn't finish the sentence as she spread the seeds on the dead dirt and then sprinkled them with water. The entire vial. Her whole collection.

Olivia bent down next to her. "Maybe this is why you've been given this gift."

Willow eyed her suspiciously. I knew she still didn't believe any of this had anything to do with her, even if Olivia and I believed the opposite.

I helped her stand a moment later, and a small grunt escaped her lips, barely audible. I wanted to steal the pain from her. I wanted it to have been me. I wanted so many things to be different.

We walked for a long time, and Olivia and I both offered Willow a steadying arm and switched off carrying her supplies. I would have laughed if you had told me a few weeks ago that Olivia would be trekking across the land carrying considerable weight and *not* complaining, yet here we were. So much had changed.

The land we traversed was just dead soil, dusty and never-ending. Very few landmarks gave you any sense of where you were. Just dust and silence. How anyone could traverse this land and not go mad was beyond me. What made it even worse, was now we knew there was *more* than this.

The landscape slowly began to change as we walked further and further north. There were now winding crevices in the earth. The stream beds were small at this point, but they slowly started to widen, and the branches began to merge as we walked, turning from stream to river. The land started to slope upward on either side of the river, creating a small valley.

Willow continued to pick up seeds along the way, beginning to fill her empty vial again.

We stopped to eat, but it was a quick stop before we began again. I wanted to reach the farthest point I'd ever been before we set up camp for the night. We were racing the daylight at this point, and we were all exhausted. Willow's injury slowed us, but she refused to stop.

"There's a point just ahead tucked between two large rocks. It will offer some protection from the elements," I finally said, sensing that Willow was in far more pain than she was willing to admit.

"Good, because I'm pretty sure my feet are going to fall off," Olivia responded, and I smiled at her reaction. "Hey, I have a question," she added. "Why do you look like you've just woken up from a restful night's sleep? And Willow and I look like we might fall down dead at any moment?"

I stared at her and shrugged.

"That's it? No explanation? No thoughts on the matter?"

"I don't know. Honestly, I don't."

Olivia eyed me skeptically.

"Maybe it's the same reason I can somehow make plants grow and water flow?" Willow cut in, meaning it to be a joke as she took out her sleeping bag and spread it on the dirt.

When we didn't respond, she looked up and found us both staring at her.

"What?" she asked.

"Well, at this point, nothing sounds crazy anymore. You could be right. I think you two were meant to find each other," Olivia replied.

Willow turned her gaze on me, but I was looking at Olivia now. Something about her words struck me and brought me back to the first moment I saw Willow. How I felt something then, even though I'd never met her.

Willow remained curiously silent.

"I'll keep watch," I finally said when we finished setting up our camp for the night, and I made sure Willow was as comfortable as she could be.

Olivia laughed, "Your energy is never-ending." She turned, winking at Willow. "It's no wonder you like him."

Willow rolled her eyes, and I laughed despite everything.

Chapter Twenty-Seven

Willow

The feeling of flowing water flooded my entire body. I felt like I was floating in it.

My eyes snapped open, pulling me out of the in-between dream space.

"Willow?" Liam asked, a hint of concern in his voice. His chest was pressed against my back, his arm resting limply over my torso as we slept on the hard dirt together.

"There's water here. I can feel it. You were right. And there's more underground. It's trapped there." I put my head in my hands, exhausted and confused. Not able to voice what was happening to me.

His only response was to hold me tighter, squeezing me until the tension melted away.

"I've been thinking." I paused, wrinkling my nose. "What if the place and the people we find are no different from the Elite?"

I felt Liam take a deep breath. "I don't know."

I shimmied out of his grip, turning to face him. "What if there is no safe place?"

He buried his face in my hair, his words muffled as he spoke. "There has to be."

I wanted to believe him as I held myself against him, but the knot in my stomach wouldn't ease.

After a few hours of walking, something in the Earth shifted, and I was surprised to find that I could feel it somehow.

"I think we're almost there," I said while Liam called out simultaneously, "animals." He pointed to tracks on the ground.

When we rounded the bend, there, in the middle of a dry and barren landscape, was a deep hole filled with water. The water spilled out from the striated rock and into a large pool. It was a natural spring that had somehow reached the surface. The water in the pool was muddy but looked clear as it poured from the rock.

Liam walked over to the edge and pulled something from his bag.

"What's that?" I asked him.

"Water test strips. I'm going to see if it's safe to drink."

"Please let it be safe. I need to get this awful dust off of me," Olivia said and shuddered.

The test strip remained white, indicating no toxicity, and Olivia let out an audible sigh.

"Olivia, you can bathe first. I'm going to check out the area surrounding this place. See if I can find human prints," Liam explained.

"I'll come with you," I said to Liam, and Olivia gave me a not-so-subtle smirk and a wink. I gave her my standard eye roll and stalked off to follow Liam over the rocks.

Liam eyed me as we continued walking. "How are your ribs? They seem much better today."

"They're surprisingly better. I have almost no pain," I said, keeping pace with him.

"You think it's the herbs? I wouldn't expect them to have healed that fast on their own."

I shrugged. "Your guess is as good as mine. It may be the herbs, or maybe it's something else. Maybe it's more than one thing."

I could tell Liam was just as confused as I was.

After a moment, Liam's gaze returned to the ground and the land in front of us. "There's a lot of activity around the pool. I wouldn't be surprised if we find human activity too. I'm counting on it. Otherwise, we'll need to make a different plan," he told me as we scrambled over more rocks and landed in dust on the other side.

"Liam, are we just walking into a trap?"

He halted, searching my face.

"I don't know," he finally responded. "We're headed in the same direction the Elite did, but I have to believe there are good people out there, Willow. Otherwise, what's the point? What are we trying to save? There has to be more, and I refuse to believe otherwise." He looked at me with such pain and love it took my breath away. "I have to believe there is more than the Elite."

I nodded, not saying anything.

"Come on, I'll show you a few more things about tracking."

Liam stopped near two sets of tracks. "That's rodent," he said, pointing, "and that looks human."

We followed the direction of the human tracks away from the rocks and the pool. They seemed to be headed northwest. We spotted other tracks, too, likely birds and some kind of larger mammal.

"Well, at least we have a direction," he said.

"What're you smiling about?" I asked him when his gaze lingered on me.

"I was just wondering if I look as disgusting as you do?" He let out a short laugh.

I smacked his arm, smiling too.

"Better get this nasty dust off of us, huh? Not sure when we might get another chance." There was a hint of mischief in his voice now. He grabbed my hand, and we walked back to the pool of water together.

Olivia was clean and dressed by the time we got back. "Did you find anything?"

"Human tracks heading northwest," Liam said to her.

"Oh good, at least we have a direction now." She paused, looking between the two of us. "You both look like hell just froze over. You might want to wash yourselves off." She chuckled. "I'll keep watch, but I expect you to keep your hands to yourselves." She laughed even harder as she turned and scrambled over the rocks to the other side, leaving us alone.

Liam turned to me, and he had a sinful grin on his face.

"I know that look," I said, smiling at him, stripping off my dusty clothes. "Let's at least get clean first," I added with a laugh.

I felt him watching me as I slipped into the water. I knew he was assessing my healing body just as much as he was admiring every inch of my bare skin.

The water was cold but refreshing. I heard him come in behind me, and then his hands were on my back, gently and slowly washing away the dust and sweat. I tilted my head back a little, savoring the feeling, and then his mouth was on my neck, trailing kisses down to my shoulder.

My breath caught at the feeling, but I pulled away slightly and faced him.

"Turn around," I commanded him, and he grinned at me before complying without a word.

I scooped water into my hands and poured it over him. I watched as the water flowed in small streams down the contours of his back, washing away the dust and revealing the details of his many scars. I scooped more water, and, this time, my hands followed the streams down his back. I felt him lean into my touch, but he didn't turn, waiting for me.

"Now, the front," I said softly.

He turned slowly and was so close I could hear his breathing. I felt him watching me, but I didn't look at him. I scooped more water and watched it flow down his chest this time, taking the dust with it. I followed the flow of the water with my hands, and his breath caught.

He leaned forward and whispered lightly in my ear, "Your turn again." His voice was a low grumble.

Burning heat pooled in my core and between my legs, and I swallowed as he scooped water, pouring it over my shoulder. It ran down my chest and between my breasts. He watched the water fall but made no move to touch me.

"Not fair," I whispered breathlessly as his eyes hungrily roamed my body.

He did it over and over again until I was squirming with need.

He grinned at me, finally leaning down to kiss me, but his lips only brushed lightly against mine—teasing.

I groaned in protest, but that only made him pull back. I was forced to stare at the desire in his eyes—the light in them burning brightly even in the daylight.

He placed his mouth irritatingly close to my ear, his breath warm against me. "Tell me what you want."

"You. I want you," I replied breathlessly.

He smiled as he finally stepped into me, crushing my chest against his, and then his lips were on mine. Hungrily exploring like it was the last time he'd ever taste me.

He lifted me, and I wrapped my legs around his waist. He walked us over to where the water was falling into the pool. We were so wrapped up in one another, he didn't notice the rocks and my back crashed into them. I let out a small yelp, my still-healing ribs barking in protest, but somehow, the pain was nothing compared to his lips, his skin, his body pressed against mine.

He pulled away slightly, concern rising, but I grabbed his face again and pulled his mouth to mine. I didn't care if I ended up with a million bruises on my back or more broken ribs.

With one arm holding me securely to him, Liam reached between us, finding my center and pressing lightly. I arched my back, hips meeting every stroke of his fingers. I could feel him, hard against me. The teasing was tortuous. The heat building was almost unbearable.

"Liam," I moaned. "More, I need more."

He didn't remove his fingers from that delicious bundle of nerves but finally pushed himself up into me. I almost screamed as he seated himself fully. Every sense latched onto where we were connected, and I met his movement with my own until both of us were completely lost in each other.

That's when I felt the thread that connected us. It grew in strength and intensity as if it were also burning. It amplified the feeling of him. Amplified everything. Though Liam didn't say anything, I knew he felt it too. His movement suddenly became more demanding. I couldn't help the sound that escaped my lips, and he groaned in response.

His mouth found me again, and he nipped at the space where my shoulder met my neck, and then he kissed and licked me down to my collarbone.

"Liam," I warned. Every touch, every movement, bringing me closer.

He met my gaze, his hips and fingers moving at an unbearable speed. "Willow," he whispered breathlessly, giving his own warning.

My name on his lips was all it took. "Fuck, Liam," I called out, louder than I intended, as I tumbled over the edge. He fell shortly after me, and I grabbed the rock behind me for stability as I trembled in his arms.

He lifted his head, and I noticed his eyes locked on the rocks behind me.

I didn't have to look to know what was happening. Somehow, I could feel it. But I turned slowly, anyway.

Spreading out from the rock where my hand had touched were tendrils of green. They spread and wound in and out of crevices, rocks, and dead earth. As we watched, plants grew larger and larger, reaching for the sun and unfurling their leaves. It didn't take long for the entire landscape to change, and we both stared at it in amazement and utter disbelief.

We heard Olivia yell, and I knew the green had reached her. She came running and stopped at the pool's edge, looking from me to Liam and back again. Then, she burst into laughter.

She barely choked out, "So, how'd you do it?" Then she paused before adding, "The plants, I mean," and laughed even harder.

And, because I felt completely ridiculous and confused, I just laughed with her.

"I don't know." I paused, trying to get out the last of the explanation through fits of laughter. "We just . . . you know . . . and then . . . and then I touched the rock, and things just started growing."

If possible, Olivia started laughing harder. Her entire body was spasming with it. It took her a few moments to calm herself down enough to say, "So, all you have to do is have an orgasm?" and then she was cackling again.

"But, seriously, is that it?" Olivia asked a moment later, trying desperately to calm herself.

"Well, that would make sense, given what everyone observed." I was also trying hard to hold back my laughter. "But, no, I don't think it's that simple."

"Simple, huh?" And the laughter escaped out of her again.

"Stop making me laugh!" I yelled at her, but it felt so good to laugh this hard. "Let me think!"

I turned to Liam, who was casually leaning against the rock, his arms crossed, a wide grin on his face.

Damn.

As I stared at him, something began to tug at the edge of my consciousness. "I think it's related to my connection between the two of you." Something felt right about that. "Connection . . . to Liam, to you, to the plants, to the water . . . feeling . . . the Earth. It's somehow all connected. I'm some sort of channel or bridge, I think." I shrugged, and they were now wide-eyed and staring at me, their laughter forgotten.

"Let me try something. Olivia, will you throw me some clean clothes from my pack?"

She searched through my bag, took out a clean shirt and pants, and threw them my way as I exited the water.

I put them on and then walked away from the pool toward the edge of the green.

When we reached the dead dirt, I sat down, closed my eyes, and placed my hands on the earth. I concentrated, trying to recreate the feelings and connection I had just felt a few minutes before, calling something invisible inside the Earth. An invisible thread. Similar to the one I felt between Liam and me.

Nothing happened immediately, but soon I felt something traveling upwards, listening to my silent call. The green tendrils burst through the surface and spread outward in a spiral pattern. A familiar pattern. One I had seen many times in Celtic lore. The Celtic Spiral. A symbol of harmony with the Earth. A symbol of strength and progress.

"I think my connection to Liam amplifies it." I shrugged and stood up.

"Yeah. No big deal. You just made stuff grow out of nowhere," Olivia said, pacing back and forth, looking at the ground like it was some sort of foreign object.

When she paused, a chuckle escaped her again. "I have to admit, I really wanted it to be the orgasm."

I rolled my eyes, but I laughed with her.

"Well, that's a nifty trick. Maybe practice will make it stronger?" Olivia asked.

"I don't know. To be honest, I think I'm in shock."

Liam walked over and put his arm around my shoulders. I smiled at him, and he leaned down and kissed me softly.

"OK, so what now?" Olivia asked.

"We head northwest," Liam said, and I knew that wasn't what Olivia meant, but we all nodded in agreement because we didn't quite know what to do with everything that had just happened. Especially me.

Chapter Twenty-Eight

Willow

The following day, we left our little oasis and headed northwest, following any signs of humans. Every time we stopped to rest or eat, I tried working on making plants grow. I was successful every time but couldn't seem to expand them much further than ten feet away from me.

"I can leave you two alone if you want," Olivia said, smirking.

I rolled my eyes. "No, I have to figure out how to do it on my own." I paused before adding, "I may not always be with you."

They both looked at me, the unspoken fear etched on their worried faces.

"Can you make specific plants grow?" Olivia asked, avoiding the subject.

"I don't know. I haven't tried."

Olivia's brow furrowed like her entire head was filled with unanswerable questions. "Any thoughts on how you got this ability?"

"I feel like there will be things I'll never know or understand. I fear the answer to that question is one of those things."

As much as I yearned for the answer to that question, there was no way to answer her. My only clues were the Celtic symbols, and the journal I had packed out of instinct. Perhaps now, I could piece some of it together into something that might help.

"Water," Olivia said.

I must have looked confused because she quickly added, "You said you could feel the water. The waterfall at the house. That had to be you. Do you think you can control water too?"

"I don't know. Maybe. Probably. But I don't know how because each time I try to call something from the Earth, it's always plants that answer."

"What happened the night before we found the waterfall?"

I thought back to the night in the library with Liam. "We were both really sad."

"Feeling. Connection . . . sadness is a feeling. You were both con-nected . . ." She trailed off.

I let out a long sigh. She was onto something, but I was so mentally and physically exhausted from everything, it was too much.

Liam came over and placed his hand on my shoulder. "Rest," he said, and I didn't have the energy to argue. "Olivia and I will scope out the surrounding area and make sure we're on the right track."

I knew we were on the right track. We all did. The number of human tracks heading northwest had increased, but I was grateful for the space.

I didn't even realize I'd fallen asleep until I heard Olivia scream and Liam yell, "Run!"

I didn't think. I just sprang up from where I was lying and turned in the direction of their voices. They were running toward me at full speed. Behind them, the Claeg were inching closer and closer. Maybe fifty of them.

"Run! Toward those rocks!" Liam yelled again as they approached me.

I took off in the direction of the rocks. I could hear the grunts of the Claeg getting closer and closer with each step I took.

We reached the rocks, and Liam paused momentarily, looking around.

"There!" he yelled and pointed to an opening. It appeared to be a small cave.

We ran as fast as we could toward it, and Olivia barreled ahead of me. Liam was last. He looked around in the dim light for something to block the opening. When he didn't find anything, he went back out.

"No!" I yelled after him.

The next thing I knew, he had pushed a large rock in front of the cave's opening, concealing it and plunging us into total darkness.

"It won't keep them out but will slow them down," he yelled from outside.

"What're you doing?" I screamed at him, panic gripping me.

"Buying you time," he shouted back, and then he was gone.

"No, no, no. I can't do this," I said into my hands, and then I heard sword hit sword outside, and my stomach dropped.

There were too many Claeg, and Liam knew it too.

"Willow!" Olivia called into the blackness, "Where are you?"

"Over here," I said in barely a whisper.

She groped around in the complete darkness and finally found me. I was shaking with tremors that consumed my whole body.

"I can't do it," I said to her.

She wrapped her arms around me. We heard Liam let out a roar of pain, and if it weren't for Olivia holding me up, I'd probably have collapsed.

"Fear is a feeling, but I doubt it will help you in any way. I'm guessing it's actually a block." She was surprisingly calm.

I knew she was right, but I didn't know how to stop being so afraid.

"Let go," she whispered into my hair.

"How?" it came out as a broken plea.

"Use me."

I didn't know if it would work, but she felt calm and strong, and I latched onto it. I somehow found her thread and my connection to her. I used her as a bridge between myself and the Earth, winding the three of us together and blindly grasping for any thread of life I could pull to the surface. I pleaded with the Earth to comply as I used Olivia to keep me steady.

Just when I was about to give up, I felt it. Life pulsing to the surface. It came so quickly that the energy of it almost knocked us over.

Olivia gasped, and then there was an awful screeching and hissing noise coming from outside the cave. We could hear the sound of running.

I slowly opened my eyes, and the cave glowed as if thousands of stars were attached to the walls.

"Glow worms," I whispered, looking around.

"So, not just plants?" Olivia asked.

I shrugged, but then reality hit me. "Shit. Olivia! Help me move this boulder!"

We both ran to the cave's opening and put all our weight into the boulder blocking the entrance, but it didn't budge.

"How did he move this by himself?" Olivia asked, still straining against the boulder.

"Liam!" I yelled, desperately hoping he was still conscious.

A few moments later, the rock moved enough for us to slip out, and Liam collapsed beside it. I fell on my knees next to him. He had a hand clutched to his side, and blood seeped through his fingers, soaking his shirt in crimson.

"Olivia, grab our packs!"

She didn't hesitate, running back to where we had left our stuff, leaving us next to the glowing cave.

The landscape was eerily silent where fifty Claeg should have been.

"Pretty impressive," Liam said, struggling to talk through the pain.

"Shhh, please don't talk," I replied, moving his hand and putting pressure on his bleeding wound. He was losing so much blood.

"I have sutures in my pack. They were in the house. I thought they might be useful. I would pat myself on the back if I could." He could barely speak, and he was trying to make a joke.

I wanted to smack him, but I smiled instead, tears pooling in the corner of my eyes.

"Lucky for you, I'm very terrible at sutures," I responded, and he let out a small laugh and grabbed his side instinctively from the pain of it.

"Is that cave glowing?" he asked, his head turning toward the opening.

"Glow worms."

"You did that?"

"I think so." My voice was wavering.

"You're amazing," he said tenderly, reaching up and placing his clean hand on my cheek.

I leaned my face into his hand and could no longer keep the tears from falling.

"They haven't gotten me yet, Willow," he said, but I heard a drop of fear in his words.

I couldn't stop crying long enough to answer.

"Your plants turn those monsters to ash." He nodded in their direction.

I turned my head toward where he was motioning, and there were piles of ash on top of the green.

"Compost," he added with a wink.

I smiled through the tears, impressed he even remembered what compost was from my constant mumbling about plants, soil, and ecology. But maybe it shouldn't have surprised me that he listened to my every word.

As my tears continued to fall, despite a considerable effort to stop them, a trickle of water began to make its way out of the cave and wind its way through the landscape. We both watched silently for a moment as it carved a trail through the green, finding the path of least resistance and filling the space with a soft trickling sound.

"You did that too," he said. It wasn't a question.

I nodded, but I still couldn't find any words. I could feel the water bubble up in connection with my tears, but it seemed so trivial compared to the blood that was pouring from him.

He noticed my gaze on the blood that was now soaking the earth beneath him, and with as much humor as he could muster, he said, "Also compost."

Instead of laughing, I cried even harder.

"Hey, please don't cause a flood. I can't move very fast. I don't want to drown." He was grinning despite everything.

"I hate you right now," I said through the tears and laughter.

"I don't believe that for one second."

"Where's Olivia?" I said to no one in particular.

"We ran for a while," was all he offered.

"Liam?"

He gave me a questioning look but didn't speak.

"I can't lose you," I barely choked out.

Before he could respond, Olivia came running back, out of breath. She threw me the bags, and I grabbed Liam's, rifling through it as quickly as possible.

"What do you need me to do?" Olivia asked me.

"Keep pressure on the wound. As much as you can. When I'm stitching him up, find my herbs."

Olivia nodded and bent down, putting pressure on Liam's side. I found the sutures and quickly opened them. I struggled to calm my shaking hands as I pulled back Liam's shirt. The blood hadn't slowed, and there was so much of it. I couldn't stop my growing panic, but Olivia placed a hand on my shoulder, and it was enough to steady me.

I stitched up the wound as best as I could. Liam didn't make a sound, but the tension in his body gave away his pain.

"You're right, you're terrible at this," he said through clenched teeth, trying his best to smile at me.

"I'm better at this," I said, holding up the herbs that Olivia found among my stuff.

He barely nodded, and then the energy seemed to completely drain from him. He let his head fall back and his eyes closed.

"Shit," I whispered as I rummaged through my bag of herbs. I grabbed yarrow to help stop the bleeding. I made a poultice by chewing the leaves and placing them on the wound. I covered it with a clean shirt, wrapping the shirt around his waist and pulling it tightly to help staunch the bleeding. When I finished, I grabbed our sleeping bags and covered him.

For the first time in my life, I prayed. I didn't know who to pray to, so I prayed to the Earth. I prayed for her to spare his life. I burned his bloody shirt, and I spread the ashes on the Earth as an offering. I promised to devote the rest of my life to her and whatever purpose she chose for me, and then I cried until I was too exhausted to stand.

The tears brought a rain I had never experienced before, and because I didn't know how to stop the rain, Olivia silently helped me move Liam into the cave. She didn't utter a word, only offering support through her presence. Her face was as solemn as mine as she watched his unconscious form.

I curled up next to him, offering whatever heat I could give him, and I finally fell asleep to the sound of the rain, the soft glow of the cave, and the heat of Liam's body next to me.

Chapter Twenty-Nine

Liam

"Willow?" I said softly, raising my head a little to get my bearings.

We were in the cave. The soft trickle of water echoed off the stone walls; the glow worms created enough light to see by. It was still dark, but I could see the first signs of dawn as I stared past Willow toward the cave's opening.

I could just make out Olivia's shadow as she stood guard outside.

"Liam!" Willow yelped in surprise, instantly sitting up.

I gave her a gentle smile, but my voice still felt weak and gruff. "You haven't gotten rid of me yet."

"Let me check you and change your bandage," she said, rummaging through her bag, grabbing supplies, and piling them at my side.

I pulled back the blanket and was surprised to find that the bandage was not soaked with blood. Willow sighed with relief as she noticed the same thing.

I winced as she unwrapped the bandage. The wound was red and swollen, but the bleeding had completely stopped.

"No blood or infection, but I'll wrap it with another poultice to help speed the healing. I'll have to remove the stitches once it's healed."

I nodded. I didn't trust my voice as I felt the weakness in my entire body. I hated the feeling. I felt too vulnerable. Too exposed. And I couldn't protect them if I was weak.

"I'm going to get you something to eat and make a tea to help build up your blood," she said, popping up again, concern on her beautiful face as she paused to stare down at me. I knew she could see right through me. See all of the things I couldn't say.

"Willow?"

"Yes?"

"We can't stay here."

"You can't move."

"I'll have to."

"No," her tone was firm.

"They know we're here. We left a perfect trail for them to follow. It's my fault. I should've seen it coming . . ." I trailed off, suddenly feeling dizzy.

"Liam, we can't hide anymore. I can stop practicing, but to completely stop, I would have to leave you and Olivia, and that's out of the question."

I didn't say anything right away. The thoughts swirled in my head as I tried to evaluate every option. Evaluate the risks.

"I think our best bet is to continue and find allies. People we can trust. People who can help us. Protect us," Willow continued.

I considered her words as she walked over to the dying fire they must have built last night.

I watched as she heated water and placed some herbs in it to steep.

"There has been no sign of anyone or anything," Olivia said, entering the cave from outside. "How's the patient?"

"The bleeding has stopped, and it's not infected, but he lost a lot of blood. He's really weak."

"Oh, so he's a normal human now?" She winked at me, and I saw Willow roll her eyes, but a smile tugged at the corner of her mouth.

"What now?" Olivia asked.

"I don't know. He can't move yet, but he doesn't want to stay. I think he's afraid that the soldiers are not far behind the Claeg."

"I have a feeling he's right." Olivia let out a big sigh.

"We can't hide anymore unless we split up. We have no choice but to continue on our same path."

"How much time does he need?" she asked, both of them acting like I wasn't even there.

"I don't know. A normal person would need at least a week. I'd love to give him that, but the best we can hope for is at least another day. I'm hoping he will have enough strength to walk a considerable distance by tomorrow, but he won't be able to help protect us if we have another encounter with a large pack of Claeg or soldiers."

Olivia let out a long breath. "I'm not sure what would be worse, more Claeg or humans with guns."

"I don't think the humans would kill us."

She shook her head. "You're too valuable. No, they would just torture you and try to use you as a weapon for their own gain. I'm not sure that's better than death."

Willow shuddered, and a tiny piece of my heart broke.

"We need allies. But, in this world, do those even exist?" Willow asked no one in particular.

"We won't find the answer by running or hiding, but I'm afraid we are walking straight into their hands."

"They're herding us. Using the Claeg to lead us right to them. They know now that the Claeg won't be able to kill us."

Olivia nodded. "We have to be on our guard."

"Allies won't be easy to find," I finally said across the cave. "They're hiding, but we can draw them out."

"How?" Olivia asked.

"Willow needs to show them what she can do. They won't be afraid to fight if they have something to fight for. If they have hope." I paused for a moment and then added, "But our enemies know this, and they will publicly try to prove that they have control over you. They will instill fear back into the people to keep them from putting up any sort of fight. They'll try to break you and then use you."

"So, what can we do?" she asked me. There was dread in her voice.

"I don't think there's anything we can do," I said, feeling completely defeated. "We can walk right into the trap and fight like hell, split up and hide and bide some time, but it won't be long before they find us . . ." I trailed off again.

"They'll use you two to manipulate me, won't they?" she asked, but I could tell she already knew the answer. "I can't ask the two of you to go through that just because of me. I'll go alone. They can't use you two if you aren't there."

"Willow, you can't do this alone," Olivia whispered.

"I can't lose you both. I wouldn't be able to live with myself if your deaths were my fault. I can't have more people I love die because of me." I heard the silent plea in her voice.

I could tell she was in a war between her head and her heart as mine continued to break at the realization that we were stuck. There was no getting out of this. Not unless we wanted to spend the rest of our lives running.

"Bill and your parents' deaths were *not* your fault," Olivia said, her voice rising.

"If it weren't for my stupid obsession with books, they'd still be here! Why do you think I never took you to the library all those years!? I won't have more blood on my hands."

Olivia shook her head sadly. "So, you'll risk your own life? The one life that could actually change this hell hole?"

"Yes!" Willow shouted back. "Because you're worth more to me than all the plants I could ever create. And I could grow back every inch of this planet, but if the people don't change, then what's the point? We'll be back right where we started."

Olivia sighed deeply and shook her head. "You just don't see."

"See what?" Willow snapped at her.

"See what you've already changed," she whispered.

"What have I changed? We lost everyone in Coria! All the work I did to help the Forgotten. What was the point when they were slaughtered!?"

"Marcus," she replied, her voice still a whisper.

"What about him?" Willow growled.

"You changed the mind of an Elite, Willow. That's no small feat. You know he put that tracker on you to save you. It couldn't have been anyone else. The shit he put up with for you. How he got you everything you ever asked for, helping the Forgotten beside you and risking his status and his life for you. Because he saw, just like Kat and I have *always* seen, how people like you have the power to *change* things for the better. You are *blind*, Willow." She let out a harsh breath, clearly exasperated.

Willow turned away from her, grappling with her own thoughts.

"You two are all I have left," she whispered, not daring to look Olivia or me in the eye.

I couldn't hide the sadness in my voice. The pain I felt at the realization that I couldn't protect them anymore. Not alone. Not like this. "Willow's right."

Olivia snapped her head around, readying for a fight, but I kept going, "It's not just her. It's me. I'm a target just as much as she is. Splitting up will confuse them. It will lead them in different directions. It will draw them away from Willow. It will buy us time to find help and supplies and make a solid plan. And if I'm truly the primary catalyst for the trail of plants, then it will be safer for Willow, for all of us, if I'm not with her."

"You really think we're better off apart?" Olivia gaped at both of us.

"For now," I replied, pausing and staring up at the glowing cave for a moment before adding, "Hopefully not for long."

She sighed deeply. "So, I'm just going to let you leave alone, Willow? Into a city full of Elite? And just trust that this will all work out?"

Willow nodded. "I'll find someone to help me, I promise Olivia. You can stay with Liam. He'll keep you safe. You'll keep each other safe."

Willow looked at me, and I looked away, unable to meet her gaze. Afraid of the pain I'd see in her eyes.

"Liam, you can't possibly agree with this?" Olivia was pleading with me now.

I didn't say anything. I didn't know what to say, and Willow's tears slipped free, spilling down her cheeks.

"I'll keep a low profile for a while," she said, choking out the words, "I'll get information, find people willing to help me. I'll stay unnoticed as long as possible. It'll give Liam time to heal and maybe time for the two of you to find help. It's the only way . . ." she said, trailing off.

"She's right," I finally responded, and my cheeks were wet now, too. "Do you know why I decided to take you two with me when we found each other in the wall? Why I had a sudden change of heart?"

Willow shook her head.

"I had every intention of leaving you there"—I gave her an apologetic look before continuing—"but when I saw the Elite tracker on your shirt, something in me snapped. I couldn't leave you with them. I didn't even know you, and yet, I just couldn't bear the thought of them getting their hands on you, squashing your heart and your tenacity, and turning you into something I wouldn't even recognize." I paused again and looked away for a moment. "I didn't want them to turn you into me."

She leaned down and kissed me lightly.

"When does she have to leave?" Olivia interrupted. She sounded resigned.

We both turned to her.

"In the morning. We'll leave shortly after and follow another path." There was so much sadness in my voice now. "They'll be on us if we stay any longer."

I turned back to Willow and added, "Bring your bow, but it'll most likely be taken when you reach Tarraco. And try to blend in as best as you can. Don't give your real name; keep your eyes and ears open. Plants and water will give you away, so practice letting go of all emotion. And if all else fails, fight like hell and show the world what you're capable of."

"This is bullshit," Olivia said, shaking her head. "Fuck this world; it doesn't deserve you, Willow."

"No, it's me who doesn't deserve the two of you," she responded, getting up and wrapping her arms around Olivia. Olivia buried her head in her shoulder and cried.

After a while, she finally let go. "How can I help you? How do I take care of Liam once you're gone?"

"I'll show you, follow me," Willow told her.

We spent the next couple of hours preparing for our departure. Swapping gear, going over different possible scenarios and obstacles we might encounter. Olivia and I finalized our plan, and Willow showed us both how to care for my wound and taught us about the herbs that might prove useful. Willow didn't take any herbs because plants would give her away, and I doubted she would get far without her bag being searched. I only hoped she could call it up from the Earth if she needed an herb.

She gave us the edible plants book, but she kept the journal.

As the day faded to night, the knot in my stomach grew.

We silently prepared for bed, and Willow cared for me, forcing me to drink one more cup of tea. Olivia volunteered to keep watch again, and neither of us argued with her.

When she was gone, Willow lay down, curled against me, and rested her head on my chest. We were silent for a while, unsure what to say to each other.

"Will you show me what the Earth feels like? Can you even do that?" I finally asked, unsure why it was the first thing I thought of.

She sat up and looked at me thoughtfully. "I don't know. I can try."

Hesitantly, she reached for my hand, and I felt something akin to a slight pull as she closed her eyes and concentrated. Her eyes moved under her eyelids, and her hand warmed even more. I closed my eyes.

Then I felt it. Something entirely different from the feeling of her.

My eyes snapped open, and I stared at a large plant behind her, growing in the darkness of the cave.

She slowly turned to see what we had created together, and we watched as the petals of a single flower slowly unfurled. The flower was the color of blood.

"Rose. A symbol of love and medicine for the heart," she said softly, tracing her fingers along the petals, down the stem, and over the thorns.

I watched her as she studied the plant, burying her nose in the flower, inhaling its intoxicating scent that I could smell from feet away. Then she walked back to me and curled up into my side. Her warmth filled me instantly. I wrapped a protective arm around her.

"I don't want the night to end," she whispered.

I kissed the top of her head and took a deep breath, trying to memorize every part of her.

She traced circles along my chest and arms as if doing the same.

"You need to sleep," I finally whispered into her hair.

She shook her head. "I can't." Her words came out choked.

"I'll find you again," I said softly, my own emotions threatening to crack.

She said nothing, and we just lay there holding each other. As her body stilled and sleep began to take her, I whispered, "I love you."

I felt her smile against my chest, and a thread of blue light poured from her fingertips into the soil beneath us. She didn't notice, and I thought maybe I was hallucinating, but then a sound so choreographed filled the cave.

"Crickets," she whispered. "The night symphony."

I closed my eyes, listening to the sound of the world waking up, holding the person responsible for it, and suddenly I knew what I had to do.

When dawn broke, I woke Willow gently, and I could feel my body rapidly healing. Willow prepared to leave in complete silence, not looking at Olivia or me.

When she was finally ready, we reviewed the plan again. There were so many unknowns, I knew the plan wouldn't work out as we had hoped, but I still clung to it for reassurance that I would see her again.

Olivia held out her arms to Willow, tears streaming down her face. "Don't risk your life. I can't lose you too." Her voice was shaking.

Willow nodded. I didn't think she could talk. She wrapped her arms around Olivia, letting a tear run down her cheek.

"Love you, Willow," Olivia said so softly that it broke my heart.

"Love you too, Liv."

And then she broke free and turned toward me. I could now stand and move around a little, but weakness lingered. She quickly looked away from me, and I didn't think I could say goodbye.

I walked over to her and lifted her chin, so she had no choice but to look at me. She closed her eyes, desperately trying to keep the tears from falling, and I kissed her lips softly. "I'll find you."

She nodded but still didn't open her eyes. It was only when I pulled away that she dared to open them.

I didn't know how to tell her everything I wanted to. I didn't think I had the words, but then they just came spilling out of me. "I will fight for the world you dream of. I will fight with all I have to make sure you get the chance to live in that world. To make sure there is a vase of fresh flowers next to your bed every morning. To make sure it's the first thing you see. To remind you that it's all because of *you*."

The tears now poured out of her eyes, and the rain began to fall in sheets outside the cave, but all I could see was her. All I could feel was her. All I wanted was her, even though I knew I'd have to let her go.

"Show them what you can do, and they will fight. They will fight for that. They will fight for you," I whispered to her.

"And what if they don't?"

"Then they aren't worth fighting for."

She looked up at me with wide eyes and tear-streaked cheeks.

"I'm terrified." Her admission was barely audible, whispered on a soft breath.

"I am too, and I'm terrified to let you go." I kissed her deeply one last time.

She shuddered as I pulled away, but her tears had stopped, and the sun began to trickle into the cave again.

She said nothing else as she dropped her arms from mine, turned, and walked out of the cave.

She didn't look back, but I heard her words as she disappeared into the sunlight. "I love you too."

PART II

Chapter Thirty

Willow

I woke on the second day at the first sign of dawn approaching. I ate quickly before packing up and continuing on as the sun slowly rose above the horizon. I collected more seeds as I went, adding them to the almost-full vial in my pocket. The simple act reminded me why I was doing this. Why I had to let them go.

As I walked, it became clearer that something had shifted inside me. Where growing plants through some sort of channel of energy had been a completely crazy concept even two days ago, it now seemed like a part of me. Something that had always been there.

I felt the channels of energy everywhere and in everything. The constant exchange of those energies and the waiting, as if the energy was holding back for some unknown moment where it would finally unleash itself. My mind moved in a million different directions, trying to piece together some logic around it. The only conclusion I could come to was that it was just an entangled, moving, changing, chaotic net of energy that seemed impossible to figure out, let alone control.

As morning faded into afternoon, the human tracks steadily increased, and now they were moving in various directions, but the main path was still clearly Northwest. I kept following the trail, putting one foot in front of the other, my unease threatening to turn me back around. Back to Olivia and Liam.

Back home.

When new tracks began to appear, I bent down to study them. Though it seemed impossible, I was certain they were the tracks of a wheeled vehicle pulled by a single horse. I had thought horses went extinct when the grasses did. It was another item I added to the growing list of things I didn't know outside the walls of my very-sheltered life in Coria.

I stayed slightly off the main path, traveling close to rocks and a dried-up stream bed. I used all the skills Liam had taught me to keep myself hidden. The goal was to blend in and get into Tarraco unnoticed. Not knowing what I was up against, though, was a disadvantage.

It didn't take long before I heard what sounded like a wheeled vehicle heading toward me. The air was dusty, so I couldn't see very far ahead. I took cover behind some larger rocks and positioned myself to watch them pass.

Two men in an open, wooden cart soon appeared through the dust. A beautiful black horse pulled the cart. Whatever the men were transporting was under a large blanket in the back of the cart. The men were busy chatting casually and completely oblivious to my presence.

I also noticed how different their clothing was. They were wearing what appeared to be a knee-length, T-shirt-type dress with a rope tied around the middle. One man had a cape draped over the seat behind him. The colors of their outfits were both a shade of gray.

I'd seen that clothing somewhere in my books. I was certain of it. I just couldn't place it. They were clothes from some lost civilization that existed thousands of years ago.

Those thoughts brought me to a harsh realization—I was in trouble if I couldn't somehow steal some clothes. I doubted my dirty T-shirt, brown pants, and men's boots would help me blend in.

I kept further off the main path, afraid I'd be spotted. More and more carts began to pass, and I had to stop to hide multiple times. Most carts were pulled by men, and some began to head off in different directions. I decided they must be on trade routes, but who were they trading with? Wherever they were going must not have been far because none of the people or carts seemed prepared for a long journey.

It didn't take much longer to reach the city's outskirts. And city was an understatement. The place seemed at least three times the size of Coria. A huge stone wall surrounded it and blocked my view of the interior. Everyone appeared to be going in and out of one large main gate.

I discreetly moved from rock to rock, finding a spot close to the gate where I could sit and scope out the people going in and out. It was around noon, and I figured I should plan on trying to sneak in around dark. I had a few hours to figure out my next move, so I found a spot large enough to sit up and stay hidden. I unpacked my lunch and ate as I watched.

I noticed four guards with guns at the gate and at least four more on the top of the wall. Most of the guards at the gate were chatting and casually checking what appeared to be papers from everyone entering or exiting. The guards on top of the wall were still and appeared to be watching every movement.

Snipers.

Most of the movement was out of the city, not into it, but after a few hours, empty carts began to make their way back into the city. The carts entering were all thoroughly searched, as were the people on foot.

Stowing away seemed out of the question.

As I continued to watch, I became more and more discouraged. There was no way I could get in without being noticed. I had to get in on foot somehow. Without papers or the proper clothing.

I was so lost in thought, mulling over every plan that hatched in my head, that I didn't hear the footsteps approaching from behind me. Somehow, though, I sensed whoever approached a moment before they grabbed me, and I whirled around, my daggers already in hand.

I noticed the surprised faces of the two soldiers a split second before I struck, slicing my blade toward the abdomen of the soldier closest to me, but he turned, and the dagger caught him in the arm instead.

The soldier let out a yelp before the other advanced on me.

I knew our fight would attract the notice of the snipers if I didn't get us out of sight, so I spun under the second soldier's arm as he reached to grab me and rebounded off the rock slightly. I kept my back to it, holding my daggers in front of me.

"Bitch," the first one mumbled, the blood spilling from his arm.

Then, the two soldiers advanced at the same time. I readied myself for what I knew was inevitable.

Only a few paces from me, the soldier on the left suddenly went down, an arrow sticking out from his back, and in the brief moment the other soldier turned to look, I swept my knife across his throat, and he fell with a loud thud, blood pouring into the dirt where he lay.

I stared blankly at the two bodies before me, not even noticing two female figures approaching.

"Your first?" a soft voice said, stopping a few feet from me.

I turned slowly to find a woman looking at me with sympathy. The woman was draped in a long dress, tied with a similar rope that had tied the men's clothing. She had long, brown hair that covered her muscular shoulders beneath. She was maybe thirty years old, and behind her was a girl about ten years old. She instinctively hid the girl behind her. Sympathetic but wary of me.

All I could manage was a slight nod, and then I turned my gaze back to the soldier's body. The first human I had ever killed.

Something twisted in my gut.

"You never get used to it. Even if they all deserve that fate." Her voice was strong, but she could not conceal a deep-seated grief behind her words.

I looked back at her, and all I could offer her in return was another nod.

"If you're trying to get into the city, you won't be able to. Not with the bow and arrows or those clothes," she said, taking a hesitant step toward me.

"I'm not from here."

"Mom," the girl whispered, tugging on her dress, "she looks like those new people that came here."

I raised my eyebrows. "I'm from Coria, a city about a five-day walk from here. Southeast."

"And you survived that walk alone?" She sounded skeptical. I didn't blame her.

I nodded but didn't elaborate.

"Impossible," she murmured. "Why didn't you come with the others?"

"Others?"

"Yes, others from Coria. They arrived a few weeks ago. Maybe a hundred of them."

The Elite and soldiers.

"Follow me. I can take you to them," she said, setting down my bow and turning to leave.

"No, wait!" I yelled after her. "Please, I don't want to be taken to them. I need to enter unnoticed."

She stopped and considered me for a moment.

"Mom?" The girl asked hesitantly, and her mom turned to her. "I don't think she's one of them." She paused, and I couldn't see the look on her mother's face. "She's too dirty and doesn't have a gun."

All true. I smiled at the girl's keen observations.

Her mother studied her daughter, then addressed me. "We'll get you some clothing, and you can enter with us. After entering, we'll part ways. I don't want any trouble you'll bring; do you understand?"

I agreed, not sure what she meant by trouble. But, then again, she wasn't wrong. Trouble did seem to follow me wherever I went. As was evidenced by the two dead soldiers at my feet.

"Wait here and move the bodies closer to the rock. Keep them hidden. I'll be back before sundown," she said.

They were both gone as quickly as they had appeared. I sat back down to wait and watch.

It didn't take long for the mother to return. Her daughter wasn't with her this time.

I quickly put on the dress she offered and left my old clothes under a rock.

"You have to leave your bow too. You'll be arrested if you're found with any weapons, but you should be able to sneak in the daggers. Keep them in your boot," she instructed me.

I placed the bow and arrows with my discarded clothes and tucked the daggers into my boots, concealing them with the skirt of the dress, and then I slung my bag over my shoulder. The journal remained in the bag; I refused to part with it, even if it might lead me into the Elite's hands.

"Follow me, and don't say anything unless I tell you to." She began walking, not even waiting to see if I was following.

"Wait!" I said, "I don't even know your name."

She stopped and faced me. "Elise."

"Thank you, Elise, I'm Gwen." I hated the lie as it left my lips, and I wondered if her name actually was Elise.

She studied me as if she could see right through me, then abruptly turned toward the gate and continued.

I stuck close to Elise and didn't say a word. The line moved quickly. My stomach was in knots as we approached the guards. Elise was rigid, and her face was unreadable. I wondered how often she had come in and out of here and what she may have been risking for me.

I thought of her daughter.

"Papers," one of the guards said to the couple before us. They were dressed similarly to us, but their clothes were torn in a few places, and they desperately needed a bath.

The man handed yellowing papers to the guard at the gate with shaking hands.

The guard looked down at the papers and then back at the couple, a sneer suddenly twisting his harsh features. "These papers are old."

Was that glee I detected in his voice?

The guard held up his hand in some kind of signal, and before I could react at all, two bullets passed through the heads of the couple in front of me. I watched in horror as their bodies crumpled to the ground, and without thinking, I took a step forward.

Elise's hand shot out and grabbed my arm, halting me. She shook her head silently, her eyes pleading.

I stared at her hand on my arm and then back at the couple as two more guards came and hauled their lifeless bodies away.

No one said anything behind us. No one even moved.

"Papers," the guard said again, this time looking at Elise and me.

Elise handed him papers, her hands steadier than I imagined they would be, as mine began to shake behind me. The guard looked at them briefly, then at her and over to me, his gaze unreadable.

"What about that one?" he asked Elise, inclining his head toward me.

"Cousin," she replied in a firm tone like she'd had this same inter-action with this guard before.

He looked at me again. This time, his eyes traveled from my face to my feet and back up again. I struggled to keep my face impassive but held still.

Finally, he returned his attention to Elise and waved us through the gates.

Elise's shoulders instantly dropped as we walked past the guards, and she let out a long stream of air as if she had been holding her breath the whole time.

"In this alone, it's good to be a woman," Elise mumbled under her breath.

I raised my brow at her statement. "They believe women to be harmless and worthless, so they're more willing to let them in without papers. The couple should have come in separately with people who had legal papers."

I couldn't quite comprehend what had just happened, let alone her words, as she continued through the city.

I followed her a little further, not getting a chance to look around me in an attempt to keep up with her. It wasn't long before she stopped. "This is where we part ways. Good luck."

She effortlessly disappeared into the crowd before I could even thank her.

I stood there, completely lost, unsure of my next move. At the very least, I was hoping to be able to ask her where I might be able to find temporary lodging. With no other plan or option, I decided to try to get a sense of the city. I finally looked around and discovered I was in some sort of plaza.

People moved in all directions, heading down various cobblestone streets extending from the plaza. The buildings were relatively small and spaced closely together. Some even seemed as though they were connected.

Everything was made of stone and mud, except for the roofs, which were made of metal. The city seemed designed to look old, but based on wear and tear, I could tell the buildings were relatively new.

The more I noticed, the more familiar the place seemed, but I still couldn't place it.

I followed a large group of people away from the plaza. We walked north toward what I believed must be the city's center.

As we approached, the streets began to widen, and more and more people were out and about. There were stands lining the edges of the roads filled with goods that people were selling. They were filled with food—primarily grains and some dried meat, clothing, colorful pottery, and artfully crafted furnishings. Some were even selling art. I smiled at the sight of such beauty and abundance. We did not have anything like it in Coria.

When I reached the city center, I stopped and looked around me. To the west was what appeared to be a large arena or stadium. It must have been the city's main attraction, as it was the largest building.

I was trying to piece everything together with what I knew about ancient history when a flash of blonde hair crossed my peripheral vision. I quickly turned my head toward it, and just ahead of me was a woman walking through the market. She was familiar somehow. I dropped the thoughts of the stadium and raced after her.

She wove in and out of the people and colorful market stands, heading east. She was so far ahead that I tried to catch up but couldn't. There were too many people and too many obstacles in the way. The best I could do was keep her within eyesight.

When she reached the edge of the city center, she briefly swiveled her head to the left, and I caught a glimpse of her profile.

I stopped dead in my tracks.

I *did* know her. I had known her almost my whole life. It was Kat. I'd know her anywhere.

She ducked into a side alley before I could shout her name.

I raced to catch up to her, slamming into a few disgruntled people and mumbling my apologies before running on, but when I reached the alleyway, she was nowhere to be seen.

Chapter Thirty-One

Liam

Olivia hadn't said anything to me all day, and I didn't blame her for avoiding me. We were both grieving in our own way, but I hated the sudden awkwardness between us.

"How'd you and Willow meet?" I finally blurted out, my voice raspy from emotion and lack of use.

Surprise flashed across her face briefly before a sly smile began to form. "I met her through Kat. Willow and Kat were best friends. They grew up together and worked in the lab together before I arrived. I met Kat in a training session for a lab position. She taught and trained new employees."

Olivia sat down, pulling her bag onto her lap, mindlessly sorting through the herbs Willow left us as she smiled at the memory.

"The moment I walked into the lab, I knew I had to be with her. She was beautiful and smart and a force of nature." She paused and let out a short laugh. "In fact, I think you two would have gotten along great."

I snorted and she winked back. "After the training, before I lost my nerve, I walked up to her and asked her out. No small talk, no introduction, no flirting." Olivia laughed again. "And you know what she said? Without hesitation, she said yes. I was speechless. I stood there just gaping at her like an idiot. She smiled and asked what I had in mind, and you know me, I don't really hold anything back, so I said maybe dinner and a make-out session at my place. She laughed and asked if that was all, with a wink, and right then, I knew I loved her." She paused, and her smile slowly faded. "Sorry. I just haven't thought about our first meeting in a very long time."

"You don't need to apologize."

She gave me a subtle nod, mindlessly separating the bags of herbs now haphazardly spread across her lap and the rock next to her. "We went on our first date, and after that, we spent every day together. She told me about Willow on our second date. I have to admit, I was jealous of the way she talked about Willow. Jealous of their closeness, of all the time they'd spent together. I was scared as hell to meet her. Totally intimidated." She chuckled. "Can you even imagine being intimidated by Willow? She is just the kindest and most gentle person, maybe a little passionate at times, but completely harmless."

I laughed then too, and Olivia's eyes lit up a little.

"I met her at Kat's apartment one evening, and I knew. Just as I knew I'd love Kat forever, I knew Willow would be my best friend." She stopped and looked up from the herbs. I kept my face blank, but my stomach was in a knot.

"After that, the three of us were inseparable. It only took a few months before Kat proposed, and I said yes. Willow married us and threw us the most wonderful wedding reception." Olivia suddenly inhaled deeply, and I could tell the next part of the story would be hard for her.

"We weren't married long. Just a few months before Kat was recruited and gone. We didn't have long to say goodbye, and Kat made me promise to stay and take care of Willow for her. But the thing is, it was Willow who took care of me." I could tell Olivia was desperately trying not to cry.

I walked over and put my hand on her shoulder. She looked up at me, and then her head was on my chest. I wrapped my arms around her.

"I can't lose both of them," she whispered into my chest.

"You won't. I won't let it happen."

"How can you promise that?"

"I can't promise, but we're going to build an army to protect her, and I won't stop until she's safe."

Olivia looked skeptical and yet slightly hopeful. "And how do you propose we do that?"

"Steal weapons, of course," I said with a wink, "and find people on our side. My goal is to get them to see what Willow did back at the house, use that community as a home base, create a defense system, and pray that people will join us once they see what we have and can do. Hopefully, Willow can find people and get information on what's really going on, so maybe we can take down the systems of power from the inside. That's best-case scenario, of course."

"You have a lot of confidence in yourself, don't you?" she replied with a laugh.

"I have no choice." But I was smiling too.

Olivia sighed and pulled away from me. "Well, we aren't going to get any of that done if we don't get moving. Are you able to travel?"

I gave her an awkward thumbs-up.

Olivia scoffed, and I knew she was unconvinced. "OK, well, we'll move slowly. Where are we going first?"

"We should follow the trail to a crossroads. If I'm correct about trade routes, we should see a split in the trail. I'm hoping there's a town due west of here. We can start there. Ask around, get information, acquire weapons, then head south again."

Olivia nodded, but I could tell she wasn't fully convinced of my ability to accomplish everything in my state. Hell, I wasn't convinced myself, but it had to be enough.

I had to be enough.

As we left our cave sanctuary, we both looked back one last time. Olivia had tears in her eyes, but she didn't let them fall. Leaving the plants behind meant leaving the last remaining piece of Willow.

After a brief pause, we both turned and followed the trail Willow had the day before. It didn't take us long to find a crossroad. Once there, evidence of horse and cart tracks were everywhere. Proof of trade and larger cities and populations.

As I expected, a path headed west, away from the main path that continued north to Tarraco. The size and use of the path suggested Tarraco was much larger than I expected, and a sudden wave of panic hit me as I imagined Willow there by herself. Everything in me screamed to follow her, but I knew I wouldn't be able to keep her safe on my own. I needed help.

So, we turned west. Away from Tarraco. Away from Willow.

Travel to the town was relatively easy. The landscape was flat, barren, and hot. We stopped often to change my bandages and drink water, so our progress was slower than I'd hoped.

"How'd you meet your wife?" Olivia asked after a while of silent walking. I knew the question was coming; I was shocked she hadn't asked me before.

The truth was, I hadn't thought about my wife in a long time. I loved her, but I was such a different person now that I wondered if we would even have been together at this point in my life. It made me a little sad knowing that, but also grateful that the grief had finally passed.

"I was always fighting, as you know, and people started betting on me. I would get in on the gambling action a bit too. At one point, I got into financial trouble with her brother. He threatened to have me killed." I laughed a little, remembering her brother's face as I dodged his attempts to beat the shit out of me. His anger grew with each failed attempt. "Valeria stepped in. She paid my debt to her brother. She wasn't afraid to put me in my place. She hated me so much that I couldn't help but love her."

Olivia choked on a laugh. "Of course you'd fall for someone who didn't want you. You egotistical bastard."

I eyed her and gave her the middle finger, which only made her laugh harder. Then I continued, "I stopped fighting then and turned my attention to winning her over. She didn't give me the time of day."

Olivia's lips twisted into a sly smile. "Smart girl."

I rolled my eyes, which had Olivia chuckling again.

"It wasn't until I stopped trying to get her that she started to see me more. I was a foolish kid thinking I could somehow win her."

"No shit."

I shook my head, rushing the story before Olivia decided to comment on every word out of my mouth. "After a few years, I finally had the balls to tell her I loved her. To my foolish surprise, she told me she loved me back. Shortly after that, we got married. As with you and Kat, it was only a few months before she was gone. I couldn't stand the grief, so instead of dealing with it, I got back into fighting. Only, this time, it was in the war against the Claeg. I discovered I was just as good at fighting the Claeg as I was at fighting people. Until I met Willow, I didn't know I could love anyone anymore."

Olivia's face turned serious as she stared thoughtfully ahead of us, and we continued walking silently for a while.

"You truly love her?" she finally asked me, like she had been struggling with my confession.

There was no doubt in my mind. "I do."

"I swear to the gods . . ." she began, but I cut her off.

"I would rather die than see anything happen to her. Her. Not her magic. Not what I could gain from it. Just her. Every beautiful, smart, wonderful, flawed inch of her. I could care less about this insufferable world, but *she* cares. She cares so much that it makes me care, too. It makes me want to create a better world for her. The one she dreams about. The one she reads about." I stopped and drew a long breath, finally noticing how fast my heart was beating. "She gives me hope, and I'm not sure I've ever felt that."

It was the truth. One I had never considered before now.

"Well, shit . . ." Olivia trailed off, shaken. "I'm sorry for doubting you. But you know what I'm *not* sorry for?"

I waited only a moment. "I'm not sorry you found us. I'm not sorry for choosing to follow you. I'm not sorry for any of it because it brought you to her. To us."

"Well, shit . . ." I echoed Olivia's words, and she smiled, patting me on the shoulder.

"With all of these tracks, you would think we would have run into someone by now." Olivia suddenly changed the subject, staring at the ground in front of her. A small furrow in her brow appeared.

She was right. Something seemed amiss, and I instinctively stiffened. "There might have been a recent attack. People may be a little more cautious."

"Oh, great. Just what we need, people who will probably throw us out on our asses *and* hungry Claeg." Sarcasm was dripping from her every word. "You can't fight, and all I'm good for is my sarcasm."

I chuckled quietly, and she threw her hands up in frustration.

We reached the outskirts of the town, and we still hadn't seen any sign of life. I was worried that the town may have been empty, evacuated, or worse. I didn't say anything to Olivia, not wanting to alarm her. We hadn't seen any sign of conflict, but that didn't mean the trouble didn't come from a different direction.

I held up my hand to stop her and put my finger to my lips to ensure she stayed quiet. I motioned to some larger rocks to the left of us, and we quietly headed toward them.

Out of earshot of the main path to the town, I finally spoke. "There's no sign of anyone, but there's also no sign of conflict. Stay here while I check the town's outskirts. If you get into trouble, just run. Do you have your daggers?"

Olivia nodded, taking one out of her boot and holding onto it with a death grip.

"It's probably nothing," I reassured her, "but I just want to make sure."

She nodded again but didn't say anything and didn't loosen her grip on her dagger.

"If I'm not back in an hour, don't come looking for me. Head back toward the crossroads and find Willow."

I patted her on the shoulder, a meek attempt to ease her fear, and then headed toward the main gate. All kinds of tracks surrounded the town, from cart, human, and animal tracks to a few Claeg tracks.

The main gate seemed to be directly ahead of me, the largest path of tracks leading directly toward it. Other tracks that appeared human and Claeg veered off to the left and right of the gate, heading around toward the other side of the town. There were no cart tracks.

As I approached the gate, I could tell it was sealed shut. I couldn't see any people on top of the wall, in front of it, or guarding the gate.

Not a good sign.

Following some human footprints, I skirted around the wall to the other side. Compared to Coria, this wall was small but seemed mostly intact. There was some minor damage here and there, but no major breach so far.

The thing that unnerved me the most was the silence. Silence usually meant death. There was no movement, no voices. Nothing. Even the wind had silenced itself.

The town was not very large, so it didn't take me long to curve around toward the back. When I rounded the corner toward the western edge, I stopped.

The wall was completely blown apart. Large pieces of stone lay everywhere. There were a few bodies among the rubble. Some were intact, but the Claeg had scavenged others. I counted maybe thirty, mostly male. Given the state of the bodies, the attack had happened recently. Within the last two days.

I was so used to seeing this kind of destruction, but this time it hit differently. My stomach twisted at the sight of the half-eaten bodies and the blatant attack on innocent lives. It wasn't just that, though. After spending weeks in a living world, the dying one felt wrong.

I carefully stepped over the rubble, keeping my ears open for any sign of people or lingering Claeg. I still didn't hear anything. The town seemed completely deserted. Except for the dead bodies near the blast, there were no more.

I was missing something.

I stopped for a moment and looked around. Human footprints were mixed with Claeg, but no sign of conflict existed. Aside from the guards at the wall, it was as if the Claeg found the city deserted, but that didn't make any sense.

A set of children's footprints captured my attention. I bent down to study them. The child wore no shoes, and its feet were no bigger than my hand. He or she must not have been more than four or five years old.

I stood and followed them into the heart of the town. Children were rare in this world, and they were the most protected. The adults wouldn't have let the child be seen or taken if the Claeg had breached the wall, so I hoped those prints would lead me somewhere.

The tracks zigzagged through the buildings, leading to a modest house close to the center of town. It was an earthen house made of mud with a metal roof. Nothing about it stood out except the tracks leading to it from all directions. There were too many tracks for such a small house.

I wondered if it was a place of trading or business, but that didn't seem to fit the evidence either.

I slowly opened the door and cautiously stepped inside. The curtains were drawn on the windows. I let my eyes adjust to the darkness.

The house had a small kitchen, some chairs, a small bed in the corner, and a well-kept dirt floor. The kitchen had been recently used, as the wood oven emitted some warmth. There were footprints of all different sizes on the dirt floor. Many people had been here, more than should fit in this small house.

There was definitely something I was missing.

I examined the prints more closely. Only a few sets of prints were near the kitchen, and the rest were everywhere else, but a pattern began to reveal itself as I observed them further. The general direction of the footprints was toward the bed, and many led to it but did not return to the door.

I was so absorbed in solving the mystery that I didn't hear the person creep up behind me as I approached the bed. Before I knew it, there was a knife at my throat. I silently cursed myself. I knew better.

My injury also seemed to be still affecting me. I noticed the weakness in my muscles, as I instinctively threw my hands up to show they were empty.

I knew that if the person wanted to kill me, they would have already done it, but despite that, my heart rate increased, and my entire body went rigid, ready to defend myself if need be.

"We don't like strangers poking around our town uninvited," said a male voice trying to sound tough, but I could hear the slight tremble beneath the words.

"I mean no harm," I responded, keeping my voice low and calm.

"You have a soldier's jacket on," he observed, the knife digging in further.

"Stole it. It's practical," I said, inwardly cringing at the lie.

"What do you want?"

"Looking for temporary shelter."

"Just you?" he asked and then looked around the room.

I took the brief lapse in his attention to get the knife off my throat. I twisted his arm away from me and disarmed him so quickly that he just stood there, blinking in surprise.

"I have no intention of hurting you or anyone else," I said, turning the knife over in my hand and handing it back to him.

He continued staring in disbelief as he slowly reached for it.

"My friend and I are looking for a safe place to stay and a way to purchase or trade for some supplies if you have any to spare," I told him. "Oh, and you should tell whoever is in charge to hide your tracks better next time."

That statement triggered something in him because he finally responded, "We didn't have enough time."

"What happened here?"

He considered my question, obviously trying to determine how much he should reveal about his people.

"You better come with me," he finally decided as he ushered me toward the bed.

I followed him, very aware that it could be a trap, but his manner suggested otherwise. His youth and inexperience with a blade told me that he was relatively new to the guard position.

He pushed the bed aside, and beneath it was a sizable trap door. He opened the door, and the steps were barely visible, leading further into the Earth than I expected.

"After you," he said, motioning toward the opening.

Thirty minutes. I had thirty minutes to get back to Olivia.

Chapter Thirty-Two

Willow

I was woken abruptly by a kick to the shins and the harsh tone of a male voice.

I must have fallen asleep sitting against the side of a small stone building facing the city center. I must not have been asleep for long because it was still light outside, though it was fading fast. Most of the city center was emptied of stalls and people.

"Get up! You cannot sleep here! Go, get out of here!"

I looked up at the man kicking me. He looked like a male librarian, with glasses not so different from the ones I used to wear, carrying papers in the crook of his left arm, and staring down at me as though I was something that needed to be squashed.

I instinctively replied, "OK, OK, I'm going. No need to get your panties in a bunch." In hindsight, I shouldn't have said that, but I blamed it on the grogginess that clouded my mind.

"What did you say?" the man growled at me.

"Nothing. Sorry. I meant no disrespect." I abruptly stood and dusted the dirt off my dress. A small crowd began to form around us.

"Who are you? Where do you live?" he asked me angrily. He wouldn't let me go easily.

"My name is Gwen, and I live down that way," I said, pointing toward the alleyway Kat had disappeared down.

He stared at me for a long time, and I tried to keep my face from giving away the lies. I hoped he wouldn't ask for an exact address or a last name. I hadn't gotten that far with my false story.

"There you are!" a female voice boomed behind me, a second before she grabbed my arm and held on tight. I turned to face her, my eyes widening in surprise.

She squeezed my arm in warning, and I quickly wiped the shock from my face.

"You know this woman?" the man said to Kat.

"Yes. My apologies. She works for me." She paused for a beat before adding, "She's new and must have been lost."

He looked at me again, for far longer than was comfortable, before addressing Kat. "Keep your employees in line, or you won't have any."

She gave a silent, curt nod, and he finally stalked off. The crowd began to disperse shortly after.

I went to say something, but Kat dragged me down the alleyway before I could utter a word. She didn't say anything, and she didn't turn to look at me. Her pace was almost too fast; I struggled to stay on my feet.

She was clearly angry, but I couldn't imagine why.

Still, I kept my mouth shut.

We passed many buildings, and as we got further away from the city center, they became smaller and more disheveled. The stench of garbage and human waste filled the air. I reached to cover my nose, but before I could, she jerked me to the right down another small alleyway.

This one didn't smell as bad, but the buildings were just as un-kept as the ones we had passed.

She finally stopped before a small, ordinary-looking earthen building with a scrap metal roof and knocked on the door.

A petite, silver-haired woman with the beginnings of wrinkles opened it. She looked at Kat, then me, and then back to Kat.

At the question in her eyes, Kat said, "She's an old friend. She isn't a threat." Her eyes searched my face for a long moment before she focused back on the older woman. "At least, I don't think she is."

My mouth fell open. "A threat?" I choked out. "How could you say that?"

Kat responded, "We'll get to that later." She said to the woman, "So?"

The woman opened the door wide enough to let us enter, and Kat pulled me through the door, still holding onto my arm tightly. Without another word, we walked through what appeared to be an art store and toward the back of the building. We entered another room that looked like a closet, but Kat shoved a supplies shelf to the side, revealing another door. She pulled me through it and down a short staircase.

Kat finally stopped at the bottom of the stairs and faced me. "What are you doing here?" Her voice was not at all joyful.

"What am I doing here? I could ask you the same question! I thought you were dead!" I yelled back louder than I intended.

She let out a huge sigh and dropped her head into her hands. "I'm sorry. I didn't mean to be so harsh. I just didn't expect to find you, of all people." She paused and raised her eyes to mine. There was pain in them. Pain I instantly wanted to erase from every line on her face.

I waited for her to continue.

"I was taken here against my will, and I've been trying to get back to you and Olivia ever since." She stopped for a moment, and then added hesitantly, "Is Olivia alive?"

"Yes." It came out as barely a whisper as my emotions finally bubbled to the surface, threatening to spill.

She put her head back in her hands and let out a silent sob, and that's when I finally permitted myself to wrap my arms around her.

She pulled her hands away and buried her face in my shoulder, and then we were both sobbing.

We stayed that way for a long time, crying and holding each other, before I finally asked, "A threat?"

Kat let out a short laugh-sob before saying, "Of course you aren't a threat, not to me, but in this city trusting people is hard, even ones you truly thought were on your side."

I must have looked completely shocked because she laughed again, adding, "There's a lot to explain, so let's get something to eat and talk."

I followed her down a small corridor. The passageway was narrow, and the ceiling was low. It was lit by torches attached to the stone walls. At the end of it, there was another door. Kat pulled out an old brass key and opened it. The room beyond was quite large. There was a small kitchen and sitting area. The floor was dirt, and the walls were stone. The air was cold inside, but the stove was lit with a small fire, offering a little warmth. The space was large and open, housing only a small table and a few chairs.

"This is where I live, but it is also where we meet," Kat explained.

"Meet?"

"I meet with a group of people trying to get out of here. Mostly women. We compile information and supplies. We've been organizing and working for years. We're close."

I found that she was staring at me with tears in her eyes, "What?" I asked her.

"Oh, it's nothing"—a pause—"it's just that I can't believe you're here. And to think that I was going to go back to you in a few days."

"You were all going to leave in a few days?"

She nodded, a smile on her face.

My stomach sank at the thought. "Kat, Coria doesn't exist anymore."

She looked at me in surprise.

"There were thousands of Claeg camped outside our walls. We were forced to fight. The Elite stayed locked up in their fortresses, leaving only once the battle ended. They came here. A few hundred of them, as I was told. The rest were killed. It was sheer luck that Olivia and I survived."

Kat shook her head, eyes wide with shock.

"Kat, I think we need to change some plans quickly. There's a lot you should know, and I have many questions for you too."

She nodded her agreement, and I walked to the kitchen to find something to eat. I hadn't realized how much I was missing the extra food at the house until I started rummaging around her shelves. Though I spotted dried meat, the rest of the kitchen was filled with nothing but grain.

Kat came up behind me, wrapped her arms around my waist, and put her head against my back. I paused my food search.

"No matter what, I'm just glad you're here," she whispered into my back.

"Me too."

It took me fifteen minutes to whip up something quick to eat. Kat helped me, and we fell into our familiar banter. She talked about her art, I talked about my books, and it felt like nothing had changed between us, even though *everything* had changed.

When we finally sat down, I told her everything that had happened since she left, until she saved me in the city center. Hours had passed by the time I finished my story. Kat said nothing the entire time. Occasionally nodding or offering a sad smile.

When I finished, she was teary-eyed and exhausted, but she whispered, "You can really make plants grow?"

I smiled at her. "Would you like me to show you?"

She nodded eagerly.

I sat beside the table, placing my hands on the dirt. I reached out to the Earth below me and smiled at the life I could feel beneath the surface. I gave a small tug, and I felt some of that life begin to travel upward. I opened my eyes, and a tiny green shoot began to push above the ground. Kat gasped as we both watched the leaves unfurl before our eyes.

"A strawberry plant!" I said with delight.

"Can you grow whatever you want?" she breathed in amazement.

"I can't choose what grows. I don't know how yet," I responded.

"You realize this changes everything, right?" Her voice was more serious now.

I saw the hope in her eyes, but I also saw the fear. "Yes, that's why I left Olivia and Liam, why I'm even afraid to be with you."

Kat regarded me briefly, and I could tell she was struggling with something. "You can't do this alone, Willow. There will always be someone they'll be able to use against you. Though I understand why you three decided to split up. It sounds like Liam is valuable too. If both of you were here together, and they found out, we'd be hard-pressed to get you out of here alive. But, regardless of what happens or the threat, I wouldn't think of leaving you alone here."

I stood up and wrapped her in a big hug. "I'm so glad I'm not alone," I whispered into her hair, which smelled like a fresh summer breeze.

I followed her back up to the shop, and we took the stairs to the second floor above. It was a modest room filled with boxes of art supplies and a small bed pushed up against a wall. A small window sat just above the bed.

I looked at her expectantly, but she wasn't looking at me. She was staring at something out the window. She appeared lost.

"You OK, Kat?"

She shook her head, and a tear escaped down her cheek. "Yeah, I'm better than OK." Her voice was shaky. She paused for another moment before continuing, "I'm beyond happy to see you. You have no idea how much I've missed you, and I'm so relieved that Olivia is alive, but"—she put her head in her hands a let out a small sob—"I'm just so scared, Willow. You have no idea what we're up against."

"Tell me."

She shook her head. "I just don't see a way out."

"There's always a way," I responded, trying to sound strong and hopeful.

She shook her head. It was then that I realized just how exhausted she was too. She had heard my story, but I knew nothing of hers. I had no idea what she'd been through or what she might still be facing.

It was as if I was staring at a stranger. That the distance between us was more than just space and time. What we faced without each other had changed us, and I wondered if she felt that, too.

After a few moments, she looked at me again, her face unreadable. "Get some sleep, I'm going out." A hint of determination had returned to her voice.

"You should rest too, Kat."

"No time," was her blunt reply, and before I could argue, she was heading for the door. She looked back briefly and quietly added, "This changes everything. *You* change everything. There's a lot that needs to be done."

And then she was gone.

Chapter Thirty-Three

Liam

The guard had brought me to the town's remaining survivors. There were fewer people than I expected, and they all looked exhausted and hopeless. They stared at me in silence while I took in my surroundings.

We were in an underground room that was nothing but dirt and stone. There was only one entrance where the tunnel we entered from above met the room we were now in. There were supplies everywhere. None of it organized. Everything had clearly been done in haste.

"Do we trust him?" I heard one of them say.

The guard had taken aside a few people, likely to discuss what to do with me. I pretended I couldn't hear them, but their voices still made it to my ears—ears that heard better than most.

"Is there anyone we can trust anymore? We were sold out," another said.

"They clearly trained him." The guard said.

"Yes, but he's alone."

"He said he was traveling with a friend." The guards voice again.

"The jacket, though . . ."

"You found him. What do you think?"

A long pause.

"If he had wanted to harm me or any of us, he would have done it already."

"Yes but harming us may not be his goal if he's alone. Maybe it's to gain information."

"Enough of this." A woman's voice this time. "This is all speculation. We need to talk to him, and then we can determine if he is trustworthy or not. I don't care what his *skills* may be. He cannot overtake us all."

Silence, then their group was moving toward me.

They all stopped before me, assessing me with wary eyes as they waited for the woman to speak.

Before she could mutter a word, though, Olivia strolled into the room, trying to act like she owned the place. Heads snapped in her direction.

I sighed.

"You aren't going to get much out of him," she said, as everyone appeared to not know what to do.

She bowed to them, smiling. "I'm the friend."

I shook my head but couldn't help my half-smile at her dramatic entrance.

"You were longer than an hour," she said over everyone, staring only at me.

"You weren't supposed to come find me. You were supposed to go find Willow." I tried to make it sound like a reprimand, but I was too relieved she'd found me instead.

"We can have this argument later. We need to get moving, and all this idle talk is taking too long."

Everyone was still gaping at Olivia, but no one moved to grab her.

"Do you want the long or short story?" she asked them.

They all blinked at her, and it took a few moments before the woman answered, "Short."

"I have no idea if we can trust you, just as you have no idea if you can trust us. But I can tell you we're not here to hurt anyone. We're here for supplies and, hopefully, your help. What we have is worth fighting for." She paused for a moment, and now everyone's attention was on her. Even the children paused their games.

"This part of the story you won't believe, but I ask that you hear us out. We have a friend who has unique abilities. She can make plants grow and water flow wherever she goes. I know that sounds impossible, but it's the truth. We have been hunted ever since we left Coria. That guy over there," she said, pointing her thumb in my direction, "he abandoned his military officer position and got us out of the city safely. Still, we were never quite safe, constantly hunted by Claeg and soldiers. Yes, they were hunting us. Following the trail of plants we left in our wake. We split up with our friend to get help and to split up the forces trying to hunt us. As far as we know, she's hiding in Tarraco, and we're here to ask for your help protecting her. In return, we can all live where food is abundant, and the Earth is once again living."

I let out a loud sigh, shaking my head again, trying to hide my laughter.

"What?" she asked me.

"Brilliant story," I replied sarcastically.

"What? They asked for the short version," she said, shrugging. "You do better, then. You've been gone for over an hour, and I got more accomplished in two minutes than you have the entire time, so don't look at me like that."

"Do you have proof?" the woman interrupted, looking between the two of us.

I nodded and pulled the pack from my back. I took out some dried herbs Willow gave us and handed them to her. She stared at them for a long time. Everyone else was dead silent, craning their necks to get a look at the plants in her hands.

"I know this is a lot to process," Olivia added. I continued to shake my head at her, the corners of my mouth twitching as I tried to hold back a smile.

Olivia glared back at me.

"How?" the woman finally responded. Her words were barely a whisper.

"It has something to do with him," she said, pointing her finger at me.

"Hey, don't bring me into this. I have no idea how to answer that question, either. I'm not even sure Willow could."

The woman looked between us again, clearly contemplating what to say next.

The silence was so awkward and uncomfortable that Olivia started staring at her feet and moving them back and forth across the dirt floor.

I snorted at her again, and she instantly snapped her head toward me long enough to give me her best look of disdain. Of course, it only made me smile wider.

"May I offer more information?" I finally said to them, directing my question to the woman.

"By all means," the woman responded, and it became clear that she was in charge. She commanded everyone's attention in the room, and they all waited for some sort of signal.

She was tall, with broad shoulders and long blonde hair tightly pulled into a ponytail. She was beautiful, but she appeared to have a permanent blank face. It was as if she didn't feel any emotion at all. She wore practical clothing and weapons only slightly concealed beneath her brown leather jacket, similar to mine except for one key difference. It wasn't a soldier's jacket.

"There's an abandoned village southeast of here. A few days' walk. There's a large house on the cliff that overlooks the village. It's completely intact—no structures damaged, simply abandoned. However, there are no fortifications to protect the village besides a broken electric fence. The large house still has some resources in the way of food, and the houses are all furnished. There are no weapons. While we stayed there, Willow, grew an entire forest of plants, and the water has returned and is clean enough to drink." I paused, giving them a moment to process everything I had said.

"We plan to bring people back into the village and work on fortifying it as best as possible to make it a safe place. We haven't mentioned yet that the living plants provide safety from the Claeg. The Claeg turn to ash if they touch any part of the living Earth. I know that also sounds impossible, and I have no proof other than our word." I stopped briefly, watching their reactions closely.

Most people were in silent shock. I could see by their blank stares and frozen bodies.

Their reaction was expected.

I continued, "We need people, weapons, and any resources you can spare. We don't expect you to trust us blindly, but we don't have much time. I fear our enemy is much greater than we expected, and they are closing in. Willow will not be able to hide forever, and we cannot protect her on our own."

The woman studied me as if she could read my very soul, and I shifted uncomfortably in my seat. It did not go unnoticed by Olivia as I heard her trying to stifle a giggle at my awkwardness.

Finally, the woman responded. "We lost almost everything in our last attack. What you see in this room is all we have left. We have been attempting to collect whatever resources we have from the village above, but it is slow because we don't have the manpower. Our weapons were severely depleted over the years, and our food stores are low. I fear we will not be much help to you, but at this point, I don't think we have any other option but to trust you." She paused, and it was my turn to gawk at her. I was not expecting them to agree so easily or so quickly. I had thought it would take days to get them to agree.

"We won't survive long without another source of incoming food, and our trade has stopped with Tarraco due to increased Claeg attacks. Until you showed up, we planned on abandoning the village and risking the trip to Tarraco. Given what we know about the city, it was not a very good option, but it was our only one. It seems you have given us another choice, and though there is a possibility you're leading us to our deaths, I'm willing to risk it." She sounded completely and utterly exhausted.

I began to say something but was interrupted by a loud banging noise from the tunnel leading to the room. Everyone whipped their heads toward the opening.

"I forgot to mention that I didn't encounter any guards when I entered," Olivia said, sounding panicked.

The woman looked at me, fear in her eyes.

"Do you have any weapons down here?" I asked her.

"Over there." She pointed to a corner of the large room. "Noah, make sure everyone is armed."

Before I knew it, chaos erupted around the room, and people were running in every direction.

"We need to block the entrance as much as possible to funnel them in individually. Hopefully, it's only one pack," I shouted over the commotion before rushing toward the entrance.

Olivia clearly had no idea how to help, so she stood there frozen.

"Olivia!" I yelled, "Your daggers!"

She pulled out of her momentary state of shock and ran toward me as people began pushing heavy things in front of the entrance to the room.

"Is there another way in or out of here?" I asked the woman who had joined in blocking the entrance, though I already knew the answer.

She shook her head.

We were trapped.

"We didn't have time to build a second exit," she added.

I only resumed my task, though I increased my speed, fear settling into my bones.

Olivia caught my eye briefly, and I saw her glance at my injured side. I tried not to wince.

"Liam!" she yelled, but that was all she could get out before the Claeg tried to hurl themselves through the opening.

"Positions!" I heard the woman yell over the commotion, and everyone formed a semi-circle around the opening, some hiding behind various furniture or boxes. Some pulled out bows. Others readied knives and swords. Olivia followed suit and crouched behind a large box beside another woman.

My only thought was that there were children in here with no way out. That Olivia was in here, too, and Willow wouldn't survive her death.

If it killed me, I was going to protect them.

I threw myself at the first Claeg, who pushed through our barrier. We clashed, and my sword easily cut through its skin. When it fell, another took its place.

I kept going, trying to keep up with each one as they started to push me further back.

With every inch gained, the Claeg came at me in greater numbers, clashing with their swords, teeth, and bodies. I knew they were tearing my skin. I could feel the blood soaking my shirt, but I didn't stop.

Bodies were beginning to pile up at the entrance as I continued to hack away at the endless stream of Claeg. I could tell my speed was not what it usually was. I was still hurting, and I didn't know how long I would be able to keep it up.

I prayed it was long enough. It had to be.

Even with the bodies blocking more of the entrance, the Claeg kept coming, pushing everything aside. I could feel myself begin to falter, unable to manage them all by myself.

"Stop standing there gawking at him and help!" Olivia's voice boomed over the sound of fighting, and a moment later, people were racing to my side, their swords and daggers colliding with any piece of the Claeg they could get their hands on.

Next to me, I saw the woman, their leader, and now I knew why they had picked her to lead. She was fearless, confident, commanding, and clearly skilled with a sword.

More and more of the Claeg fell, but so did some of the humans. I heard their screams as the Claeg tore into their flesh.

Their leader next to me picked up her pace, sensing the urgency. Sensing our failing defense.

Despite our efforts, a Claeg broke through the entrance to the room. I pushed forward despite it. Hitting limb after limb and ignoring the now searing pain in my side.

I didn't notice the exhaustion. I didn't notice the dead bodies around me or the smell of blood. I didn't count the people lying on the ground. I didn't look for Olivia. I simply kept going.

It seemed like an eternity before I saw the end of the tunnel and no more Claeg racing down the steps.

There are only a few more, I repeated that over and over in my head as more and more blood spilled from wounds that spread across my entire body. I didn't know how I was still standing, let alone fighting.

The last Claeg put up a hell of a fight, even after I'd cut him down to his knees. He snarled at me and kept swinging, almost slicing a huge gash in my abdomen, and I stumbled backward over another fallen Claeg before I saw a flash of steel before me.

Everything instantly stilled around us. No more Claeg entered the room. The only sound was my ragged breath and the screams and groans of agony from the injured people around me.

I stood there, unable to move. My breathing increased, and I felt I couldn't pull enough air into my lungs. I collapsed to my knees and listened to the rattling breath in my chest. A hand clasped my shoulder, and I stared up into the face of their leader. I realized I didn't know her name, and because I didn't know what else to do, I asked her.

"Leeann," she replied, trying to give me a small smile.

And then I fell, no longer able to support my own weight.

Leeann grabbed for me, bracing the worst of my fall, and gently laid me on the ground.

I stared up at her normally blank face. There was a hint of worry there, but my vision blurred, and I knew I couldn't hold my consciousness much longer.

"We'll get you help," was all she managed to say through her heavy breathing as she put her hand over my side, trying to staunch the blood from my earlier wound.

"Liam!" I heard Olivia's panicked voice, and something in me finally relaxed.

She was safe.

It was the last thing I thought as my eyes involuntarily closed. Everything darkening.

Chapter Thirty-Four

Willow

"**S**hit!" I swore into the darkness as my eyes snapped open, and the reality hit me. What I was feeling in the space between dreams—It was Liam. It was his pain. And somehow, I knew it was real.

Even outside of the dream now, the pain poured into me, and I didn't know what to do. I was momentarily paralyzed by it. I was shaking and sweating and crying all at once.

Fear seized me, tightening its hold.

Use me. Olivia's words echoed in my brain. I tried to shake away the memory. I was alone this time.

You're never alone. The message was barely a whisper. A whisper that I knew somehow came from deep inside the Earth.

Use me.

I stumbled out of bed and felt my way blindly to the stairs. Somehow, I managed to make it down the steps and through the shop without damaging anything. I found the closet and the hidden staircase and went down, using the wall to guide me.

Desperate to feel the dirt under my hands. Desperate to reach that voice. Desperate to stop the pain.

At the bottom of the stairs, I snaked my way into the large, hidden room, and I laid myself on the dirt floor. My tears fell in a torrent, soaked up by the Earth under my head.

I felt his pain. I felt death at the doorstep. I could do nothing.

I instinctually reached out to the Earth below me, as I had done dozens of times when I called the plants, reaching for any lifeline I could find.

When I felt the pulsing energy of the life that waited patiently below the surface, all I could manage was one word, "Please." It was a whispered plea.

A few moments passed, and then I felt a familiar shift in the earth below me. Something was moving upward, but something was also moving outward. Away from me.

When the energy hit me, it felt like pure sunlight. It enveloped my entire body with a warmth I could never describe. I felt my body relax. The tears stopped, the shaking stopped, and the fear eased.

Save him. Save him. Save him. Was all I could think as I finally passed out on the dirt.

"Willow," a soft but hesitant voice whispered. A hand was on my shoulder, shaking me lightly.

I groaned, not wanting to open my eyes or move my body just yet.

"Willow," the voice said again, this time a little louder, and I reluctantly opened my eyes to see Kat crouched next to me.

I blinked a couple of times, trying to focus. The first thing I noticed was the color green, and I groaned again.

"I assume all of this was you?" Kat said, motioning around the room.

I sat up, trying to shake the sleep from my eyes. When the room finally came into full focus, all I could do was laugh.

Kat gave me a questioning look.

"It's borage—a lot of borage. Apparently, the Earth thinks I need a heavy dose of courage." I laughed again at the beautiful, green plants with blue, star-shaped flowers that filled the entire room.

"What happened?" she asked. A careful question.

Her question brought the memory back, and my panic grew.

Kat noticed my wide eyes and the stiffness in my posture, and she said in a more demanding tone, "Willow, what *happened*?"

I responded in a shaky voice, "Something happened to Liam. He was hurt. I think he was, or is, dying. I don't know." I couldn't stop the tears from flowing again.

"Olivia?" she asked so quietly I could barely hear it.

"I . . . I don't know." I suddenly felt so helpless.

Kat reached for me and pulled me into a hug.

"I think I need some of that borage," I finally said after a few long minutes.

Kat pulled away just enough to look into my eyes, and then she broke into a smile. "Really? That's all you have to say?"

I shrugged. "I must admit, I've been at a loss for words lately."

"I suppose I would be, too, if I were you."

When neither of us attempted to move, I added, "I think he's alive . . . barely. I don't know how I know that. I just *feel* it somehow."

Kat nodded. I saw the concern in her eyes. She didn't say anything, though, and I knew it was because she was just as much at a loss for words as I was.

We sat in silence for a while longer, with Kat holding me close until our hearts resumed their normal pace.

An amazed whistling noise came from the passageway, and the two of us turned toward it. The same silver-haired woman who let us into the shop yesterday stood at the room's opening. I glanced around me and realized that the place looked like an overgrown greenhouse, and I let out a large sigh.

The woman watched me, and instead of surprise or shock, she just looked angry. "Your doing, I suppose?"

"Yes, unintended," I responded, not moving out of Kat's arms.

The woman narrowed her gaze.

"Cass, she wouldn't put us in danger if she didn't have to. This was the unintended consequence of trying to save someone's life. Someone important, " Kat said to her, finally releasing me and standing up. She brushed the dirt from her pants and walked toward Cass.

"Important to whom?" Cass asked her as if I were not in the room.

"To all of us," Kat snapped at her. "She wouldn't have this ability without him."

"Maybe that would be better," Cass shot back.

"You can't be serious?" Kat said incredulously.

Cass sighed. "No, I'm not serious, but this is a problem, Kat." She motioned around the room. "She needs to control it. We won't last long if these things keep popping up everywhere."

"You're right," I said, standing up, annoyed that they were talking about me like I wasn't even there. "Do you have any idea who might be able to help me *control* this?"

Cass glared at me, and I struggled not to flinch under her gaze.

"Cass, she isn't putting us in danger *on purpose*. But we do need to figure out if there is anything that might help her." She paused for a moment before adding, "What about Circe?"

Cass's face softened a little. "That's a good place to start."

Kat addressed me, explaining, "She has a hidden library. If there's information that might help you, it'd be there, though I doubt you'd find much. Circe has been collecting books from all over the place for the last thirty years or so, but I've never heard anything about this." She motioned around the room.

"I've been all over bookstores and libraries, and this is the closest I've come to finding anything remotely related to what's happening to me," I responded, walking over to the pack I had dumped on the floor when I arrived.

I opened it and rummaged around until I found the journal. I pulled it from the bag and handed it to Kat.

She looked at the cover and opened it to the first page. She flipped through the pages, her brows wrinkling as she studied it.

"Do you know what *any* of this means?" she asked me.

"Some. I'm familiar with the plant information. Their healing properties. But the rest . . ." I trailed off and shrugged.

"May I?" Cass asked.

I nodded, and Kat handed the journal to Cass.

She flipped through the pages, her face blank. It took her a few minutes to reach the end.

"I don't understand one lick of this, but the handwriting is familiar," she said, thoughtfully.

"Really?" Kat asked her.

"I've seen many handwritten words in my life. Placing this would be nearly impossible." Cass stopped briefly, giving me a contemplative look. "Start with Circe. Show her this. She might have more handwritten journals or texts that match the handwriting or the content."

Cass paused and turned to Kat. "Have you told her yet?"

"Told me what?"

Kat didn't look at me. She just shook her head.

Chapter Thirty-Five

Liam

Within the darkness, I felt a slight pull, so faint that I almost dismissed it. But then, the pull got stronger, more insistent. I tried to ignore it this time, content with staying in the emptiness before me, but the pull continued to become stronger and stronger, and with it came the pain.

Excruciating pain.

I was stuck in the darkness and couldn't tell if I was screaming. The pain was all-consuming. I wanted to go back. Back to the darkness and the emptiness, but the pain just kept coming. And then, all of a sudden, something soothed the pain. Not entirely, but just enough.

I was suddenly aware of my broken body and mind.

Willow. I reached out, but I couldn't feel her.

The pull finally ceased, and I felt like I was falling into that darkness again.

Willow. It was the only thing that kept me from the emptiness in front of me.

Light, so bright it was blinding, pulled me back to consciousness. I tried to turn away, but I couldn't. The light hit me, and I could feel the energy pouring into me—a warm, healing energy filling me up.

Suddenly, I was gasping for air, and I could hear people talking all around me. A warm hand was on my chest, and a voice called my name.

"Liam!" It was a desperate plea.

I didn't want to open my eyes. They felt so heavy. I could barely breathe, and my body wouldn't move. The pain wouldn't stop. I wanted to go back to the emptiness.

Willow.

She held me here. Somehow, she was my lifeline.

I reluctantly opened my eyes and groaned at the effort it took.

I stared up at a stunned Olivia, her face streaked with tears. She let out a loud exhale. "I thought you were dead."

I struggled to get the words out. "I was. Almost." My voice was gravel. Each word was a dagger in my already painful body.

Olivia must have noticed my struggle. "Shhh, don't talk, just rest. I have Willow's herbs with me, and she left a note instructing us on how to use them in case of emergency." She smiled then, grabbing for her pack and pulling out a bag full of dried herbs, and with it, a long handwritten sheet with Willow's handwriting on it.

She took a few moments to scan the paper before she dug around in the bag of herbs, grabbing what she needed. I briefly turned my head to survey the damage around me. The pain prevented me from saying anything or asking questions. Still, I could gather enough information from the smell of blood, the dead bodies around me, and the occasional roar of pain coming from within the tunnel.

There were no hurried steps or sounds of fighting. How many others survived, I didn't know. I saw a few of her men fall next to me, but it was all a blur, and my memory was failing me. Everything felt like a mist was concealing it all.

"I have to get these clothes off of you. I can't tell where the blood is coming from. There's too much of it, and I don't know how much of it is yours or theirs," Olivia said, nodding toward the dead Claeg next to us.

I didn't have the energy to respond, so I gave her the slightest of nods. She pulled out a pair of scissors and carefully cut the shirt away from my body.

"Shit, Liam. You re-opened your previous wound, and you have a million others." I could hear the worry in her voice. "I'll start with the original wound. It seems to be the leakiest."

I raised my eyebrows at that, and the slightest of smiles formed on her face. "What? Do you have a better word for it?"

I tried to smile back, but it probably looked more like a snarl.

She let out a snort at my effort. "Just keep still, OK? I'm not as good as Willow at this, and I don't want to carve you up further. Willow would kill me if I ended up killing you by accident, especially since she wrote very, *very* detailed instructions on what to do in this situation. It's as if she *knew* this would happen to you." I could hear the sarcasm in that last statement.

I huffed out a breath, the closest I would come to a laugh.

She placed her hand on my chest. Bracing me, or bracing herself, I couldn't tell.

"The stitching will hurt," she told me determinedly after preparing the needle and thread.

"Can't possibly hurt more than the rest of me," I barely got out.

She smiled at me, "I don't know, you haven't experienced my first-aid skills."

I huffed out another breath of air, trying not to make the pain worse.

She smiled slyly at me. "Is that a laugh?" she asked in that mischievous tone, and after a short pause, she said, "You ready?"

I shook my head, and she laughed. "I don't think you have a choice. I'm your only option."

Olivia was meticulous, constantly checking the instructions Willow had left her. She cleaned, stitched, added herbs, then bandaged all of the lacerations on my torso. After a while, it was clear that she was correct about the number of wounds. I must have looked like a carved-up piece of meat.

It took her hours, and I didn't make a sound through all of it. I clung to that lifeline that I now knew Willow had sent me. I had no idea how she did it, but somehow, she pulled me back from death.

Eventually, I passed out. I wasn't sure if it was from the exhaustion, the pain, or both.

When I woke up, I was on some sort of cot. Olivia was asleep next to me, sitting on a chair, her head and arms on the cot beside my legs.

I looked around me. There wasn't any movement, and the room was mainly silent except for the occasional groan of pain.

I swiveled my head toward the tunnel. It was sealed shut with a wooden door and iron nails.

That won't help for very long, I thought to myself, but I knew it was the best they could do with what they had.

Leean must have sensed my movement because she was standing over me when I turned my head back around.

"We weren't properly introduced before." She studied my face, before adding, "I'm Leeann, and you're Liam."

I nodded, not yet trusting my voice.

She continued, "I'm the unofficial leader of these people."

I nodded again.

She sighed, running a bloody hand through her hair. I realized at that moment that she must be exhausted. She'd been too busy tending to her people to wash her hands.

"Rest," I managed to say. "You," I added, lifting my hand to point at her, finding even that slight movement difficult.

She sighed again and nodded, a distant look on her face. "You're right. I cannot do anything else right now. There's no point in wearing myself down further. I'll leave you to rest."

She turned to leave but then stopped. When she faced me again, she was struggling with something. "I don't know how you did what you did, but . . . Thank you. I don't know if we would have survived without you."

I shook my head at her, and because I couldn't get all the words out, I struggled to say, "No, we led them here. I'm sorry."

She looked at me, her brow raising slightly. "You cannot possibly know that, and regardless, we're in your debt. I'm not sure how long we can stay here. We'll move when everyone is able."

I nodded, unable and unwilling to argue with her.

Olivia stirred beside me, letting out a sigh in her sleep.

Leeann watched at her. "She's useful. You're lucky to have her."

Though her words lacked emotion, I nodded, sensing that Leeann might not be so different from me.

"Goodnight," she added, walking away without waiting for a response.

I exhaled slowly and closed my eyes again, letting the exhaustion lull me into oblivion.

When I woke, there was a lot of commotion all around me. People were hurrying to pack up whatever they could.

I still couldn't stand, but the pain had subsided greatly. I lifted my head and looked around to see if I could find Olivia. I spotted her across the room talking to Leeann. I couldn't hear their words, but their body language suggested some tension.

I turned away from them and scanned the rest of the room. I swiveled my head in the opposite direction, and my eyes landed on a small, frail woman with curly, black hair standing a few feet away from me. Her eyes locked on mine, and she wasn't moving, as if something was rooting her in place. She looked to be in her twenties. She had torn clothes and a pained look on her face.

I gave her a gentle smile and nodded, pulling her out of her trance. She slowly made her way to the cot I was lying on, but her movement was hesitant.

She opened her mouth to speak but then shut it again quickly and looked down at her feet.

"What's your name?" I asked her, not knowing what else to say.

"Emilia," she said in a small voice.

"I'm Liam."

She nodded in a way that made me realize she already knew my name.

When she said nothing further, I asked her, "Do you know what's going on with all this commotion?"

She shook her head still not saying anything.

I waited a moment longer to see if she would speak, and when she didn't, I tried again. "Do you have any family or friends here?"

"I have a brother," she said so quietly that I had to lean closer to hear her. "You saved him." She paused before adding, "Thank you."

I gave her a broad smile, and the corners of her mouth turned up slightly in response.

"Were you born here?" I asked her.

She shook her head. "We were born in Tarraco. We escaped and came here. Our father was a trader."

I nodded, trying to encourage her to continue, but she stopped and seemed content not adding any more information to her story.

When I felt like I had run out of things to say, a frail-looking teenager came up behind Emilia. I could feel her flinch when he put his hand on her shoulder, but when she saw who it was, she relaxed considerably.

"We need to finish packing up," he said to her.

She looked back at me for a moment, then turned on her heels and walked away without another word.

"You must be the brother?" I asked him, though the similarities were obvious. He had the same curly, black hair and piercing stare.

He nodded. "I'm Lucius."

"Liam."

"I know who you are."

"She doesn't say much," I said, nodding in her direction.

"She's . . . been through a lot." I could tell from the hesitation in those words that she had faced many horrors in her short life.

"We came here to try to escape it," he added a moment later. "Most of the people here have been in similar situations. This town was a sanctuary for people like her. We lost a lot trying to get here. I'm all she has left."

"She's lucky to have you."

He studied my face for a few moments. "You're not like them."

"Like who?"

"The people who wear those jackets," he replied, pointing to my discarded jacket beside me.

"Sometimes, I'm not so sure."

He considered me, and I struggled not to turn away from his stare.

"You aren't," he finally said in a way that left no room for arguing.

I was unsure of how to respond to that.

"Thank you," he said over his shoulder before walking away to join his sister, and I couldn't tell if the thank you was for saving him or talking to his sister.

Watching him walk away, I felt the emotion bubbling up. Anger, mostly, but also sadness. Anger for this fucked up world we lived in and for all of the good people who were so broken. Anger for the hopelessness I felt and for my inability to change anything for them.

Lost in those thoughts, I looked up to find Olivia. She cocked her head to the side. I knew she must have read my face.

"It's nothing," I said, looking away from her.

"Mmmhmm." I could tell she didn't believe a lick of my nonsense.

After I said nothing, she added, "They're preparing to move today. I told them it would be impossible. Too many people, including you, are too injured to walk."

I didn't comment.

Olivia studied me, gauging my emotional and physical states, before adding, "They have a few carts and a few horses that survived the attack. They'll use those to transport the injured. Everyone else will have to carry the supplies."

"They're still planning on coming with us?"

"I don't think they have a better option. Plus, you were pretty convincing yesterday despite almost killing yourself. Most of the people here think you are some sort of god." She huffed at the last statement.

I gave my best attempt at a smug smile, and Olivia gave me her best attempt at an obscene gesture.

I laughed despite the pain.

"Even with the herbs and your *godlike* body and healing ability, I don't think the bumpy ride will help you, or any of the others, heal," she said, and I laughed again. "But I can't convince Leeann. She's adamant that if we stay another day or two, we won't survive. Though she didn't say it, she really meant that without you, we don't stand a chance, and as much as I would love to disagree with her"—she gave me her best side-eye—"she's right."

I smirked at her, and she let out a sarcastic laugh.

"I really don't think your ego could get any bigger."

"Just say it," I egged her on.

"Say what?"

"That you just can't live without me."

She rolled her eyes as dramatically as possible. "Smug bastard."

I laughed again as we sat there watching everyone who was able, prepare to leave. "What can I do to help?" I finally asked her.

"Nothing. Just heal. We'll need you healthy again before we reach the house." Her expression changed. "I have a bad feeling about this. They usually don't attack the same place twice. I feel like they *knew* we were here. Like they waited for us to take the bait. Waited for us to get ourselves trapped."

"You're right. I've thought about that, too. I didn't leave any of them alive, though. If they're still hunting us, it'll take whoever's in charge a long time to realize that they weren't successful. We bought ourselves a couple of days, at least. If we can return to the house, we'll at least be safe from the Claeg. That will buy us even more time."

Olivia furrowed her brow. "Liam, at some point, they're going to realize, if they haven't already, that the Claeg cannot kill us. What will they send instead? Will they ever stop? What's their goal?"

"We cannot know their motive without getting closer or getting inside information. I *do* know that they have many more military weapons at their disposal. They won't use them if they don't have to because they're limited. They'll exhaust every option before deploying some of their other military tactics. They'll dispose of most of the Claeg before they send human armies. Humans who can truly fight are too valuable and only used in dire situations. All we can do is hope they haven't reached the point where using their limited military supplies and human armies are necessary. After all, they're only after the three of us, as far as I know. I could be wrong, but I don't think they're at the point where they'll do anything other than try to overwhelm us with the Claeg."

Olivia nodded but didn't seem wholly convinced.

"Olivia?" I asked, unsure how to present her with what I was about to say.

She raised her eyebrows, sensing my hesitancy.

"I think Willow saved me somehow."

"She saved you?"

I nodded, then told her everything that had happened while I was unconscious.

When I finished, she took a long time to respond. "*How* on earth is that possible? Are you sure you didn't dream it?"

I shook my head. "I thought so too, but I was conscious enough to know it was her. I could *feel* her."

Olivia didn't say anything for a long time, turning her attention to the busy room around us. What could she say? What could I say?

Finally, she returned her attention to me. "You rest. I'll see how I can help speed things up."

"I feel pretty helpless," I responded, hating to admit it even to myself.

"You and Willow are insufferable," she said with a huff.

I raised my brows.

"You both need to learn to accept a little help every once in a while. Us *mortals* are not completely useless, you know." She sounded exasperated, but I could see a hint of a smile.

I threw up my hands in surrender. Olivia shook her head and laughed at me. "Sleep. I'll be back in a little while."

I was too tired and in too much pain to argue with her.

Chapter Thirty-Six

Willow

"Tell me what?" I repeated when Kat didn't respond.

She sighed. "I think it's about time I tell you my story."

Kat walked over to the little kitchen, trying her best not to trample the plants growing everywhere.

I looked back to where Cass was standing, but she was already gone.

Kat waved me over to a table next to the kitchen, and while Kat made us something to eat, I heated water to make tea from the borage plants. We didn't say anything as we worked, but once we sat down, Kat began her story.

"When I was recruited, I thought there was no chance of survival. I was only part of a small group of people. Mostly women. When we left the city, the men in our group were separated from us, and a group of soldiers took us. They didn't explain anything. I thought it was strange that they had separated us from the men, but I was too afraid to ask."

I could see the struggle within her. The apprehension, the fear, and the grief were all plainly written across her face. I had never seen her this way and braced myself as she continued.

"We ended up walking north for hours. Everyone was silent. When darkness fell, we slept on the dirt. Some of the soldiers fell asleep with us, but some of them dragged a few of the women away from our camp. They came back a short while later, and I could hear their sobs. The next morning, I saw dried blood on their legs, but I could do nothing to help them."

Kat paused for a few moments, rubbing her temples. When she returned her hands to the table, I covered them with my own. She looked up at my face, and tears shimmered in the corner of her eyes.

"The next day was the same. We walked the entire day without food and with very little water. Luckily, we came to a small community of houses. From what you said earlier, it must have been the community you stayed in. I thought it would be better to stay in a place with beds and blankets, so we didn't have to freeze, but it wasn't. It only made it easier for them to . . ." She trailed off and the tears were falling now. I found that my eyes were no longer dry either. I squeezed her hands harder.

"I was only able to save myself by hiding. I didn't sleep at all. The fear and the screams of the women kept me awake. I considered staying in my hiding place in the morning, but I knew they would find me. I saw them checking our trackers each morning and night."

When she stopped, I could see her reliving every decision she made. Her eyes were pinched at the corners and tears glistened in them. Grief warred with anger, and my heart broke for her.

"After the second day, I couldn't help but think it would have been better to have been killed by the Claeg than to endure this."

"Shit, Kat," I said, as I moved my chair right next to hers and wrapped my arms around her. She told the rest of the story with her head on my shoulder.

"The third day was the same. Walking with no food and very little water and trying to sleep on the cold dirt while the women were pulled from their sleep to *service* the men. The third night, I could no longer keep myself awake. I was too tired and too weak. I covered myself with dirt to look less desirable. I was desperate. Somehow, my luck held."

She pulled away from me slightly, sipping the tea I made for her. Her eyes widened in surprise as she swallowed, and I grinned.

"This is amazing," she said, and I could hear the awe in her voice.

"This plant will calm your nerves and give you courage. I think maybe the plant was meant for both of us." I gave her a weak smile.

She gave me a grateful nod before continuing her story. "I prayed the fourth day would be the last day of our journey. I was starved, dehydrated, and completely exhausted. Just when I felt like I couldn't keep going, a girl collapsed. The men laughed, and when she couldn't rise, the men started kicking her. For *sport*. Another woman tried to help the girl stand, but the men got so angry that they started beating her, too. When they were done, the men ordered us to leave them there. So, we just left them. We *left them to die*, Willow." There was so much anguish in her voice now as she let out a strangled sob.

I squeezed her hand, which was now clammy beneath mine.

"That night, we reached Tarraco. We were taken to a small, mostly empty, building. About fifty cots were lined up on a dirt floor. There was a small bathroom the size of a closet. The men dropped us off and, to our relief, left shortly after. We instantly collapsed onto the beds. A few minutes later, five women, wearing these insufferable dresses," she said, motioning to her attire, "came in and gave us a meager meal and a cup of water. We were so starved that we didn't question anything."

Kat pulled her head off my shoulder and looked into my eyes. "Willow, no one did *anything*. No one said a word. No one comforted the crying or injured women. We barely *breathed*."

I gave her a solemn nod. "Fear. It does crazy things to you."

Kat gave me a thoughtful look before leaning down and resting her head on my shoulder once again.

"For days, no one told us anything. The days passed in the same way. Three meals a day, shower once a week, and lots of sleep. There was nothing to entertain us, but it took us all a long while to even begin to speak to each other. Slowly, though, we became close. After the first month, it was clear what we were doing there. The women who brought us food daily came in one day and demanded to see our undergarments. We all knew what it meant if we started bleeding. Even though I wasn't bleeding, we knew there were two of us who were. We went to great lengths to keep it hidden, but now we couldn't do anything but watch as those women were stripped and then taken away in tears."

Kat's own tears soaked my shoulder, now.

"We did *nothing*. We just watched them leave in silence. Our friends." Another sob escaped Kat.

I turned so that I could pull her into a hug, and I let her cry on my chest. I stroked her hair and waited.

Her words were muddled with her sobs now. "After that, we all tried to stop eating, but when we did, they force-fed us. If they couldn't force-feed us, they beat us. All I could do was hope that my cycle wouldn't return. A few more months went by, and my luck held. By this point, though, half of the women had started bleeding and were taken away. Before I knew it, six months had passed. After their weekly bleeding check, they informed us that we were free to go. They kicked us out onto the street with just the clothes on our backs and nothing else. We hadn't even seen the city, and we had no idea where we were or where we were supposed to go. It was then that Cass approached us. She knew right away where we had just come from. She offered us food and shelter. She had been rescuing women like us for a long time. A huge network of women all over the city are dedicated to helping each other. They take in the women who are kicked out and the women who are forced to breed and bear children without any help from the men."

Kat shook her head. "They rape the women until they are pregnant, and then they kick them out on the streets to fend for themselves and raise an unwanted child alone. It's unforgivable."

"After Cass took me in, I spent a lot of time painting. It was the only way to keep myself from falling so far into the horrors we all faced. Finally, I told Cass I wanted to do more than just take women in and give them a place to live and food to eat. I wanted to start a rebellion. I wanted the women to learn how to fight back. Of course, It wasn't that easy. It took time to convince the women to start gathering to discuss how we should move forward."

Kat paused and let out another long breath, steadying her words. "It hasn't been easy. Our ultimate decision was to find a way to escape Tarraco together. We had been preparing to leave, but then you showed up, and now our plans need to change again." She sighed.

"Why do they need to change? You still have a place to go, even if it isn't where you originally thought it would be."

Kat looked at me for a long time before responding, and I could see the sadness in her expression. "It's too dangerous. You expose us. Your *gift*, as amazing as it is, leaves a perfect trail. We'll never be safe. All these women want is to become invisible to anyone who might hurt them again. No offense, but you put the spotlight right on us."

Her face fell, and she looked as lost as I felt. "Willow, I just don't know what to do. You're a wonderful gift to this world. You have an amazing ability to heal what is so very broken with this Earth, but at the same time . . . we're all scared." She shook her head again. "Cass means no harm. She's just worried that you'll expose us and everything we worked so hard for, mainly the trust of these women."

"I'm sorry," I whispered.

"Willow, I don't mean it like that. I'm just in a tough position right now."

"What can I do?"

"That's what we were discussing late last night. I met with the other leaders. Most want you to lay low. Stay hidden. I argued that that would greatly waste your talent and what you could offer. Cass suggested that you spend time researching and figuring out how to control your . . . powers?"

"I understand the fear and the hesitation. None of these people know me, so how could I ask them to trust me? On top of that, I don't even know the extent of what I can do, and controlling it?" I shrugged.

Relief washed over her face. "I would love for you to meet everyone, though. And I know they would love to meet you, too. In the meantime, I'll show you the library and introduce you to Circe."

I nodded, my mind still reeling from everything Kat had just told me.

Chapter Thirty-Seven

Willow

A few minutes later, we were out the door and snaking our way through the city, avoiding the major streets whenever possible. I noticed immediately that most women kept their heads down and avoided eye contact. The men, on the other hand, seemed to always be watching. It was as if they were waiting for something. A mistake. A reason to flaunt their power over us.

I followed Kat across the city. I noted our path so I could find my way without her, and as I noticed another side street, I almost ran straight into a tall man. I silently cursed myself, muttering "sorry" as I kept my head down and continued, picking up my pace to increase the distance between us.

"Willow?" A surprised voice called from behind me.

I stopped dead in my tracks, and Kat stopped ahead of me but didn't turn to face me. Instead, she turned toward a shop window and pretended to be interested in what was inside.

I slowly circled toward the man.

"I knew it was you!" said a cheery voice.

I trailed my eyes up to his face, and I must have looked completely shocked because he let out a short laugh. "It's good to see you too."

"Sorry, I just didn't expect to see . . . *you*," I responded, unable to keep the disbelief from my voice.

"I didn't expect to see you either, if that helps. I was sure you were dead, but I'm pleased you aren't," he added quickly, trying to sound less awkward.

I noticed Kat angled her body toward us, but she didn't move closer.

Marcus cocked his head to the side slightly, and I realized I hadn't said anything.

"Sorry, I'm just still in shock. Is there a place we can talk out of the way?"

"Yeah, of course. Follow me," he said and walked left down a small street.

As I passed Kat, she mouthed, "What are you doing!" I could tell she didn't trust him.

"I'll be fine," I mouthed back to her quickly before picking up my pace.

We didn't walk far before he stopped in front of a stone building with a door but no windows.

He looked around quickly before opening the door and waving me in.

As I crossed the threshold, a hand grabbed me and pulled me back out the door. Marcus turned his head in surprise but didn't make a move to stop them from taking me.

"What are you doing!" hissed Kat in my ear.

"Talking?" I responded, unsure of my motives or why I even asked to speak to him.

"Talking? Are you crazy! He's an Elite!" Kat released my arm, aware that Marcus was watching us. "How do you know him, Willow?"

"He was my boss at the lab. He came in right after you left."

She looked between us, and Marcus nodded in confirmation. He still didn't move.

"And you trust him?"

I shrugged. "I used to." I saw Marcus raise his eyebrows at that.

Kat sighed, then stepped aside, waving me in the door. "But I'm coming with you," she said as she stalked in after me, leaving no room for debate.

Marcus shut the door and turned on the lights.

"Welcome to my office," he said, laughing at our reaction.

His office was a dimly lit room filled with tables, and on those tables were countless computers. All of them were lit up and beeping away, no doubt running their programs without the help of any people.

"I thought you were working on food crops? That's what you were doing back in the city," I said, confused.

"I was, but that wasn't my main job. I got the food crop position after your previous boss disappeared." He looked sympathetically at Kat before continuing. "I didn't want the position initially, but they told me it was more to watch you, Willow, than to do anything else. I think they knew the food crops were a dead end."

Kat blinked at him, as surprised as I was.

"What do you mean, watch me?"

"My main job is to track people. I keep track of everyone, but I mostly keep an eye on the people they tell me to. I'm given a list of names and have to record their movements. They asked me to watch you. I was told to watch you long ago, but for some reason, they wanted me to keep tabs on you, in person, while you worked."

"Well, that's not creepy or anything," Kat said with a hint of sarcasm.

"Why me?" I asked him, ignoring Kat.

He looked between us before answering. "You have to know you were the best at your job, Willow. You created a larger crop yield than any other team in Coria. Double, if not triple, the amount anyone else could produce. The Elite wanted to know how and why. They wanted to know if you were hiding something."

"Wait, so you reported *all of* my movements to them? Since before you were my boss?" My panic rose with each revelation.

"Yes and no." He shrugged again.

I raised my eyebrows, waiting for him to continue.

He seemed to get the hint. "I didn't report *everything*. I gave my usual report of you going to work, home, and occasionally to Olivia's apartment."

"That's it? No *other* places?"

"No. I didn't feel it was necessary to report any of your other movements." The way he said it, I knew he was well aware of my trips to the library in the forbidden part of the city.

"Why?" I asked, completely dumbfounded.

A flush of color reached his cheeks, but he didn't answer me.

"Willow?" Marcus said carefully after a few moments. "How did you come to be with Liam?"

I must have looked startled because he continued, "I've been tracking him for years. He was at the top of my list. I had to give the most detailed reports about him. He's well-known with the Elite."

"Um, it was by accident," I responded, unsure how much I should reveal to him.

I could tell he knew I was not giving him the entire story, but he continued, "Listen, you were never supposed to be out there that day. I was supposed to keep you in my office, but with the chaos, I couldn't stop you. I even put an Elite tracker on you to make sure if you somehow slipped past me, you would be stopped before you reached the gates." He sounded almost sad, like everything that happened was his fault somehow.

It hit me then. The reason the soldiers called after us when we ran away from them.

"I didn't know that, but you must know I would never have left Olivia," I said softly.

"I know, but I still hoped I could've saved you from all that."

"Thank you. I mean it," I said, and I did. "But what would the Elite have done with me if I *had* stayed?"

Marcus grappled with something before he responded. "I would have kept you away from the worst of it."

I opened my mouth to ask what he meant, but Marcus changed the subject. "Is Olivia alive?"

I nodded once, still unwilling to give up more information than that. He seemed to understand because he didn't ask anything else about her.

"And Liam?"

Kat shook her head at me from behind him. She didn't want me to reveal anything else.

"I don't know," I said, and it was the truth for now. For all I knew, they could both be dead.

He nodded, but his brow furrowed.

"Why are they so interested in him?"

"I can't tell you much. There's a lot I don't know. But before I answer your question, can you answer one of mine?" he asked me carefully.

"I'll try."

"Why were you with him?" It was almost as if there was fear or panic in his voice.

"He saved us from the Claeg and led us out of danger. We split up just south of here," I said. None of it was a lie. Marcus looked away for a moment before answering my question. "He's dangerous, Willow. He's done a lot of bad things. Unspeakable things. I just wouldn't want him to hurt you."

I didn't react to his statement, so he added, "He was their crony. Always doing things for them without questioning. He has a lot of blood on his hands. I was asked to watch him because they feared he might turn on the Elite. Even though he followed orders, they didn't trust him. They know he's alive, you know. Even without the trackers, they know. They also know what he plans to do. Or rather, they think they do."

Liam was right. They were always one step ahead.

"Marcus, can I ask you a favor?"

I saw Kat behind him shaking her head and mouthing the word, "*No,*" but I ignored her.

"I'm in a bit of a . . . *situation* . . . and I'm wondering if there's any way you might be able to help me?"

"I'll try my best, but I cannot promise anything. I may be one of the *Elite*, but I don't rank very high on that list." He pointedly looked at Kat, who smirked back at him.

I chose my next words carefully. "I'm afraid they might be looking for me too. I don't think they know *who* they are looking for, but I need to know if they're tracking a person related to, well, *plants.*"

Marcus's eyes went wide.

"Shit," I responded.

"That's you?" He could barely get the words out.

I nodded. "Listen, can you possibly get them *off* my track somehow? Get them interested in a different location. I just need you to do that for a few weeks. I know it's asking *a lot*, but it's important." I was practically begging him.

"I can do that, but, Willow, if they find out it's you and know you're here, you'll be arrested. You're high on their list of most wanted. Along with Liam. Most people on that list are never seen after arrest." Concern filled his eyes.

"I won't get caught. I'll stay out of trouble."

Marcus's mouth twisted into a slight smirk.

"OK, OK, I'll *try* to stay out of trouble," I said sarcastically, rolling my eyes.

He laughed. "And I'll try my best to keep them off your trail."

I reached out and touched his arm. "Thank you, again. I mean it."

The color rose to his cheeks a second time. "It's good to see you, Willow." I could hear the sincerity in his voice.

I released his arm. "You too, Marcus. Tomorrow, I'll meet you here at the same time."

When we were a safe distance from Marcus's office, Kat turned to me. "What the *hell* were you thinking?"

"We need his help, Kat, and you know it. If I can keep them off my trail, it keeps everyone else safe. It buys us time to get everyone out of here."

"Yes, but can you trust him not to give you up?"

"He won't give me up," I said, and I truly believed every word of that.

"I mean, it's obvious he likes you. Let's hope that's enough," she said, and there was no sarcasm in her voice this time.

"Oh, and your boy, Liam, sounds like a real catch," she added, giving me a sideways glance.

"Yeah, you kind of have to warm up to him."

Kat laughed loudly and then clamped her hand over her mouth to silence it.

I smirked back at her, and she hit my arm, still smiling.

"We're still going to the library, right?" I finally asked her.

She grinned. "Would I deprive you of your favorite hobby?"

"You better not." And then we turned down one more alleyway and ran into a dead end with an old wooden door and an old brass handle.

Kat approached the door and knocked five times.

We both waited silently, and the door took a few minutes to creak open.

It was then that I was staring into familiar eyes. Eyes I had never seen but somehow knew.

Chapter Thirty-Eight

Liam

I didn't know how long I was asleep, but I woke to find the room mostly empty.

I sat up, probably too quickly, because the dizziness blacked out my vision for a second, and I had to brace myself to keep from falling off the cot.

"Easy there," Olivia chided.

I turned to face her and found her looking disgustingly dirty and smirking at me.

"What's with the shit-eating grin?" I asked, slightly annoyed at the headache forming in my head.

"Oh, you'll see soon enough." She winked. "Are you ready to move?"

"Ready as I'll ever be."

"Do you need to be carried out of here? Because I would need some help with that," she said, and there was no mocking or sarcasm in her words, only concern.

"No, I think I can manage." I swung my legs over the side of the bed and paused for a moment. It had been two days since I had moved my limbs, and I needed to get the blood moving again. I reached down and massaged my legs a bit.

"Did you notice what supplies they have? Do they have enough weapons?" I asked her.

"Ha! Enough? Absolutely not, but we're not helpless. Though we could really use you back to your old hot-headed self." She winked at me.

"I missed you too," I replied sarcastically.

She laughed, and then her face turned serious again as she watched me. "Can I help you?"

"I might need a steadying shoulder to get my balance once I stand up."

She came over and stood next to my cot. I reached out to grab her shoulder, and she hunched a little. I pulled up to stand and stayed there, letting the lightheadedness pass.

"The dizziness is the worst part."

"Well, that isn't surprising. You hit your head pretty hard. Multiple times, no doubt, and you lost a lot of blood. An entire human's worth of blood."

"Yeah, thanks for reminding me that I got the shit beat out of me."

"No problem. Just here to keep you humble," she said with a sarcastic smile.

I started walking slowly. Olivia stayed by my side in case I needed her for balance.

By the time we reached the stairs, I was beginning to feel sturdier. It took my eyes a moment to adjust to the light once we were outside, but, when they did, I noticed a fair amount of supplies strapped to people, dogs, and horses and shoved into the back of carts.

"More than I expected," I said to no one in particular. "Where to, doc?"

Her smile returned. "That cart over there." She pointed to a simple wooden cart pulled by a severely malnourished white horse. Every rib showed through his loose skin.

"Can that thing even pull me?"

"If you're being serious, then yes. He's stronger than he looks."

I walked up in front of the horse and slowly reached out my hand. I had seen horses before but had never been this close. He seemed to consider me before touching my outstretched hand with his nose. I stroked the top of it for a minute before walking around to his side and stroking his fur. He didn't object.

"He likes you. That's shocking, actually," Olivia said with a hint of humor.

"I'm more gentle than I look."

She scoffed as I walked around to the back of the cart and hopped in.

Olivia had prepared everything. There was a pack of bandages and herbs, a pack of food, and a canteen of water, along with blankets, a change of clothes, and a few weapons.

"Thank you," I said to her after assessing the cart.

"You're welcome." She stopped and stared at me for a few moments. "You seem to be a living contradiction."

I sighed. I knew exactly what she meant. Who I was. Who I *truly* was didn't align with many of the actions I had taken in the past.

"People here are in awe of what you did. But there are also rumors. It seems people have heard stories of you. No one can quite seem to figure out what the truth is. Many don't want you to come along.

Others feel we won't make it anywhere without you." She ran her hands through her dusty and blood-caked hair. "I'm not sure what to think. The things I've heard are not good, Liam. Not good at all. But what I know of you the last couple of weeks and what you have told us . . ." She shrugged.

"The rumors are probably true."

She raised her eyebrows at that.

I sighed again. "I did *a lot* of things that I'm not proud of. Both before I volunteered to fight and especially after I did. I was so broken and lost, I didn't think about my actions. I simply followed orders. I never questioned them, and I never denied them. I didn't feel like I deserved to live, and I didn't think I would survive very long anyway. It took me a long time to realize that I was wrong."

"The women?" she asked me hesitantly.

I was shocked that she would think so ill of me, and I'm sure it showed on my face. "All of that's a lie. I've never laid a hand on a woman without her consent. As for my men, well, it's true I didn't stop them, at least at first. As I said, there are many things I'm not proud of. I will spend a lifetime trying to make up for it all, and even then, it won't be enough."

It took Olivia a moment to respond. "I trust you. Willow trusts you. Just don't . . . don't blow it, OK? Willow *loves* you. And I'm starting to become rather used to having you around."

I couldn't help but smile at her response as she glanced awkwardly in my direction. I reached over and pulled her into a hug.

"Hugging is probably not our thing," she said, awkwardly pulling away from me, and I let out a short chuckle. "We should stick to a handshake or something. Also, I meant to thank you for the dagger-throwing lessons. I don't feel so helpless anymore."

"I'm happy to kick your ass anytime you want."

Olivia went to open her mouth, likely about to spew something sarcastic, when we were interrupted by Leeann.

"How're you feeling?" she asked me in a formal sort of tone.

"Better." Which was the truth, but I didn't think I'd be up to fighting standards for a few more days.

"Good." She assessed me. "We're ready to move out. I sent scouts out ahead of us. They left an hour ago. I'm going to lead the procession and place you in the rear." It wasn't a question. It was an order.

She then abruptly turned, shouted a few orders, and headed to the front of the group.

It wasn't long before the cart jerked forward, and we were heading south.

Back home.

The scouts returned with nothing important to report. They were replaced by new scouts who ran out ahead of the group.

"Shouldn't they be sending scouts behind us too?" Olivia asked, walking next to my cart.

"Yes, but I doubt they have the manpower. Leeann probably sent scouts out before we left and believes that there's no way anything could catch up to us in such a short time because they didn't find anything. She'll likely send scouts in all directions once we stop for the night. At least, that's what I would do."

Olivia nodded. "Still, it doesn't seem like enough."

"I agree, but she's doing what she can with what she has. She's covering the most likely scenarios. It's a smart move."

Olivia stared straight ahead, lost in thought.

We were silent for a while, scanning the horizon behind the procession of people and carts. Visibility wasn't great. The winds had picked up, and more dust kicked up into the air. Our tracks were wiped out the instant they were made. It was a good thing in case anyone was tracking us, but bad because we wouldn't know what was coming.

Eventually, Leeann made her way to our cart again. "Any ideas on where we can stop for the night? I'm afraid some of the injured are not faring so well."

"If I remember correctly, there's a rather-large rock outcropping about a half-mile southeast of here. It should be large enough for everyone and offer protection from the wind and the dust," I replied.

She shouted a few directions ahead to one of her men, then without looking at me, asked, "How're you faring?"

"Feeling better by the minute." I was still too weak to be useful to anyone, and my headache was my constant companion. I didn't tell her any of this, though, and Olivia eyed me warily.

"Good," was all she said.

"Leeann, we're sitting ducks without scouts on the rocks."

"I'll make sure there are scouts up high and facing all directions," she said tersely.

I simply nodded, though she still wasn't looking at me.

A few more moments went by, and then she inclined her head, picked up her pace, and made her way through the procession of people and supplies.

"Is that how most people talk to you?" Olivia asked, seriously.

"My superiors? Yes."

"Is she your superior?"

I didn't answer right away. "These are her people, not mine. Plus, as you said earlier, she probably doesn't know whether or not to believe the rumors about me. She's taking a huge risk. She's seen my skills firsthand and probably feels like she has no choice but to follow us, but I don't think she's happy about it. I don't think she trusts me at all."

Olivia sighed. "And *how* exactly do we earn her trust?"

"By sticking to our word. It's the only thing we can do."

"I don't think politics is my thing."

I huffed. "No shit."

She narrowed her gaze, but her smile gave her away.

Fifteen minutes went by, and the rocks began appearing to our right. They grew in size and number as we headed further south. They soon opened into a large area, and all the people and carts filed in.

Sticking to her word, Leeann sent scouts up on the rocks, scattering them in all directions. After everyone settled and the fires were lit, Leeann returned to us.

"The injured are not doing well. I'm afraid tomorrow will be slow-moving. We might not reach the community tomorrow as planned."

"I'll go see how I can help," Olivia interjected and was off before anyone could respond, Willow's bag of herbs in her hands.

Leeann watched her go in silence but didn't make a move to follow her or leave my side.

"Many rumors are floating around about you. I tend to ignore that nonsense, but some people are afraid. I don't want or need any explanation or testimony from you. I just want your word that you'll not lay a hand on any of them." She nodded toward a small group of women huddled beside a brightly glowing fire.

"You have my word." Defending myself with words would do nothing to convince anyone.

She paused to study my face, like she was trying to root out the truth, and we were silent for a while, watching the people prepare food and tend to the injured. I saw Olivia pulling out herbs, checking Willow's notes, and gently tending to the worst injuries. I could see the exhaustion in the slump of her shoulders, but she hid it well, always smiling and maintaining her sarcastic banter. A few of her patients laughed and smiled in return.

Leeann watched her people mill about, helping one another. She was stoic. Unmoveable. No one could deny that she was a good leader. Her people knew it, and they placed all of their trust in her decisions. I knew she had the final word on whether to trust me when the rumors began to spread. I needed to thank her for that one day.

"I'll leave you," Leann said a moment before Olivia strolled up to the cart.

Olivia tapped on the wood to get my attention. "Make sure you eat before you fall asleep."

I gave her a tired smile. "Thanks, doc."

"I think I'm getting the hang of these herbs," she said, exhausted too but beaming.

I winked at her as I swallowed a mouthful of dried meat.

We silently watched everyone settle in for the night. Some people were still eating, others were setting up their sleeping arrangements, others were chatting, some were laughing, but most were somber and exhausted. Beaten down from two brutal attacks and the losses they were feeling. It was always so much more than the physical exhaustion. This kind of life and loss sank deeper. It sank its teeth into your very soul.

Olivia finally broke our comfortable silence. "Tomorrow, we get a piece of her back." The light returned to her eyes as she said it.

"Yes." I didn't know why I sounded so sad. I didn't know why I felt so sad.

I was woken just before dawn by loud talking near my cart.

I slowly raised myself to sitting and peered over the cart's edge toward a group of people in deep conversation. I couldn't make out their words, but I could tell there was some disagreement. In the middle of the group was Leeann. She wasn't saying anything but silently considering everything that was said.

I knew it was not my place, but I slowly moved my body off the cart, glancing at Olivia, sound asleep beside me. I was careful not to wake her as my feet hit the ground. I steadied myself for a moment before walking over to the group.

As I neared them, a few caught sight of me and stopped talking.

"Please don't stop on my account," I said casually.

Some eyed me, and others ignored me and continued their discussion. They were discussing what the scouts had reported. Apparently, a rather large pack of Claeg were following our tracks from the north. The debate was whether we should find a place to hide ourselves or if we could risk moving quickly to get to the community before they caught up to us. That is if what I claimed about the plants and the Claeg was true.

I could tell not everyone believed me.

I listened. I didn't speak. I had already decided it was not my place to offer my opinion. Not yet anyway.

Suddenly, Leeann shifted her gaze to me. "What do you think? You seem to have the most experience with these creatures."

All eyes turned toward me.

"There are too many of us to be able to hide effectively. We'll be found," I said matter-of-factly. "And I'm too weak to defend everyone. As are the rest of the people here. We wouldn't survive a third fight."

"As I expected." She sounded conflicted.

Everyone was silent, waiting for her to make a decision.

"Get everything ready to move out. We leave at first light," she finally said, and everyone instantly moved to follow her command, sensing the urgency.

As some of the group passed me, a few of them mumbled about my statement and how I had any right even to have an opinion. I didn't blame them for their skepticism.

Once everyone dispersed, Leeann continued to stare off into the distance. I knew she was thinking about every possibility. "Do you think we can outrun them?"

"No." There was no need to sugarcoat it.

She nodded once, and then she was gone, offering help to whoever needed it.

I stood there for a moment, knowing I would be needed today, but unsure if my body would be up for the task.

I was lost in thought when I saw a small figure in my peripheral vision. I swiveled my head, and my eyes landed on Emilia. She was silent and staring at her feet. I knew she wanted to say something to me.

"Hi, Emilia," I said, offering her a smile and a chance to speak.

"Will you protect us?" She lifted her head toward the group of women I saw last night by the fire. The women I was supposed to stay away from.

"I can't promise anything, but I'll give my life trying to protect you. *All* of you. Do you believe that?"

She looked at me then, and I almost flinched under her piercing stare.

"I trust you," she said in a slightly stronger voice than before.

The truth was, I didn't know if I could keep my word, but I knew I'd die trying. They deserved a chance at a better life. Maybe we all did.

Without another word, Emilia headed back to her group.

"Thank you," a quiet voice said behind me.

I turned to see Emilia's brother standing behind me. "She doesn't trust men, but for some reason, she trusts you, despite the rumors."

"I'll do my best not to lose that trust." It was all I could think of to say.

He nodded, then changed the subject. "I was the scout that found out we're being followed. There are a lot of them, Liam, and they're moving fast."

"I know." I hesitated. "I'm scared too."

He looked surprised at my answer.

"We can't hide everyone, though, and we certainly can't fight them under these circumstances. We have to try to outrun them. It's our only choice." I stopped temporarily and watched him. "You did well. We might all be dead if it weren't for you."

A bit of color reached his cheeks.

"Let's help everyone we can so we can get out of here as quickly as possible," I said.

He looked like he was about to say something but thought better of it because he turned and left me standing there.

I let out a large sigh before I turned and tried to make myself useful.

We were on the road within an hour. The conditions were no more favorable than yesterday, and I cursed the wind. The visibility was piss poor. I couldn't see more than a hundred feet in front or behind me.

We continued south, navigating by the sun that was barely visible through the dust. Somehow, we managed to stay together, and everyone seemed to know the urgency because our pace was faster than yesterday despite the injuries and exhaustion.

It was eerily silent as if everyone awaited the first scream. I kept my eyes and ears peeled behind us. I felt the tension in Olivia, who had decided to join me in the cart, keeping watch as well.

"I hate this place. I hated it the first time, and I still hate it. It seems to suck the life out of you." There was dread in her voice.

I remembered this place too. It was maddening, and the ominous silence stretched out before us.

Most of the day passed in the same way. Luckily, as sunset neared, the visibility improved slightly. The mood also improved, as we could now hear a few people chatting, and laughter drifted our way occasionally.

"I think we'll make it," Olivia said, and I could hear the hope in her voice.

I didn't say anything, too afraid to let myself hope.

Just then, Lucius came running up beside the cart with a wide smile. "We can see the community! It's just as you said it would be! Less than a mile to go!"

At the same moment, Olivia's face paled, and I knew what she saw.

I didn't even think. I grabbed my sword and a couple of daggers, strapping them to myself. I jumped from the cart and turned to face her one last time.

"Run!" I yelled. "Tell everyone to run!" Then I turned and sprinted toward the huge pack of Claeg, who were gaining on us rapidly.

"No! Liam! Stop!" I could hear her shout desperately behind me, but I didn't stop.

I only needed to buy them time. I didn't need to fight. I just needed to slow the Claeg down. I kept running, and I didn't think of the pain that was screaming for me to stop.

"Shit!" I heard Olivia scream behind me, but she listened because the next moment, I heard her barking directions as everyone's pace picked up, and I increased the distance between them and me.

There must have been over a hundred Claeg, and they were gaining on us faster than I expected. I stopped in my tracks, preparing myself and waiting for their onslaught. I only needed to distract them, get their focus on me, just long enough for everyone to reach the field of green ahead of us.

I closed my eyes, trying to regain my balance and vision. My head was still reeling from our earlier attack, and I wondered if I could avoid their blows for as long as I needed to.

I didn't have much time to think before they were on me. When the Claeg saw me, they slowed their pace. A few of them closest to me prepared to attack. I easily dodged their initial blows, slashing at their legs and feet. I made contact with a few of them, and they let out wails of anger and pain. Their roars drew the attention of more of them. The group slowed their pace even more.

I backtracked each time I dodged a blow. There was no way I could survive their onslaught for long, so I continued to retreat as slowly as possible.

I was somehow able to kill a few of them, but there were too many, and I had caught the attention of most of them now. I knew I would soon be surrounded, but I continued my retreat while sweeping down their line, slashing at their feet as I went.

It didn't take them long to realize what I was doing, and they changed their strategy. Their line began forming a semi-circle around me, trying to trap me in the middle.

I changed my strategy too, aiming for the opening in their line that was quickly closing. I slashed a few of them as I ran full speed toward it, willing my injured and tired body to keep going.

I barely made it through, and a sharp, cutting pain greeted me as I broke free from their line. I let out a roar as I continued as fast as I could toward the field and all the people racing for safety.

I felt the blood spilling down my leg, but I didn't dare look down. Leeann's people were just about to cross into the field, but they were still moving too slowly. I knew they wouldn't all make it unless I did something.

Olivia turned toward me, and I shouted, "Faster!"

She immediately focused on everyone before her, instructed a few people to drop their belongings, and pushed them faster. Everyone else seemed to catch on as the rest of the bags, boxes, and carts were abandoned.

I used the abandoned supplies to my advantage and led the pack of Claeg through the debris, grabbing what I could and hurling it toward them. Some lost their balance and tumbled to the ground, taking out a few others on their way down.

It wasn't much of an obstacle for them, as they were still gaining on us, but a few seconds could mean life or death, so I continued to haul supplies at them and tried to dodge their blows simultaneously.

As I grabbed another crate from the ground and continued my retreat, I looked up to find that most people had reached the field. I was now only a few hundred feet from Olivia and the remaining people. She was urging them forward as fast as she could, but I saw a few limping and unable to move any faster.

I hauled the crate behind me, and I heard it splinter against the head of a Claeg. I heard the body fall, and a few others tripped over it and tumbled to the ground.

There was nothing else I could do to slow them down, so I picked up my pace to reach Olivia. Some of the others were waiting in the field, encouraging us, while the rest retreated to the houses. Leeann was with Olivia, helping anyone she could.

I reached them a second later and yanked a limping teenager from Olivia's grip.

"Run!" I shouted at her, and for a split second, I didn't think she would obey me, but she suddenly turned and sprinted for the field.

I grabbed the injured teenager, hauled him onto my shoulders, and ran as fast as I could.

Leeann reached the field with a few of the remaining injured people, and they collapsed on the grass. Olivia was right behind them.

When she reached the field and turned toward me, I saw the fear on her face a split second before she screamed, "Liam!"

Only a few more steps, I told myself before I launched into the air. At the same time, my head collided with something solid, and everything went black.

Chapter Thirty-Nine

Willow

"I've been waiting for you," said a voice that sounded so ancient, it almost didn't sound real.

"Sorry we're late, Circe," Kat said behind me, but from the look on Circe's face, I wasn't so sure she was talking to Kat.

Circe opened the door to let us in. As I passed her, a shiver escaped down my spine. I tried my best not to let it show.

Circe slammed the door behind us, and I had to wait a moment for my eyes to adjust to the dark interior.

She led us down a hallway into a small sitting room with two red, velvet chairs and an elaborately carved red velvet couch. I saw the detailed carvings on the legs and arms as I approached. They were covered in intricate vining plants and flowers.

I couldn't stop staring at the carvings. Kat came over and explained, "Circe is quite the artist. She's been carving her entire life. Wood, stone, anything she can. Wait until you see the library shelves."

Kat made her way over to the kitchen, where Circe was boiling something that smelled like death. I wrinkled my nose as I caught another whiff of it.

It can't be the same.

And yet, the carvings looked identical to those in the house. But she'd been here over thirty years. Liam said the village was abandoned only five years ago. It didn't make sense. Something wasn't adding up.

"I hear you can make those come to life," Circe said behind me, and I almost fell over in surprise.

I caught myself and stood to face her. She shoved a bowl of the most awful-smelling soup into my hands and looked at me with those ancient eyes. I wanted to cower and hide from her stare but held my ground.

"Thank you."

She said nothing, clearly waiting for me to respond to her previous question.

"Oh, I don't think I can do that," I said awkwardly, stumbling over my words, "I can't seem to control what grows."

"Mmm," she responded, still staring at me as if waiting for me to say something else.

I shifted awkwardly on my feet.

Kat broke the uncomfortable silence. "I have to meet some of the women. Willow, I'll be back to get you in a couple of hours." She looked between the two of us. "Go easy on her, Circe, she's confused and lost. Just as we all are."

Circe nodded but didn't break her stare.

Kat gave us one more concerned glance before she turned and walked down the hallway. The door opened and shut before Circe said, "Why don't you try?" It was more of a command than a question.

I sat on the ground next to the couch and placed my hand on the vines encircling the legs. I tried to ignore Circe's piercing gaze as I closed my eyes and concentrated.

It took me a moment to calm myself enough to feel the Earth pulsing beneath me. Once I felt it, I asked the Earth, not with words, but with images, of what I wanted, and then I pulled.

Moments later, I felt the familiar rising of life to the surface. I opened my eyes to see what might be growing from that rising energy, and to my astonishment, the vines began to transform into living plants. Leaves unfurled, and small, red flowers bloomed. The entire couch seemed to come alive.

"What did you do differently?" Circe asked me. Her voice hadn't changed. She was clearly unimpressed.

I stumbled over my words again, "I—I don't know."

"Think."

I looked back at the vines that were now fully formed. I didn't know how long I studied them before finally answering her. "I asked. That was the only thing I did differently."

Circe nodded, clearly satisfied by my answer. "Follow me."

At the end of a second hallway was another wooden door. The door was also intricately carved, but this time, it had an eye at the center and a circular pattern spiraling out from it. It was eerily similar to the eye on the house's front door back in the small town.

Once inside, she closed the door behind me, pulled a metal bolt across it, then walked toward the back of the room. The room was dimly lit, with no windows or doors to the outside. It must have been her bedroom because a small bed was pushed against the far wall. Aside from the bed, there was not much in the room. Only some wooden crates whose contents I couldn't make out. Oddly enough, the room didn't have any of her carvings.

She waved me to the back corner and pushed aside the wooden crates. Beneath them was a small wooden hatch. She yanked on the handle, and the hatch sprung open. All I could see was a ladder leading down into the small opening in the floor.

She paused with the hatch open, waiting for me to descend the ladder. I opened my mouth to ask a question but then decided better of it. I peered down into the opening. It was black as night down there.

I stepped onto the ladder and when I reached the bottom, I moved out of the way and laid my hand on the wall beside me.

Circe descended the ladder a few seconds later, closing the hatch above her as she did, and we were both plunged into darkness.

When she reached the bottom, light suddenly appeared along the walls of the passageway, as if somehow the place itself was enchanted.

She stared past me and then walked further into the passageway. I decided now might not be the best time to ask her any questions.

We walked only a few hundred feet until the passageway opened into a large, cavernous room. The room lit up when Circe crossed the threshold, and lining every wall were shelves and shelves of books.

I forgot about the lights and was instantly drawn to the books. Kat was right about the shelves. They were beautifully carved, just as the legs of the couch were.

After a few moments of silence, studying the carvings and books on the shelves, I turned to Circe and asked, "Have you always lived here?"

She looked at me as though it was a dumb question. "No."

I refrained from asking my next question and instead turned my attention back to the books. She had books of all kinds. History, art, literature, science, the list went on. Some of the books were written in languages I had never heard of.

I grazed my hands over their leather bindings as I walked around. Circe didn't stop me, and she didn't say anything either. I took my time, pulling books out that sparked my interest and flipping through them as I would have back at the Coria City Library.

After a few minutes, or maybe more than that, I stopped at a particularly intricately carved shelf. It was different from the others. Instead of being carved with vines and plants, it was carved with two black snakes twisting around each other as if in an embrace. The scales on the carving seemed to shimmer and change with the light, making it seem as though the snakes were alive and moving.

I faced Circe, and she was still watching me. I wasn't sure what she wanted me to do or say. Suddenly, I remembered the journal. I shrugged the pack off my shoulders and let it fall to the ground, and then I crouched down and rifled through it.

"Cass wanted me to show you this journal I found. She said you might know who wrote it or where it came from," I said, standing up and handing it to her.

Before it reached her hands, I saw something shift in her expression. She turned the journal over, running her deeply wrinkled hands along the soft leather. "I haven't seen this for a very long time."

"You know it?" I asked her, surprised.

She looked up at me then, and I could see that her eyes had softened a bit. "Yes, I know it because I wrote it."

My mouth practically dropped to the floor.

"I suppose it's about time I tell you a little about my story," she said, and when I didn't respond, she moved to two chairs near the center of the room, and we both sat down.

"I was born a very long time ago. It was so long ago I can hardly remember how old I am. The world was not broken back then." She must have noted the look on my face because she quickly added, "You must suspend most of what you believe to be true if I am to continue with my tale."

I did the math in my head. That would make her over one hundred fifty years old. It was an impossible age, but the questions were too many to ask at this point, so I was resigned to continue listening.

"My mother named me Circe after the Greek enchantress who should have been a goddess. I think she knew what I was, even before I was born. I would not be surprised if my mother were a seer, but even before the world broke, it was dangerous to reveal such things. I was born into a living, albeit dying, world. Weather patterns were extreme. One year, we would be completely without water, and the next, we would be drowning in it. We had taken so much from our living Earth that she resigned to fight back. It became relentless. People lost their homes, livelihoods, and lives. Out of fear, people foolishly followed their city leaders, who claimed they could help those of us who suffered the most from the extreme weather. We were pushed into small cities and told exactly what to do. The fear kept everyone from questioning what was happening. Before we knew it, no one was left in the living world to help care for it. We watched from overcrowded cities as the world died around us." Circe paused for a moment, coughing lightly, and I waited patiently for her to continue.

Not many books were written during this period, so most of what Circe said was new to me.

"When I was a child, I studied plants. I would draw them, I would carve them, I would write about them. When I reached the age of fifteen, we were forced to move to the city. It was then, I realized something was different about me. When I walked into rooms, fires would roar to life, candles would randomly light, and lightbulbs would switch on in my presence. I couldn't control what was happening, and, at first, I didn't believe it was me. Afraid for my life, my mother kept me hidden from the outside world."

Circe shifted in her seat as if the story made her uncomfortable, but I refrained from saying anything, though I was dying to know more about her powers.

"I spent a lot of time trying to figure out what was happening to me. I snuck out of my room during the night and broke into bookstores and libraries in search of anything that might help. During this same time, the city's leaders declared war on information, and books were plucked from shelves and destroyed. For me, it was a race against time. Unsurprisingly, all books about magic, the healing properties of plants, stories of a living Earth, and certain histories disappeared." She let out another raspy cough.

I reached into my pack and handed her my bottle of water. She nodded her thanks before continuing.

"I religiously studied the books and came across a few that mentioned elemental Earth magic. These were not academic works, mind you. They were works of fiction that wove information about elemental magic into their stories. Despite my logical brain telling me I was silly to follow this information, I decided it was my best shot at discovering what was happening and how to control it. So, I began to write down everything I learned from those stories. I added my notes, observations, and personal experiments and tried to understand it all. That's what you see in the journal you brought back to me."

Suddenly, what I had been reading in her journal began to make more sense.

"Soon after I wrote that journal, I got into trouble. I got caught in a bookstore after dark, and when I was detained, I accidentally lit the entire building on fire. The fire allowed me to escape, but my parents knew it was just a matter of time before they discovered me, so they packed us up, and we escaped the city. That was just before they started putting trackers in everyone. We built our own community far from the city. It was at this time that I began to hone my craft and was able to control the fire. I used it to my advantage, running away to neighboring cities, starting fires as a distraction, and stealing supplies. We built our community on those stolen supplies. Everything was peaceful for a while. We lived happily in a beautiful house on a cliff. I spent my days carving the walls, the doors, the shelves. Whatever my parents would allow me to. That was also the time I fell in love with a boy. He shared my love of art and books and was unafraid of my fire. I was determined to spend the rest of my life with him." She stopped and looked past me to the bookshelf carved with the two snakes.

"We had many years together as we watched the world die around us. The house had a life of its own, and we held tight to the joy we made there. From what I gather, the house still has a life of its own." She chuckled lightly. "Whatever magic it was made with seems to still be burning."

My questions about the house bubbled up. The food. The lack of dust. The feeling of aliveness. All of it seemed so impossible, yet here she was talking about magic and admitting that the house seemed to be sentient. I opened my mouth to ask about it, but she continued.

"We had four children and watched our community grow. When our children were grown and had their own families, the peace ended. The cities ran out of resources and sent highly trained soldiers to raid neighboring areas. We saw it coming, though not quickly enough. We were a peaceful community and had no weapons to defend ourselves, so we sent out an alarm and got most of the people out of the community before the soldiers descended on us. I stayed with my husband, and my children refused to leave, so they sent their families with the evacuees and stayed to help. I had already decided to use my fire to protect us, but it wasn't enough." There was a hint of sadness, or maybe it was regret, in her eyes.

"I surrounded the community with fire, but bullets can pass through fire."

My heart dropped. I knew what had happened without her saying it, but she continued anyway.

"I told them to run, but they refused. I watched them fall. All of them. And I was resigned to fall with them. They were my family. I had nothing else to live for. I was shot in the back, and I blacked out, but I was spared for reasons I still do not know. I was taken to Tarraco and imprisoned for a very long time. When they deemed me too old to put up any sort of fight, they released me. I began my old habit of stealing books again and looking for my grandchildren. I heard nothing of them, and for a while, I had hoped they had gotten away safely. I know now that they were intercepted not far from here and shot on sight." She stopped her story and studied me.

I couldn't stop the tears that began to pour from my eyes.

"Girl, stop your tears. Do not pity me. I lived a good, long, happy life with them. Your tears will only get us found out."

"But I cried the other day, and nothing happened," I mumbled as I wiped my face with the end of my dress.

"Did you not hear of the old city wells suddenly running with water again?" She huffed, clearly annoyed at my lack of knowledge.

"I'm not finished with my story. I left the most important part for last." Her voice changed once again.

"What I discovered about my powers was that they are intimately tied to my emotions. Anger seems to be the strongest instigator of fire. The stronger the anger, the stronger the fire. Other emotions affect the details of it, but anger is the spark. We will start there," she said matter-of-factly.

"So, controlling my emotions controls my ability?"

"You can no more control your emotions than you can move a mountain. No, the goal is not to control your emotions but to channel them."

I raised my eyebrows at that.

"In my journal, you may have noticed drawings. Lines connecting various points. Those lines are channels of energy. They connect every living and non-living thing. Energy can be transferred or channeled into any object or living being. Emotions are energy, so they can be channeled, too."

Suddenly, it all began to make sense. The connection I could feel between myself and other people, the energy I felt rising from the Earth when I called it, my ability to call life to the surface . . . all of it.

Circe must have noticed something had clicked into place for me because she asked, "You've seen these channels, haven't you?"

I had no idea how she knew, but I nodded. "But why emotion? Why does emotion make it *stronger*?"

"I don't know for sure, but emotional states have always been linked to energy states and elements."

"Yes. Yes, like the energetics of plants and tissue states. It's why you use certain plants to heal certain conditions. Hot plants will only aggravate hot tissue states. Hot is also associated with anger and fire."

Circe nodded, encouraging me to continue.

"Water is associated with turbulent emotion, sadness, and tears, which is why it's amplified when I cry. The harder I cry, the stronger the water." I considered what earth might be associated with.

Circe still didn't interject.

"Earth must be associated with love, or pleasure."

Circe raised her eyebrows slightly, and the corner of her mouth kicked up for the first time into a smile.

I continued my train of thought. "My powers of earth are amplified when I'm with Liam. They're more than doubled, especially after . . . a night together."

Circe's smile remained, but she didn't speak or interrupt me.

"Anger, as you said, must be associated with fire."

Circe nodded again.

"Air. I can't quite figure that one out." I looked at her expectantly.

"Air is associated with using your voice, standing up for yourself, and your creative flow. The elements are controlled by more than one emotion. Many things can control them at once, though it's true that they respond more strongly to certain emotions. You can change the element's strength, purpose, direction, and composition by combining different emotional energies."

"But you said you can't control your emotions. You can only channel them. What does that mean?"

"Since you've discovered your power, has there been any time you were overwhelmed and unable to call on your power?"

"Yes. I believe it was fear that blocked it."

"And did you overcome that block?"

Suddenly, I knew where she was going with this.

"Yes. At one point, I used Olivia, Liam, and the Earth herself."

Circe nodded, then explained, "You used them as a channel. You used their emotional energy and channeled it for whatever purpose you needed it for. When your energy is blocked, you can use the energy from others, even the Earth herself or the rocks you sit upon. Everything has an energy you can channel. And you can, and most likely have already, channeled your emotions in the opposite direction."

My eyes widened. "When I felt Liam dying, I . . . I think I somehow sent energy to him. I don't know how I did, but I felt it moving outward."

Circe nodded, "Yes, exactly. Now, it's a matter of practicing when and where to channel that emotion. If you need to hide it, it's best to channel it into a non-living object, such as a rock, so it will pass unseen among mortals."

A question was still burning inside of me. I suspected the answer, but I feared it. "I know I can manipulate earth and water, but do you think I can also manipulate fire and air?"

Circe didn't answer me right away. "Earth and water seem to come easily to you. If you have fire and air abilities, something may be blocking them. We can explore that, but we need to make sure you can channel the energy safely and effectively."

I asked one final question, not really expecting an answer. "Why me?"

Circe sighed. "I don't know; that's something I have been studying since I've been here. The myths suggest you and I have Fae blood, so we can call the elements. Beyond that, there is no more explanation."

I remembered my Celtic mythology books and how drawn to them I felt, but I never expected there may have been some truth to them.

"And Liam? He seems almost inhuman. I suspect Kat has told you about him?"

Circe nodded again. "The Fae were not only a magical race, but they were godlike in their physique and movement. Many ancient people worshiped them as living gods."

"What happened to them?"

"They disappeared as the Earth began dying. Long before I was born. No one knows if they died or if they're simply waiting."

"Waiting for what?"

"For people to remember."

"Remember?"

"Them. How to care for the Earth." She shrugged.

We were silent for a few moments, and I was unsure how to process everything.

"Let's start with channeling energy into safe objects so that when the emotion hits, you can use it or disperse it safely," she said. Then, she launched into a series of simple directions for channeling my energy.

I practiced repeatedly until I felt I had a small grasp on it. Circe didn't say much beyond barking directions or giving her opinions on how I did. By the end of it, I was so exhausted I could barely stand.

"We'll stop here for the day," Circe finally said, and I let out a sigh of relief.

"Food. You need food," she said, standing up and walking toward the door.

I followed her through the passageway and up the ladder to her room. When we reached the sitting room, I collapsed on the couch. She shuffled into the kitchen and came back with the awful-smelling soup. This time, I didn't hesitate. I was too hungry to care what was in it.

By the time I finished eating, Kat knocked on the door. Before she took me back to her place, Circe called after me. "Practice tonight. Practice as much as you can. If the tears must fall, use a stone to absorb the energy of it."

I nodded, too tired to answer, and Kat gave me a questioning look. I waved my hand at her, letting her know I would explain later.

Chapter Forty

Liam

"Liam?" A familiar, hesitant voice woke me from my deep sleep.

I groaned, not wanting to open my eyes. My body felt significantly better, but my head pounded.

"Wake up." Olivia's voice was more demanding this time.

I groaned again and opened one eye, squinting up to find a concerned Olivia bent over me, her dark hair spilling all around her face.

"What?" I grunted, pushing myself up to sitting and finally opening my other eye.

Her hand flew at my shoulder, punching it hard.

"Ow, what was that for?" I asked, rubbing the place she'd hit.

"That's for almost dying and leaving me alone."

"I'm still here, aren't I?" I argued.

She huffed. "That's not the point, Liam. You can't throw yourself at a hundred Claeg, injured no less. It's reckless!"

I heard the desperation in her voice, and it threw me. Gone was her sarcasm, replaced by real fear.

I sighed, placing my hand over hers on the bed next to me. "I'm not going anywhere."

Olivia looked away from me and was silent for a long time, but she didn't pull her hand away.

The willow tree over the bed looked as though it had seen better days. The leaves were wilted, a few branches fallen and sprawled across the floor. Whatever magic Willow had given this place seemed to be fading.

Olivia pulled me out of my thoughts. "If we don't start caring for these, they'll die."

"How?" I asked, studying the wrinkled bark of the tree. It looked dry.

"I'm going to ask Emilia and her friends to help find the information we need to keep the plants alive. I know a bit about it from Willow, but not enough."

"Liv?"

She finally turned toward me, glancing down at my hand on hers, and then met my eyes. I could see the tears in hers. "What's really wrong?"

"It's tense, Liam. Really tense. It feels like we're walking a fine line between order and chaos. There's a lot of angry people."

"Fear will do that to people," I said calmly.

"Fear is all anyone's ever known," she whispered back.

I squeezed her hand. "Then let's show them something different."

A tear slipped from her dark eyes. "How?"

I gave her a weak smile. "Show them the life we had here, as fleeting as it was."

"No offense, but I think those big, burly men who hate your guts aren't gonna change colors overnight because of a few plants and books."

I laughed. "There she is."

Olivia finally smirked and I let out a long breath. One I hadn't realized I'd been holding.

"Are you well enough to meet with Leeann?" She changed the subject, reaching for the bandages on my arms.

"Yes."

Olivia looked skeptical, eyeing the bandage. "May I?"

I nodded.

I already knew what she'd find, but I let her pull the bandage off. Her surprised intake of breath was enough to prove what I already felt. That I was almost completely healed.

"How?" she whispered, tearing off the other bandages.

I yelped at the force as she uncovered every inch of me to find nothing but a few angry scars.

"I don't know. I'm starting to heal faster and faster lately."

"Was it Willow again?" she asked, scooping up the used bandages.

"I don't know." It was the truth. Whatever was happening was happening fast. It felt as though I was getting stronger every day, and injuries that used to plague me for months were gone within a day. I didn't know if it was me or Willow, or if perhaps it was both of us.

Olivia shook her head, assessing me as I stood and threw on a shirt.

"How come I don't get any of this special magic you two seem to have? Seems completely unfair." She pouted.

I laughed. "You want to go up against a hundred Claeg next time?"

"That's not the point," she grumbled, standing and following me to the door.

"Lead the way, doc," I said, sweeping my hands toward the hallway.

She rolled her eyes, but I could see her smile. "Your ego really couldn't get any bigger, and now you have some sort of godlike power. I hope Leeann roasts you." She hmphed as she stormed out the door.

I followed, chuckling.

Olivia was correct. The place was tense. Everyone had decided to camp out in the main house, too afraid to leave the safety of others. I didn't blame them, but many were already at each other's throats, and it had only been a day.

"We need a plan, and we need one quickly," I commented to Olivia as we passed an open doorway where two people argued about whose room it was.

"Told you. Chaos."

I grunted my agreement as we made our way to the front of the house. People were milling about, lost, confused, or downright angry. Some people greeted us. Others shot us condescending looks.

Olivia shook her head, disappointed. "You saved all our lives, and yet, that doesn't seem to earn you the thanks you deserve."

I glanced at her out of the corner of my eye, my mouth itching to smile.

"Of course, that went straight to your head." She sounded annoyed, but she rolled her eyes and smiled as we stopped in front of the sitting room doors. Angry voices filtered out into the hallway.

Olivia wrinkled her nose.

"Will you go find Lucius and Emilia for me?" I asked her.

Olivia gazed at the door and then back at me. She nodded once, and then took off toward the kitchen.

I didn't bother knocking, I knew no one would hear it anyway.

A few heads snapped in my direction as I entered, and the room fell silent a moment later. I saw Leeann's brief look of shock before she greeted me. "You're feeling better?"

"Good as new."

She furrowed her brow, taking a step toward me, sweeping her eyes from my head to my toes. Assessing me. "Impossible," she whispered under her breath.

"I know it seems that way." I shrugged, walking over to the table everyone was crowded around. No one moved as if they were frozen to the spot. Some looked at me curiously, others were clearly wary of me.

There was a large map in the center of the table. Everyone was huddled around it. The map was extremely detailed, mapping out every landmark from here to Tarraco.

"Impressive," I murmured, and instantly knew who'd made it as his cheeks darkened at the compliment.

"This is Keenan, our cartographer," Leeann introduced us.

I extended my hand, and he didn't hesitate as he clasped it. Keenan was tall and broad shouldered. He wore glasses and his dark hand practically swallowed mine. He reminded me of Marvin and looked more like a soldier than a cartographer, but his hands were smooth and uncalloused; I knew he hadn't seen much fighting in his life.

I smiled. "Good to meet you."

He returned the smile. "You too."

"We were discussing safety," Leeann cut in, as I dropped Keenan's hand.

I opened my mouth to speak as the door swung open again. Olivia walked in with Lucius and Emilia in tow. The latter looked a bit fearful and out of place. Lucius had a comforting hand on her shoulder.

Leeann shot me another surprised look.

"They can help," was all I offered in explanation, waving the three of them over.

Leeann sighed, then continued, "As I was saying, this house is our safest place. The houses in the valley are too far apart and too exposed. It's safest to keep everyone here for now."

Many of them nodded in agreement. Emilia and Lucius remained silent and still, as did Olivia.

"Some of the people here will be at each other's throats if they remain crammed in this house for much longer," I interjected, and everyone turned to stare at me. ·

I saw the frustration rising in Leeann, but I continued anyway. "Furthermore, these plants will die without our help. They're already starting to. I have no authority with your people, Leeann, but I have information about this place that might be helpful."

Leeann sighed and nodded her head, permitting me to continue.

"Olivia is the best person to ask about caring for the plants. The library also has information about them. I suggest anyone interested in the plants be put to work on caring for them before they're lost. It will keep many of your people busy and occupied and, therefore, less likely to be at each other's throats. Emilia"—I turned to her—"would you and your friends be willing to take care of the library? You all can be responsible for finding the information we need. No one will be permitted into or out of the library without your permission, and there will be no exceptions to that rule." I addressed the last part to everyone in the room.

Emilia's wide eyes were the only sign of surprise. "We would love to do that. Thank you."

When no one objected, I continued. "Other people should be put to work on getting the electric fence back up and working. This place runs on geothermal electricity, and I have already done extensive work on the system to get it working again. Small fence repairs are most likely the only effort needed. Anyone who has a propensity for getting into physical altercations should be sent to me. I'll train them and put their energy to better use. Scouts should be put in various locations around the cliffs above us. The cliffs offer an unobstructed view in every direction. We'll see an attack coming long before it reaches us. I've scouted the cliffs and will mark, on Keenan's map, where the best lookouts are located."

Keenan nodded his approval.

"We need cooks and people to tend to the injured, and if you have any people who are skilled in technology, I could use them to look at some equipment we found in storage." I paused, and everyone was still staring at me. Many of them looked shell-shocked.

"I'll be in charge of the injured, and I'll help Emilia and her friends on where to start with tending the plants," Olivia said, and she nodded in Emilia's direction.

Emilia inclined her head slightly.

"Lucius, I need you to get me a list of every person who is likely to create trouble," I told him.

Lucius nodded but remained silent.

Finally, Leeann spoke. "We'll follow your advice, Liam, but first, I think we all want to know what's going on."

I sighed, running my hands through my hair. I knew the questions were coming. I just didn't have the answers I knew they wanted.

"I wish I could tell you. I honestly don't know. I suspect Willow knows more now and could shed some light on the situation, but I can't. I know that doesn't help, and that's reason enough for you all not to trust me, but I have stuck to my word and will continue to do so."

No one said anything for a few moments. I felt the tension in the air as everyone waited for Leeann to say something.

"I trust you," said a small voice beside me, and everyone whipped their heads in her direction.

Emilia shrunk a little bit from their attention but held her ground. "I trust him," she said again, a little louder, and this time to the group.

No one spoke, but no one disagreed with her either. That was a start, at least.

Leeann sighed again, "We need more people."

"I know," I responded. "It might be time we start planning on reaching Willow and hoping she has a large group willing to join forces with us."

Olivia looked at me in surprise.

"Can you handle training, managing, *and* planning an escape for Willow and who knows how many other people?" Leeann asked me.

"He doesn't sleep," Olivia responded.

I shot her a seething look. She just grinned back innocently.

"We need to prioritize getting everyone settled and safe before we plan anything else, but I agree that we need to start thinking about getting your friend out of Tarraco. If she is who you say she is, and I'm very much starting to believe it, given this," Leeann said, motioning to the house and the plants and the living valley below, "then she's in danger there, and the longer we wait, the more likely she is to be imprisoned or harmed before we reach her."

Out of the corner of my eye, I saw a slight smile on Olivia's lips despite Leeann's warning about her safety.

"Liam, you will give Keenan the locations for the scouts, then you will make sure Emilia's women are settled and safe. After that I need you to explain the electricity and the fence to a few of my men so they can begin repairs. Then, you are free to train the dissenters. I wish you luck with that." Leeann gave me a slight look of concern and skepticism before wiping her face of emotion.

I inclined my head, acknowledging her command.

Leeann turned her attention to Olivia. "Olivia, once the injured are settled and stable, you can help Emilia's group get started with the library and the plants."

Olivia nodded.

"I'll see to the cooks, the sleeping arrangements, and the management of the supplies," Leeann added.

"Emilia's group is going to take this room," I told Leeann.

Emilia's mouth fell open, but I directed my attention to Leeann.

Leeann looked at me, likely deciding if it was worth arguing about. "We'll find another place to meet," she finally said, then addressed the group, "you're all dismissed."

Everyone glanced at me briefly before rushing out to accomplish their tasks.

I followed them, but Leeann grabbed my arm.

"There's a lot of hatred aimed at you, and for no good reason, in my opinion, but I have been unable to sway them," Leeann said quietly to me. Emilia was still standing next to me, and I could feel her shiver at Leeann's admission.

"I've always loved a challenge," I said, trying to lighten the mood.

She dropped my arm. "Just be careful." She turned and walked out of the room after the others.

I could see the fear in Emilia's eyes. "They frighten us."

I knew exactly who she was referring to. "I won't let them touch you."

Chapter Forty-One

Willow

I sat up and noticed the light just beginning to seep through the window. Kat was still fast asleep beside me in the small bed. I felt the warmth of her against my back. I carefully turned over and stared at the ceiling.

My thoughts drifted to Liam. Within the joy, there was also a profound sadness. A longing and an ache that wouldn't leave. It felt, now more than ever, as if a piece of me was missing.

When it all began to feel like too much to hold, I sat up, needing to get out of the cramped space and get some air. I slowly slid off the end of the bed, careful not to wake Kat. When my feet hit the floor, I glanced back at her.

It wasn't her that caught my attention, though. It was the color red. I stared, dumbfounded, at the small stain on the bed where I used to be.

Then, I felt it running down my leg, and it finally sank in.

"Kat," I whispered, leaning over to shake her gently.

Kat let out a quiet groan before reluctantly opening her eyes. "What is it?"

I pointed to the bed.

A gasp escaped her lips, and she instinctively clamped her hand over her mouth. She turned back toward me, and the surprise on her face slowly turned toward something resembling glee.

I narrowed my eyes.

"Despite the story I told you, this is good, Willow. It really is. It means we can heal. It means your plants help us to heal." She paused for a moment and then added, "We'll get you cleaned up, and no one will know."

Kat got out of bed, stripped the sheets, took my hand, and led me downstairs into the secret room behind the closet. She then proceeded to heat water, adding it to a small tub tucked in the corner of the room. When full, she instructed me to strip off my clothes and get in.

I let Kat care for me. I was too tired and too emotional to say anything. Kat seemed to understand this because she didn't say much and refrained from asking me any questions. I wondered if this was what the women here did for each other. How they supported and cared for one another despite the risk. Despite every horrible thing in this world.

After my bath, she gave me a new dress and some neatly folded cloth to add to my underwear to catch the blood.

"You'll need to change that every two hours or so. Before it's completely soaked through."

I nodded, still not wanting to say anything. Not knowing what to say.

Kat looked at me with some concern and then came over and wrapped her arms around me. I rested my head on her shoulder, and then the tears came spilling out of me.

She didn't speak, and we stayed that way for a long while.

When the tears stopped and I felt completely spent, Kat led me to the table.

"I'll make you some breakfast." She looked around the room thoughtfully.

"Do you think you could grow some plants for tea? Something that might help?" She sounded as if she didn't quite know whether it was a good idea.

"I could try."

I eased myself off the chair onto the dirt floor and considered how to grow what I needed. I was well aware of the plants that might be useful or helpful in this situation, but instead of asking for those plants, I decided to ask the Earth to send me what I needed.

I opened the channel, and it didn't take long for the energy to rise. When I felt it reach the surface, I opened my eyes to various plants beginning to grow and unfurl their leaves. I watched them in silence. Kat paused her cooking to watch, too.

When they finished growing, I collapsed among them, inhaling their scent, and whispered, "Thank you."

"They're beautiful," Kat said in wonder. "Do you know what plants these are?"

I nodded and pointed to each one. "That is motherwort, that one is mugwort, the one over there is yarrow, and this one in front of me is nettle. Don't touch her because she can give you a nasty sting. Over there is red raspberry, and this one is red clover. And that last one in the corner is rose. It seems she knows that on top of supporting my menstrual cycle, I might also need some heart healing. I'll gather some of the leaves and flowers to make tea. You should drink some, too. These are highly nutritional plants."

When breakfast was ready, we sat down, ate, and sipped our tea. Kat's eyes widened at the taste of the tea, and I smiled into my cup.

"Thank you," I said to her.

"For what?"

"For everything. For taking care of me. I feel much better."

She smiled, and I wanted to soak in this time with her. The time we had stolen from us. I wanted it all back, but the reality of our situation sunk in. We had a lot to do. "I should get to Circe's before meeting with Marcus."

She furrowed her brow, and I knew she was still worried about Marcus.

"You have to trust me. I know this sounds ridiculous, but I think I can feel it when someone is lying to me. Plus, I know him. I know he won't betray me."

"I know, I know. I just can't shake this feeling that he'll lead us down a path we don't want to take."

"We need his help. We need the Elite to look away from us. I don't think we can get everyone out without him."

"I know. I know," she said again, wiping the table and reaching for my empty plate.

"I would give my life before giving you all up." I didn't know why it came out so quietly.

She fell silent at that, her hand stopping. I could see the unshed tears glistening in her eyes. "I know you would. I'm afraid of that, and I don't want to lose you when I've finally found you again."

I couldn't take it back because it was the truth. All I could offer her was the simple truth. "I'm afraid too."

Kat left the dirty towel on the table and walked around until she stood before me. She was taller than me but not as tall as Olivia, so I had to crane my neck slightly to meet her eyes. "We'll succeed. We have to. We have no choice. There is no alternative but death."

It was a truth I didn't want to admit to myself, but now I couldn't deny it. There were only two options—we escaped, or we died. Escaping with everyone depended on many factors falling into place perfectly. Marcus keeping Elite eyes away from us, Liam surviving and finding help, Kat organizing and getting everything in place in time, and me keeping my powers hidden from curious gazes.

It seemed an impossible task.

Kat handed me a few more folded pieces of cloth, and I stuffed them into the pocket hidden in my dress. Then, we both walked up to the shop above.

Kat halted beside me, and I found her face suddenly drained of all color.

"What's wrong?" I asked, panic gripping me.

She pointed out the window in front of us.

"Shit!" I yelled. "How could I have been so careless?!"

Kat walked over to the door and opened it. The rain drifted softly inside, and the scent of the wet Earth wafted toward us. We both inhaled deeply without realizing it.

"It's beautiful, and smells divine," Kat said.

"Yes, but now they know I'm here."

"You don't know that." Again, her voice was calm and soothing, like she could read my thoughts. "You can't be expected to be perfect all the time. You're still human, after all. Well, at least, I think you are."

I didn't know what to expect when I knocked on Circe's door, but the scowl that greeted me was information enough.

When Circe slammed the door behind me, I somehow felt her anger, which felt like a burning inferno. It was the first time it hit me that this woman was truly powerful, and her flame could bite.

"I'm sorry. I wasn't thinking when the tears came." I already knew it was a weak excuse.

Circe didn't say anything, but her look was enough to make me shrink away from her. "If they didn't know you were here before, they certainly do now."

I swore the lights began to burn a little brighter.

"Follow me," she said, walking toward her bedroom and the library hidden below.

As we went through her room toward the secret hatch in the floor, I said to her back, "I started bleeding this morning for the first time."

Circe halted and slowly turned toward me, her face softening. She studied me for what felt like minutes before responding. "That explains the rain."

I must have looked confused, because she continued. "Your powers will ebb and flow with your cycle. Certain times within your cycle will increase your powers, and certain times will decrease them. There will be times when earth will be more powerful and times when water will be. Water is powerful while you bleed."

"This is all so confusing." I dropped my head into my hands, the tears threatening to fall again.

Circe walked over and gently put her hand on my shoulder. "You'll get the hang of it. You'll learn to live with the cycles. This is where the core of your power comes from. Do not forget that."

Circe directed her lessons toward my cycles and how I could use them to my advantage. She explained that water would be strongest while I bled, and earth would be strongest when I ovulated. If I had the powers of air and fire, air would be the strongest leading up to ovulation, and fire would be the strongest leading up to my bleeding. She explained that I could use these to my advantage, and I should not try to fight the cycles. Fighting would only lead to unintended consequences.

We also practiced channeling energy into stones, but she kept that lesson light as she sensed my lack of energy.

After a few hours of practice, we collapsed into the library chairs. Circe let out a loud exhale.

"Circe, may I ask you a question?" I was hesitant but didn't quite understand why.

She waited for me to continue.

"Why is that shelf carved differently from the others?" I asked, pointing to the shelf with the two entwined black snakes.

Circe didn't answer right away. Emotion bubbled up inside her. An emotion that felt like grief but older. Almost like it was ingrained into her very being. "I carved them to remind myself of the cycles of life, death, and rebirth. It gave me a little bit of solace after I lost my family to know that when one life ends, another begins. The snake represents fertility, healing, wisdom, and the cycles of death and rebirth. It felt important to carve them."

I nodded, not knowing how to respond.

"You need some hearty food before you leave," she said suddenly, getting up from her chair.

I didn't argue with her and followed her back to the kitchen.

"I brought you some herbs," I said when we reached the kitchen, pulling out the ones I grew earlier.

Circe carefully reached out and took them. She turned them over gently in her hands, studying each one. She then raised them to her nose and inhaled deeply.

She let out a long sigh, and I noticed a tear slip from the corner of her eye.

"Thank you," she said. "It has been a long time since I've held these plants. I never thought I would see them again. I'm honored." She bowed her head slightly.

I smiled at her, and she stared back at me for a long while. I didn't know what she was looking for.

"You're truly a gift to this world. I pray you never forget that." Her words were clipped and short, but their meaning hit their target, and my chest clenched at the weight sitting on my shoulders.

Circe returned to the simmering pot on the stove, unaware of what her words did to me. She carefully chose some herbs and tossed them in.

I fell onto the couch, suddenly overcome with exhaustion.

I didn't realize I had fallen asleep until Circe's hand gently woke me. She didn't say anything, just handed me a bowl. The soup seemed much more appetizing this time around. I happily downed it.

"I need to go meet with someone. May I see you tomorrow?" I asked her when I finished.

Circe nodded, a hint of a smile on her lips.

"Thank you," I said to her before opening the door and entering the city. I was greeted by a harsh and blinding sun. It looked like it had never rained, and I was glad of it.

I knocked on the door to Marcus's office, nervous.

Marcus opened the door carefully. His face changed from concerned to delighted when he saw that it was me.

I smiled back as I walked in, and he closed the door behind me. This time, he bolted the door.

"I was afraid you wouldn't come," he said, seemingly embarrassed by that revelation.

"Why wouldn't I come?"

He shrugged and walked over to his desk, but I didn't press him further. Instead, I got right to business. "Why are the Elite hunting Liam and I?" I didn't know if he knew the answer, but I needed to know if I was going to stay hidden.

Marcus paused for a moment, studying my face, and I realized I could feel his emotions shift with the mention of Liam's name. It was fear and something else I couldn't place.

Realizing that I could *feel* his emotions made me almost fall off the chair. Before this, I thought I was simply good at reading people, but now it was obvious that it was so much more than that. I could *feel* them almost as if they were my own.

"Are you alright?"

I waved off Marcus's concern, straightening myself and taking a deep breath.

Marcus eyed me with slight suspicion. "He's interested in using you and Liam to increase his power and influence over the people of Tarraco. If he can grow plants that will keep the people fed and relatively happy, a revolt against him is less likely. If he has Liam, he can build an army stronger than any seen in human history."

"And who is he?"

Marcus shifted in his seat, "He calls himself the emperor."

"He's building a new Roman empire." Here was the confirmation of what Liam told us and I suspected.

Marcus raised his eyebrows.

"The Roman empire was the longest-lasting empire in human history. Some say it was the most dominating empire. It changed, well, *everything*. But it had quite the downfall. Historians coined the term 'dark ages' to describe the time after the fall of the Roman empire," I explained.

Marcus looked at me with a hint of shock, and I could *feel* his confusion, which I tried to ignore.

"I suppose you know this from all of your visits to the forbidden part of the city?"

I nodded. "I have a bit of an obsession with reading," I explained with a grin.

He smiled back at me before saying, "The emperor got rid of most books."

"Easier to manipulate people if they have no idea they're being manipulated."

His brow furrowed slightly as he considered my words.

"Marcus," I finally said, and I could feel his heart skip a beat, "I need a way out. I need a way to escape, and not just me. A very large group of people is looking to leave Tarraco, and I want to help them do that."

I felt his surprise. I knew he was expecting that from me, but maybe he wasn't expecting it so soon.

"You can come with us," I added.

His heart skipped another beat, but before he could respond, I *felt* them coming, and I swiveled my head toward the door.

"What is it?" Marcus asked, just before there was a loud knock.

I felt Marcus's panic. The panic was not for himself, though. It was for me.

"Is there anywhere I can hide in here?" I whispered to him.

He shook his head. "This is a one-room office with only one way in and one way out."

"Were you expecting visitors?"

He shook his head again.

"Well, they don't seem very friendly."

His eyes held a question in them, and before I could explain there was a louder, more insistent knock.

"You better get that," I said, readying myself for the three people I knew were about to enter the room.

Marcus walked over to the door, and slowly slid the bolt free of the lock. He opened the door a crack, and he tensed. Fear washed over him, and it was almost too much for me to hold. I had no idea how to stop the flood of emotions coming from him.

Through the crack in the door, I heard Marcus say harshly, "What're you doing here?"

The voice that answered sounded disgustingly sadistic. "Did you miss us, techy?"

Marcus flinched.

"Let us in before we break down the door," another voice said, and there was violence in those words.

Marcus reluctantly obeyed.

The three men who walked through the door reminded me of Liam, except they felt wrong. Like they were twisted and broken and spit back out somehow. Like they were *made* to destroy. They reminded me of the Claeg, except, instead of purely an instinctual need to kill, they could also manipulate and control.

They didn't notice me right away, and I made sure to remain perfectly still and silent.

"What do you want?" Marcus asked them again.

"The emperor isn't happy with you. He wants to see you. He thinks you've been keeping some vital information from him," I could feel the fear twist and change within Marcus. It went from an immediate fear to a deep-seated one.

It was then that one of them spotted me.

"So . . ." the soldier said, walking toward me, "you *have* been keeping something from us."

Marcus wheeled around and stepped in front of the soldier walking toward me. The soldier stopped and glared at him.

"Pretty little thing isn't she?" a second one said, circling Marcus, coming closer. Marcus backed up slowly, keeping them in front of him.

"Mixing with the peasants, I see. *Tsk, Tsk*. Isn't that against the rules?" The first one asked, shaking his finger mockingly.

Marcus still didn't say anything as he came to stand next to me, so close that our arms touched.

"Maybe we should take her with us. Have a little fun of our own," one of them said, grinning savagely at the others.

"You won't touch her," Marcus said firmly, standing a little taller.

The soldier who just spoke got up into Marcus' face and spit. "Who's gonna stop us? You?" He let out a short huff of a laugh.

"Back off," I said, quickly pulling a dagger from the belt of my dress and pressing it firmly into his abdomen.

"Whoa, kitty has claws," he said sarcastically, and the other two laughed at his remark.

The soldier made a move to grab my wrist, but I yanked it free faster, making sure to angle the dagger up as I pulled away. The move sliced a gash in his wrist and hand, and he let out a gruff yelp. I saw and felt the anger rising in him.

"Put a leash on your pussy cat, Marcus, or we'll do it for you," he growled, clutching his hand to his chest.

"I will do no such thing. She's with me. As you seem so concerned with rules, might I remind you that you have no authority here? You're simply a messenger. Touch her, and I'll have you destroyed."

Their demeanors instantly changed, and they all took a step backward.

"You have delivered your message. Now get out," Marcus said in an equally savage voice to theirs.

They backed up toward the door, but their anger grew with each step.

Marcus followed them and opened the door, motioning for them to get the hell out.

They didn't say anything, but they obeyed. They had murder in their eyes as Marcus slammed the door shut and bolted it. His shoulders slumped, and he let out a sigh. I could feel his fear subside a bit, but it was still there. He ran his hands through his hair and stared at the floor.

"What can I do?" I practically begged him.

He shook his head, completely hopeless. "They'll report that you were with me. Those thugs will make sure I pay for what happened. They'll find you, Willow, and I don't know what I can do about it."

I walked over and placed my hand on his shoulder. He didn't flinch from my touch, but I felt something move within him.

"We don't have much time," I said. "We need to figure out how to get out of here. Both of us."

"I'll have to meet with the emperor tomorrow. I can't put it off longer than that. I can probably convince him that you're nothing. That you're a peasant girl that I found . . . appealing." Color rose to his cheeks. He looked at me apologetically. "Those men won't disagree with me. They're too dumb. You're dressed like a nobody, so they'll think you're a nobody." He paused again, cringing now.

"The problem is," he continued, "the emperor wants to see me. That means he suspects I've been withholding something. I can probably convince him otherwise and feed him misleading information that will keep him busy for a while. Even if that works, though, it won't work for long. It'll buy us a week or two, max. After that"—Marcus shrugged—"he has more forceful ways to get the truth out of me."

"So, we'll plan on one week and hope it's more like two," I said.

"I'll keep his dogs sniffing around far from here, but I don't know how long that will last. No new plants have popped up here, so they're suspicious. They have a feeling you're here."

"Well, the rain certainly didn't help." I was suddenly irritated at my mistake.

Marcus's eyes widened. "That was you?"

I nodded. "I suppose I forgot to mention that I can also manipulate water. I assumed you knew because I assumed *they* knew."

Marcus shook his head. "No, but you may be right in thinking that they now suspect it's related to you. If that's the case, we may have less time than I think. The meeting with the emperor should give me a good gauge of what they're thinking and how much time we have."

"I agree, time is no longer on our side. We need a plan to get us all out without raising suspicion."

Marcus stared at me thoughtfully. "I've been thinking about that. I think we can give them a reason to look in the opposite direction. A decoy of some sort. Then, we might be able to get everyone out relatively quickly and discreetly."

"You mean a decoy, as in plants?" I asked, anticipating his plan.

"I know it puts you in considerably more danger than everyone else, but I don't know if we have any other option."

I didn't hesitate. "I'll do it. Do you have a location in mind?"

Marcus suddenly looked and felt sad again, but he responded, "You plan to head south, correct?"

I nodded.

"There's an abandoned town just north of here. It's located up in the hills. There are many places to hide and avoid detection up there. If you can make it up there and leave a trail for them to follow, then hide out for a day or two before heading south again, I think we could distract enough of them to get everyone out. I can turn their gaze northward before you leave, and I can track their exact route, so you don't get caught in their path."

"I'll do it and make it back." I tried to reassure him. "But how are you going to get out?"

The look he gave me and the sadness in his heart made me realize he didn't believe he could make it out. "I have to stay here long enough to track all the soldiers. We're in trouble if they somehow catch on and head south before we suspect. I won't be able to leave until everyone is out, and even then, the window may be too small. They'll figure out what's happening, and they'll know it's me."

"That scenario can only exist *if* they discover they've been led astray. If I do my job well enough, they won't be heading back toward the city until you're long gone," I said, trying to sound hopeful.

"I fear that the sheer number of people that will suddenly be missing might tip them off."

"Then I create a large rainstorm to keep everyone inside for a day or two. So no one notices the lack of people until we're far away."

Marcus looked at me, contemplating what I just said.

"Willow?" he asked cautiously.

"Yeah?"

"I haven't asked this question because I'm afraid of what the answer might be, but now seems like an important time to ask." He took a deep breath. "*How* are you planning on supporting and protecting all of these people?"

I knew what he was afraid of, but if he was going to come with us, he needed to know.

"There's a community south of here, just a few days' walk. It has some basic security already in place and working electricity. Many resources are already there, and because of my last visit, it's now a thriving ecosystem, creating enough food for everyone. Liam and Olivia are collecting weapons, resources, and people to help us," I explained.

Marcus sighed, "And you trust him?"

"Yes. I cannot explain *how* I can trust him, but I do. I hope you can take my word for it."

He sighed again but didn't push it further.

I walked over and put my hand on his arm, looking up into his eyes. I felt the surprise at my touch, but he didn't move away.

"Thank you. Sincerely. I don't know what I would do without you." The color rose to his cheeks again, which I found somewhat endearing.

And then I felt something else. Something, or someone, much bigger approaching us.

My head turned toward the door and the knock that followed. "Shit."

Chapter Forty-Two

Liam

I spent the rest of the day giving Keenan the best locations for placing the scouts and then helping the women settle into their rooms. I didn't interact with any of them except Emilia. As I moved beds and other supplies into their room, I kept my head down. Most women avoided me entirely.

When I finished, I went to the makeshift infirmary set up in one of the larger bedrooms.

"How's everything going," I asked Olivia, who poured over Willow's herbal notes.

At my voice, Olivia gave me a tired smile. "It's going. Most people are recovering well, but two have made a turn for the worse, and I'm afraid I may be unable to help them. I need more herbs, but I don't know where to find them out there," she said, waving her hand toward the window.

"Didn't Willow leave that foraging book for us?"

She paused, thinking. "She did. I just have to remember where I put it."

"I can help you collect some of the herbs later. That might also give us the time to start figuring out how to get Willow out of the Tarraco."

A spark of hope and joy lit her eyes. "I would love nothing more than to spend the evening with you," she said with a wink and her usual sarcasm.

"In the meantime, do you have some time to head to the library and get the women started on their research?"

Olivia looked around the room at the injured people being tended to by a few volunteers. "Yes, I can be up there in a few minutes. I just need to give instructions to some volunteers before I leave."

I nodded. "I have to deal with the riffraff. I'll meet you in the library in two hours."

I saw the unease on her face as she stared at me.

"If I can handle a herd of Claeg, I can handle a few delinquents."

"The Claeg are one thing. Men with a chip on their shoulder is something else entirely. Just be careful."

"I'm always careful."

She rolled her eyes, but she was smiling as I walked out.

It took Lucius a while to collect all the men, but somehow he managed it. I saw the exhaustion and frustration on his face the second I walked into the kitchen. The men were all gathered at a few tables and looking at them made it obvious why the women were afraid of them. They were brooding and intimidating.

They were split into a few separate groups and didn't even pretend they liked each other. I instantly spotted each group's leader, and they were my main focus. The others were just the muscle.

I had dealt with many men like this, but the difference was that these men were not only violent and dangerous, they also wouldn't mind if I were dead, and I was sure they had discussed that topic extensively.

They all locked eyes on me as I approached the tables. Their anger and disgust were all aimed at me. My goal was to say as little as possible and stay the hell away until their anger settled.

Lucius let out a sigh of relief as I approached. I gave him a quick nod, dismissing him, before I faced the men. He didn't hesitate, getting up and rushing past me out of the kitchen. I heard a few of them snickering after him. I ignored all of it.

"As I'm sure you've heard, you are stuck training with me." Before any of them could comment, I added, "But I have no intention of following through with that. I've decided to let you train yourselves. I'll give you two days to form a collective group, choose a leader, and create a training program. If anyone gets severely injured or dies, or you fail to complete those three tasks, you will be stuck with me."

I didn't give them a chance to make any retort as I turned and walked out of the room. Surprised murmurs followed in my wake.

As I exited the kitchen, I almost ran straight into Leeann, dodging her at the last second.

She looked at me and then back through the door at the group of motley men in the kitchen, already beginning to argue with one another.

I shrugged. "I thought I would give them two days to see if they can organize and train themselves. I suspect they'll be at each other's throats in less than an hour. Better to make them think they have power and control."

She grinned. She actually grinned.

"I expect there'll be no more people added to the infirmary," she said firmly, but I could hear the amusement in her voice.

"No, ma'am," I responded with a smile and a wink.

She nodded, and her grin was still there when she left me, heading toward the library.

I slumped against the kitchen wall, staying out of sight, listening to the men and their endless arguments.

It didn't take long for things to escalate. I didn't expect the men to get along, but this was surprisingly fast. I sighed and stood, preparing to step between them to stop the brawling. Their screaming caught some people's attention, and they paused fleetingly, looking at the kitchen before looking at me. I gave them a reassuring nod and then waved them on.

I didn't move when I heard the first punch land, but I've known men like this long enough to know that it wouldn't end with just one punch. I waited, and it didn't take much longer before it was a full-out brawl, with everyone throwing punches in every direction.

I inhaled deeply before entering the room, slowly walking toward the mass of flying limbs and words. No one saw me. They were too involved in their brawl to notice anything other than their anger and the face of the person closest to them.

Without much thought, I grabbed a chair and snapped the leg off. I casually walked over to the edge of the group, and it took no more than a minute before most of them were lying on the ground, panting and staring up at me.

"I gave you two days. You didn't last one hour." I dropped the leg of the chair and stepped over some of them.

Most stared at me, dumbfounded. Some were writhing in pain and clutching broken bones or split lips.

"Get up," I said without looking at them.

Most rose, but some remained on the ground, seething. A few spit in my direction.

I gave the men a curt nod. "Wise choice," I said before lowering my gaze to the others. "Now, I'm going to say this slowly, and I'm only going to say it once"—I paused, looking at every one of the men still on the floor—"you either stand the hell up, or you leave this house, this community, this place, and you never come back. And if you refuse, I'll force you, which won't be fun for anyone."

I hadn't thought about what might happen if they *all* refused to stand.

Slowly, though, the men began to rise. I could see the baffled and angry looks of the men remaining on the floor. Not surprisingly, those were the leaders who had now just lost their muscle.

"My patience is running thin." I kept my voice sounding bored and walked over to pick up the leg of the chair again.

A few men flinched as I stood up, and a few more reluctantly stood. Now, there were only two remaining on the floor.

I walked over and stared down at them. "Is this your choice?"

Neither of them moved, but they didn't respond either. A few of their men behind me began to plead with them to stand. I didn't say anything, waiting for them to make their move.

After a few more moments, they both rose slowly, mouths twisted in identical sneers.

I ignored them and addressed the group. "You all have the new title of protectors. Your job will be to train in the military arts daily and protect this community with your life. I'll guide you through that training, but it's up to you to do the work. If you fail, this community falls, which will be on your shoulders. I'll meet you every morning in the front hall at sunrise. You have until the morning to tend to your wounds. However, you are not to take up the volunteers' time in the infirmary. Get what you need and tend to yourselves. I don't want to have to remind you what will happen if you disobey."

With that, I left them standing there, mouths open in shock.

I passed Leeann again on my way to the library. She didn't say anything, but her eyebrows rose. I gave her a quick nod, and she smiled before continuing with her duties.

When I reached the library door, I gave it a quiet knock and waited for a response. I heard footsteps approaching the door, and Olivia's voice gently giving directions.

The door opened, and Emilia's eyes stared back at me through the crack. She smiled quickly before opening it enough to let me pass.

"Are you sure it's OK I'm here?" I asked her as I tentatively passed through the door, and she shut it behind me.

Emilia nodded, still smiling.

"This place is incredible," she said, and I smiled back at her. I wasn't sure I had ever seen her smile.

"Olivia has been a great help in pointing us in the right direction. I'm afraid we may be slow to start, though. There are a lot of books we've never seen before, and the girls are busy looking through all of them," Emilia explained, her voice full of excitement.

"No rush," I told her, my eyes falling on Olivia.

"How's it going?" I asked Olivia as we approached.

She looked up from a book she was explaining to one of the girls, and, once again, there was exhaustion on her face, but she smiled. "It's going great."

I caught the girl next to Olivia looking at me tentatively as a bit of color rose to her cheeks.

"You need a break," I said, stating the obvious.

Olivia sighed, then stood up. "This one is great for basic plant care. It isn't specific, but it'll give you a good background knowledge," she said to the girl next to her, and the girl peeled her eyes away from me and back to Olivia. She gave a quick nod before grabbing the book, bowing her head in our direction, and walking over to a group of women sitting on the couch.

"I think you may have some admirers," Olivia said with a wink.

"You as well." I inclined my head toward a woman who couldn't seem to peel her eyes away from Olivia.

Olivia's cheeks turned pink. I didn't think I had ever seen her blush.

She saw my grin and sensed what I was about to say, so she quickly interjected. "Let's go," grabbing my arm and pulling me toward the library door.

I gave Emilia an apologetic look and a quick "thank you" as I was dragged out the door.

After it shut, Olivia said, "Don't say it."

"Say what?" I was grinning from ear to ear.

"Don't be a smartass," she responded, but she was grinning too.

We took the long way down to the valley, taking note of places that needed more care and ones that were thriving. Olivia added notes to a journal she had taken with her.

"What plants do you need most?" I asked her as we walked.

"Yarrow, echinacea, calendula, comfrey, and herbs with a high nutrient value." I could hear the exhaustion still lingering in her voice.

"Maybe first, we sit under the big oak tree by the creek?" I suggested. She sighed but didn't argue.

We lazily made our way down to the tree. Olivia picked some yarrow along the way, clearly able to identify it now. We didn't talk. Both of us needed the silence, I suspected.

When we reached the tree, Olivia plopped down at the base of it and leaned her back against the broad trunk. We breathed in the scent of the earth around us, and I could see Olivia's shoulders slacken. Still, I said nothing.

Eventually, she pulled her pack close to her and took out Willow's foraging book. She flipped through it, marking a few pages.

"How can I help you?" I finally asked her.

"I just want Willow back." She looked northward as if she could see her. "I take it you at least have a slight idea of how we might get her back?"

I nodded. "But it will take some pieces falling into place."

"You mean those men?" she asked, unease in her voice.

"I don't need all of them," I told her, trying to sound hopeful, "but I can't do it alone, and I can't keep this place protected while I'm gone without them."

"I'm going too," she said after a few moments of silent contemplation.

I didn't try to argue with her. I knew it would be pointless.

"How long?" she asked.

"A week or two at best. It depends on how things go with the training. I have no idea what skills they possess besides brute strength and a whole lot of anger."

"Men," she said, shaking her head.

I raised a brow, and a small smile tugged on the corner of her mouth.

"I just want to sleep for an entire week," she said, sounding exhausted again.

"I know. Me too." It was all I could think of to say to her.

She eyed me wearily for a moment before standing up and holding out her hand. I stared at her hand for a moment before taking it.

"Let's find what we're looking for and get back to work," she said with slightly more determination.

We spent the next two hours before sunset finding and gathering the plants Olivia needed for the infirmary. When Olivia was satisfied with what she had collected, we slowly made our way back to the house, admiring the setting sun, the sound of the waterfall, and the scent of the plants.

It was nearly dark when we reached the door.

"I need to get these plants to the infirmary," Olivia announced.

I grabbed her arm. "You're eating first," I said, leaving no room for argument.

She didn't bite back, so I gently led her to the kitchen.

We walked over to the stove, and she handed some nettles to the cook. I knew she wanted to cook, I could see it in her eyes, but was too tired to add anything else to her list. After things settled down, I hoped she'd have the opportunity to do it again.

I pulled out a chair for her before finding my seat. She dropped her head into her arms on the table, and I let her doze for a few minutes while the food was prepared.

I took my time looking around the room at the various people gathered. The mood seemed better than it had this morning, but some men still glared at me from their tables.

I sighed at the work that would need to be done to unify them, and I turned my attention back to Olivia, who was now, very clearly, asleep in her chair.

"Excuse me?" said a tentative voice behind me.

I turned slowly, and the girl from the library was standing behind me. A rush of color reached her cheeks, and she quickly looked down at the floor. She had come alone.

"How can I help you?" I quietly asked her.

"No one told me to come. I came on my own," she explained, slightly panicked and still looking at the ground.

"I won't tell anyone."

She looked up at me, the color still bright on her cheeks. "I was wondering," she paused, taking a breath, before continuing, "if maybe you could also train some of us?"

I held back my surprise at her question. "I can do that."

A small smile appeared. "I thought maybe it would help us feel . . . less afraid."

"Are there more women interested?"

She didn't say anything immediately, and I waited.

"I don't know." She sounded almost embarrassed.

"That's OK. Even if it's just you, I would be honored to help however I can."

The color on her cheeks turned brighter. "Thank you."

"Why don't you ask some of the other women, and I'll meet you in the library after lunch tomorrow?" I suggested.

I saw the growing excitement in her face before she turned and headed out of the kitchen.

I watched her go.

Before I could get up to retrieve food, a hand reached around and placed a bowl of soup in front of me. I twisted in my chair and found Leeann staring down at me.

She gave me a small smile before walking around the table, carefully putting a bowl of soup in front of Olivia, who was still asleep, and sitting beside me.

"I just wanted to say thank you," she said, the authority in her voice softening a bit.

I took a bite of the soup, waiting for what I knew was coming.

"Before you make any plans for your trip to Tarraco, I wanted to give you some information that might be useful," she said, looking at Olivia.

"She needs sleep," I explained, and Leeann nodded.

"There's one main gate, which, as far as anyone can tell, is the only way in or out. The walls are unscalable, and please don't ask me how I know that. There are four to six guards at the gate and four to six snipers on top of the wall by the gate. There are papers you need for entering the city. Before our attack, we participated in regular trade with Tarraco, and a few of our merchants have papers that allowed them to enter." She ran her hands through her hair, a nervous look forming on her face. "I'm afraid those papers won't work anymore."

I raised my brows.

"I have a sneaking suspicion that Tarraco orchestrated the attack on our village. I have no proof, obviously, but the more I think about it, the more obvious it becomes. That being said, I don't know if you would be welcomed into the city using our papers."

"Do we have any other options?"

She sighed, and suddenly, I could hear the exhaustion in her voice too. "No."

"Do we have anything of real value to them that we might use if the papers fail us?"

She took a few moments to respond. "I see where you're going with this. I have a few ideas. I'll see what I can come up with." She paused. "Are they going to recognize you?"

"Unlikely the guards will, but there are people in the city that will."

She nodded, contemplating what I had just said. "This seems like more risk than it's worth."

"I'll take precautions to make sure I . . . we," I said, looking over at Olivia, "get out safely if things don't go well at the gate."

"I trust your decisions," she said before rising from her chair. "I'll see to the trade goods I can offer them and will secure the papers. Is there anything else you need from me?"

I shook my head. "Is there anything else you need from me?"

She stared at me for a few moments. "You already have, and are, doing more than enough." With that, she turned and left me with an empty bowl of soup and a friend still fast asleep in her chair.

Chapter Forty-Three

Willow

Marcus gave me a panicked look, temporarily frozen in place.

"Were you expecting anyone else?" I asked, though I already knew the answer from the look on his face.

Marcus shook his head and finally looked away from me. "But I think I know who it is, based on your reaction."

With shaking hands, he finally moved toward the door and cracked it.

"Getting into arguments with my men now, are we?" The man's voice sounded oddly soft with a hint of amusement.

"They stuck their noses where they didn't belong," Marcus replied, opening the door wider for the man on the other side before adding, "Captain."

My heart skipped a beat at the title, but a moment later, a huge man I didn't recognize stepped through the door and scanned the room until his eyes landed on me.

Marcus had relaxed significantly, which I noticed with some intrigue as the captain smiled brightly at me. The corners of his eyes crinkled as he did, and suddenly, I didn't feel like I was in the presence of a ruthless warrior, but instead, a big teddy bear. He was the largest man I'd ever seen, but somehow, his edges were soft and his eyes sympathetic.

"Who do we have here?" he asked, stepping toward me.

Out of instinct, I stepped back, and the captain instantly stopped, his grin almost disappearing.

"Did my men attack you?" I sensed anger in his question.

I kept my voice steady as I held his stare. "They tried."

His mouth kicked up into a grin again. "It was you who gave him that nasty slash across his hand, wasn't it?"

I nodded, and the captain's smile only grew. "I'm sure he deserved it. It's a shame, though. It's his fighting hand. He'll be no use to me now."

The captain didn't seem too torn up over it.

When I said nothing, he continued. "I'm Marvin. Captain of the military here."

He waited for me to introduce myself, but I remained silent.

He eyed me with a slight smirk still on his lips before he turned and addressed Marcus. "I came to warn you that whatever you have planned to say to the emperor, you better make it twice as good. He won't be happy with anything less than hard evidence."

Marcus's eyes darted to me briefly before returning to the captain. "I have a new lead." His voice did not indicate the fear I felt in him, lingering just below the surface.

The captain didn't miss a beat as his eyes met mine again. "That's good to hear."

I could tell he knew something was up, but he didn't question or demand any answers. His next question to Marcus made my heart stop completely.

"Any news on Liam?"

Marcus couldn't help his wandering eyes once again, and this time, his eyes landed on me and held as he replied to the captain, "No news, I'm sorry."

I hadn't realized I wasn't breathing, but when Marvin looked at me again, I sucked in a deep breath, bracing myself for the question I knew was coming.

"You know Liam?"

I don't know what possessed me; maybe it was his gentle demeanor or concern for Liam, but I suddenly blurted, "He's alive. Or, he was a few days ago."

Marvin visibly relaxed, dropping his shoulders. He seemed so relieved I almost started crying, but his warm smile stopped me.

"A woman who knows how to conceal and use a dagger. I knew either you're one of the bravest or dumbest women alive, or Liam taught you. I suspect it may be a little of both." He gave me a wink.

I smiled back at him. "He was a good teacher."

"Good. I'm glad. Looks like maybe he's doing something more valuable with his time." His tone held a hint of mischief, and I suddenly wondered if my feelings for Liam were also written all over my face.

I shifted my gaze to Marcus, who paled. In fact, he looked horrified.

"I won't ask for details. I wouldn't want to be the one to get him caught. I'm just glad he's alive. Too many forces have been sent after him. I wouldn't want to make that worse. I take it you've been with him since Coria?"

I nodded.

He looked both relieved and mortified by my confirmation. "Then you've been involved in the Claeg attacks against him?"

My eyes widened. We had suspected as much, but to hear it confirmed still sent a shockwave through me.

"Yes." It came out squeaky, and I cleared my throat. "How? How can they control the Claeg like that."

Marvin looked like he shouldn't tell me or more like he didn't *want* to. "The general gives them villages to raid. He feeds them, essentially."

None of that was a surprise. Liam suspected it. He'd seen the villages with people served up to the Claeg, but it still twisted my gut; innocent lives served as pet food to monsters.

"They sent a hundred at him the last time," Marvin commented.

My eyes shot to him, and panic gripped me. "When?"

"Two days ago."

"No. No. No." I felt like I was going to pass out.

Marvin took two giant steps and was instantly at my side, putting a steadying arm under my elbow.

"I take it you weren't there?" His voice was quiet. Almost comforting.

I shook my head. A hundred Claeg against only Liam and Olivia without my help. They'd never make it out of that alive.

Marvin must have read my face. "They attacked a village on the edge of collapse. We don't know if anyone survived, but he wasn't alone. There were still survivors to help him, and knowing Liam, he got out of there in one piece."

"And you can't do anything to stop them?"

Marvin dropped my arm, taking a step away from me. "I've tried. I've told the general they are going to kill him accidentally, but he won't listen. The general is trying to herd him here. He knows Liam won't come willingly, and he knows Liam won't get himself caught. Liam would kill every soldier before allowing anyone to touch him."

"They're right, but what kind of logic is that? To send more and more Claeg after him?"

"Shitty logic, if you ask me. He's done with all this. He'd rather die than allow them to manipulate him anymore. I saw it in his eyes when he left."

Now, I could really see the sadness in Marvin's eyes. I saw how much it was killing him not to be able to help Liam.

"You're friends?" I don't know why I asked. The answer was obvious.

Marvin laughed almost self-consciously. "I'm not sure he considers me a friend, but he's gotten me through some very tough spots, so I'd consider him my friend."

I gave Marvin a weak smile. "We're going to get him back." I sounded far more confident than I felt.

Marvin looked skeptical, but there was hope in his words. "I cannot help you much because I'm being watched as closely as Marcus is, but I'll do what I can."

I don't know why, but I stepped forward and wrapped the man in a hug. My arms barely made it around his waist.

Marvin tensed but then laughed before wrapping his arms around me in return. If my arms barely made it around him, his arms could have wrapped around me twice.

"Please tell me you have a really good plan," he whispered into my hair.

I pulled away enough to look at him. "It's not perfect, but it's going to work. It has to."

I reached into my pocket, rummaging through the stones Circe made me carry around, the vial of seeds, and extra pieces of cloth for my cycle before I felt the familiar crinkle of paper. I pulled it out, stepping back from Marvin and holding it out to him.

"What's that?" Marvin asked, hesitantly reaching for it.

"It's Liam's vision for what this world could be. What it should be." It was the truth. I'd saved the picture. The one he loved so much. The one that depicted a field of flowers and blooming trees. Lavender and rosemary flowers dotted the picture with purple, while the pomegranate trees bloomed with large crimson blossoms. Citrus trees were sprinkled with small white flowers, and poppies bloomed beneath their branches in colors that ranged from orange to red. The entire Earth was sprinkled with color.

One day, when I could control what grew, I would give him this vision and so much more.

Marvin unfolded the paper and stared down at the picture. His brow wrinkled, but he didn't look shocked at what he found.

"I saw something like this. That man. One of the Forgotten who was apprehended right before the . . ." He trailed off and didn't finish the sentence. "He had a book. A book just like this picture."

I couldn't help the tear that slid free as I nodded. "That was my fault. His death was my fault."

"You. You are who Liam found that day. The person he couldn't turn in. You were his last straw. You were the reason he left." His voice held a hint of awe as he looked at me for a few moments before his voice changed. "His death was not your fault. It was ours for allowing someone to be murdered for possessing something as innocent as a book." His voice sounded like it might crack, like he might also break.

"I have to ask," Marvin said, tearing his gaze away from me and glancing back at Marcus. Marcus looked as if he already knew what he was going to ask. "How can you give him this?"

I knew I shouldn't tell him. I knew it was dangerous. For him and me. But if he was Liam's friend, then he deserved to know. He deserved to know what we were fighting for. What we could gain if we succeeded, but also what we could lose if we failed.

I closed my eyes, reaching for the Earth. The feeling of the Earth felt so familiar now, almost like an extension of myself, and, sure enough, the life pulsed just below the surface. I pulled gently, asking for one of the plants in the picture in Marvin's hand. A lavender plant.

When I opened my eyes, Marvin and Marcus were staring in shock at the green shoots sprouting from the dirt floor.

By the time the small purple flowers bloomed, the entire room smelled divine. The scent wrapped around us all like a blanket, soothing and comforting.

When Marvin finally pulled his eyes away from the lavender, his cheeks were wet. "How?"

"I don't know, but I do know that the Claeg die if they come into contact with plants. We are safe from them if we restore the Earth to its healthy and balanced state. If we create what's in that picture," I said, pointing to the picture now forgotten in his hand.

Marvin looked down at the picture and then the plant before finally meeting my eyes again. "I don't know how or why or . . ."—he struggled with his words—"but I . . . I want in. I want to help. I want this world too."

"Then we have to keep her protected." Marcus finally broke his silence, stepping to my side.

"I'll keep my men away from her. The soldiers won't be a problem."

"And I'll find a way out of this place. A way to keep the emperor's and the general's eyes away from it all," Marcus added.

I turned to Marvin. "There are around two hundred women and children I need to get out of here too."

Marvin's eyebrows rose. "Two hundred?"

"You know what they do to women here. That number can't be surprising. In fact, I wish it was more."

"Fuck." Marvin suddenly looked worried.

I placed a reassuring hand on his arm. "We have a plan."

He smiled down at me. "I do not doubt that if Liam is involved in any of this, things will work out exactly how he planned them."

"I'm not sure he expected me to take so many people with us. This may throw him for a loop."

"He may not expect it, but I'll bet he's prepared for it."

I sighed. "Let's hope so. More importantly, let's hope he's still alive."

"The sun is setting. I need to get Willow back," Marcus cut in, looking at his watch.

Marvin stepped away from me. "I need to get back to base. We'll be in contact."

Marcus and I both nodded as Marvin made his way to the door.

He stopped, his hand on the knob, and faced me one more time. "I knew. I knew there was something special about him, and it doesn't surprise me one bit that he found you. That you two found each other.

I really hope your plan works out, and I can play a role in it, no matter how small."

With that, he was out the door.

I continued to stare at the closed door, tears threatening, as I choked out, "You trust him?"

"About as much as I trust anyone in this city," Marcus replied, watching me intently.

I inhaled deeply. "Well, I guess we'll find out soon enough."

Chapter Forty-Four

Liam

The days became easier. We all fell into a routine that almost felt peaceful. Although Olivia didn't say anything, the cheeriness returned to her features. The dark circles under her eyes began to disappear, and her sarcastic smile seemed permanently plastered on her face.

"Do you need anything today?" I asked her at our usual breakfast table.

She shook her head with a mouthful of food in it.

"OK, then, I'm off to tame the beasts again," I said, standing up and grabbing my empty plate.

She gave me that sarcastic grin. "You make it sound so fun."

"Beating the shit out of them gives me some satisfaction, but I have to admit, you women are much more enjoyable to train." I gave her a devious smirk.

"I won't tell Willow you just said that." She winked, stuffing the last bite of food in her mouth.

"Thanks, real big of you," I replied, adding, "I'll see you after lunch in the library."

I'll give these men credit. They all showed up daily, on time, and *mostly* without complaint. Some of them had become true allies, but most still loathed me and wanted me dead.

As for the training, they were surprisingly talented, though they lacked discipline, and their conditioning needed work.

I remained a man of few words around them, only speaking when needed, and I rarely broke up any fights. Olivia mentioned that if they continued this way, she might have to kill them herself, as she had no room or time for them in the infirmary.

After my success in getting the men to show up, Lucius decided to join us. He was the most eager student, though his age and poor nutrition up until now had made it difficult for him to keep up. I would take the willing participant over the angry and talented one any day, though.

After a few days, I no longer needed to instruct the men. They had picked up the routine.

I observed them, noting the changes in behavior, allegiance, demeanor, and skill. The past few days had also dissolved most of their separate group allegiances. Which meant we were close to getting Willow back. I didn't want to even think about it, though, because the thought of not being able to get her back scared me more than anything. Without her, we had no chance. Even with what we'd been able to do here. Even with what *I'd* been able to do with these men in such a short time.

Training the women, however, was the only part of my day that didn't feel hard. It felt relaxed and easy. The way I hoped the entire community would feel like eventually.

Emilia greeted me at the door to the library, and with her were Olivia and Silvana, the girl who had convinced me to train them. None of the other women were willing to spend the afternoon with a man, especially not me. Though they no longer feared me, they still kept their distance.

I briefly caught them staring at me through the doorway as the three women grabbed their things and followed me out of the library. I gave them a small smile as I closed the door behind us.

"So, what are we learning today?" Silvana asked excitedly. She was easily a head taller than Emilia but seemed frailer somehow. She had jet-black hair that fell to her waist and eyes that seemed the same color as her hair. She was pale, with blood-red lips, but her most noticeable feature was the large white scar that crossed her lower lip and extended to her chin.

"How not to barf all over ourselves, probably," Olivia said sarcastically.

"Despite what you think, Olivia, my conditioning exercises are necessary for success in everything else."

Olivia didn't say anything but rolled her eyes instead.

"No one forced you to come," I said to her with a smile.

She rolled her eyes again, and I snickered lightly as we continued down the cliff to the training area.

When we arrived, the men were gone, having cleaned up their mess. It was just us.

I led the three women through a warm-up drill and then moved on to conditioning. Despite Olivia's sarcastic complaining, they had also improved significantly since starting to train a few days ago.

Having been on the run for so long and given her previous training with Willow, Olivia had the least trouble with the exercises. However, Emilia was shockingly talented at hand-to-hand combat. Her size allowed her to be quick, and she used it to her advantage. On the other hand, Silvana seemed incredibly out of place, but her determination was truly admirable.

The three made an odd team, but I would take them over the men any day.

"We're working on hand-to-hand combat again today," I explained as they finished their conditioning drills.

I heard their collective moan as I led them toward the center of the field.

"Emilia, will you help me demonstrate?"

She nodded, walking to stand in front of me.

"We're going to work on blocking today. Emilia, I want you to try to hit me."

She didn't hesitate before circling me, moving her feet and raising her fists. She threw a few punches, and I moved to block each one. After a minute or two, I stopped her and explained to all of them what I had done. They listened intently, and then I motioned for them to practice with each other. I stepped away, watching them carefully. I only interjected a few times to offer advice.

After an hour, I stopped them and dismissed them for the day. Emilia and Silvana thanked me before locking arms and returning to the house. Olivia lingered and waited for me to join her.

"You look tired, even for you," she told me.

I sighed but didn't respond.

"Are you meeting with Leeann tonight?"

I nodded.

"Have you chosen who's coming with us?"

I nodded again.

"We're leaving soon, then?"

"Two days."

Olivia's eyes widened, and a smile broke out on her lips.

When we reached the house, Olivia returned to the infirmary, and I went to Leeann's meeting room.

I knocked lightly on the door, and the cartographer, Keenan, opened it.

I nodded at him, and he nodded back in silent acknowledgment as I entered the room. Leeann was seated at her desk, and Keenan was the only other person there. Leeann had converted one of the smaller bedrooms into a working office. A desk was brought in, along with shelves, and a large table sat in the middle of the room. The table was full of maps and correspondences, and though the space was filled with things, Leeann had meticulously organized it all.

Without looking up from her desk, Leeann said, "You're dismissed, Keenan."

He made to leave, but I interjected. "Actually, I'd like him to stay."

Both of them looked at me with mild surprise.

"I have some tasks for him," I added.

"I take it, you've decided who you're taking with you?" Leeann asked.

"Olivia, Lucius, Cato, Emilia, Silvana, and Keenan here."

Keenan's mouth dropped open, but Leeann only responded, "Are you sure?" She didn't sound shocked at my choice, but nor did she sound confident in it.

"I'll take allegiance, intelligence, and collaboration over strength and skill any day," I said matter-of-factly.

Leeann looked thoughtful but replied, "I have the papers, supplies, and clothing ready."

"Thank you. I plan to leave in two days. I'll use tomorrow to prepare the others."

Leeann stood from the chair behind her desk, and I could see she was struggling with what she wanted to say to me. I waited.

"We haven't discussed what might happen if you don't return."

"The men are unified. They'll follow your orders. If I don't return, Cathal will replace me. You have the supplies, the information, and the technology to weather any storm. That being said, I *will* return."

She considered my statement for a few long moments, and though I could still see the concern in her eyes, she finally waved me out the door.

"Meet me in the kitchen in one hour," I told Keenan as I passed him.

He dipped his head slightly, as I entered the hallway and closed the door behind me.

I let out a big sigh as I headed to collect the others.

They were all surprised at my having selected them. Of all of them, I expected Silvana to say no, but she didn't. None refused, despite the danger.

I spent the evening explaining the plan, their roles, and various situations that may not go as planned. Olivia and I were the only ones entering the city, I explained. Keenan was in charge of getting us to and from the city undetected, as he knew and had studied every map of the area. Cato was our best sharpshooter, so I assigned him as our sniper in case we needed help. Lucius was our scout and spy in case we needed to make a hasty retreat. Emilia and Silvana were to be messengers between us, as they were the least likely to be suspected of being anything but helpless women.

Aside from the occasional nod or look of surprise, no one made a sound while I explained the plan to them. It took me well over an hour to map everything out.

My last instructions were to give them all a list of needed supplies, and then I dismissed them to begin their preparation.

After my dismissal, no one moved. They just stared at me.

Olivia looked around at them before her eyes landed on me again. "Liam? I think that maybe everyone is wondering *why* you chose them. Don't get me wrong, I love everyone in this group, but I don't think we seem like the obvious choice."

To be honest, I was expecting the question. "The main point is that you all *are not* the obvious choice. It's easier to remain under their radar that way. Second, you are all capable and good at your individual roles. Third, you are all able to work well with others, and lastly, and most importantly, I trust you all with my life." I scanned their faces, before adding, "The question you need to ask yourselves before you fully commit is if you feel the same way. If there is *any* doubt in your mind, don't come. Doubt will get you killed faster than anything else."

They didn't respond right away as they silently looked at each other.

I waited.

It was Emilia who spoke first. "There's no doubt. Because of you, there's no doubt in my mind anymore. I thank you for that." She bowed her head slightly.

One by one, the rest of them said a variation of the same, and then they rose from their chairs to prepare themselves for what was ahead.

Only Olivia remained seated with me.

"You ready?" she asked me.

"No, I never feel ready."

She gave me a knowing smile, and I knew she understood some of the weight I was carrying. "Get some rest. You need it the most." She stood and took the empty plate from in front of me.

I nodded but didn't reply, and as she walked over to deposit the plates in the sink, I headed toward Willow's . . . our . . . room.

Chapter Forty-Five

Willow

The next few days were a blur. Kat was constantly meeting with various groups of women, making sure everyone was prepared for the unexpected. I continued to meet with Marcus, making sure everything was on track, and making sure we wouldn't be blindsided. Marvin kept to his word, and there were no more incidents with the soldiers.

Marcus's meeting with the emperor went as expected. The emperor suspected that information was being withheld, Marcus assured him that wasn't true, and gave him evidence of new information. It seemed to pacify the emperor, as we had hoped it would.

I continued to meet with Circe, as well, and I started to feel as though I could *control* the energy now. The stones worked wonders, and I found that the energy I put into them could also be taken out of them. I spent the evenings practicing moving the energy around until it felt like second nature to me. I became more and more aware of energy channels, and I found I no longer had to think about them to access them. The web of channels seemed to grow and shift as if it were a living, breathing, entity. I found that the energy could be affected by almost anything, and it seemed to permeate everything, but what once felt like a tangled and confusing mess, seemed normal now.

As the day I was to leave for the north inched closer, Kat started to disappear more often and came to bed only rarely. Cass ignored me completely, and, besides Marcus, I didn't interact with anyone else.

Marcus had become a good friend, though I knew he wished we could be more. It wasn't a subject he had brought up, but I could feel it within him. I could also feel his fear growing as the days passed. Despite my reassurance, his fear didn't subside.

Amid all the chaos and planning, the thought that this was too easy clung to me. I couldn't shake the feeling that we were missing something. Everything had become too peaceful. Too calm.

"I need you to come meet the women today. After breakfast," Kat said through a mouthful of food, three days before I was set to leave.

I'd harvested most of the plants growing in the secret underground room, and those we hadn't already used were hanging along the walls. Their wilted leaves and petals left behind an earthy scent I was getting so used to that the streets suddenly smelled dead and barren.

I looked at her in surprise. "I thought Cass didn't want me meeting any of them? I thought you all wanted me to stay away. For everyone's safety?"

Kat put her food down and stared at me thoughtfully. "No one wants you to stay away, Willow. Cass was worried you wouldn't be able to control any of it and that it would give us away, but you've proven yourself. More than proven yourself. Plus, the women need to meet you. They need to know what we stand to gain by leaving."

"You want me to show them what I can do?"

A wide smile grew on her lips. "That's exactly what I want you to do."

The thought of what I'd show them grew in my mind, and a smile bloomed on my own lips in response to hers.

"We need to get more people out of the breeding building," one of the women shouted as I stood in the back corner of the secret meeting room.

I leaned against the wall, my arms crossed, observing everything. The women, the morale, their body language, how they reacted to Kat and their leaders. I sucked up all the information I could. Anything that might help us all escape Tarraco.

Kat was running a logistics meeting to review the plan Marcus and I had set up. Though it was my plan, these women still didn't know me, and given the looks shot my way, they didn't trust me either. Kat allowed me to come to the meetings now that I had better control of my powers, but it was obvious not everyone agreed with that decision.

Kat ran a dirty hand through her hair. "We can't. We're too close to escape. It's too risky."

"So, you're just going to leave this new group of women?" The woman asked incredulously.

Kat shook her head, looking conflicted.

Another woman's voice rang out somewhere across the room. "I'll do it. I'll take a small contingent of women with me. Any we can spare."

The woman's voice was familiar, and as the crowd parted slightly, I saw the young girl clutching her mother's hand and smiling up at her. Elise and Lily.

Kat shook her head. "I can't ask you to do that, Elise, not when you're already risking your life helping us all get out of here."

"You don't need me until the day we leave. I have time. Plus"—she paused, looking down at her daughter—"I need to do this."

My chest squeezed watching them, and Elise's silent confession.

"I'll go!" I shouted before I could stop myself.

Thirty-five heads all turned at once.

I cringed at the attention but cleared my voice. "I'll go," I repeated. "I'm handy with a bow and daggers."

No one could argue with that. Elise had seen me kill a soldier, and I'd told Kat about Liam's training. I was arguably better than most of the women here when it came to wielding weapons.

Kat shook her head but didn't argue. "Elise, you'll take Willow, me, and two other volunteers. We'll get as many out as we can."

I wanted to argue with Kat about coming with us, but the stern look she threw at me made me snap my mouth shut. Now wasn't the time to argue with her.

Elise nodded, but another familiar voice rang out before Kat could move on with the meeting.

"I'll be going, too."

Circe stood a few people away from me, a smirk plastered on her face.

"Circe," Kat began, but Circe held up a hand, silencing her.

"I've stood idle long enough. My fire will soon no longer be a secret. At least let me be a last resort if everything goes to shit."

She wasn't wrong, and I smiled at the old woman.

Kat looked like she wanted to argue, but Circe held her gaze, and I knew Kat would relent under the same stare I received daily.

"Fine." Kat waved her hand, signaling she was done with this part of the meeting, and then began ticking off other items on the agenda.

The feel of a small hand in mine had me looking down into curious eyes, and I smiled at the girl who seemed to have no fear.

"I'm glad you're going with my mom," she whispered.

I smiled. "Me too."

"Can you really make plants grow?"

I nodded. "Do you know what plants look like?"

Lily's smile grew, and her eyes lit up. "Circe showed me in her books."

"Do you have a favorite?"

"Lily's, of course!" she whispered. Her mother gave Lily a stern look from across the room, which caused her to throw her hand over her mouth and giggle.

"Perhaps one day I could grow you a whole field of them. What do you think?"

Lily's mouth fell open, and she nodded enthusiastically.

Perhaps one day, I could give all of these women what they deserved.

"I'm just so tired, Willow. I just want this to be over with."

All the women had left the meeting in two or three small groups. It was a way to be less conspicuous.

I took a few hesitant steps toward Kat until I was within arm's reach. Her eyes were rimmed with exhaustion I tried to ignore, along with my own weariness.

"I just don't know how much longer I can hold on," she explained miserably, her eyes losing their usual stern firmness. It was a vulnerability Kat only reserved for Olivia and me.

I grabbed her shoulders, pulling her into a rough hug. "One week. We can do one more week."

She nodded against my shoulder, stiffening a moment later and pulling away. "Any news with Marcus?"

I shook my head. "Everything is going as planned. No new developments."

I didn't realize I was furrowing my brow, but Kat immediately picked up on the change. "You're worried?"

It wasn't a question, but I answered anyway. "It feels too easy right now. It has me on edge."

"I feel the same."

I shivered, and the energy around me seemed to do the same. The dirt on the floor shifted under our feet, making Kat jump and yelp.

When she met my eyes, hers were wide.

I had no explanation. All I knew was that my power was growing, but I had no idea what that meant for all of us.

We were running out of time.

After a lengthy briefing and a detailed map of the building we were attempting to break into, I sat on the ground with Elise, Kat, Circe, and two other women I'd just met who were Elise's most trusted spies. Lily's head was in Elise's lap, watching me intently across from her.

I'd wink at her every once in a while, then return my attention to the rest of the women. She'd giggle as if she and I were spilling secrets. Sometimes, I forgot she was just a child. Her attention to detail and observational skills were above those of most adults. She could instantly read a person, knowing their exact intentions. Though I was proud of her, it was not lost on me that those were necessary survival skills in our world, and the fact that she had to have them at all was evidence of just how fucked up everything was.

Despite the easy atmosphere, I felt everyone's fear. It felt like a tug of something wrong in my chest. I wasn't used to feeling the energetic emotions all around me yet, and I was still working out what each sensation meant. Fear was so prolific here that it was the first emotion I could easily read.

Circe watched me with curious eyes as Elise finished up with our plan. I didn't meet her eyes, unable to face what I'd find there. I knew she could sense some of my new abilities, but I hadn't been given the chance to tell her yet, and now was not the time.

"Willow, you'll come with Kat and I to lead the women out. Based on our intel, we'll enter during the night staffing change. I've mapped out the hallways with no cameras. The route is longer, but we're less likely to be caught. It's in and out. We take out any soldier we see but leave the staff. They're just as much slaves as the women are." Elise explained, immediately turning and directing her attention to the next person.

She was efficient and clearly experienced at running this thing. Though I would undoubtedly encounter soldiers, my hands were unusually steady.

"Circe, Bellona, and Aurora will be lookouts and will create a clear exit for us. Circe will be our last resort," Elise continued.

Circe nodded, smiling at the thought of finally using her fire again. I was secretly, or maybe not so secretly, looking forward to seeing it.

When Elise finished, and I made to leave, Lily stopped me. "Are you afraid?" she asked.

"I'm always afraid, but you know what I'm more afraid of than those soldiers or getting caught?"

Lily shook her head, her eyes widening with anticipation.

"I'm more afraid of not fighting to help these women."

Lily's eyebrows bunched in an adorable, childish way, and my heart lit up at the sight. "I think I understand."

I patted her on the shoulder. "Good. Now it's time to go kick some soldier butt."

Chapter Forty-Six

Willow

All of us wore black clothing to blend in with the shadows. Our hair was swept up and tucked beneath more black fabric, and our clothes were loose, concealing any curves. The idea was to be seen as men so the women we protected wouldn't be suspected if we were spotted. It went without saying that if any of us were caught, we'd never reveal each other, no matter what torture they put us through.

We crept through back alleyways, carefully avoiding the soldiers on curfew watch. These women had clearly done this before. It was as if they could run this route blind.

Elise used silent hand signals to direct us and let us know when the coast was clear. We made it to the breeding building without a hitch, and I felt more confident in this mission than I probably should have.

Elise waved a hand, and her, Kat, and I split off from Circe, Bellona, and Aurora.

Just as we planned, the sound of a door opening and closing, along with soft voices, filled the air around us. The staff was changing. Now was our time to move.

Elise waved us forward, and we heaved the large wooden back door open only enough to let us slip through.

I led the women through pitch-black hallways that wound around the main holding rooms. Most women were held in a large area, waiting for their cycles to return. Once they did, they were taken to private rooms for monitoring and the required servicing from men without their consent.

I felt the soldiers long before they rounded the corner and signaled to Kat and Elise to retreat. We all quickly backpedaled down the dark hallway and turned left into a different passageway. This one was lit with a few flickering torches, illuminating a long row of closed doors. It made me sick thinking about what was happening behind those doors.

We stopped, huddled together, waiting for the soldiers to pass. Except, they never did.

My heartbeat thumped in my chest as I peered around the corner to find them chatting and leaning against the wall.

"Shit," I mumbled, turning to Kat and Elise. "They aren't moving, and we don't have time to wait for them."

"How many cameras are in this hall?" Elise asked.

"Two. One above us and one at the other end," I explained.

"Take out this one. I'll take out the one at the end of the hall," Elise said, preparing to sprint down the dimly lit passage.

I shook my head. "That will alert the entire building."

"What choice do we have?" Elise argued.

I pinched the bridge of my nose. "What if I take out the soldiers instead?" I asked.

Kat and Elise exchanged a glance I couldn't see.

"Do it," Elise said.

I nodded, pulling two daggers from my thigh and assessing the soldiers' positions. Luckily, they stood facing each other. Theoretically, this should be easy. It rarely was, though.

I nodded to Kat and Elise and stepped out into the hallway, instantly releasing my first dagger. It collided with the first soldier's head, and he fell against the wall behind him. Before the second soldier could react, my second dagger was flying. With the turn of his head, the dagger pierced through his eye.

"Damn," Kat said, her eyes wide at the scene in front of her.

"Let's move," Elise said, returning to the dark hallway where the two soldiers' bodies lay, unmoving.

I didn't follow her. Not when a blood-curdling scream snaked its way down the hallway and into my ears. Not when I knew what was happening behind that closed door. Not when the whimpering followed.

Kat shot me a look, shaking her head. But, I couldn't listen to her. I couldn't leave that woman. I couldn't leave any of them.

Kat's eyes widened, as I whirled around and left her and Elise standing there in shock.

"Get to the main room. Get them out!" I shouted before my leg kicked in the first door.

Yanking another dagger from my belt, I was on the man in an instant, running the blade across the soft skin of his neck. Blood gushed and spilled all over the naked woman he was holding down.

She screamed, her terror rendering her frozen.

"Cover up and follow me. Quickly!" I shouted. Now was not the time for soft words. The cameras likely already alerted a much bigger problem.

I didn't wait for the woman, hoping she'd follow, as I kicked in another doorway. I went through the same routine as I made it slowly down the hallway. Half-naked women covered in blood stumbled down the hallway after me. Their fortitude and courage in the face of a horrible situation kept me going. I didn't think about the number of men I killed. I was determined to get to the last door.

That's when I felt them—two more soldiers. Close enough that I knew there was no hiding.

I pulled the bow from my back and halted my steps, aiming for the corner they were about to round. The women froze behind me. A few sobs pierced the silence, but they followed my direction without a word.

I pulled the arrow back, but then a breeze flowed over my fingers, halting my hand.

Instead, I aimed for the camera above the soldiers that suddenly appeared around the corner. The camera fell with a large thud in front of them both.

"You were almost a dead man," I whispered harshly to the larger of the two soldiers, unwrapping the fabric around my head and revealing my face.

Marvin dropped his gun, heaving a large sigh. His other soldier, however, did not lower his weapon.

I eyed the unknown soldier, raising my bow a few inches.

"Lower your gun, Private," Marvin barked, and the man slowly obeyed, not taking his eyes off me.

"What the hell are you doing here?" I asked Marvin.

"I could ask you the same. Marcus didn't warn me about this."

Fair point. This was a last-minute decision.

"I didn't have time to warn Marcus."

Marvin nodded and then looked past me to the women. His eyes widened slightly as he put together why I was here.

I inclined my head, confirming his suspicions.

"Shit." Marvin turned his attention to the soldier behind him. I couldn't see his face, but I saw his shoulders tense.

This private was a liability, and Marvin knew it.

Marvin stepped closer to me so the soldier behind him couldn't hear. "You tripped the camera. I got a call to come check it out. My entire regiment is not far behind."

"Fuck."

"You need to get out of here before they show up." His voice was pleading as he stared past me at the terrified women.

"What the fuck?" the private interrupted.

"Not now, Private," he growled, motioning for me to get the women out of here.

Marvin must have read the question on my face. The question of why he was risking everything for us. "My wife was taken here. She never made it out."

I squeezed my eyes shut, emotion wanting to rise to the surface.

The rustle of many feet had me averting my attention. Elise and Kat stood there, out of breath. Around thirty women followed close behind them. They both stared at me, afraid but waiting for my direction.

"We get to the exit point. Warn Circe she might have a large group of soldiers on our tail," I said.

Kat and Elise nodded, and then began herding the women toward the back exit.

"I'll get your ass put in the arena for this!" The private no longer felt the need to be quiet as he shouted in Marvin's face. I had no idea what he meant by the arena, but I didn't have time to ask.

I raised my bow, aiming for the private's head.

Marvin tilted his head in my direction, smirking. "Watch yourself, Private, or you'll end up with an arrow through your eye."

The private scoffed. "She'd miss me by a mile."

Marvin sneered. "Do you want to test that theory? She just freed all of those women. By herself."

The soldier reluctantly stepped away from Marvin as the last woman disappeared down the hall.

I shot a questioning glance at Marvin, still holding the soldier hostage under my loaded bow.

"Go. I'll take care of the rest," he said, a hint of exhaustion in his words.

That's when the private made his move, whipping out a gun and pointing it in Marvin's direction.

He didn't get a chance to get a shot off before my arrow was protruding through the side of his head. He fell to the ground with a quiet thud.

"Damn," Marvin said, staring at his fallen soldier. "You're better trained than half my unit."

I snorted, then slung the bow across my shoulder and stepped to Marvin's side. "I'm sorry about your wife."

Marvin's eyes were suddenly glassy. "I just wish I had fought for her harder."

I understood what he meant. I wish I had fought harder for my parents, for Kat when she was taken, for Bill, and for every murder I'd witnessed.

"You're fighting now." It was all I could offer him.

"Go," Marvin whispered.

"What about you?"

"I'll be fine. This is easily pinned on an unknown group of rebels. There sure are enough of them now."

My eyebrows rose—some information to file in the back of my head. We weren't the only ones fighting back.

"You've been keeping eyes on more than just us?" I didn't know why I hadn't noticed it earlier.

Marvin's smirk reappeared, lighting up his whole face. "Go."

This time, I smiled, not arguing with him, and then I turned and sprinted back to our safe house.

Back to the fight that suddenly didn't feel so impossible.

Chapter Forty-Seven

Liam

We left at sunrise. The pace we set for ourselves meant we would reach the gate in two days.

The first day was uneventful. Keenan steered us away from the plants Willow had left in a trail to Tarraco, as they were likely being watched. When we stopped for the night, luckily not encountering any Claeg, Olivia came over and plopped down beside me.

"I know what you're thinking," she said to me.

I raised my eyebrows.

"They know the risk. And we won't lose any of them. But Liam?"

"Hm?"

"Don't endanger the whole mission just to save one of us."

I looked down at my feet for a few moments. Every soldier knew that rule. I had followed that rule in the past, but I had never been attached to the people I was commanding. Not like this, anyway.

I finally gave her a curt nod.

"Not very convincing," she said with a hint of sarcasm.

I shrugged.

Olivia's eyes narrowed as though she saw right through me. "Let me guess, you're on watch?"

I nodded again, but a hint of a smile reached my lips.

"We'll be there tomorrow," she said to no one in particular.

I swallowed my reaction, and she gave me an amused smirk before walking over to her sleeping bag next to Emilia and Silvana, who were already asleep.

Shit, I thought to myself, because I didn't know what to do with all the rising emotions.

We reached the gates late afternoon the next day. Lucius and Cato left us to proceed to their scouting positions. Keenan found a hiding spot out of the way, and Emilia and Silvana walked with us until we reached the rendezvous spot. All of them promised to keep out of sight and follow the plan, no matter what happened to Olivia and me.

Olivia and I both approached the gate in silence, and as we waited in line to get in, our trading goods with us, a small hand suddenly grabbed mine and yanked me to the side.

It took me so much by surprise that I stumbled and almost fell.

When I regained my balance, I looked down at a young girl no older than twelve.

She put her finger to her lips and whispered, "Are you Liam?"

I nodded, eyes widening.

A young woman I hadn't noticed came up behind me and whispered in my ear, "You won't get in without our help. I've already looked at your papers. They won't work. Follow us. We'll take you to Willow."

Olivia looked at me, and I shrugged. I had no idea whether we should trust them, yet they knew Willow.

Olivia slumped, clearly resigned to the change of plan.

I waved my hand toward Emilia and Silvana, signaling to let them know we were OK.

The girl grabbed my other hand and held on tight. The young woman grabbed Olivia's arm and held on to her elbow.

When we reached the front of the line, the men recognized the young woman and the girl, waving off the papers the young woman tried to hand them.

"Who do you have with you this time?" the guard asked, somewhat annoyed.

"This is my daddy," the girl said cheerily, and it took all of me not to make a noise or change my facial expression.

"And this is my sister," the young woman said, inclining her head toward Olivia but not letting go of her arm.

"And *why* are they out and about?" he asked suspiciously.

"They were told to collect some supplies from the village to the west." The young woman shrugged indifferently.

The guard walked over and opened the box in Olivia's hands, rifled through it for a moment, and then waved us in.

I silently thanked Leeann for the goods as we passed into Tarraco, the largest city in this area and possibly the world.

No one said anything as we wound our way through the cobblestone streets. Olivia looked around in amazement as we passed vendors selling all kinds of goods.

We walked for fifteen minutes before stopping in front of a small building resembling an art supply shop.

"This is Kat's house," the woman explained, and then she grabbed the girl's hand and turned to walk away.

The girl stopped her and said with a smile, "It's nice to meet you finally!" And then she was gone.

All the color drained from Olivia's face. "Kat?" She sounded as though she were on the verge of sobbing. "Could it be the same Kat?" Her voice was now bordering on panicked.

I put a comforting hand on her shoulder. "Only one way to find out."

Olivia and I stared at the door for a few more moments before I worked up the nerve to knock. Olivia's face was still pale, as she tried to stop herself from shaking. I held onto her shoulder as a striking blonde woman opened the door. In an instant, tears were streaming down their faces as we were pulled inside. Olivia buried her face in the woman's shoulder and sobbed.

I waited.

Eventually, the woman turned toward me and smiled. "I'm Kat," she said, her voice trembling.

"Liam," I responded, and she nodded, still smiling, though her face was soaked with tears.

Kat pulled back enough to look at Olivia. Olivia smiled and then pulled Kat's lips to her own. I took a few steps back, feeling I should give them privacy. When Olivia finally pulled away, there was color in her cheeks again.

Kat looked at me and explained, "Willow is meeting with a correspondent of ours. She should be back in an hour or so."

"I'll just see myself around," I said awkwardly, heading toward the door.

Neither responded as their lips locked again, and I slipped out.

I paused at the front door and smiled before turning around and heading back toward the main square.

I told myself I was just getting a lay of the land, but the truth was that I didn't know what to do with myself, so I just kept walking. I wound through the main square and down another random alleyway. As I rounded the corner, I saw her and halted. She stared at me as though she already knew I would be there.

Chapter Forty-Eight

Willow

As Marcus was walking me home, I felt him long before I saw him. He felt like sunlight on a warm summer day, and I could taste the honey on the tip of my tongue. It was a sensation that now felt a part of me. Something I couldn't pull myself away from, even if I tried.

I halted abruptly, and Marcus stopped next to me.

"What is it?" he asked, his concern growing.

I didn't respond and stared toward the corner that I knew Liam was about to round.

And then he was there. Alive. Whole. Beautiful.

He stopped and stared at me like I was a ghost.

I felt Marcus's surprise, and something else I couldn't quite place. He looked between us, and I couldn't tear my eyes away from Liam.

Liam finally noticed Marcus, and he looked between the two of us. I felt his recognition, his confusion, and his question.

I didn't think about the fact that I could now feel *everyone's* emotions because all I wanted to feel was Liam. All I could focus on was him.

Marcus cleared his throat, and I finally tore my eyes from Liam, stepping forward and grabbing his arm. I felt him tense at my touch.

"You shouldn't be out here," I whispered. "You'll be recognized."

I pulled him down the cobblestone street and turned the corner toward Kat's house. Marcus followed, just behind us, and no one said a word.

When we reached her door, I addressed Marcus. "I'll see you tomorrow. Nothing changes. We move forward as planned," I said, knowing how uneasy Marcus felt about Liam's sudden presence.

Marcus looked between us once more before nodding and walking away.

Liam watched him until he rounded the corner, then turned and looked down at where I was clutching his arm and then back to my face. There was nothing but pure wonder in his eyes as if he hadn't expected to see me again.

"Come on," I said, opening the door and leading him inside.

I heard voices upstairs and shot Liam a questioning glance.

A wide smile broke out across his lips. "Olivia's here."

I wanted to rush to her, but she needed to see Kat more than she needed to see me, so I grabbed Liam's arm and led him to the back of the house, through the closet, to the secret room below.

When we finally reached the room, he let out a soft whistle. "Been busy, I see," he said, motioning to the array of plants hanging around the room.

I smiled, and we stood there looking at each other for a long time, unsure what to say or where to start. He looked the same, yet I felt something different about him. A confidence I hadn't felt before. A sense of peace.

"I'll make us some tea," I said awkwardly, stepping away from his gaze and walking over to the stove.

He watched me go, then walked to the table and settled on one of the chairs.

"You look good. I mean, you always look good, but you look . . . healthy," he said awkwardly and then looked away from me.

I almost laughed at the compliment but finished the tea, walked over, handed him a cup, and sat on the chair beside him.

"Tell me everything," he finally said, so I did.

I didn't know how long I had talked, but before I finished, I had drunk three cups of tea and felt exhausted.

Liam didn't say anything while I talked, only offering a smile or a light touch here and there.

"Tell me about you and Olivia," I said when I finished my story.

He smiled and recounted everything. From finding the village and the people, saving them, almost dying, taking them back to the house we found, almost dying again, and then building something beautiful with them. My heart felt full listening to him, knowing that we'd found our people. That there were people who wanted the same thing and were willing to fight for it. Willing to work toward the world we dreamed of.

"We have a safe place, Willow," he said with such hope that it almost broke my heart.

"I can't wait to see it, to meet everyone . . . all of it," I said, emotion threatening to spill over.

He reached out and grabbed my hand, and the thread between us, the channel, seemed to open of its own accord, and before I could register it all, his lips were on mine.

The need I felt, the need he felt, was so overwhelming that my tears threatened to spill.

Liam pulled back and looked at me as a tear escaped down my cheek. He watched it fall, and then his lips were tracing its path. His touch was so gentle, I felt my body melting into him.

He traced his hands down my back, pulling me closer, and then his hands stopped at my pockets. He pulled back, puzzled at what he felt.

I laughed briefly before explaining, "The rocks I use to channel the energy."

He smiled. A devious sort of smile. "So many of them,"

I shrugged. "Circe thought I'd need them."

He smirked, and then his lips were on mine again.

"Wait," I said into his mouth, placing my hand on his chest.

I knelt, placing my hands on the ground. I called up a bed of moss from the Earth, and we both watched as the moss spread across the bare dirt.

"We don't have a bed down here," I explained, and he laughed again, reaching for me.

"Wait," I said again, taking the stones out of my pocket and placing them in a circle around the bed of moss.

"So they're within easy reach," I explained. "Don't want to grow a forest in the middle of the city."

The joy in Liam's eyes made me melt once more. I pulled him down on top of me, and when our mouths met again, everything else disappeared, and it was only him and me and the incredible joy between us.

It wasn't what I expected. I thought the need for each other would be all-consuming, but we went slowly as if discovering each other for the first time. The moss was soft beneath my back, and I could feel its energy swirling with our own—changing, growing, expanding—but it stayed within the stone circle; I wondered if Liam felt it too.

We were so careful, so tentative, but we found a rhythm that was both gentle and satisfyingly intense. It consumed us until the energy was too much to hold. Our collective release had me gasping for air and grabbing the closest stone. The energy poured into it in an endless stream, and I felt it overflow the rock I was holding onto, then spill into the one next to it. I could feel the energy as it circled us, and I opened my eyes to find Liam wide-eyed, staring at the stone circle. It was glowing brightly.

When my eyes met his again, I saw the amazement. I felt it too, and I laughed because I didn't know what else to do.

I pulled his mouth to mine once more, and he collapsed into me gently before rolling off of me and sinking into the moss next to me. I lay my head on his shoulder and traced circles around the muscles on his chest, marking the new scars on his torso.

We didn't speak for a long time as we lay among the glow and the soft moss beneath us, memorizing each other once again.

"Um, Willow?" Liam's voice sounded almost afraid, and I tensed, raising my head.

Liam was looking at the table and the containers of dirt I'd planted my seeds in. The seeds from my vial. Hoping I could somehow get them to sprout despite my years of failure.

I almost dismissed him when I noticed tiny sprouts, pale green and barely reaching above the surface of the dirt. Searching for sunlight.

I shot to my feet and raced to the table.

Sure enough, they had sprouted.

I turned and smiled so brightly that Liam laughed.

"I did it."

"You did it," he repeated.

"I did it." I couldn't believe it.

"Willow?" Liam's voice was soft and hesitant, and I somehow tore my eyes away from the sprouted seeds to find him watching me. "I just want you to know—" He stopped, unsure how to continue.

I lay back down, resting my head on his shoulder, and he finally continued so softly that I had to strain to hear him. "I've gotten a taste of the world you dream of. I've gotten a taste of you. And I won't stop until I can have it every day for the rest of my pathetic, undeserved life."

I didn't reply. I didn't have to. I let my body speak for me as I wrapped him up in my embrace.

Never again would I let him believe that his or anyone else's life was undeserved.

Never again.

Chapter Forty-Nine

Liam

Willow woke abruptly, sitting up. It jerked me out of my deep sleep.

"What's wrong?" I asked, sitting up with her.

"Shit. Shit. Shit," was all she could say.

"Willow?"

She looked at me then, and suddenly, she was crying. The sobs wracked her body. She grabbed the rock next to her, and it began to glow fiercely. Sucking up the energy that would turn into rain if she didn't do something with it.

"They have Marcus. They're torturing him. They know we're here. They know . . ." She could barely get the words out between sobs.

"Willow, we need to get dressed," I said, my voice calm but commanding. All I knew was that we had to get out. We might have already been out of time if he had given up any information.

I held out my hand and pulled her to her feet. We dressed quickly in silence.

"Olivia and Kat," Willow said, suddenly panicked, "we need to get them out of here."

I nodded, and then I was racing toward the door. My own panic grew despite my efforts to quell it.

Willow followed on my heels.

We didn't knock when we got to Kat's bedroom door. We just barged in. Olivia instantly bolted upright in the bed.

"What is it?" she asked, panic beginning to rise in her voice as she noticed our faces.

"Where's Kat?" Willow pleaded.

"She went to meet with someone early this morning," Olivia explained, then added more forcefully, "Willow, what's wrong?"

"They have Marcus. They know we're here. They're coming. We have to go. *Now*," she explained, walking over and picking up Olivia's clothes from the ground.

Olivia didn't hesitate. She grabbed the clothes and threw them on.

As we walked down the stairs, Willow stopped dead, and I knew she felt something.

"Shit," she whispered as Olivia and I halted behind her.

"Those three assholes are here," she mumbled to us.

"Is there another way out?" Olvia asked, the panic still in her voice.

"There's a window in the back room. We can sneak out that way." She waved her hand for us to follow her.

We didn't make it into the room before the three soldiers burst through the door. I briefly caught sight of their faces. Each of them was familiar to me. My men.

The three of them didn't hesitate, and before I could do anything, they released an all-consuming gas. I saw their savage grins through their masks as everything went black.

Chapter Fifty

Liam

I was expecting one of my men to question me. Possibly even the general. What I wasn't expecting was Marvin.

He gave me a sad smile as he sat down on a chair by the door to the cell. I noticed he kept it unlocked.

"This wasn't part of the plan." His words caught me off guard.

"Plan? Your plan?"

"Willow's plan. Our plan." He motioned between the two of us.

"You're in on it?"

He gave me a subtle nod. "Of course, I am. How could I not? When I found out it was her. The girl with the books . . ." He trailed off, rubbing his smooth head and glancing at the sunlight streaming through the tiny window above my bed. "And then I saw what she could do." He finally met my eyes again. "How could I not? How could anyone not? And then I found out she knew you, and not just knew you, but I knew she loved you. I . . . I . . ." He couldn't finish his sentence. "You can still get her out of here if you comply with their wishes," he said, changing the subject.

I saw through his lie. "You know that isn't true. Whatever I choose, she dies, or worse, she becomes their slave. I have no choice anymore."

I let my head fall, its weight suddenly feeling like too much. "I can't do it, Marvin. I can't be their pawn anymore. I can't kill more innocent people. I won't."

"So, what are you going to do?" His sadness permeated each word.

"Fight."

Marvin's silence made me snap my head up. I found him studying me, grappling with what he would say next.

"It's the two of you against the emperor, the general, the military, and the Elite. Tell me how you will fight your way out of that?"

He wanted me to have a new plan. He wanted me to tell him there was some way we all walked out of this alive and free.

I couldn't give him that, so I remained silent.

Marvin sighed. He knew the truth. "The general will be in to see you since you've declined. I begged to be the first one to talk to you. I thought maybe I could convince you somehow. Silly of me to think you'd stop fighting, but you know what the general will do."

I nodded. I did know. I remembered that no one met the general and saw another day.

"I wish I could do more for you," he began, but I cut him off.

"You've done enough. You've done more than enough." My voice began to crack as I spoke.

"I've not done nearly enough, Liam. Not. Nearly. Enough."

I stood up, taking a few short steps until I was right in front of him. I put my hand on his shoulder, forcing his gaze to mine. "If all you'd done was be my friend, that would have been enough. But you've done more. For Willow too, I suspect, and I cannot ever repay you for that."

Now, it was Marvin's turn for his voice to break as he placed his hand on my opposite shoulder. "I wanted that world too."

I patted his shoulder lightly. "I know, Marvin. I know. And it's not over yet. Somehow, I'll get her out. Somehow, I'll give you that world. Both of you."

I saw the tears Marvin wouldn't shed, his eyes glossy with them as he stood to leave.

My question halted his hand on the door.

"Have you ever been married? Been in love?"

He didn't turn toward me, but his voice still reached me across the room. "Her name was Iris, and she was small but mighty. She fought every damn day of her life." He paused and opened the door. "Don't stop fighting for her like I did."

Those were the last words he spoke as the door shut behind him.

I knew eventually I'd be visited by the general. I expected a contingent of soldiers, but what I didn't expect were . . . scientists?

They are here to test your abilities, Captain. They're here to test if you're human or not." I almost forgot how sadistic the general sounded, and a chill ran down my spine.

I angled my head, setting my mouth in a firm line, not wanting to say a word to him.

"Let's see if you bleed the same color as we do," the general drawled as he circled where I stood shirtless in the middle of the cell. My arms and legs were both chained to the floor, allowing me very little movement.

The three people in white coats approached me. They were hesitant, eyeing me like some sort of monster. The leader of the three, a small man with wire glasses and limbs like twigs, pulled out a scalpel.

"We need to test your blood, Captain," he squeaked out.

Did they really think I didn't bleed the same color as them? I guess I was about to find out.

The man sliced my forearm enough to collect a few drops of blood and then quickly stepped away from me. He blindly reached back and handed the blood to the youngest woman on his team, who looked like the vial might explode at any moment.

Their fear of me almost made me laugh, but then I remembered the stories most people had heard about me, and their fear made sense.

The general watched me like a hawk, obviously waiting for me to react in some way. I wouldn't give that to him, no matter what they tried.

"Seems you do bleed the same color as we do," the general commented as the blood composition was tested on some sort of small machine.

I remained still, noticing they hadn't made an effort to bandage my bleeding arm. The blood dripped slowly onto the concrete floor and the shackles holding me in place.

"Our next test is a rather interesting one. Did you know there are rumors you cannot feel pain, Captain?"

Oh shit. Though I knew of those rumors, I didn't actually think anyone was dumb enough to believe them.

I eyed the general with disdain. After all I'd done for the bastard, he would see me suffer. It didn't surprise me, only made me angrier. But I refused to speak. I refused to give him any ammunition.

The man with the glasses approached me again, even slower than the last time. I saw the slight tremble in his hands. He held out a few wires attached to adhesive pads at the end. The wires extended to a box with a series of dials and buttons.

The scientist noticed my gaze and explained. "This will pump small amounts of electricity into your body in an attempt to elicit a pain response."

I glared at the man, and he shrunk back as though I'd reach out and eat him alive.

"He can't hurt you. Proceed," the general snapped at the scientist.

The man jumped at his voice and then quickly secured the sticky pads across my chest and arms.

I prepared myself for the pain. I'd been in pain countless times. I would endure this.

When the scientist flipped the switch, I wasn't ready for the kind of pain it elicited. I was used to deep lacerations, hits to the head, even stray bullet wounds, but this was different. This pain snaked its way through every nerve in my body making me twitch uncontrollably.

I didn't shout. All that came out of me was a surprised grunt.

The two assistants furiously jotted down notes on my responses as the lead scientist increased the intensity of the machine.

I didn't register how long this torture went on for. My brain, luck-ily, shut out the worst of it.

"Enough!" the general finally shouted, taking me out of my trance.

Clearly, my lack of screaming angered him far more than the actual results of the test.

"Cut him open," he snarled at the scientist.

The man halted, his eyes widening in surprise. "Excuse me, but is that wise? He could bleed out."

The general waved a hand at him. "I don't give a shit. I need answers."

"I don't mean to push, sir, but what are you trying to get out of this?"

The general, got up in his face and shouted, "I will not have this traitor stand in silence while there are other traitors out there that he isn't helping me find. He will suffer for his silence."

It didn't matter that he hadn't even tried to ask me for the information. He knew I wouldn't talk, and I was guessing Willow wasn't talking either. Her little rebellion was safe for now. Perhaps that was the silver lining. They could still escape this hell hole even if we couldn't.

That thought didn't save me from the pain, though. His scientist tore into my torso like I was a piece of meat he was meticulously cutting up.

It took all of me not to scream, but for Willow, I'd endure this.

The sadistic bastard watched the entire thing, marveling at the blood and torn muscle that I feared might never heal correctly.

He talked, too, revealing far too much, but it didn't matter. I'd likely be dead by morning anyway.

My brain heard bits and pieces of how he and the emperor weaponized the Claeg and seized control of neighboring cities. One by one killing those he deemed unworthy. He glorified his breeding program as though he were creating the gods themselves through rape. He even talked of Willow and what she'd discovered about increasing food production and how he would use that information to make the masses believe he was some sort of all-powerful god. It was sickening to listen to. Everything was a power grab for them.

There wasn't a spec of humanity in the man.

It was then that I realized maybe I wasn't the monster I thought I was.

At least now I was fighting for the right side.

Though I didn't make a sound, eventually the blood loss meant I couldn't stay on my feet any longer. I fell hard on my knees, wondering if the bone cracked at the force of it. Then everything went black.

I felt her again, in the space between dreaming and death. She poured her energy into me, and I bathed in the bliss and pain all at once, realizing there was nothing I wouldn't do to get her out of this place.

I woke up on the concrete floor, lying on my back. It was dark, but the light from the moon filtered through the small window near the ceiling.

"I thought I might have lost you." Marvin's voice cracked as though it were full of emotion, or perhaps it was from lack of sleep.

I turned my head just enough to see him sitting in the corner of the cell, his legs tucked under him on the floor.

That's when I felt them—bandages all over my chest and arms.

"You cleaned me up?" My voice was rough from disuse.

Marvin stood and approached me, squatting down so I could see him.

"I did. The bastard carved you up and then left you to die."

I grunted, trying to sit, but Marvin placed a hand on my chest, holding me in place. "I thought he wanted you to lead his army, but I'm beginning to think there's something else he's hiding from us."

"He doesn't think I'm human. He claimed he was experimenting."

"You're serious?" Marvin sounded as though he might laugh.

"I wish I weren't. The real problem is he might not be wrong."

Marvin's eyes widened, and his lips parted as though he wanted to argue with me, but when I sat and started peeling off the bandages, his gasp was enough to confirm what I already suspected.

"They're gone?" Marvin yelped.

I nodded. "It's not all me. Willow somehow helped. She'd done it before. But even without her, I'm healing faster every day. My strength is increasing too."

"What does it mean?" he asked, though he knew I didn't have the answer.

"I don't know, but what I do know is I need to get Willow out of here."

Marvin looked pained. "There's no way, Liam. Every soldier in the city is tasked with keeping the two of you here. All units."

"Kat and the women?" I asked him.

"Vanished."

"Fuck."

I wasn't ready to admit defeat, but this situation just got a hundred times harder.

Chapter Fifty-One

Willow

The first thing I noticed was my pounding headache. I kept my eyes shut, not wanting to open them just yet, afraid the light might burn a hole through my head.

There were voices, and I kept myself perfectly still, straining to hear them.

"He's awake, but he isn't giving us any information, and he won't agree to any of our terms." I recognized the voice of one of the soldiers.

"Make him," another voice replied. One I didn't recognize.

The soldier didn't respond, and I heard his footsteps as he walked away and closed a door behind him.

My head ached so badly that I wanted to go back to sleep, but I slowly opened my eyes instead, too worried about Liam and Olivia to give in to the pain.

As the room came into focus, I noticed I was on some sort of cot pushed up against a cold stone wall. There was a small, barred window above me, letting in very little light. As I slowly turned my head, a small, bald male came into view. He was seated on a chair in the opposite corner and was wearing deep-purple robes that were embroidered with gold detail. He looked well-fed, with a potbelly that stuck out at his midsection. When he noticed my eyes were open, a savage grin formed on his face.

It took all of me not to spit on that face, but I didn't. Instead, I tried to sit up.

"Careful. Take it slowly," said the man, but his tone held no concern, only steel.

When I finally raised myself to sitting, I spun my legs off the cot, so my feet rested on the ground and looked at the man in the corner.

"What do you want with me?" I snarled at him, not masking my anger.

He smiled again, but there was no sweetness. "I think you know what I want."

"You can't have it," I said bluntly.

"I thought you might say that." He stood up and couldn't have been more than five feet tall. "I think you'll change your mind in time, especially if you want to see your friends again. Until then, you'll stay here."

"You aren't to touch them," I growled, still unable to stand.

He grinned again. "What are you going to do about it? Grow a flower?" He let out a wretched laugh, and I spit at him. That only made him laugh harder.

"Eat, drink, get your strength back, and then we'll talk again," he said, opening the door and walking out, not allowing me to reply.

I slumped back on the cot and rubbed my eyes. The headache was so bad I couldn't think straight. I reached for the cup of water next to the bed and sucked it down in one gulp, and then I lay my head back down on the pillow.

I didn't know how long I slept, but I was woken by the latch of the door turning.

I opened my eyes, and luckily, my headache was gone. The short, bald man returned to the room and shut the door behind him.

"How are you feeling?" he asked, without emotion.

"Fine," I responded shortly.

"Good. We have many things to discuss," he said, then paused, awaiting a response.

When I didn't reply, he continued. "As I'm sure Marcus has told you, I need your services. As you can see, the city and the people are struggling." He paused and looked for a response again.

I glared at him; I could feel my anger rising at the mention of Marcus.

"People will die if we cannot find a solution to our food shortage," he continued. "You'll be compensated, of course. Handsomely so, if I might add."

He waited for a response again, but I kept my mouth shut.

He sighed. "You could help this city thrive. You could help us build a new world."

"Whose world? Yours? For whose benefit?" I finally interrupted him.

He looked slightly surprised. "No, it's for all of us. I'm only trying to help these people."

I let out a short laugh. "Help? And how are the women who are raped and forced to birth babies being helped? How are the thousands of people you slaughtered being helped? How does your alliance with the Claeg help anyone but yourself? How is hoarding the weapons, resources, and technology for your precious Elite helping anyone else?"

"What do you know about ruling a city?" he practically spat at me.

"I don't know much, but I know genocide and rape aren't the answer," I responded, my words dripping with spite.

"With your help, we would have enough food to support all of those people," he said, calming his anger a bit. "No more killing necessary."

"You're sick, and I would rather die than help you," I replied, and I didn't care if I sounded like a child.

"So, you'll condemn all these people to death?"

"You already did that, and, as you said before, what's growing a flower going to do?"

"If nothing, it gives people hope," he responded.

"Ha! So they won't fight back. So they'll *bow* at your feet."

He shook his head. "You just don't see . . ."

"No, you're right. I *don't* see because *I* don't have the *privilege* of living with all the resources I could ever want, staying locked up in my tower with my guards who have guns, killing people at will, and stealing their resources to feed my endless want for power and control. Well, you know what?" I said, my voice rising angrily. "Control is an illusion, and you have fallen for it! You will watch this city crumble beneath you, and I'll enjoy watching it happen."

He didn't respond right away. He just laughed again. The sound trickled down my spine, making me shiver. "And with what army will you make this city crumble?"

"I don't need an army. If you had read the history books you destroyed more closely, you would know that your city will crumble of its own accord from the inside out. Nothing lasts forever. Everything turns to dust eventually. Your *Empire* will be no different. I just hope I'm here to witness it." I gave him a feral grin.

He looked at me, his impatience growing. "If you won't help of your own free will, then you leave me no choice," he said, standing up and reaching the door. "Before this is over, you'll be on your knees, bowing at my feet."

"Unlikely," I replied, my words dripping with disdain. "I'd rather die."

He raised his eyebrows at that. "You may just get your wish, but I think watching your friends die one by one will be much more satisfying for me. You have until tomorrow to change your mind."

With that, he slammed the door, not giving me any chance to reply.

Chapter Fifty-Two

Willow

I was woken again the next afternoon by the emperor.

"Rise and shine. Time to get dressed. We have somewhere to be," he said, but there was no cheeriness in his voice.

"I have no intention of going anywhere with you."

He looked at me with a sideways grin. "Oh, I think you'll want to see this. Been a long while since we've had someone *worthy* of their opponent."

It dawned on me what he planned to do to get me to comply with his demands. "You wouldn't."

He smiled even broader. "You have the power to stop it," he said, shoving a dress into my arms.

I stared blankly at the dress, my mind racing with what I should do.

"I would erase any illusions you have of getting out of this. Your friend, or is it your lover? He may be powerful, but he's still human, and humans can be broken and tamed. The people will enjoy watching him, I think."

I lunged at him, and he pulled a knife from his shirt sleeve and pressed it against my abdomen.

"Tsk. Tsk," he said, shaking his head. "Perhaps we'll need to take you in chains."

I spit in his face, and he stepped back and slowly wiped it away with his sleeve, glaring at me.

"I'll enjoy your reaction the most, I believe." He turned and walked out.

I sank back onto the cot, and it took all of me not to collapse on the floor.

As we approached the stadium, I felt everyone staring at me. I was part of the spectacle, just as much as Liam was, I realized then. For what purpose, I had no idea.

I kept my gaze aimed ahead of me and didn't say anything.

The soldier looked over at me occasionally, and I could tell he was enjoying every moment of this. I held in all the snide remarks, but I made a silent promise to myself to ensure he suffered, especially for Marcus.

"You were playing us the whole time," the soldier said, and I finally looked at him. "I suspect you aren't exactly what you say you are, nor do I think Marcus knows exactly what you are."

I turned my gaze forward again, not bothering with a response.

When we reached the gate to the stadium, I looked up at the familiarity of it from the history books, and a shiver escaped down my spine. What kind of person would replicate such a horrible spectacle?

The soldier led me through the gates, and we emerged into the stadium as it began filling with people. The sheer size of the stadium—it was unfathomable.

The arena at the base was circular, with a dirt floor. The walls surrounding it were tall enough that no one could escape it, and within those walls were various gated rooms spread out along the perimeter. Liam was in the room opposite me. I felt him without needing to reach out anymore.

"Come on," the soldier spat at me, yanking on my chains and practically dragging me up the stairs, intersecting the rows and rows of stone seats.

We wound our way slowly to the top. There was a large, covered area clearly made for the Elite. It was adorned with precious stones, fabric of various colors covering the area, blocking out the sun's harsh rays, and I saw tables of food spread throughout the entire area—enough food to feed the whole stadium if they had wanted to. There were cushions on the stone seats and what looked like alcoholic drinks beside them.

I didn't try to hide my disgust as we approached the area set aside for the emperor. I felt his eyes scanning me from head to toe, and the same predatory smile erupted on his lips. "You look delicious, just as I'd hoped," he drawled, clearly drunk.

I glared at him but didn't dare respond.

"Have it your way," he slurred as he waved his hand at the soldier who led me to a seat next to the emperor's chair.

The soldier shoved me onto the hard stone and fastened the chains around my wrists to an iron loop welded into the stone seat beside me. It was obvious I hadn't been his only prisoner here.

I settled into my seat and got my bearings. Most of the Elite were dressed finely and already drunk. The majority ignored me, but I noticed a few curious glances and wondered how much they knew about me.

As I scanned the rest of the stadium, I realized how big this city was. The sheer number of people took my breath away.

"Impressive, isn't it?" the emperor said, plopping beside me. "This could be yours, you know," he continued.

"Like I said earlier, I would rather die."

He looked at me for a few moments. The alcohol had melted some of his savage exterior, making him appear much more human.

"I think I'd like to marry you," he finally said.

"That's the alcohol speaking, and you're a fool."

He laughed. "A fool who has built all this." He awkwardly swept his hands around the stadium.

I kept quiet with my eyes on the arena floor.

He stared at me silently until a soldier I had never seen before came up and whispered something in his ear. I saw him nod out of the corner of my eye, and then he got up and walked away.

I let out a sigh of relief as he moved out of sight, and I turned my gaze back to my surroundings.

I noticed the Elite had split into two main groups, and the looks they gave each other made it evident they didn't get along. As I suspected, the leaders he'd assigned to keep the other cities and towns under the emperor's control were split on his actions. He was losing his people's support, not just the peasants but also the Elite. He needed Liam and I to regain his favor with them.

Unsurprisingly, the general stood in the center of the Elite group that favored the emperor. He was laughing and looked drunk, which took away some of his intimidating demeanor. A girl wearing nothing more than a slip clung to his arm as if her life depended on it.

It probably did.

I shifted my line of sight further from the general and found fifteen to twenty guards stationed throughout the Elite area, all with weapons. Luckily, it didn't look like any of them had guns. Marvin was among them, and though he talked casually to those around him, I could tell by his rigid stance that he was afraid.

He caught my gaze briefly, offering a weak smile.

I returned the smile and then continued scanning the stadium. Guards were stationed on top of the walls. Luckily, there were only ten of them. They were the ones that likely had guns.

As for the rest of the people below, only a few soldiers were scattered among them. The people outnumbered them one hundred to one, easily.

I felt him before I saw him, and his pain was overwhelming.

I snapped my head toward the stairs leading to the Elite area, and a moment later, two soldiers emerged, dragging Marcus along with them. His face was so swollen it was almost unrecognizable, and I could tell he had a broken arm and a few broken fingers by the way his arm hung limply beside him.

The soldiers walked over and dropped him next to me. He let out a low groan at the impact.

"I thought you might want some company." Disdain dripped from the emperor's voice as he came up on my left-hand side and sat down beside me. "An example of what's to come if you continue to deny me."

"And for a second there, I thought the alcohol might have made you more likable," I replied sarcastically.

The emperor laughed. "Quite the tongue for someone in your position."

I shrugged, grabbing Marcus's good hand and giving it a reassuring squeeze. The truth was I was terrified, but I refused to show it.

Marcus stared at the point where our hands met, then looked up at me and tried to smile.

I gave him a quick nod and then returned my attention to the emperor.

"Well, since you've not changed your mind, we might get on with the entertainment for the evening," the emperor said.

The people around him who heard him let out a loud cheer that had a domino effect around the stadium.

My stomach turned to knots as the cheering got louder.

The emperor gave a wave, and a soldier standing at the edge of the arena below walked toward one of the gates.

The crowd grew silent.

Chapter Fifty-Three

Willow

The soldier opened the gate, stepped inside, and threw something over his shoulder. As he emerged, I noticed it was a person. It was Olivia. Her body was limp, and there was blood dripping from her wrists and soaking the dirt below her as the soldier walked to the center of the stadium and dumped her on the ground.

I heard him growl, "Get up."

"You bastard!" I yelled at the emperor beside me, standing and yanking on the chains holding me.

He only laughed. A sadistic sort of laugh. One that made you realize that this dead world had stolen every ounce of humanity from him.

I watched Olivia try to stand and fail. The soldier kicked her, and my gut clenched.

The crowd began yelling at her. At first, it felt like they were cheering her on, but as I listened closer, I heard shouts of disgust.

"You and your people are going to rot in hell for this," I snarled at him.

The emperor laughed again. "Like I said before, the choice is yours," he waved his hand again, and another gate opened.

Liam came rushing out of the gate, armed with a sword and shield and wearing gladiator armor. He spotted Olivia and rushed to her side. He put her arm around his shoulder and helped her stand, and then she looked at him, and my heart cracked in two.

My family. My whole world.

A third gate opened, and I heard them before I saw them. Claeg. Attracted to the scent of Olivia's blood. She was the bait. The damsel in distress. A way to force Liam to fight them, to save her.

The entertainment for the evening.

When they emerged, five of them, the crowd erupted into cheers and whoops. My stomach recoiled again.

I couldn't take my eyes off them as the Claeg rushed toward Olivia.

Liam whirled around and blocked a few blows before taking down two in one stroke.

The crowd went wild.

The other three were no match for him either; he quickly dispatched them and rushed back to Olivia, trying desperately to get the bleeding to stop. He tried to tear a piece of her clothing to make a bandage, but the gate opened again, and ten Claeg rushed out.

This was the game. The bastard was going to find his limit while showing off his greatest weapon to the people.

I swiveled toward the emperor, hate dripping from my words, "You won't win this. He won't let Olivia die without also going down with her. You'll lose both of them."

The emperor shrugged again. "I've already won the support of the people, as you can hear for yourself, and I've made it this far without him. He would undoubtedly make me more powerful, but even he's dispensable."

The crowd erupted again, and I turned back toward the arena, unable to sit down. Liam had already taken down the ten Claeg, and the gate opened again, revealing twenty more.

Olivia could not hold herself up anymore and collapsed on the ground again. The crowd booed her, and for an instant, Liam turned, distracted; a Claeg swung its sword and slashed a considerable gash through his leg. He howled with pain but turned quickly and cut the Claeg's head off in one stroke.

The crowd erupted again.

Despite his injured leg, he felled all twenty Claeg in minutes, and then the gate opened, revealing forty more.

"I've heard the rumors, but it's even more impressive to see in real life," the emperor said, making a low whistling sound.

As the Claeg closed in, I couldn't take it anymore. I didn't see any other way out.

I turned to the emperor, and he looked up at me, triumph already on his face.

"OK . . ." I started, and then I felt a hand grab mine.

Marcus was nodding his chin in the opposite direction.

The crowd let out another cheer, and the emperor became temporarily distracted.

I looked where he was nodding, and then I saw them. *All* of them. All two hundred women spread out among the crowd.

I looked closer at the Elite area and saw Kat just outside it. Weapon in hand and tears streaking down her face. Elise and Lily were with her, as was Cass, who had a supporting hand on her shoulder.

The rest of the women must have had weapons carefully concealed in their hands, behind their backs, or in the folds of their dresses, and looked like they were waiting for her signal, but she appeared frozen.

They came. They had a chance to escape, but they came.

And then I felt the anger rising. Anger for all the injustice, for all we had lost, for Liam, for Olivia, for Kat, for these women who had become family, for the Earth who had lost more than any of us had.

The crowd gasped, and I turned toward the arena to find that a few of the Claeg had gotten past Liam and were headed straight for Olivia. He was too overwhelmed to help.

And then everything I felt, all the anger, all the heartbreak, all the love, erupted into a loud roar that escaped my lips. Everyone briefly looked toward me before a sound so deafeningly loud drowned out everything else.

The sound barreled through the stadium on wings of air, and chaos erupted. People fell over, tables turned and shattered their contents, the cloth shades ripped from their poles, and when the wall of air reached the arena floor, it was so strong it halted the Claeg's movement.

Liam covered his face at the assault of dust and wind that pushed him toward Olivia.

I turned toward Kat noticing she had given her signal, and among the wind were two hundred women taking down the soldiers in the stadium.

The emperor regained his balance and wits, and it took him a moment to understand what was happening.

"No!" he shouted, but the wind swallowed his words.

He gave a hand signal to the soldiers on the top of the stadium, and the gunshots started. People panicked and fled for the exits.

I saw a few women fall as I turned back toward Marcus, who hadn't released my hand. Despite his pain, he had held on.

And then I saw him. Marvin. He pulled a gun from his belt and started taking down the snipers. One at a time, he silenced their guns, protecting the women who were fighting the soldiers.

I thought it would be a sniper that took Marvin out, and my heart stopped as I saw what he didn't. The general pushed aside the panicked people, making a beeline for Marvin.

A disgusted look spread across his features, twisting his mouth into something vaguely resembling the Claeg.

My shouts weren't enough, though I yelled with everything I had. He couldn't hear me through the commotion.

Everything happened in slow motion, and I was powerless to stop it. It felt like my heart stopped the moment the general drew his sword. An instant later, he swung it through the air, catching the light from the sun, and the whole world paused. Images of the life Marvin might have had flashed through my mind. A life with us. A life with a million bear hugs and broad smiles. A life he deserved. The hot tears streamed down my face as the world turned once again. Not truly stopping for anyone or anything. And then, there was nothing but blood. The general had cut Marvin's head right from his shoulders.

"No!" I wailed, taking a step toward him, still chained to my seat, unable to reach him.

Unable to save him.

"Willow!" A shout so loud and familiar that I felt it in my core—in our connection to one another. I swung my gaze toward the arena floor.

Liam was struggling to protect Olivia now that the wind had begun to die, and they were nearly on top of them.

I started to panic again as my chest constricted at the sight of Marvin's dead body, the women falling in heaps under the soldiers' swords, and Liam and Olivia seconds away from being devoured by the Claeg.

And then the silent voices.

Use me.

Use me.

Use me.

Hundreds of them.

It finally dawned on me.

I closed my eyes and quickly opened up the energy channels between me and *all* of the women in the stadium, along with the channels that connected us all to the Earth. Then I saw it. This beautiful web of energy pulsing with life and pulsing with power.

I called it. An energy so great, it couldn't be stopped. It couldn't be controlled. Not even by me.

The shouts grew more frantic now.

My eyes snapped open to find massive vines sprouting on the arena floor, forming a cage around the Claeg. I heard them screech as they touched the vines, their arms, legs, and bodies turning to ash on contact.

I blinked, not quite believing what I saw, but then the emperor groaned behind me, and I faced him. Without asking, a vine crawled up his body and fastened him to his chair. The same vine crawled up my chains and broke me free of them.

I let go of Marcus's hand and walked over to the emperor. He was wide-eyed, panic written all over his face.

"I wouldn't move if I were you," I said as I noticed him struggling against the thorny vines, blood beginning to drip down his hands.

"You have a front-row seat to the fall of your empire, as promised." There was nothing but calm in my voice now. "Oh, and here's the flower you wanted," I added as a poppy sprouted up at his feet and bloomed in crimson.

I didn't give him another thought as I called the fire next. I found that the flames had been patiently waiting for my call. Anything and everything combustible suddenly burst into flame.

I watched the chaos as the vines pushed themselves into cracks and crevices around the stadium, crumbling the rock beneath them and taking the soldiers with them. I watched the fire as it consumed everything flammable in its path, leaving nothing but ash.

Out of the corner of my eye, I saw the general. He was still fighting through the people, scrambling to get out. He aimed for the staircase in front of him, taking out everyone in his path.

It took little more than a thought. A thick vine grabbed him by the ankle, making him fall onto the hard stone. When he tried to swipe at the vine, another caught his wrist, squeezing until the sword fell from his hand. He shouted something I couldn't hear, and another vine wound around his mouth, silencing him.

I made a move toward him. I wanted to be the one to kill him, but then Marcus's hand was in mine again, and I snapped out of my single-minded rage.

Kat was running toward me, shouting something I couldn't hear, and I looked back at the arena floor as it began to crumble.

"Run!" I shouted at Liam over the commotion. He might not have heard me with his ears, but he *felt* my meaning. He instantly grabbed Olivia's limp body and threw her over his shoulder.

Kat stopped and glanced at them, something like relief blooming on her face, before turning back toward me.

"We need to get out of here!" she shouted among the falling debris.

"Is everyone out?" I asked her.

She shrugged.

"Take Marcus," I said, transferring his hand to hers. "Get him out. Get everyone out that you can. I need to stay and help everyone get to safety."

"No, Willow. I won't let you do that," she shouted, but we were running out of time.

"I'll make it out, I promise. Please go."

She hesitated only briefly, then she threw Marcus's good arm around her shoulders, and they made their way toward the stairs. Cass, Elise, Lily, and Circe raced up to meet them.

They all looked at me, and I nodded at them. A silent order.

They all nodded back in quick understanding before turning and descending the stairs toward the exit.

Only Circe didn't follow them. She made her way slowly toward me.

She grinned at me. "I never thought I'd live to see this day," she explained. "I'm not going to miss this."

I tried to interrupt her, but she waved her hand at me. "I'm old. Too old. I'm just grateful I got to meet you, Willow. My story is complete now. It's time to write your own."

A tear escaped down my face as the world around me crumbled. I couldn't lose her, too.

"Save those tears for creating a living Earth, and never underestimate yourself. You have such a beautiful gift. *Feel Everything*, and don't hold back. *That* is your superpower."

"But the stones . . ."

She waved her hand at me again. "No need for those. You don't have to hide anymore. I saw the web you created, Willow. I never thought it was possible to weave energy like that. Will you use me now to help finish the job?"

I nodded, unable to say anything, as the tears continued falling.

I opened the channel between me, Circe, and the Earth. I wove them together, and I felt the energy pulsing through her.

She smiled. "I'll control the fire. You control the Earth."

I nodded again, and then she unleashed herself.

Her fire was different from mine. It burned hotter and faster and longer. All those years of pain and suffering had molded her fire into something unshakable, and I felt honored to have known her. To have felt her.

I directed my energy toward the vines. I wove them in and out of the stadium, crushing everything in their path.

I heard the emperor whimper behind me and turned briefly toward him. It wasn't the look on his face that stood out the most. It was his hands. They trembled, just as mine had, and it was the first time

I realized that mine no longer shook. I didn't know when they had stopped, but I knew, at that moment, that they would never again.

I slowly peeled my eyes away from the emperor's hands, and as I continued to crush the stones, I used the vines to create shelters from falling debris for people trying to get out. Circe and I controlled the energy as much as we could, for as long as we could.

When most people were out, and our portion of the stadium became unstable, I stopped and looked at Circe.

"Go," she said, turning toward the emperor. "I'll make sure he sees it completed."

I grabbed her and wrapped her in a hug, letting out a short sob.

"Oh, child," she said, patting my head. "Remember, energy can only be transferred. It cannot be lost. You will see me again. In the flames of the fires you will set to transform the world into a beautiful living canvas." She paused and whispered in my ear, "It has been an honor," then she pulled away and shoved me toward the stairs.

I didn't look back at her, too afraid I wouldn't go if I did, but I paused at the top of the stairs, watching the stadium and the city beyond crumble.

Then I roared into the gaping hole that used to be the stadium, and a gust of wind barreled through what remained, dancing among the chaos, happy to join the fun. I heard Circe laugh behind me, and I smiled at her laughter before I raced down the last remaining staircase and out into the city.

The vines were hungrily descending through Tarraco, crumbling houses, and cobblestone streets in their path. I heard people screaming, and everyone was running toward the gate.

The vines followed me as I ran, and I used them to shelter everyone I could. I yelled after them to follow me, and they didn't hesitate as they joined me under the living roof that protected us.

I stopped when we reached the city's gate, letting everyone pour out into the barren land beyond it.

Once everyone was out, I released the sheltering vines and walked through the crowd of shocked and confused people. They didn't seem to notice me.

I didn't have to look to find them. Their energy pulled me toward them. They were away from the main crowd, circled together, their attention on whatever or whoever was in the middle of them.

I placed my hand on Cass's shoulder. She turned, and surprise washed over her face before shifting to something like relief. To my utter disbelief, she wrapped her arms around me and sobbed into my shoulder for a moment before pulling back and pushing me forward through the other women.

They quickly stepped aside once they noticed me, and I made my way to the center.

Before I saw her, I knew. I felt it in the stadium before Liam took her away. I felt the loss of her channel—the loss of her life.

Kat was sitting in the center, sobs racking her entire body. Olivia was pale as a ghost next to her and not moving. Liam was kneeling on Olivia's other side, and his face was streaked with tears.

I didn't reach them before I collapsed to the ground. I didn't feel Liam come over and wrap his arms around me. I didn't hear the crying. My grief consumed me.

Desperate not to feel this way, I searched frantically for her channel but couldn't find it. I couldn't pour energy into it if I couldn't find it.

I barely registered Liam explaining, "She lost too much blood," and then more tears fell down his face as he buried it into the crook of my neck.

I buried my face in the dirt, and I pleaded with the Earth to bring her back. I knew it wouldn't work, that it was a futile attempt, but my grief so consumed me that I didn't know what else to do. A sob escaped me, and then the tears began to fall in a continuous stream, and I couldn't stop them.

I briefly registered the rain as it began falling around us, but I didn't care if I flooded the entire world with my tears.

No one said anything or moved as the rain came faster and harder.

Energy is never lost, the Earth seemed to whisper against my cheek. *Use me.*

I continued to let the tears fall as it hit me what Circe had just told me—the energy of the living returns to the Earth once it is gone, and the Earth gives it back in the form of new life in an endless cycle.

Olivia's energy was not gone. It had simply returned to the Earth, waiting for its chance to bloom once again. *All* of the energy of those lost were waiting beneath the surface of the Earth for their opportunity to return to life once more. Whether a human, a tree, or a butterfly, an endless stream of energy was waiting to create new life.

"Thank you," I whispered as I searched the Earth for the familiar energy I had come to know and love. It wasn't hard to find it. It was just below the surface. It felt like pure love. Instead of pulling the energy up, I whispered, "Would you like to return?" offering her a choice.

The energy didn't hesitate, and as it traveled upward, I felt the channel forming again, burning brighter as it approached Olivia's limp body.

When it reached her, I felt it seep into every cell in her body, awakening everything within her.

Suddenly, I heard a gasp for air, and Kat stopped crying.

I raised my head from the ground and saw Olivia's chest rising and falling. The look on Kat's face set me to sobbing again. The rain began to fall so violently it seemed like I might really drown the whole world.

Liam grabbed my arm and pulled me into his lap. It only made me cry harder as I buried my face in his chest.

"Marvin is dead," I choked out. "I couldn't . . . I couldn't stop it.

Liam didn't say anything, but I felt his tears and his heartbreak as I continued to cry against his chest, listening to the beat of his heart against my cheek. Both of us were lost in our grief but also our relief that it was over.

Then, a soft voice made its way over to me. "Willow . . ."

I lifted my head. Olivia looked at me as she lay limply in Kat's lap. "You're going to drown us." It was barely a whisper, but she was smiling.

I let out a louder sob, and then she was laughing, and I found I was sobbing and laughing simultaneously.

"Look," someone said, pointing past us to the west.

Everyone turned, and the crowd parted. We all stared through the rain as trees and plants popped up everywhere.

"The city was built on the edge of a lake," someone observed, and I looked beyond the trees to see water filling a large crater in the earth.

The trees spread so far this time that the entire landscape transformed in minutes. A lake, mountains, trees, and a city of rubble at its edge.

No one said anything for a while, but then I noticed Lily, who had gotten up and begun to dance, cry, and laugh in the rain that continued to fall. Some of the other women joined.

"Will you dance with me?" Olivia asked Kat.

Kat laughed. "You can't even stand. How're you going to dance?"

Olivia shrugged, and Liam stood up, pulling me up with him.

He smirked at me before going over and picking Olivia up. She smiled at him and then turned toward Kat, holding out her arms.

Kat laughed, sobbed, and fell into Olivia's arms, and the three of them swayed to music only they could hear.

As I watched them dance, still unable to stop my tears, I sensed a significant presence approaching from the south. There was a large group of people, wagons, and horses not far from us.

"Liam," I said loud enough for him to hear me.

He stopped and turned with Olivia still in his arms. When he saw them, it was his turn to laugh and sob all at the same time.

He settled Olivia back into Kat's lap, and everyone watched as the group approached. A tall woman with long blonde hair, who was not much older than me, walked up to Liam and stopped just before him. They both didn't say anything for a moment, and then Liam stepped forward and threw his arms around the woman. She went rigid before relaxing into his embrace.

When they finally pulled away from each other, Liam said, "I thought you wouldn't come."

"Why would we not come?"

Liam had no immediate answer before noticing the small group standing just behind the woman. "You went back for help?" Liam said, and it wasn't really a question.

They all nodded and smiled at him.

"Thank you."

They nodded again, beaming.

"Impressive," the woman said, motioning to the trees, the lake, and the surrounding area. "We could do with a little less rain for our journey back, as the mud might pose a problem, but who's complaining?"

Liam laughed at that, and I felt joy and relief pouring from him.

"Olivia needs help," Liam said, directing the woman's attention to Olivia, who was still on the ground with Kat.

The woman nodded, and before she could say anything, a small group rushed over to Olivia, pulling out various herbs and bandages from their packs.

Olivia glanced over my way and gave me a small smile and a wink.

"Willow?" I turned toward the woman. Liam was standing right behind her. I glanced between them, and the woman continued, holding out her hand, "I'm Leeann. It's an honor to meet you."

I reached for her hand. "It's an honor to meet you, as well."

She smiled, and then Liam was at my side, grabbing my hand and squeezing it tight.

"Let's go home," she said to us, and I felt the joy and expectation that rose in Liam, and it was so strong that a few more plants popped up next to us. He didn't notice. No one did. As the rain continued to fall, the lake continued to fill, and the entire landscape transformed, I held that memory close to my heart.

"I'll organize everyone," Liam said, but Leeann put a hand on his arm, and he stopped.

"You will do nothing of the sort. You have done enough"—she looked between us—"both of you."

She walked off, barking directions. Everyone with her immediately followed, scattering around the groups of people, offering dry blankets, medical care, and any other supplies they might need.

We both sat on the grass next to Kat and Olivia as everyone else scattered. Among the commotion, the four of us were still and silent, taking it all in.

Epilogue

It took us almost three days to reach the house. It turned out the mud was a lot harder to traverse than we expected. But luckily, we all made it in one piece, and suddenly the community was overflowing with people. Too many people.

Liam and Leeann instantly got to work planning and supervising the construction of more homes. In the meantime, our house was full of people day and night, and I enjoyed it. There was more laughter, more love, and more joy filling the house than I ever expected. Circe's carvings, which I transformed into living vines, grew more vibrant in the glow of everyone's joy.

I met everyone Liam had grown to love and found it easy to love them too. I introduced Kat's women to Emilia's women, and they were instant allies and friends.

I watched them all as the days passed, and I saw new relationships forming and old ones ending, and through all of it, two main threads were holding this place together—love and hope.

Olivia grew stronger daily, as did her relationship with Kat, as they got to know each other again. As the house slowly transformed into a true home, Liam and I got lost in each other. We began to weave another story as I started to feel movement in my womb for the first time.

We kept our secret for a while, relishing it until I could no longer hide it.

Everyone doted on me and wanted to touch her. I let them.

She was the embodiment of hope for the future, and it was as if everyone already knew that. She was loved long before she made her journey Earthside.

I spent the final days of my pregnancy lying on the Earth. Dreaming. Imagining. Weaving. Creating.

She was born on the Earth under a mother oak tree and a fire sun. Her cry called the bees, and they swarmed above us as I stared down at her for the first time. She had bright red hair and her daddy's eyes, and I knew she was going to transform this entire world with her flame.

The End

Acknowledgements

The list of people who helped me get this book into the world over the last two years is long. I couldn't have done this without each and every one of them. I thought writing a book was something you did alone. How wrong was I!

I want to start by thanking the women who supported me throughout the process, starting with my Book Incubator writing group. Your encouragement and advice were priceless; this book wouldn't exist without you. To my Spicy Swap writing group. You all were there for all my crazy questions, holding me through the challenging parts and laughing with me when I shared ridiculous things. Thank you for the support and all the writing advice.

To my beta readers, Katya, your suggestions were super helpful in making this story memorable, and your encouragement got me through some significant imposter syndrome. Daph, your advice and encouragement kept me going as I neared the end. Lauren, your attention to detail helped me make the small changes needed to make the story stand out.

To my sisters, from the number of times you talked me through scenes, and the amount of times you inevitably read the same story over and over again, honestly, I would be lost without you. This book wouldn't exist without the two of you.

To my editor, Heather at Simply Spellbound Edits, you are truly a wonder. Your support and knowledge helped hone this story until it felt like it was truly the best it could be.

To my PR manager, Rumaisa, you have helped to not only take the burden of marketing off my shoulders, but you have also made it feel so fun. This book wouldn't have the reach it has if it weren't for you. I am forever grateful to you.

To my children, everything I do is because of you. You're the reason I write stories. You remind me to keep dreaming.

Lastly, to my husband, from all the late nights talking out scenes (even though you haven't read the whole thing yet) to your support and love, I couldn't, and wouldn't, want to do this crazy life without you.

About the author

Brilynn O'Neal lives in California with her husband, three children, two dogs, two cats, ten chickens, and lots of honeybees. When she's not writing spicy, emotional stories, she's outside soaking up nature and saving bees.

Follow her on Instagram, TikTok, and Pinterest

@forestsandfantasy